Ritual Abuse – Autumn

Spiritual Warfare

Lynda L. Irons

Irons Quill

Contact the author at ironsquillreader@gmail.com. Questions and comments are welcome. All emails will be read.

This book is dedicated to those who wrestle with dissociation in themselves or in someone they love. I am grateful for the holy privilege of having worked with hundreds of precious, courageous, funny, and deeply spiritual dissociative people over the past twenty-five years. Thank you for taking the risk in your pursuit of healing by becoming transparent and vulnerable during ministry sessions.

This is the first of a four-book series and is a work of fiction that is loosely based on some actual events from the author's life. Names, characters, places, and incidents that resemble that of any real persons, living or dead, business establishments, locales, churches, and so on, are purely coincidental and are the product of the author's wild imagination.

This story is not for everyone. It contains some very disturbing information. While this book is purely a work of fiction, it depicts the tormented lives of far too many ritual abuse survivors who live in our communities. The representative characters in this book give voice to these amazing survivors in a way that only hints at the horrors that they experienced day in and day out. This narrative is not meant to be sensational, rather to raise awareness that these people exist and desperately need the help of the Church.

WARNING: If you are a Ritual Abuse survivor, please be aware that some of the contents in this book could trigger unresolved programming.

TABLE OF CONTENTS PAGE

PROLOGUE

In the darkest hour of the night the abject fear that the whimpering child felt was far beyond terror. Drugged, confused, and overwhelmed; the four-year-old cried out for his mommy. Chosen for his fair hair and blue eyes, symbols of purity, he was in the center of diabolical evil. Helpless on a roughly hewn five-sided rock near the blazing fire and surrounded by menacing people, he knew that something awful was about to happen. What he did not know was that a counterfeit communion service was being prepared.

The chanting was malevolent and brought him to choking sobs. Occasionally someone would touch his quivering body. Each touch brought paroxysms of pain. It renewed his dread and the certainty that he would never see his family again.

Suddenly there was silence as an imposing and sinister man approached him and intoned words that he did not recognize. His hypnotic stare silenced the child as he motioned another to his side. It was hard to tell if the other one was a boy or a girl. There was malice there, too, but it was somewhat different because this person acted more like a robot, like one who was also being controlled by the evil.

The huge man produced an ornate dagger and placed it in the hand of the robot person and grunted an order. Chanting resumed in a low, slow cadence and quickly crescendoed. It stopped abruptly with the plunge of the knife. The child felt the burn of the blade as it pierced through skin, crunched through bone, and impaled his heart. Spasms convulsing uncontrollably, blood spurting, he recognized one last horror as the blade was withdrawn and used to nearly sever his head from his tiny body.

A chalice was brought forward to catch the crimson blood. Eyes glazed, the ravenous throng anticipated the feast. One final desecration was committed by the leader. He eviscerated the body and plucked the warm and trembling heart from its cavity. It was skillfully diced with a practiced hand and passed to the voracious mob.

They chanted their glee and partook as one before passing the chalice. Invigorated and frenzied by their blood-thirsty lust, they began to tear at clothing and lost themselves in a profane orgy until the coming of dawn dispelled the darkness. The nefarious horde dispersed quietly after having efficiently removed all evidence of their feast. Returning to their homes, they prepared to go about their daily routines in the midst of an unsuspecting community.

1

Equinox, September 21, 2006

The brilliant moon gave the already picturesque landscape a muted beauty. Abigail Steele wandered from the front porch to the back deck to take in the exquisite views, to breathe in the crisp autumn air, to listen to the irregular cadences of the crickets and frogs. A distant owl added a mournful hoot. Buster nickered his greeting from somewhere in the shadows of the pasture. "Hey, boy," she replied. She could hear the grass being snatched from its patch as he went back to grazing.

She heard Dude's high-pitched yawn as he stirred in his hideaway under the deck. "Hey, Dude," she said softly. She never really got around to naming him. The first time she saw the shy pup and picked him up, she said, "Ooh, you're such a cute little dude." Abigail thought that she would name him once she got to know his personality, but years later she was still calling him Dude.

The little farm had become a sanctuary of sorts to Abigail. All the desires of her heart had materialized on this remote ten-acre parcel of land. She enjoyed watching Buster roam the woods and pasture. His lean-to was built next to the tack room and a small barn had been added more recently. It kept him sheltered in the really bad weather, and it also housed her four-wheeler, an assortment of tools, and bales of hay. She had good neighbors, her first dog, an orchard, a small vineyard, and a garden that she steadily enlarged year after year.

Situated on top of a hill, the farmhouse gave her a fabulous view of fields and woods to the west, the pond and valley to the north that swept up the hill to the Milner's place, and the overgrown fields across the road to the east. A fairly thick stand of woods blocked the view to the south unless the leaves were down. The gravel driveway wound in lazy curves parallel to the road across the front of the property.

The farmhouse was probably as old as her father, but it was solid and snug. She asked her neighbors to the north, Earl and Jan Milner, about the age of the house. They said it was built about the time that Beulah Washington was born. When questioned about the year, Jan told her that she was not sure, and told her how to find the cemetery in which Beulah was buried behind the Baptist church a few miles away at the end of their road.

Local lore said that when James proposed to her, Beulah refused to marry him until he provided her with indoor plumbing. Now all that was left of the old outhouse was a rectangular slab of cement with a round hole in the middle of it which was overgrown by the various grasses and weeds that invaded the back yard. The Washington farmstead originally included Earl and Jan's fifteen acres, the twenty-five acres that her neighbor to the south owned as well as eighty acres across the road and the hundreds of acres behind their properties that was owned by yet another neighbor who lived past the Milners.

Abigail's reveries were interrupted by a low growl from Dude. He heard the distinct sound of the four-wheelers before Abigail did. She scanned the woods in the river bottoms across the hundred-acre corn field to the west and saw headlights. They flickered like strobe lights as the vehicles wound their way along the wooded trails. Over the years four-wheelers had cleared good horse riding trails in the bottoms. Abigail, Buster, and Dude spent many happy hours exploring all of the different trails on their excursions.

Dude joined her on the deck and shook the sleep off before sitting alertly next to Abigail. "Just night riders," she said, "settle down boy." She reached down to scratch his ears, and heard his tail thumping on the wooden deck.

It was not unusual for the locals to take a night ride on horses or four-wheelers. Sometimes she could hear them late into the night and wondered how they could work on such little sleep. But riders would be expected on a gorgeous night like this. Who knows how many more nights would present the perfect combination of brilliant moon light, relatively dry trails, and mild weather?

Abigail reluctantly went back into the house since she needed to get ready for work and get some sleep. Rarely deviating from her daily routine, she went to bed and woke up about the same time all of her life. Having come from a large family in which a regular schedule kept things from getting very chaotic, she retained the ingrained habits.

The reflection in the mirror imitated her as she brushed her teeth and frowned at her unruly locks that rebelled against combs and brushes, curling irons and gels. Her light brown eyes and tanned skin complimented what she called her dirty-dishwater-blonde hair. Abigail judged herself to be somewhere between pretty and coyote-ugly; an average gal who could be attractive with a little make-up and a good hair day. Blessed with long limbs, she was athletic and competitive; both necessary traits to survive life with all of her brothers.

Abigail finished her evening routine and went to bed. Tonight, she preferred the single bed in the back bedroom because it faced the west. Better breezes came through the windows and she could watch the night critters that emerged long after the sun went down. She could catch glimpses of Buster grazing and Dude patrolling his territory in the glow of the yard light. She was grateful for that yard light because the pack of river bottom coyotes came a bit too close for comfort whenever the electricity failed.

Flipping on her bedside radio, reading her Bible, she gratefully slipped under the covers and prayed out loud, "Lord, thank You for another beautiful day. We have an intense day tomorrow. I pray for favor with some of Carrie Sue's and Amy's hostile parts. Please bless all of us with a good night's sleep. Abba, they've endured so much; if there is any way to short-cut their healing processes, please show me."

She soon dozed off and slept well, but heard the four-wheelers through the open window. She roused just enough to make a mental note, but not quite enough to roll over and look out the window.

They came by four-wheeler and horseback on trails that crisscrossed the river bottoms on the west side of the road. They used the trails that were formed along the edges of fields behind the farms that lined the east side of the road. A few of them arrived in pickup trucks. There was one distinct full-sized county-owned sedan.

An intangible cord drew each one to the same site. On certain days the tug was irresistible. The pull began in earnest at dusk and crescendoed throughout the evening. By ten o'clock most of them were well on the way. By midnight everyone was present.

Some of the participants were mystified by the restlessness that plagued them during ritual days. They did not consider the possibility that they had been programmed during various rituals to which they had been subjected previously. Many of them were just like Carrie Sue. Her father was a devout Satanist. He came from a long line of them. It was all they knew.

Her mother was chosen as his mate because she had been sexually traumatized as a small child. The combination of the trauma and her high dissociative ability produced multiple personalities. Although she had spontaneously dissociated because of childhood trauma, most of the subsequent alternative personalities had been created and were now controlled through programming by her husband and his cult comrades.

Her mother had initially been used as a "breeder" to produce infants for their rituals. Now it was Carrie Sue's time. Dissociation was a blessing in that it allowed for the host personality to function fairly normally in society because alternate personalities bore the horrific memories.

Carrie Sue was subjected to the incantations, hexes, covenants, curses, drugs, hypnosis, and more. They were part of the rituals from the time she was permitted to be conceived by the regional master. She was one who was allowed to live to serve their purposes. Her older brother was being groomed for leadership in their local cult. His participation in the rituals included tormenting Carrie Sue. He did not mind using his status to do despicable things to her when she still lived at home.

Males held higher status than females. This bias had its origins in Genesis 3:15 where God cursed Satan. *"And I will put enmity between you and the woman, and between your seed and her seed; He shall bruise you on the head, and you shall bruise Him on the heel."* Satan poured his hatred onto Eve and all future potential Messiah-bearers.

Satan needed to thwart God's plan. There were several times in history in which the Messianic line was down to one man. He almost succeeded. When the Messiah was born despite Satan's best efforts, he incited King Herod to order the murder of all male children under the age of two based on the wise men's calculations. He failed in that mission but continues his tirade against women.

Carrie Sue never noticed the ordinary word that came up in the phone call from her father. It was used to trigger the switch into a cult-loyal personality who would get her to the ritual. She "disappeared" and knew nothing of the activities that occurred while she lost executive control of her body.

That night a personality named Yeoman was present. He was designed to participate in the rituals, to do violence, to willingly drink blood, to act at the bidding of the master. He was the antithesis of Carrie Sue who loved the Lord Jesus. There were many other dissociated parts of Carrie Sue who were also programmed as he was.

The drumming was not very loud since there were neighboring farms to consider. Sound carried in these rolling hills that were filled with woods and fields, creeks and bogs. They were gathered around the fire. Hooded robes were donned by the officiants and the ritual was carried out to honor the god of the equinox with their sacrifice.

By three a.m. the appropriate curses had been uttered and demons were commissioned to carry them out. Urdang did not have far to travel, not that space was ever much of a problem for the winged messenger. He hovered high over the small farm not far down the road bringing his oppressive aura with him. The horse became restless. The dog barked at nothing visible.

2

Friday, September 22

Too soon the morning light wakened Abigail. The oppression was as tangible as the morning fog. "Lord, this is the day that You have made and I will rejoice and be glad in it despite my feelings. Abba, I plead the blood of Jesus Christ over this property, the air above it, and the ground beneath it. I plead the blood of Jesus over me and all the stuff You have given me. I ask that You would assign Your warring angels to escort me wherever I need to go today."

Urdang shrieked his curses as he retreated from the property that was dedicated to his enemy. The nefarious curses did not alight. Abigail went about her morning routine unscathed.

Today was Friday and Abigail was mentally reviewing her day. Even though her work schedule was not very full, she was always glad when she could get back to her little farm. Today she was going to meet with three of her clients. Two of them had been abused practically from conception. They were raised by Satanists and had dissociated into multiple personalities, most of whom were programmed to be cult-loyal. The third client was a teenager who had issues with her step-father.

Abigail checked the water level in the trough to make sure that Buster and Dude had enough to last until Saturday. It was full enough but really ought to be scrubbed to get rid of the algae and dead leaves. Tomorrow. She slid through the wooden fence and jogged down to the tack room.

Buster saw her and galloped up the pasture with mane and tail streaming behind him as he ran straight at Abigail. It was a game they played. She would throw up both of her arms and at the last minute he would rear up and paw the air. After he settled down he would nuzzle her looking for a treat.

Abigail filled Buster's bowl with a measure of sweet feed from the tack room and secured the floppy old wooden door with two chains. Buster had figured out how to get the lower chain loose and nearly foundered by eating too much sweet feed a year ago, so she added the second chain. Dude materialized from somewhere in the woods and danced around Abigail as she made her way back up to the house to give him his ration before she ate her own breakfast.

Slipping her tiny leather purse into her front pocket, she grabbed her keys and headed out to the truck. Abigail grinned nearly every time she got into the sleek gray pickup truck. Her father was very traditional and girls were just not supposed to drive trucks. They were supposed to wash dishes and boys were supposed to take out the garbage and mow the lawn. Abigail was not being rebellious, just enjoying the freedom of driving a truck and running the tiller and her riding lawn mower. Actually, she was quite pleased to do everything around the little farm.

She arrived at exactly 9:55 a.m. for her ten o'clock appointment with Carrie Sue Wagner. Carrie Sue was already there, leaning against her car in a masculine pose. *It must be Marty, the teen-aged driver.* Abigail reached behind her seat and grabbed her office-in-a-bag which contained her Bible, notebook, datebook, and pens. With a practiced move she flung the leather bag over her shoulder, shut the door, and readied her keys to open the side door of the Springfield Baptist church.

Being one minute late used to mean Carrie Sue's hair-trigger rejection button would be pushed. That would also mean facing one of her child parts that was anxious about abandonment or else an angry personality that would ream Abigail out. This was annoying but not unexpected when working with ritual abuse survivors. Fortunately, Carrie Sue had received much healing in the last couple of years and that had not happened in a long time.

One time a particularly vulgar and hostile part began to ream her out, telling her to do some things that were anatomically impossible. Abigail calmly collected her things and firmly stated that Carrie Sue should call her to reschedule their next appointment. Abigail left and a more composed and apologetic host personality called and rescheduled. Funny, it never happened again; at least not that badly.

After settling into their chairs and finishing with small talk and some light-hearted bantering, Abigail opened with prayer. She always prayed with her eyes open. She learned to "watch and pray" because she never knew who would switch in when she was not looking. Carrie Sue had an unstable system in some respects. The host personality was displaced quite often when other parts were inadvertently triggered or wanted to speak up.

Abigail finished her prayer, "Lord, start us where we need to start today, amen."

It was apparent that a child alter had switched in. Carrie Sue's face seemed fuller, her eyes rounder, and her wrinkles faded. "Lizzie?" Abigail asked.

"Yep. You're getting good at telling us apart."

"It's rough, y'all look alike," she replied with a grin and a wink.

Lizzie exploded with the pure laughter of a five-year-old. Abigail was always amazed at the sense of humor, the kidding around, and the fun these dear survivors had. What a blessed recompense for all the trauma they had endured.

"How are you doing today?" Lizzie had shown up very distressed in the last couple of sessions. She had deep pain. Whenever they got close to going to the memory, she would shut down and another personality would take over. It was usually her protector, David; a fierce young man who was now one of Abigail's greatest allies in the system. But David owed his first allegiance to Lizzie and the other little ones in his charge.

"I don't like to think about what we talked about last time."

"I know it's hard, but it's the only way I know that you can be healed and not have to think about it every single day. Do you think we can try to go there today? Jesus promised that He would never leave you or forsake you. He's the same yesterday, today, and forever."

"Yeah, but I didn't see Him there," she protested ruefully. A pout formed on her lips.

"I believe you, Lizzie. The cult guys didn't want you to be able to see the real Jesus there. He really was there, but I believe that He was blocked from you because of the bio-dad."

"Then he's stronger than Jesus." Lizzie was trying to grasp principles of spiritual warfare that most mature Christians do not understand.

"Okay, Lizzie, here's the problem. God made all people with a free-will. We get to make choices. God set it up so that moms and dads have responsibility and authority. When parents make crappy choices, kids get hurt."

"That's not fair!" she protested.

"I know," Abigail agreed, "but the only other choice that God had was to make us into robots or puppets. I like to make choices; don't you?"

"Yeah, but..." her voice trailed off as she tried to grasp God's risky double-bind.

"Another part of the problem is that the scuzzie uglies have a so-called legal right to hurt a kid if her parents give them that permission. The Bible says that Satan is like a roaring lion seeking whom he may devour. Lions in the jungle don't go after the bulls or the fast ones or the ones who are all together in the herd. They go after the little ones who are slow or hurt or alone. Scuzzie uglies didn't go after your bio-dad, they went after you. That's why we need to go back to that memory so we can get rid of them and you can see the real Jesus."

Children were subjected to so many double-binds. Good was bad, up was down, right was wrong, Satan was good and Jesus was bad. They were introduced to a false Jesus who would harm the child or direct the cult members to harm the child. Then the child was "rescued" and informed that it was Satan who told them to save the child. This was reenacted in innumerable scenarios so that the child would never trust a true *or* a false Jesus and certainly not anyone who claimed to represent the true Jesus.

Abigail worked hard to gain the trust of Carrie Sue's alters. She had to walk a delicate line to encourage prayers to the God who was thought to have orchestrated their life of hell-on-earth. And, they protested, even if He did not devise her torment, why didn't He stop it? Why did He put her in that family? Abigail also had to walk a fine line between pushing too hard or too little. She had to be careful not to force any decision because that would then make her no better than the Satanists who forced their will upon them.

David switched in to protect Lizzie. "She's still thinking about it," he reported. "It's probably not going to happen today, but there's something more urgent, I think."

"Well," said Abigail, "I'm disappointed. It just grieves me to think that she's got to carry that load every day. So, what's up?"

"You remember Scooter?"

"Yes," Abigail replied with a grin, "the little nark." It seemed that every system had an observer, a little one whose job it was to spy within the system. Just like any ordinary three or four-year-old who seems to unobtrusively watch what goes on with the grownups in his or her world, so these little ones seem to be able to slip around undetected and know what happens inside the system. They may not always understand everything, but they certainly have a sense of whether or not it is good or bad.

"Will she talk to me directly, or would she be more comfortable talking through you?" Scooter was very shy and wary of both outside people and inside personalities; especially hostile ones. She had been subjected to punishments of the internal persecutors enough times to be afraid.

"She'd rather let me tell you," David replied.

"What's going on?" Abigail had to conceal her impatience. Sometimes it was like pulling teeth. Why couldn't they just come out and say something? But she knew that she was constantly being tested. Was she trustworthy? Would she believe? How would she respond?

David hesitated, eyes downcast, "Well, she said that we were at a ritual last night. Equinox, you know. We were pretty sore this morning and kind of figured that something happened." She could tell that he was frustrated when he could not protect like he wanted to.

He had a warrior's heart but had limited internal jurisdiction. He could only do so much to protect them.

"Oh-h…" Abigail sighed. One step forward, a hundred steps backward. When will it end? When will they be free from the programming and the cult control? "Do you know who got accessed?"

"Yeah, it was the Equinox Quints."

"Are they available, or is their protector available to talk to?" Abigail asked. She was hoping to be able to pray with them to minimize the damage. This would not have been the first Equinox ritual to which they had been subjected.

"They're kind of shaken up, but they are willing to have you pray for them. They'll listen in while I stay here. They're not mine, but they know me and saw how I helped my little ones get healed and integrated. They're tired and hurting and ready."

"Excellent." Abigail was encouraged. Sometimes it took lengthy negotiations to get to the point of prayer. "Ready?"

"Yes," David replied.

Abigail approached the throne of grace in the name of Jesus the Christ on behalf of the Equinox Quints. She appealed to the Lord to render all verbal assaults null and void - all the spiels, hexes, chants, curses, oaths, assignments, covenants, and especially the programming. She asked that all direct and indirect unholy unions, soul ties, and flesh links would be broken. She prayed for all other forms of torment, for things ingested, for body memories, and for all the emotional pain to be healed. Abigail pled the blood of Jesus over all the strongholds associated with every sin against each of the Quints. She asked that the Balm of Gilead would soothe and heal all their body memories. "Holy Spirit, please come now and seal what has been healed. Fill each of them with Your presence. Restore innocence and purity, peace, light, and truth. In Jesus' name, amen.

"How are they doing?" she asked.

"Whew!" David sighed. "Relief! They're smiling and don't look so beaten up."

"Praise God! Are they ready to go back inside where they came from so they can't be accessed anymore?"

"I'll ask them." David conferred with the Quints and then reported, "Yes, they said, 'get us outta here, we don't ever want to do another Equinox.'"

"Cool. Let's pray." Abigail prayed for the Lord to reknit them back into their rightful places in the core person or a protector. She always deferred to the Lord's placement and timing. Sometimes it was evident that there was integration, sometimes the absence of the parts was all that confirmed it.

"Thanks, see ya later." David switched out and Carrie Sue's host was back in executive control.

They closed in prayer and then made an appointment for next week. A careful hug at the door concluded their session. Abigail was judicious about hugs or touches. She never knew if another part might be co-conscious with the host or might even switch in for a second. That part could be male or female, adult or child. If that new part did not know Abigail, the hug could be misconstrued.

Abigail checked to see if Brittany had arrived yet. Both she and her mother were already there. "Come in, good timing," Abigail invited the perky teenager. Her mother smiled from the waiting room and was already busy checking her cell phone. Brittany had made some progress in previous sessions working on her anger issues, but there was more work to do.

Despite outward appearances, Brittany was an angry young lady; and rightfully so. She discovered that her step-father had actually bored a pencil sized hole in the wall between the back-to-back closets of her room and the spare bedroom. She had wondered why her closet door was always open and clothes separated a bit. She felt embarrassed, infuriated, tainted, and more by his voyeurism. Gross!

"I'm just not ready to forgive the jerk-face."

"I don't blame you for being angry, but you are the one who will suffer if you hold onto bitterness."

"If I forgive him, it'll be as if he got away with it," she objected.

"Not exactly," Abigail countered, "God will take care of him. Your job is to forgive him. You know the definitions - to loose away, to cover, or to grant an unconditional grace to someone who does *not* deserve it and has not asked for it."

"I know; I'm just not ready."

They set that discussion aside for the time being and prayed about another issue. Brittany was at least willing to think about forgiving her step-dad and come back and discuss it again next time. Abigail closed with prayer and consulted with her mom to set another appointment for the following week.

Abigail shuffled a few papers. She loved the ministry sessions and despised what she referred to as administrivia. Of course, if it was not documented, it did not happen; so she carefully recorded her session notes while she waited for Amy.

Amy consistently arrived six minutes late for her appointments. It was a control thing. It was an anger thing. It was a number six thing. Amy was tough and she had mostly male alters. Her system was very closed and secretive. Like so many others, she had a finely tuned gift of sarcasm – yet another form of anger – which leached into most exchanges.

Once again F. Amy Bolton arrived six minutes late for her two o'clock appointment. She flopped down on the couch and crossed her legs and arms. Amy never used her first name and wouldn't tell anyone what it was. She despised it, in fact. This was very common with SRA survivors who usually used their middle name or some variation of their given name.

Abigail often wondered what the F. stood for and noted that it was the sixth letter of the alphabet. Was that just a coincidence? Or was there some diabolical symbolic significance to it? Sometimes the cult would use FFF instead of 666. Someday it would come out if Amy stuck with the healing journey long enough.

Oh, Lord, this looks like another tough session – favor, please! Abigail breathed her prayer and then greeted Amy, "Hey, how are you doing?"

"Oh, just fine and dandy. Life's just great!" Amy replied with an exaggerated grin and a sarcastic edge.

"Let's open with prayer then and get started," Abigail smiled back and ignored the sarcasm. Abigail led the prayer with eyes wide open but directed at her Bible which was open to the Scripture verses that she incorporated into the prayer. Amy did not close her eyes either and thinly disguised her disdain for God stuff. She was here for something other than healing.

"So, when are we going to get some healing for the little ones?" Abigail asked.

"It's not that easy. They are being watched by a bunch of guards. They're in the inner cells and we can't get to them." Amy, or whoever was in charge, was not being particularly uncooperative, indeed, any information she let out brought additional danger to any informant. It could also bring retribution on those in the cells. She was being careful.

Amy's internal system resembled a large prison complex. There were six buildings with six stories of cell blocks. There were sixty blocks on each floor and six hundred so-called prisoners. 666. The number six was repeated in her system in many and various ways. There also were tunnels and mazes that ran underneath the buildings and the outlying lands. There were interrogation rooms, work rooms, and other rooms for other functions. There were guards, wardens, and sentries throughout the prison system; most of whom were persecutors and cult-loyal.

Outside of the prison complex there were houses and other structures that accommodated the non-cult-loyal personalities. They were traumatized, but not due to ritual abuse per se. Abigail was just beginning to grasp the extent of the evil that was perpetrated upon Amy that caused her to have such an oppressive internal structure. It would not be pretty to see what was in the subterranean levels of the prison.

"Can you get a message to the head warden for me?" Abigail boldly asked.

"What! Are you nuts? Even if I wanted to get a message to him, you wouldn't want to meet with him. He's not nice."

"I have a hunch that he's listening in because we're talking about his jurisdiction. I want to help him out with something. I need to talk to the head honcho because I don't want to go behind his back or force something without his consent," Abigail countered.

Amy's countenance and demeanor changed abruptly. "Who do you think you are busting in here and summoning the head warden?" a voice growled.

"Hi, are you the head warden or are you one of his assistants?"

"I ain't telling you nothing," he snarled.

"Well, as long as you're here, do you mind if I lay out a proposal? You have nothing to lose except a couple of minutes." Abigail bargained with him and prayed for favor. She would also be able to pick up clues about the personalities in this sector.

"Like you have anything we need," he spat, "but I'll give ya one minute."

"Okay, thanks." Abigail talked fast. "Here's the deal – the head warden has a bunch of crying, hurting little ones in there that take a lot of his time and attention. He also may not know that they are a big part of the reason that he is so well monitored and punished for his so-called failures. They're probably programmed and demonized just like everyone else. Their demons nark on your operations and let Satan and his allies know how things are being run in there. I can help him with both issues."

The brief look of surprise was quickly disguised. "How do you know about that?" he demanded.

It was a bit of a gamble, but Abigail knew the basic strategies of cult control. They create and program personalities. They groom some of them to rise to power in the cult by giving them assignments both internally and in the outside world. Power is the lure. Power is what is supposed to keep torment at a minimum. She knew there would be plenty of pre-borns, new-borns, infants, toddlers, and kids. Every SRA survivor had them. The cult counted on the survivors themselves as well as their counselors being unaware of their existence.

"This ain't my first load of pumpkins. I have a bit of experience with others like Amy. Besides, the Holy Spirit will sometimes give me the discernment and knowledge I need to help you."

Mentioning the Holy Spirit enraged him, but he controlled his tongue.

"Well, I promised you I'd only bug you for one minute. What do you want to do?" Abigail wanted to build trust. They had been betrayed innumerable times. She did not want to be one more in a string of controlling, deceiving, disappointing people.

"I'm listening," he feigned disinterest in his tone and demeanor.

"You got a name?"

"You can call me Caleb" he said.

"Thanks; that's a good name for a leader," she said and continued despite his quizzical look. "Caleb, I know you're not the head warden, so I'll give you the gist of my proposal and you can get back to me after you confer with whoever you have to."

He nodded.

"Head warden and all of you under his jurisdiction have assignments. You try to do them to the best of your abilities, but likely feel as if you have both hands tied behind your backs. You get punished for not doing what you can't really do no matter how hard you try. What I propose is that he considers allowing the little ones to get healed and consolidated into their sector heads, protectors, or whoever would be appropriate. Then you won't have to be distracted with the kids, they'll be out of their misery, and more importantly; the outside cult guys have fewer ways to access you and jerk you around."

"What's the catch? What do you want? What's in it for you?" he asked suspiciously. Nobody in his world did anything for free. Everybody wanted something - power, control, sex, money, status - yes, everybody wanted something.

"I want the kids to be healed and safe. I want all of you to be healed and safe."

Caleb had been played before by people who called themselves Christians. It was a cleverly designed cult ploy to make sure that in the event that Amy or any one of her parts ever met a genuine Christian who actually knew how to deal with SRA survivors, they would not be trusted.

Duplicity. Double-binds. That was all they knew. Why should Caleb trust this lady? And yet there was something about her that was different. Her eyes; yes, that was it. They were different. They were not the eyes of the malevolent people he'd encountered time and time again.

"I will give your proposal to the head warden and let you know," he said with less hostility.

"Thank you. You want to do that right now or get back to me next time I meet with Amy?"

"I'll catch you next time."

With that, Caleb slipped into his internal place and the host Amy reappeared.

"Hey," Abigail greeted Amy. "You okay?"

"You're a crazy lady! I cannot believe that you had the nerve to talk to Caleb. And that he gave you the time of day."

"I like the biggest, baddest ones the best. They can't admit it, but they usually have the most tender hearts and are enraged at the things that were done to the little ones, especially. They just can't admit it or they'll be perceived as being weak and get punished by their demons. Besides, there are no bad parts, just parts with bad assignments. They are all parts of F. Amy Bolton and I will love them all." Abigail said some things because she knew that others were listening in and needed to hear that message.

Amy gave an involuntary shudder when Abigail spoke her full name, "Please don't say my whole name. I hate it."

Abigail agreed, but now knew that there was something more behind the name that was disturbing her. There was programming of some kind at the very least.

Suddenly, Head Warden was there. "I heard what you were saying to Caleb," he said gruffly and with an authoritative air about him. "What gives you the right to barge in here?"

"I didn't think I was barging in on anyone. If you recall, I asked permission to lay out a proposal. Did Caleb tell you?" Abigail kept steady eye contact.

"Yeah, yeah, I heard everything," he said with exaggerated impatience.

"What do you want to do? I realize that just talking to me could get you into trouble, especially because of the access the masters have to your system through those little ones." She knew that bluntly laying it out would make him uncomfortable, but she also wanted him to know that she knew exactly what it would cost him. Abigail gave him time to process the information.

He shifted uncomfortably in his seat. He knew that there was a leak in his system, but he did not know how the masters knew what was going on. It was both infuriating and scary. He knew that his world would never be the same again after talking with this woman, but as uncomfortable as his world was, it was all he knew.

Abigail persisted, "I'm not asking you to change your allegiances or your job, just trying to help out."

"Why?" He demanded suspiciously.

"I just happen to believe that kids - or anyone, for that matter, should not have to suffer. I happen to like Amy and all of you are a part of her. If you say yes, I'll pray for their healing. If you say no, I'll leave you alone."

He acted as if he was reluctant. His pride would not allow him to appear to concede too easily. "All right, but if this is a trick, you'll be sorry."

"No problem. If you think I'm doing something wrong, step in and stop it, okay?" He nodded his assent so Abigail started to pray a comprehensive prayer that renounced the strongholds and demons associated with all the verbal, sexual, and physical assaults that had come against the little ones. She prayed for the healing of their body memories and emotional pain. She asked the Holy Spirit to fill them with the fruit of the Spirit. She paused and asked, "How are they doing now?"

Head Warden's countenance softened a little as he said, "They've stopped crying and writhing around."

"Good, I'm glad for them. Are you okay with asking God to kind of consolidate them into a leader or protector? That way they can't be accessed again."

"Sure," he agreed less grudgingly.

Abigail continued to pray, "Lord we ask that You complete and correct anything prayed incompletely or incorrectly and that You would then bring them together into the right leader, amen."

"They're gone!" he said with alarm. He looked at her suspiciously and demanded, "What have you done with them?"

"Well, they're not really gone, no one completely disappears; they just take a different form. Check with your leaders and they can probably tell you whether or not they felt them integrate into them." Abigail waited while he consulted with his leaders. It always amazed her how rapidly complex internal transactions could take place.

"They said that they're in. They also said that they feel better and don't understand it."

"When the little ones got healed and got rid of their pain and went into the others, they brought their healing with them. Do you remember that I prayed that they would be filled with the fruit of the Spirit? Some of that fruit is love, joy, and peace."

"Yeah, that's what we feel. Thanks. Er, sorry for giving you such a rough time."

"No problem. If it's all right, maybe we can talk again some time."

"Sure," he said and then stepped back into his internal world.

Amy emerged again. They finished their session with small talk and set up their next appointment. Abigail prayed a prayer of protection over Amy and all the parts before they left. Then Abigail finished her paperwork, locked up her office, and headed to her truck. "Thank You, Lord Jesus for all the break throughs today."

The fresh air was particularly invigorating. Abigail grinned as she headed out of the parking lot and headed toward home. One quick stop at the Kingston IGA ensured that she would not starve that weekend. Abigail hated to shop so she procrastinated until she absolutely had to go to the grocery store.

She cruised down Kingston Road and followed the curves over the knolls and the numerous bridges that crossed the branches in the river bottom area. A right turn onto York Creek Road brought her within two miles of home. The picturesque ride up the hill and around the bend, past the big barn and finally down the hill to her driveway was never tiresome. She slowed to make the turn onto her gravel driveway and followed its curves up to the house.

Buster lifted his head and cantered around the orchard and appeared along the fence closest to the place she parked her truck. Dude gave a huge yawn, stretched his back legs behind him and sleepily trotted over to her. *What a nice welcoming committee!* Abigail grabbed the two grocery sacks, walked over to Buster and patted his muscular neck as he rooted for goodies. "Not today, boy, but tomorrow we'll go for a good ride and I'll give you a treat. You, too, Dude."

The little beggars!

Abigail put the groceries away and grabbed a homemade granola bar before changing into her play clothes. There was still ample work to do in the garden and today was still mild enough to do some weeding. The compost pile was getting taller as the garden was getting thinned out. There were still a few handfuls of beans and a few tomatoes braving the cool weather. A number of quart jars were already lined up nicely in the basement. The pressure cooker that she purchased last year preserved green beans which would be savored this winter.

The evening came all too soon. Abigail especially loved dusk. There was something calming about the day coming to a close. Sitting on the back deck with Dude watching the sunset, she remarked, "Earlier and earlier, Dude, pretty soon it'll be dark at this hour." He looked at her with the devotion only a dog could have. It didn't matter what she said, he always seemed to agree.

"Well, Dude, it's time for me to go in." She gave him a hug and ruffled the fur behind his ears before standing up. Abigail secured the door and began to close windows that had let the fresh fall air in all day. Dinner was simple, but nutritious. After cleaning up the kitchen Abigail checked her emails and began her bedtime routine. *Tomorrow will be fun, maybe we'll check out that new trail I saw last time.*

3

Saturday, September 23

Abigail's eyes popped open. *Saturday!* Even though she had six-day weekends, Saturdays still felt like a special day off after working forty plus hour weeks for so much of her life. She had a fairly regular routine for house work that reflected her philosophy. The house got dusted sometimes and vacuumed on most Saturdays. The bathrooms always got attention. Inside work got done more thoroughly in inclement weather and outside work got done in nice weather.

First things first. Grabbing a sweatshirt, she quickly scooted out the back door to take care of her critters. The stray cats had to fend for themselves, but Buster and Dude needed regular care. It was still nippy and she could see her breath as she made her way down to the tack room. Buster was expecting her. "We're going to go a little light on the sweet feed for now, but you'll get more later," she promised.

On the way back up to the house she drained the trough. Dude scampered out of the woods acting as if he had not seen her for days. He danced on his hind legs and pawed the air just in front of her before dropping down and getting his ears scratched and sides thwacked with open palms. "Come on, let's get your breakfast." He happily circled Abigail all the way to the deck and sat impatiently thumping his tail while she filled his bowl.

Inside, Abigail prepared a hearty breakfast and ate it while reading her morning devotional. Then she quickly wrestled the hose out to the trough, sprayed out the leaves and gunk, righted it, and began filling it. She jogged back to the house.

Dragging the old vacuum cleaner out, she plugged it in, pushing and pulling it across the floors in all of the rooms on the main level. The bathrooms were sanitized in record time. Abigail always got excited about a ride with her two favorite guys. She put on her riding boots and decided how many layers she should wear. She could always shed them and stow them in the saddlebag. Her Walther was on her belt along with her Winchester pocket knife in its sheath.

She used the bathroom and put the toilet seat down before she flushed; a habit long established after a doily accidentally got flushed. Ducking back into the kitchen to grab her water bottle, she took one more quick check around the house and then headed back outside. The trough was full enough. She shut off the water, wound up the hose, opened the gate, and went down to catch Buster with Dude by her side. Dude could sense her anticipation.

Buster saw them coming and met her at the tack room. Abigail grabbed the bridle in one hand and a small scoop of sweet feed in the other. As he lowered his head to go for the feed she put her right arm around his neck and deftly slipped the bit into his mouth with her left and looped the leather over his ears. With the reins dropped onto the ground, Buster would not roam away. Abigail went back into the tack room and grabbed the curry comb for a quick brushing. Then she shook out the dusty saddle blanket and tossed it over his broad back. One more trip into the tack room was required for the saddle. She gave him a knee in the ribs to make him exhale as she tightened the cinch. As good a horse as he was, he still tried his little tricks from time to time. Picking up the reins, she put her left foot into the stirrup, did a bouncing hop and swung up into the saddle. She was fairly tall, but he was fifteen hands high.

"All right, guys," she said as she slipped the water bottle into the saddlebag, "we're going out the front gate today to do some exploring."

The trails through the river bottoms were fairly challenging but familiar; sometimes it was nice to try different trails. The farmers along both sides of the highway were tolerant of horses and four-wheelers as long as the crops were not trampled. Most of them rode four-wheelers or horses themselves.

Nudging Buster lightly, they walked along the curved driveway. When they got to the end of it, they carefully crossed the road. Buster's shoes made their distinctive metallic sound on the asphalt as she guided him to the opposite shoulder. They made their way southward toward York Creek and watched for an opening in the scrub trees along the overgrown field to the east.

The wiry young man mounted his borrowed horse. His mission was arranged two nights ago. He guided the large animal northward, crossed the road before York Creek, and picked his way through the brush that lined the road until he found the trail that led toward the river bottoms to the west. When he had traveled about half a mile deep into the woods, he turned to the right and followed the fields on that side of the road to the large hundred-acre corn field.

He was certain that he was not being seen as he dismounted and opened the back gate. He deftly remounted and rode up the trail that led to the barn area. After tying his horse to a tree at the edge of the woods, he cautiously walked up to the back of the house, approaching from the wooded side to ensure that the old couple to the north would not see him. He entered, quietly rearranged things and then disappeared as quickly and quietly as he had come.

Just before the little, mostly dry York Creek they found an opening and picked up an already established trail. They had been on this side of the road before, but usually followed the trail straight to the east which kept their backs to her house. There were several fields back to back with hedges or creeks that separated them. Today Abigail wanted to go back about two fields and then explore the one she had spotted across the creek to the south. The road would be roughly parallel to these fields. She was curious about whether or not she could see the distant neighbors' houses from the back.

Dude always put on a minimum of three times the mileage that Buster and Abigail did. He would range far to the right, come back for a while and then scoot off to the left scaring up rabbits or birds. Sometimes he would trot on ahead and carry himself as if he knew exactly where they were going. He was wondrously clueless and it was refreshing to watch him live in the moment. Abigail envied him. Too many times her mind would wander back over daily concerns or disquieting thoughts about a client that needed prayer.

Today, however, Abigail intentionally absorbed everything her senses could take in. The sun was warm on her face. Many of the weeds were brittle and crunched under Buster's hoofs. As they went through a low area closer to the creek, she listened to the rhythmic squelch and sucking sounds his hoofs made in the mud. Their presence startled scores of fleeing grasshoppers that scattered in every direction as they fled the unforgiving hoofs.

Abigail looked down occasionally to see if she could spot tracks of deer, coyote, fox, dogs, turkeys, horses or other critters. Most of the tracks had been obliterated by the four-wheelers, but there were still quite a few hoof prints. They seemed fairly fresh, as if all this traffic had come this way recently. *Oh, yeah! Thursday night. I'll bet this is the way the night riders went. Must have been a party around here.*

Splashing across the creek to explore the field to the south, they encountered a narrower valley with low wooded hills on either side. There was evidence that quite a bit of the horse and four-wheeler traffic also followed this trail recently. The first field ended with a brush hedge. They navigated their way through a worn gap and followed the trail that opened into another slightly larger field. Abigail had no idea that there were so many fields back here. At this time of year soybeans and corn were still drying on the stalk.

Dude seemed excited about a trail that led up a fairly steep incline to the right. *Perfect, maybe I'll be able to see the back side of someone's house.* She made a subtle movement with her wrist which put gentle pressure on the left side of Buster's neck. He turned obediently to the right and began the climb. She did not want to intrude on anyone's privacy, but as long as there were no fences, she was sure that it would not be a problem to explore a little. Riders were considerate of their neighbors.

Dude was about two hundred feet ahead of them and had stopped under a large oak tree. He was intently sniffing the ground and running circles around something that looked like a large rock.

Buster suddenly lifted his head, flared his nostrils and laid his ears back. He was on high alert for some reason. Abigail reacted by scanning the woods and trails all around her but did not notice anything unusual. Maybe there was another horse on the other side of the fence which was coming into sight just beyond the tree.

Abigail urged him forward. There was tenseness in his whole body. "Easy, boy, we're okay." He did not seem to believe her. When they got closer, she felt the hair rise on her arms and the back of her neck. Looking at the rock that Dude was so excited about, she saw that it had been chiseled to make it into a rough pentagram shape.

"Oh, Lord! Oh, Jesus, this is not good," Abigail breathed a prayer. She got a quick glance at the top of the roof of the house and a large barn that was set to the side. *Blue roof; black barn.* "Oh, Lord, my neighbor is a …" she did not finish the sentence. *Who could it be? Do they know me? Do they know some of my clients?* Her adrenaline-fueled thoughts and questions raced through her mind.

"Dude! Come on boy, let's go home." She turned Buster and had to keep him from bolting down the trail. They both knew what "home" meant and she knew exactly what "like a horse to a barn" meant.

They got down to the bottom of the incline without incident. Both animals could go home without any guidance from Abigail so she gave Buster his head and he took off in a gentle lope. She loved that gait the best because it was like sitting in a rocking chair. Slowing him as they crossed York Creek, making the turn back toward the highway, they covered the ground quickly. Buster did not like to walk the length of the last field, but Abigail wanted him to start cooling down before they got back home.

When they reached the gate, Abigail dismounted and threw the reins over the saddle. Buster trotted down to the tack room and waited impatiently for his treat. Abigail focused on the tasks at hand. She did not want to wrestle with the implications of their discovery that morning.

After the gate was secured she walked down to Buster. He was already nosing his bowl. *Can horses feel entitled?* Abigail wondered. She gave him a small measure of sweet feed and then turned her attention to the saddle, blanket, and bridle. He happily munched while she curried his sweaty hide and talked to him.

With everything stowed away, she gave him a final pat on the rump and walked back up to the house. She kept the front door locked, but the door in the back was usually left unlocked when she was home. Today was no different. She stepped inside and put the water bottle on the counter after she drained it. *Gotta drink more water,* she reprimanded herself.

Lunch time was long gone and she was famished after the ride in the invigorating fall air. She made a grilled cheese sandwich, put some bread and butter pickles on it and ate without tasting it. Her mind was elsewhere. When she was finished, she grabbed a cola and went to her study to think and pray.

It wasn't long before the water and the cola worked their way through her system. She got up and went to the bathroom. She froze. The toilet seat was up as if a man had used it. *I know I put that down, I always do.* She quickly turned around and searched through the rest of the house, grateful that she had not yet put Walther away. She called the sweet German made Walther P .32 "Walther" as if he were a close companion.

Indeed, he was.

She peered cautiously into the living room and everything seemed to be as she had left it. The quick but systematic inspection ended in her bedroom. *Did I leave that drawer partially open? No!* She had always been somewhat of a perfectionist and liked for things to be in their proper places. Her gaze fell upon the embroidered Scripture verse that hung on the wall beside the dresser. It was crooked. *I know that was not like that.* She felt the rush of adrenaline that fear elicits course through her system.

"Oh, Lord, someone's been in here. Lord I plead Your blood over this place once again. You said that everywhere we put the soles of our feet belong to us. This is my jurisdiction and I am asking You to evict any foul spirit that was left behind by whoever was here. Lord, cleanse this place."

A thought suddenly occurred to her about how frequently cars started up her driveway and then backed down and left as mysteriously as they came. It seemed as if they backed down once they drove up far enough to determine that her truck was there. She now made the connection. *There could not possibly be that many lost people in the entire county. They've got to be cult members.*

"Lord, I am tired of them coming up the driveway, would You commission warring angels to stand at the end of the driveway to strip off any demon attached to them and even those trying to hitchhike up here with me?" Abigail sometimes felt "slimed" after her sessions with ritual abuse survivors. She envisioned two mighty angels at least twenty feet tall with their arms stretched out in front of them as they grasped flaming swords. *Very cool!*

She looked into the disturbed drawer and didn't think anything was taken. After straightening the embroidery, she personalized the verse, "No weapon formed against me shall prosper!" She was feeling quite indignant.

Going outside to see if there were any tire tracks in the gravel driveway, she doubted that it proved much more than to confirm that someone else had been here. Dude joined her. She walked all the way down to the mailbox and did not see anything conclusive. She wished that she knew someone she could get to do finger prints and thought of Sheriff Bynum. They attended the same church, but she had a strong and inexplicably creepy feeling about him.

At the end of the driveway, she remembered that she had asked for angelic protection. How she wished that she could see things in the spiritual realm better! Dude paused and cocked his head seeming to sense something as he nosed around the end of the driveway, but then again, it could just as easily be a rabbit or a mole.

After she collected the mail and wandered back up the hill, she decided to call her next-hill neighbors. They were elderly, but if they happened to be looking toward her house at the right time, they might have noticed something.

Earl answered with a cheerful, "What's up?"

"I just got back from riding and when I got back, it was pretty evident that someone had been in my house while we were gone."

"Did they take anything?"

"Well, if they did, it's nothing obvious. I have my valuables locked up in the safe. It seems like they just moved stuff around. And left the toilet seat up."

"Well, you be careful. Lock your doors. Maybe you need an alarm system or something."

"I'll be careful. I think it's just harassment."

Earl did not press her for details and seemed to down-play it but said that he and Jan would pay more attention whenever they had the chance. They chatted about other things for a little while longer.

"Okay. Say hi to Jan for me." Abigail hung up and then decided to get a good book and catch some sun on the back deck. Dude was faithfully waiting for her and curled up at her feet. Looking at her much-loved pet, she thought, *He has two speeds – sprint and nap!* He had brought her comfort and plenty of amusement over the years.

4

Rosh Hashanah, September 24

It was Sunday and the sun rose a few minutes before six. Once it cleared the ridge, it shone directly into Abigail's bedroom. She slept with the window open unless it was very cold. This morning she stretched and called out for Dude. He emerged with sleepy eyes and grunted his greeting before taking off on his morning rounds.

He was part Labrador retriever and he lived up to his name. There was an area by the oak in the front yard in which he deposited the things he retrieved - cans, bits of cardboard, fast food cartons, bones, and other trash that he thought of as personal gifts from careless litterbugs. The pampered pooch had his house on the covered front porch which gave him plenty of extra protection during even the coldest winter weather. It was a little unusual, but Abigail believed that animals belonged outdoors.

Abigail dressed for the nippy morning and headed out to take care of Buster and Dude before she made her own breakfast complete with a steaming cup of Earl Grey tea. *Oh, what shall I wear to church today?* She stood before the closet a minute before choosing some dress slacks and a matching blouse that no one would see under her jacket anyway.

As she pulled into the church parking lot, she saw her good friend and prayer partner, Cindy McCord, with her family. Cindy was very discerning and even though she sometimes raised an eyebrow when Abigail spoke of ritual abuse, she diligently prayed about the unfamiliar issues. Abigail never violated confidentiality, but it was necessary to let Cindy know about the spiritual warfare that swirled around this kind of ministry.

"Hi, Cindy," Abigail called.

"Hey, Abi," Cindy returned, "you were on my mind yesterday. You okay?"

"Boy, do I have some stuff to tell you! You just wouldn't believe it!"

"With you, I think I might," she laughed. "You want to catch up after lunch? I think Gary would be okay with the kids for a while," Cindy asked over her shoulder as she was heading to her classroom.

"Sounds like a plan, see you after church."

Abigail headed for the other door, arriving at the same time as Sheriff Roger Bynum and his family. He opened the door for his family and continued to hold it open for Abigail. She smiled and thanked him. He did not look her in the eye, but as she passed, he said in a low voice, "How's your horse? Horses have been found dead in your area lately. Maybe it's that Coggins Disease." He followed his family inside.

Before he let go of the door, she looked at his large hand. In the flesh between his thumb and index finger was a tattoo. It was a small upside-down cross. The hair on the back of her neck rose and she felt the goose bumps rise on her arms. *This man is way more than creepy!* Abigail was alarmed. *And was that a hint or a threat? And just how does he know that I have a horse?* Of course, he was the sheriff and this was a relatively small county.

Abigail was distracted during Sunday school and had to work hard to focus on worship. It was a blessing that the worship team had chosen songs that seemed customized for her troubled heart that morning. Pastor Daniel Spalding brought a message about King David's battles. "He did warfare in the natural realm," he concluded, "so that we can know how to war in the spiritual realm. Get into the Psalms and customize them for your situation. Pray them back to the Lord."

The service closed with a chorus and people began to pour into the aisles. Abigail kept her conversations short as she worked her way toward Cindy and her husband. Cindy needed to go home for lunch with Gary and to get the kids settled for the afternoon. "How about two-thirty at your place?" Cindy asked.

"Works," Abigail nodded, "see you in a bit. And thanks, Gary, for letting me have her for a while."

He picked up on Abigail's tension. "No problem, me and the kids have a project this afternoon, don't we?" He loved being a dad and cherished the time he got to spend with Traci and Bryan.

Abigail walked to her truck, put her Bible on the seat, started the engine, and followed the parade of vehicles out of the parking lot and through the town of Springfield to the road that led to her farm. Buster was waiting in the corner of the pasture. When he saw her, he turned and galloped all the way around the fenced off orchard and garden that protruded into his pasture and was waiting for her near the driveway by the time she parked the truck.

He whinnied his greeting and paced expectantly until she crossed over to him and gave him all the attention he wanted. "We'll go riding again pretty soon, not today, though. I promise." She talked to her critters as if they understood every word she said. Maybe they did.

By the time Abigail had finished cleaning up after her own lunch and taken a ten-minute power nap, it was nearly time for Cindy's arrival. She took her Bible to the front porch and sat on one of the two rockers. Dude heard her and came around to join her. He sat between her feet and looked at her with the kind of look that only a dog could give while she absent-mindedly scratched and patted his glossy coat. It was getting thicker with the cool nights.

Cindy arrived right on time. Both of them liked to be punctual. Dude gave her a royal greeting and she rewarded him with praises and pats on the head.

"Let's go to the back deck and sit in the sunshine," Abigail invited. "Water or cola?"

"Water. Good idea! Let's catch some warm rays while we still can."

They maneuvered their chairs to take advantage of the sun and the view of the barn at the edge of the pasture as well as the corn field and the bottomland beyond. Buster briefly looked up from his grazing and then went back to it. Dude settled down with a sigh as he lowered his head to his paws and looked up from time to time as if he was checking to see if his input would be necessary.

"Okay, I'm more than curious. What is going on?" Cindy began.

Abigail inhaled and let out a big breath. "Well, yesterday we went for a ride across the road. I wanted to explore the fields that are to the south," she gestured over her shoulder toward the road with her thumb. "We saw lots of four-wheeler tracks and lots of hoof prints. Thursday night I was out here and there seemed to be a lot of traffic in the bottoms. I didn't think anything of it since it was a perfect night for night riding."

Cindy remained quiet and waited for more details.

"Anyway, we crossed that little creek and followed the trails that run parallel to the road and through a couple of smaller fields. Then I saw a wide trail that headed back toward the highway and I thought we could go up there just to see which neighbor might own that land. Just curious, ya know? Dude went up ahead of us and was real excited about something under a big oak. When Buster and I got closer, Buster got real nervous and on high alert. He was snorting and wanted to bolt and run."

Cindy leaned forward slightly.

"When we got up to the top, I saw a fence and the top of a roof - oh man, was it blue or green? Blue. Yes, it was blue. There was a black barn, maybe one of those tobacco barns. Anyway," Abigail raced on with the story, "Dude was sniffing around a huge rock that was about three feet high and maybe four feet across. Oh! And get this! It was chiseled into the shape of a pentagram. Cindy, I think there was a ritual there on the Equinox Thursday." Abigail was getting very animated with her gestures.

Cindy's eyes widened, "You think your neighbor is a Satanist?"

"That's what it looks like. I'm not sure which one; it's hard to guess how far down the road it would be because of the curves. I'm not sure if I want to know, but I want to know, you know?"

"It might be nice to know who to watch out for. What are you going to do?"

"I don't know, but it wouldn't hurt to drive down the road and see if I can spot a house with a blue roof and a black barn. Some of the houses are back off the road so the buildings aren't visible from there."

They both fell into silence for a few minutes.

Abigail startled Cindy, "Oh, there's more! When I got back from the ride, I went into the bathroom and the toilet seat was up. You know how I always put it down. So, I looked around the rest of the house and found a dresser drawer opened a little and that verse on the wall next to my dresser was crooked. Cindy, I *know* that it was not like that when I left. Someone was in my house."

"We have to pray for your protection. Did you call the sheriff?" Cindy asked.

"Ooh, that's the other spooky thing. This morning at church I just happened to be going in at the same time as the Bynum family. He held the door open for me after his family went in and then he said, 'How's your horse? There have been horses found dead in your area lately - maybe that Coggins disease or something like that.' My hair stood up on end. He creeps me out. I won't call him.

"Besides," Abigail added, "I just happened to look at his hand when he was holding the door open and he had an upside-down cross tattooed in the fold of the skin between his thumb and index finger." She jabbed her left index finger into the fold of her right hand. "I'm pretty sure he wanted me to see that, now that I think about it."

"Whoa, that's interesting," Cindy nodded, "I know what you mean; he bothers me, too."

"I don't know if that was a veiled threat or not," Abigail added. "I wonder if he was the one that was in my house. I checked with Earl and Jan and they weren't home while I was out riding."

"Somebody knew you were gone riding," Cindy made a keen observation.

"That would mean that someone is watching me; someone who blends into this neck of the woods, like a neighbor or a mailman or someone who drives up and down this road a lot."

"Like your next-door neighbor? I guess we have a few things to pray about."

Abigail nodded and opened her Bible to Psalm 35 and began to customize it for her situation, "Contend, Oh Lord, with those who contend with me …"

Cindy prayed in agreement and incorporated other warring Scriptures into her prayers, practicing what Pastor Spalding had just preached.

They prayed until they had covered each aspect of the current situation and felt peace about it. Then they began to give praise and thanksgiving to their King. After the final amen, they closed their Bibles and sat in silence for a few minutes.

Cindy glanced at her watch, "I guess I'd better see how Gary is doing with the kids." She stood up, finished her water and headed to the kitchen to put her glass on the counter. Abigail was glad that her close friend felt so much at home here. She followed Cindy into the house and they walked out of the front door together. Dude raced around the house and jumped up and down excitedly as they neared Cindy's car. The two friends hugged briefly before Cindy drove off.

Dude escorted her all the way down the driveway, staying in the grass. Once she got onto the road he turned and scampered back up to the house. Abigail loved to watch him run. His ears flattened and head lowered to streamline his body for speed, he arrived at the front porch with his tongue hanging out the side of his mouth. He looked for approval for doing his escort job.

"You're the best, Dude," she said, "Come on; let's go take care of Buster. They walked around the house, past the garden, and squeezed through the fence. The evening feeding was routine and Abigail walked back to the house to get her own supper ready. The sun was going down around six o'clock already as the daylight got shorter and shorter.

Zorroz waited until dark to meet with his area master, Daggett. There were disturbing things happening to some of the key members of their group. There were disturbing things happening to key members of the regional council as well. There had never been any disruptions in their powers. Now there were signs of weakness and downright impotence both physically and in the spiritual realm.

Prinz, the regional master, was already at their secure meeting place. The remote location made it easy to slip behind the building without being seen. If there was traffic, it was easy to keep going until it was safe to turn around and make another attempt. Sunday nights were very easy and Zorroz had no trouble. He was surprised, however, to see several other vehicles already there. He parked and walked over to the dark entry way. There were dim lights on inside, but there were no windows on the ground level of this building.

When Zorroz entered the meeting room he was mildly surprised to see not only Prinz, but Darod, Levi, and Herrak from a neighboring district also in attendance. This was significant. He managed to keep his demeanor neutral as he gave obeisance to his superiors and nodded to the others.

He had not seen Mastiff at the last area gathering. He assumed that he was on assignment elsewhere. He was called Mastiff partially because he was a very large, strong man. Tonight, his great prowess was noticeably diminished.

Prinz cleared his throat and growled, "We have a problem that we need to take care of very carefully. Mastiff's daughter has been giving him information through one of her inside informers. It seems as if the precautions we have laid in place over the years have been breached. Carrie Sue has been meeting with some woman who has been able to dismantle the programming. Furthermore, as you can see by Mastiff's condition, she has been able to do much damage. We need to stop her. We need to stop both of them. Soon."

He continued, "She's also seeing one of Darod's people. He stopped and briefly looked each man in the eye. It brought internal shudders that came from both the men and their invisible powers. There was a hierarchy of rulers, powers, and spiritual world forces. The thinly veiled threat meant that failure would bring misery.

As much bravado as each one normally exuded they knew that their powers were vulnerable to The Great Power. Mastiff was distressed. This was a truly a dog-eat-dog organization. They would stab each other in the back in a heartbeat. They would climb over each other to reach the top of the ladder. He was vulnerable and it was his responsibility. He could not manage his daughter and therefore, he had brought this situation upon himself and the entire region. He vowed to increase the pressure on his enemy. The little scare tactics would have to escalate.

"You and that worthless whelp of a son of yours had better get on it," Prinz hissed, "and the rest of you as well." He did not need to spell out what the consequences were for failure. Prinz then stood and swept out of the subdued room.

The men went to their vehicles in silence and left the parking lot as unobtrusively as possible. They would meet up later at the designated gathering place. They would not let any Christian, Catholic, or Jewish religious event go unanswered. Tonight was the Rosh Hashanah ritual.

Mastiff reflected on the situation in which he was embroiled. That "son" of his was probably not even his own blood. Sure, the worthless cur was born to his wife, but he doubted that he had sired that wiry young runt who had an uncanny resemblance to Prinz himself.

5

Monday, September 25

Abigail woke Monday morning to the sun streaming through her windows. She felt very blessed to have six-day weekends most of the time. She was free to arrange her schedule according to the number of counselees she had to see. She did not *have* to work, but she loved the work and it kept her as busy as she wanted to be.

After a good stretch, she got up and pulled her play clothes on. The critters always got attention first. She grabbed her sweatshirt off the hook near the back door and headed down to see Buster. As usual Dude bounced alongside of her with enthusiasm. One would think that he had not seen her for days.

"This is the day that the Lord has made and I will rejoice and be glad in it!" she declared into the heavens. A decade ago Abigail determined to declare this verse every day whether it was spoken with pure joy or uttered through gritted teeth. It was coming up on the tenth anniversary of the accident that changed her life forever.

Halloween night … her husband was driving their three sons home from the youth activity at church … the drunken pickup truck driver … the phone call …. "Steve, Marty, Mike - Oh, God, how I miss my boys!

Darryl, my life mate …" She stopped herself before she meandered down that path too far. The settlement and insurance money provided the funds to buy this little sanctuary of a farm - yet another bittersweet thought.

Now and then Abigail thought about the possibility of another relationship but she felt like it would betray her family somehow. Sometimes she felt so lonely. She knew that Darryl would have wanted her to be happy and secure if that was God's will. She missed his companionship and intimacy, laughter and tears, and everything that made for a good marriage.

Today she missed her family.

F. Amy Bolton was on the move by two a.m. that Monday morning. She had worked late the night before. She was able to hold down her job at the pizza parlor mainly because she liked to drive and did not have to mingle with people. Deliver the pizza. Collect the money. She was able to turn on just enough charm to earn decent tips. If she just happened to switch to an inappropriate personality, she was usually able to get the right person back into executive control and keep her job. Some days were more difficult than others and she was beginning to believe that her counselor might be right about some things. There were heated internal arguments about whether or not they should trust Abigail.

Right now, however, she was not delivering any pizzas. Amy was not in executive control of the body; Issador was. The phone had rung in the middle of the night and when Amy answered it, there were a series of tones. She thought the call had been disconnected so she had hung up and gone back to sleep. She did not know that the tones triggered Issador.

Issador was driving them to a rendezvous point near the lake a few hours away. He pulled into a parking spot and casually walked to a bench near the lake just before sunrise. Soon he was joined by a man who just as casually flashed a sign. This triggered Nicholai, the commandant of one of the subterranean levels. Even though Head Warden had jurisdiction over the ground level prison, Nicholai had his spies and access to that level without the knowledge of Head Warden. Nicholai was subject to a superior and that superior answered to someone else higher up. Or, perhaps, more accurately, lower down.

"What is going on?" Herrak demanded.

Nicholai was usually very sure of himself. Today he was alarmed and feared retribution from the area master. He had no good answer for the mysterious disappearance of so many personalities. "I don't know; it has something to do with that counselor lady. She suckered Head Warden into something; I was blocked from whatever went on."

"You're not doing your job! You need to keep Amy from seeing her. Kill her if you have to. And if you can't do that, you need to create more chaos and confusion so that they can't do anything. Get them to wear that woman out. You know what's on the line here." He did not wait for an answer but abruptly turned his back and marched back to his vehicle.

Nicholai contemplated his options. He had internal power to influence a fairly large number of other personalities who would not know that they were doing his bidding. He had demonic assistance. He also knew the consequences of failure all too well. Nicholai faded back into his internal domain.

Issador was quite accustomed to what he called irregularities. One minute he would be speaking with someone and the next they were gone, leaving him to wonder if the encounter was real or imagined. *Well, I'm here now and I need to get us home.* He ambled back to their car and drove home. They were back in bed by ten-thirty.

Amy woke up shortly afterwards and noted the time. She still felt tired even though she slept ten straight hours except for the wrong number. *Why do I get so many wrong numbers? And in the middle of the night?* She sighed and started her day.

Abigail took full advantage of the dry weather to do fall cleaning outside. She turned the compost pile after she raked up the plants that were no longer productive. It put her into a melancholy frame of mind – dying things; things past their prime. She mowed the two acres of lawn that surrounded the farmhouse. It was another one of her chores that she called play. The ten-horsepower riding mower made it fun and gave her time to think and pray.

She and Earl had also finished cutting up all of the downed trees on their properties. A wild storm felled a number of oaks and shag bark hickory trees the previous fall. They both used wood stoves to help reduce their heating bills. Earl always said that wood heats you many times - when you cut it, when you split it, and when you burn it.

He was right.

They made a good team – he had the chain saws and the Jeep that could haul half a rick of wood at a time. She had the strength and stamina to load and unload the wood. He taught her how to use the smaller chain saw and to split wood. He used a minimum of effort in his practiced movements, but his heart condition forced him to pace himself. He made it look so easy. With a flick of his wrist and accurate blows the wood split into even wedges.

Abigail had good wood-splitting days and then there were her character-building wood-splitting days. The end result was five cords of stacked wood so far. She would be toasty warm as she curled up by the wood stove this winter. It was nice to have both a forced air gas furnace and a woodstove.

Abigail went to church that Wednesday night as usual and found a parking space in the side lot on one of the back rows. Backing all the way up to the hedge and grabbing her Bible, she headed into the church. She was thankful tonight that Sheriff Bynum only came on Sundays. She did not want to risk running into him again since she was not sure if she could mask her thoughts and feelings very well if he were to look at her closely.

While the congregation sang a combination of hymns and worship songs a wiry figure moved out of the shadows. He looked around briefly and dropped out of sight under a pickup truck. With a small flashlight clenched in his teeth, he pulled a hand tool out of his pocket and made a crimp in the line. He scooted over to the other side and repeated the deed. He slid out of the parking lot and casually returned to his vehicle. He liked the deeply tinted windows in the battered Chevy and the powerful engine under the hood.

6

Friday, September 29

Friday morning came soon enough. Abigail believed that she could make the outdoor chores a full-time preoccupation, the indoor projects a full-time job, and counseling full time as well. *There is so much to do, how could anyone ever be bored?* She hustled through the usual morning routine, jotted a few things on her grocery list, and got ready for work.

Abigail pulled up to the church and applied the brakes. She could not know that fluid oozed out of the two partially crimped lines each time she stepped on the brake. Carrie Sue was waiting as usual. They greeted each other and walked up to the side door of the church. Abigail unlocked it and they walked down the hall to her office. Abigail noticed that Carrie Sue seemed to be moving rather gingerly as she turned on the CD player in the waiting area.

Abigail sat with her open Bible on her lap, a steno notepad rested on top of that, and her pen was ready in her hand. They opened the session with a prayer that incorporated words from Psalm 64, "Hear our voices, O God, preserve Carrie Sue from the dread of the enemy who thinks You don't know what they are doing. Foil their schemes, Lord and start us where we need to start today."

When Abigail finished the prayer, she was looking into the pained eyes of yet another personality. She sensed that it was a female who was probably a young teen. "Hi, I'm Abigail." Abigail was quite accustomed to introducing herself numerous times.

The alter shifted uncomfortably in her chair and furtively looked around the room for clues to her whereabouts. It was not uncommon for parts who had been concealed for a long time to surface and have no idea where they were. This forced them to be very creative actors.

"You're okay; you're safe here. Carrie Sue was walking like she was hurting this morning; I have a hunch that you are carrying that pain. Do you know Carrie Sue?"

She looked even more distressed as she shook her head after looking down at her own body.

"Would it be all right for me to explain a few things to you?" Abigail began her negotiations with this one. *Oh, Lord, why does it always have to be so tedious and painful?*

She nodded her assent and looked at Abigail with eyes that begged for her to be truthful and safe.

"Thanks, I know this is hard so I'll give you some generalities and you can feel free to ask me anything you want, okay?" Abigail took a breath and plunged into her basic explanation. "You are a part of Carrie Sue. Carrie Sue was raised by Satanists. Your first memory and your last memory were probably the worst for you, right?"

She paused to give the teen a moment to reflect on her obviously painful history and got another nod.

"When the cult, your bio-dad, and those other creeps got a hold of Carrie Sue, they did horrific things to her. Made her eat or drink something that made her woozy … do you remember that?"

There was another nod and increased interest.

"They combined drugs, hypnotism, and torture – usually involving sexual stuff – and that caused you to split off of someone else who is just a bit younger than you but has the same kind of issues. So, she basically shut down and kind of hibernated and you continued where she left off until you couldn't stand it anymore. When you shut down that last time, someone else took over for you. You stayed stuck at, what? Twelve or thirteen?"

Startled at Abigail's discernment, the alter drew back in her chair. Knowledge is power. It is always used against you.

"I'm sorry; I didn't mean to alarm you. I know you've never met anyone safe before and you have no reason to trust me so I'm grateful that you are giving me a chance. Can I keep going?"

"Okay," she barely squeaked out.

Ah, a beginning. She's talking. "Carrie Sue, that's the birth name of the person who you're a part of, kept growing and aging. That's why you're a young teen sitting here in an older body. She's in her mid-thirties but you stayed stuck at your age."

Eyes widened as she began to grasp these foreign concepts. She looked down again. *That's why my body is bigger and I have …* She did not finish the thought.

Abigail did a quick math calculation. This was 2006, Carrie Sue was born in 1973, and this one must think it's about 1985 or 1986. The world had changed a lot since then. "I know that this can be very confusing; shocking even. Does this make any sense?"

"Yes ma'am." She said politely.

"Can you tell me about the last time you were out?" Abigail probed. "Like, what year it was or the time of year maybe?"

"It was cold and rainy, leaves were beginning to change color," she began tentatively in a soft voice. "I just remember my brother ..." She paused and sighed deeply. "He was mean."

"There are lots of other parts in there, too. Some of them told me about the brother. Did your memories about what he did to you happen at home or at some other place?"

"Mostly home, but sometimes he took me to the woods or a barn."

"I'm sorry, that's not the way big brothers are supposed to behave. They're supposed to protect their little sisters." Abigail was trying to expose this one to a new normal. All she had known was abuse. Receiving abuse was this personality's job and *that* was infuriating. That fueled Abigail's passion for counseling these pariahs.

"Do you know why you're out now after being shut down for so long?" Abigail asked. She had a good idea, but did not want to put words into the girl's mouth or make any suggestions that would influence her.

"Billy called my name," she admitted, "I have to obey him."

"Why?" Abigail asked, knowing that she had been programmed to respond.

"My dad gave me to him," she said ruefully.

"I'm sorry for that, too. That's not the way dads are supposed to protect their little girls."

Abigail received a look that said *what planet are you from?* "The good news is that we can get you safe today," Abigail continued, "can I tell you about it?"

She received another doubtful look along with a nod. This one had little to lose and Abigail's warm brown eyes were so different from the cold eyes that she was accustomed to seeing. She would take a chance. A big chance.

"Great. Here it is in a nutshell: when your father gave you to your brother, it was their agreement. But the Bible says that a covenant or agreement that has been previously ratified cannot be set aside. That means that if there was another covenant already made with someone else, your father's covenant was bogus. Do you know the real Jesus Christ? Not the mean, false one they may have told you about?"

Eyes narrowed and Abigail could see the confusion and hear the unspoken questions. There was so much duplicity training in play with these survivors. "They said he was the real Jesus."

"Have they ever told you anything that was one hundred percent true?"

"No," she admitted with downcast eyes.

"How about if we set that aside for now and let me finish telling you the way out. You can think about it and then decide what you want to do."

"Sure."

"Okay then," Abigail continued with the tricky conversation. Too many times the personality would switch out or a protector or a persecutor would step in. "Let's get back to the covenant thing. You have to remember that Satan and the Satanists are a bunch of legalists. So, if the real God's Word is true, then that means that when He said before you were formed in your mother's womb, I knew you, He had a covenant relationship with you. That happened before time and before Lucifer screwed up and became Satan. So, then the covenant that God had with you cannot be set aside by your father or brother or anyone else for that matter. Besides, a covenant made with a minor is bogus. A covenant made with someone against their will is bogus. A covenant made with someone who is impaired is bogus."

She began to grasp Abigail's argument and leaned forward a little, but she was not quite ready to have her hopes dashed again.

"We need to reverse their bogus deals. Here's what happened in the spiritual realm: your father and brother got power through demons that they think they are using. The demons are going along with it because they need someone to work through and are helping Satan's agenda. Other demons got you. You were the one left holding the bag. There's nothing in it for you except torment."

The young teen winced at those words as if she were being jabbed.

"They're not happy that you know this and that you might actually give me permission to pray for you, are they?"

"They're mad and they say that they'll make it worse for me."

"They're lying. Would you allow me to pray a quick prayer to prove it?"

She was feeling more torment and was desperate for relief. "Okay," she gasped, "please help me."

"Lord Jesus Christ, I plead Your cleansing blood over this part of Carrie Sue and ask that You would separate every foul spirit from her and set them aside where they cannot harm her in any way." Abigail saw the immediate relief.

"Thank you!" she said. Her cloudy countenance brightened, but she kept looking toward the corner of the room. She was seeing something in the spiritual realm that Abigail did not see in the natural realm. It was probably a bunch of angry demons.

"You're welcome. Do you have a name?"

"Yeah," she said with shame, "but I don't like it. It starts with a C."

Abigail could imagine what degrading name it was. "Jesus will give you a new name. Let me finish with the plan now that the scuzzie uglies are out of the way. You just saw what happened to you when I prayed and you got rid of the demons that were assigned to you. Demons need people to work through; that's why they bargained with the dad and the brother to get you. Now they will be going to a place where Jesus sends them – POWs I call them, and the dad and brother will lose their demonic powers because those guys will be joining these guys." Abigail gestured to the corner. "The last thing we can do to make sure that you will never be accessed again is to ask the Lord Jesus to put you back inside where you came from before they split you out."

Abigail paused as she anticipated the unasked questions for yet another foreign idea. *Poor girl, she's really hanging in there.*

"What do you mean?" she queried.

"When God knit Carrie Sue in her mother's womb, she was complete with one body, one soul, and one spirit. That's God's best plan for each of us. All the torment and torture caused dissociation on a brain level and on a soul level. The enemy wants to divide and conquer. If you're separate, you're more easily accessed and used. If we ask God to put you back inside where you came from, you can help Carrie Sue beat these creeps with your strength and character."

The beleaguered personality followed Abigail's line of reasoning.

"As long as you and all the others have those traits and character, the original Carrie Sue doesn't have access to it. When you come back together, it benefits all of you and, more importantly, it frustrates the dickens out of the cult because they can't trigger you anymore because you don't exist in the form they created. You are safe and Carrie Sue is safer. We have a ways to go before everyone is in though." *Maybe I should have been a lawyer.*

"Okay, I'm tired, let's do it."

"One more question. Remember I said there was someone that you split off of and someone else split off of you?"

"Yes."

"I have a hunch that there are probably a bunch of others who are just like you who have been listening in and who would also like to be healed and put back inside. Are you aware of them?"

"Yeah, there's a bunch of us," she admitted, "and we all want that."

"Great, let's pray." Abigail prayed her fairly comprehensive prayer that demolished strongholds caused by verbal assaults and programming, direct and indirect sexual violations, and other traumas. She prayed for the healing of body memories and emotional pain. She asked for "divine forgetfulness" for particularly sordid memories. She rebuked the demons and asked the Lord to send them to a place where they would never afflict another person again and to send reproaches back upon those who sent them. Finally, she blessed those affected personalities with light, truth, the fruit of the Holy Spirit, and unity in a bond of peace as the Lord reknit them back into their rightful places.

Suddenly Carrie Sue was back in executive control. "Wow! That was good. She was really hurting. Big brother called her out last night and was talking about payback for what we were doing to him and bio-dad. He said it's our fault that dad's getting sick. I don't know what he's talking about."

"I think I do. Were you listening in when I was explaining about reversing the legal transaction?"

"Yeah."

"Every time that you have been in here and we have been able to get your parts healed and delivered, the demons from you and from the brother and the dad – and whoever else used you as a bargaining chip – go to wherever Jesus sends them. You get set free but they lose their powers. Reproaches go back on them. Your father is in his fifties but seemed to be much younger and stronger until lately, right?"

"Yeah."

"That means that whatever power he had was from demons. No demons; no power. Satanists need power. Demons need people to work through. It's win-win for them and lose-lose for you. That's why he gave you away so many times so that his power would be built up. Your brother did that too; all of them did for that matter. They're mad and don't want you to see me. That's why they called out that young teen to punish her and the rest of you. She was hurting."

"Yeah, and so was I." The host personality often felt the physical and/or emotional pain of alters who were not always evident.

"I noticed the limp this morning. How are you doing now?"

"Good, the pain is all gone. Big brother was, er, particularly rough last night."

"I know you think I push too hard and too fast sometimes, but that's going to keep happening until everyone is in," Abigail reminded them.

"Yeah, we know, but change is hard. This is all we've ever known."

"I understand, but staying the same isn't so great either. And they know that you know now, so they'll be upping the pressure. Hey, I hate that our time is about up, so let me pray you out of here."

"Okay, thanks, we really do appreciate all you're doing, ya know."

Abigail smiled and prayed, "Lord, thank You for the break through. I pray Your highest protection over Carrie Sue and all of her parts. Abba, please do not let the enemy continue to hurt Your precious child or any part of her spirit, soul, or body, amen."

They made arrangements for the following Friday. Abigail completed her paperwork and got ready for the next appointment.

Brittany came on time as usual. Her mother made it a priority to see that her daughter got healing. She felt guilty for everything the teen had been through with the divorce from her father, and now this from her step-father.

"How are you doing today, Brittany?"

"Fine, but I'm getting really tired of talking about this," she replied. "No offense."

"Well, we can do something about that, but you are going to have to face the big F word …" Brittany's eyes widened with surprise until Abigail finished her unexpected statement … "Forgiveness." Sometimes it was necessary to get a teenager's attention.

"Seriously, Brittany, once you take care of that business, you can move on. Trust me, I know. Been there, done that, got the T-shirt, gave it to Jesus. I have peace and I am much safer without my anger."

Brittany's cheeks puffed out as she took a deep breath and blew it out. "Okay, so if I forgive the jerk-face …" she let the thought evaporate.

"Let's talk about three related issues a minute and maybe that will help you. One is forgiveness. That's the transaction between us and God. We say, 'God, I confess I have held a grudge against Jerk-face and I choose to loose the offender away, to cover the sin, to give him an unconditional grace that he has not asked for and *so* does not deserve.' The next issue is about reconciliation. The end of Romans twelve says, *'if possible, so far as it depends on you, be at peace with all men.'* Now Brittany, reconciliation is not always possible and not always wise. It's a mutual agreement between two people to renew a relationship. Trust is the third issue. That means your offender has to prove that he is trustworthy. In your case, you can choose to forgive him, but any kind of relationship with him is not going to happen because right now you choose not to. He's not safe and he's unrepentant and therefore untrustworthy. Does that make sense?"

"Yeah, I think so," Brittany had thoughts tumbling around in her mind. "But he still gets away with it and that's not fair!"

"No, he really doesn't. Romans twelve says, "*'VENGEANCE IS MINE, I WILL REPAY,' says the* LORD."

So, if you have your hands around his neck, you're getting in God's way. It's like He's saying, 'Do you want to take care of him? Or Me? You? Or Me?' When we get out of God's way, He can do the most creative vengeance."

"I'd just like to shove a pencil through that hole while he's looking! I'd just like to kick him in the …" Brittany stopped her outburst.

"Would you really do it if you had the chance?"

"No, not really, but that's how mad I am."

"God is giving you a way to be angry and not sin. Do you think you're ready to try it His way?" Abigail invited gently.

Brittany took another deep breath and released it in a long huff. "Okay, what do I have to do?"

"Well, you've been holding a grudge for a while so that needs to be 'fessed up. Then you can forgive him. Remember to use active verbs – I confess … I choose – okay? And then I'll pray in agreement."

"Okay, here goes," Brittany wasn't completely convinced. "God, I'm really ticked at my jerk-face step-father and I confess my anger. And I choose to loose it away and forgive him even though I don't think he deserves it." She made a scissor motion with her fingers.

"Lord, I pray in agreement with my sister and ask that You would demolish any strongholds created by her grudge and cleanse her from all unrighteousness and any root of bitterness that may have defiled her. We rebuke all demons associated with her anger and unforgiveness and ask that You would heal and seal all those broken places. Fill her with Your Holy Spirit and let the fruit of the Spirit – especially peace – fill her, in Jesus' name, amen.

Brittany was quiet. "Now what?"

"Let's go back to the memory of discovering the hole between the closets and ask the Lord to bring you truth that will set you free."

"Okay."

"You just focus on the memory. I'll pray and then shut up. You just let me know what you see or hear or sense," Abigail instructed.

Brittany nodded and closed her eyes.

"Lord, You're the same yesterday, today, and forever. You were there even though Brittany did not sense You then. Would You manifest Your presence in that memory right now and let Brittany see You with her spiritual eyes or hear You with her spiritual ears or sense Your presence? What is the truth that You want Brittany to know that will set her free from this pain?"

They sat in silence for several minutes before the astounded teen gave a short laugh and opened her eyes. "You're not going to believe this. I saw Jesus standing in my closet. He was plugging the hole with His finger and He winked at me!" She laughed again. "Is that for real?"

Abigail smiled, "Well, how does the memory feel right now?"

"Oh, wow!" Brittany said in astonishment, "I don't feel the shame or anger or dirty or anything."

"Are you absolutely sure? Just a minute ago you had a bunch of intense feelings."

"Yeah, I know," Brittany was mystified, "but now I can't even make myself feel them or think of anything except Jesus being there for me."

"Very cool," Abigail rejoiced with Brittany. "God uses the way He created our minds to work to give us clearer understanding. A picture is worth a thousand words. What's the truth He wants you to know?"

"That He was there. That He protects me. That He is taking care of it" she said with wonder. "Oh, I can't wait to tell Mom. Are we done?"

"One more question: What are you going to do the next time someone offends you? Because you know that sooner or later someone will offend you, right?"

Brittany flashed a big grin and made the scissors motion with her right hand.

"Go celebrate! I'm proud of you." Abigail smiled back at the jubilant teen.

Brittany bounced back to the waiting area and Abigail could hear the animated conversation. She smiled. *Thank You, Lord for letting me participate with You.* She told Brittany's mother that she thought that they could play it by ear as far as another session was concerned. If there were residual issues she should call, but she had a feeling that Brittany was good to go for now.

They left so Abigail turned her thoughts to her paperwork and then to the next appointment. Amy would invariably be six minutes late. She checked her watch. *Still about twenty minutes away.*

Amy was under the influence of Nicholai. She did not know it, of course, but she had lost executive control while on the way to see Abigail. Nicholai directed Issador to drive them back home again. Issador complied and when they got home he walked up the three steps into the mobile home. It looked more like a teenager's bedroom than an adult's abode. It was a jumbled mess of clothes, unfinished projects, empty food containers, and unwashed dishes.

They went into one of the two small bedrooms. This one was decorated for a child. The sight of the room caused Tony, one of the child alters, to switch in. He immediately found his favorite toys and began to play.

Nicholai was pleased. *We'll just waste that woman's time for now and keep her from doing any more damage.*

Abigail checked her watch. *Hmm. Unusual for Amy to be late. Hope she's all right.* Abigail had a policy of waiting for fifteen minutes. If someone did not call or show up, she would leave and wait for them to call her to reschedule. She did not hunt anyone down. That was their responsibility.

Amy did not show so Abigail closed up the office and went out to her truck. She did not notice the circle of oily drops that had accumulated under the truck. After stowing her office-in-a-bag behind the seat, she headed to the grocery store to pick up a few items. She applied the brakes as she entered the parking lot. *Hmm, the pedal went down a little more than usual.* She made a mental note to check fluid levels when she got home and went about her business.

Abigail finished her shopping, placed the groceries on the floorboard, and walked around the back of the truck. She eased out of the parking lot, timing her entry onto the highway so she did not have to wait. Her father was a trucker and he taught her how to drive. He was big on smooth driving.

She could just hear him now, "There's just no sense in roaring up to a red light and having to brake hard and then rev up your engine again. You want to be easy on your engine and brakes." She remembered how he made her practice braking without having any lurch at the end. Smooth.

She wound down Kingston Road following the curves, accelerating a bit up the hills and coasting down. She could not know that each time she tapped on the brakes more fluid squirted out. Touching the brakes before the last curve, she became alarmed when the truck did not respond much. The pedal was soft and it went further to the floor this time. *I'll definitely have to check that fluid.*

She made it to York Creek Road and put on her turn signal. She tried to brake, but the pedal was even softer. She pumped it and it seemed to help a little, but by that time she was going too fast to make the turn. She glided past the road and coasted up a slight incline and made a quick decision to turn into the church parking lot at the top of the rise. It was a blessing that there was no traffic. She impulsively decided to try to make it the last two miles home.

Pulling back onto the highway and driving the short distance to her road, she eased around the corner and accelerated more cautiously up the grade and then started thinking about the two hills that she still needed to navigate. The last one was a half mile long downhill grade to her driveway. M*aybe I should have stayed at the church and called someone. Well, too late now, I'm committed.* Coasting to the top of the last hill, she slowed the truck almost to a stop, and breathed a hasty prayer before making the final descent.

Fortunately, the driveway was not at a ninety degree angle; it was more like sixty degrees. *Oh, Lord, I sure hope I don't run down Your angels.* She readily acknowledged that she had a warped sense of humor. Gripping the wheel with white knuckles, pumping the brakes as she neared the entrance to her driveway, she went onto the shoulder to try to make the angle even more favorable.

The passenger side tires bounced off the road jolting her and scattering the groceries all over the floorboard. The gravel in the driveway crunched and skittered as the tires tried to grab some traction. The momentum caused her to go off the left-hand side of the driveway into the grass but she was able to maintain control and avoid the giant sycamore tree. As the truck slowed because of the uphill grade of the driveway, Abigail breathed a sigh of relief before her next alarming thought: I still have to stop this thing!

Oh, Lord, please don't let me run into the house. I need a little more help here. Suddenly a thought flashed into her mind. *Of course! The parking brake! That might work. Thank You, Lord.* As she made the final turn up to the house only going about three miles per hour, she pressed the parking brake. It made a loud protest as the rear tires locked up and the truck skidded to a shuddering halt.

That's when Abigail began to shake.

High overhead Urdang cursed again. Much too late he sensed another being near him and took a blow in the back before he could dodge it. His superior was not pleased by the ineffective curses, the foiled plans, and the superior enemy forces that gathered around that demon-slaying woman. Who was she?

"Thank You, Lord! Thank You, Lord, for getting this idiot home safely. I should have left it at that church," Abigail prayed out loud. She finally opened the door after her adrenaline rush subsided and the trembling stopped. She was greeted by Dude. She had not noticed her welcoming committee while she was so focused on her adventure.

After putting the groceries away and getting something to eat, she turned her thoughts to her truck problem. This was one of the times she really missed her husband. He could pop the hood and fix almost anything that was wrong.

Dad had taught her some of the basics of vehicle maintenance as a prerequisite for owning her first car. He wanted to make sure that his little girl would not be ripped off by someone wanting to charge her for changing the blinker fluid. She could top off fluids, change a tire and the oil if needed.

She always joked that doing it by herself was Plan A but she preferred Plan B. When Cindy asked her about that one day she explained, "Plan A is doing it myself. Plan B is when I start Plan A and look pitiful enough that some really nice chivalrous man comes along and finishes it for me."

She went outside and looked under the hood. Just as she suspected, the brake fluid reservoir was pretty empty. *Now the question is: why?* She went back inside and called Cindy.

"Hello, how are you?" Cindy cheerfully chirped.

"I'm okay now," Abigail replied, "but I just had another little adventure. I need Gary's expertise and I would love some prayer cover." She went on to dramatize her ride of terror in full detail. Abigail was actually kind of an adrenaline junkie and she was not nearly as upset as some people might have been - at least now that she was safe.

"I'll have Gary come over when he's done at work to check it out for you," Cindy volunteered.

"That would so be nice. I may just need to top it off, but with the suddenness of it, I wonder if I have a leak somewhere. I'd rather do Plan B, if you know what I mean," Abigail chuckled.

Cindy laughed, too. "I'll call him. I'm pretty sure that he can swing by on his way home."

"Thanks, Cindy; I don't know what I'd do without you guys." They hung up and Abigail spent the remaining afternoon hours distractedly doing little tasks. Finally, she grabbed her book and sat out on the back deck to await Gary. Of course, Dude had to join her. She was glad for his company.

Before long she heard the crunch of tires at the bottom of the gravel driveway. Dude perked up and sprang off the deck. It was Gary. He got the royal greeting from Dude and then was ignored as Dude busied himself exploring all the new smells that came with Gary's truck.

"Cindy said you had a little adventure today," he said with a worried look. "Why didn't you pull over or leave it in the church parking lot?"

"Well, I guess I should have. I really thought I'd be able to get home safely," Abigail responded almost like a busted child. "It was definitely not smooth."

"Yeah, I saw your marks at end of the driveway. I don't know how you didn't hit that tree. Your guardian angel must be dinged up. I'm just glad you're safe," he said. "Let's take a look." He popped the hood and put the support in its place.

"Definitely empty." He took his flashlight out of his tool chest and started to look down the tubing and connectors that made up the brake system. Finally, he lay down next to the truck and ran his flashlight up and down the brake line. He touched a spot and then shined his light on the glistening fluid that was pooled directly underneath it. He looked again at the line and wiped it dry with a cloth.

"Hey, Ab, come take a look at this," he said.

Abigail moved to the ground and looked where he had the flashlight beam concentrated. "Looks like a leak in the line."

"Look again," he said. "Do you see how shiny that line is there and where it's kind of dented? Like it was crimped?"

"Yeah, you think a rock hit it or I might have run over something that nicked it?"

"Let's look at the other side," he suggested. They got down on the other side and found virtually the same thing at about the same spot in the line.

"What are you thinking?" Abigail asked with rising alarm.

"I'm thinking that the cuts are too clean to be some random rock, even if it was a sharp one. I'm thinking that someone partially cut your brake lines."

"Serious?!" Abigail felt the alarm bells reverberate in her belly as she began to tick back through all the strange things that had been going on lately – the cars always turning around in the driveway, the hang up calls, the toilet seat, the discovery of the pentagram shaped rock, the last encounter with sheriff Bynum – were they related to this?

"Abigail, someone wants you hurt or dead," Gary said bluntly. "This was no accident. These brake lines were cut. If it was a full cut, you would have known right away and not gotten very far. This was intended to give you the kind of ride you had today." He reached into his pocket and took out his phone.

"What are you doing? Who are you calling?" Abigail asked in a bit of a panic. She was afraid he would call the sheriff and she did not know if he understood her reservations about the man.

"Just going to take some pictures," he said. He proceeded to snap pictures of both sides. It was amazing what phones could do these days. Abigail carried the plainest, least technical type available and jokingly referred to herself as a techno-tard.

"What are you going to do with those?" she asked.

"Not sure, but I think we need to document this for some reason."

"Thanks, Gary. Now what?"

"Do you have to be anywhere any time soon?"

"I was hoping to get to church on Sunday, but other than that, I'm good."

"Tell you what," he said, "I'm off tomorrow; I'll come by with the tow dolly and take your truck back to my shop. It won't take long to replace them and bleed the lines and you'll be on your way. It'll probably be about a hundred bucks for the parts." He could have done the work right there, but it would be easier to put it up on the rack and check for any other possible problems.

"I hate to make you work on your day off, but thanks," Abigail's relief was evident. "Let me get you some money for the lines." She went into the house and got her wallet.

He took the cash and put it into his wallet. "Ten o'clock good?"

"I'll be here. I'm not going anywhere."

"You keep an eye out," he warned.

"I have my ferocious canine and the warring angels at the bottom of the driveway. Besides, no weapon formed against me will prosper," she asserted with a grin.

Gary shook his head and headed down the driveway with Dude escorting him to the bottom.

Abigail laughed when he got back up with his tongue hanging out of the side of his mouth, "Your job is never done; is it boy?"

Prinz was not pleased. He wanted real results. Things were beginning to shift in his little kingdom and he felt his grip weakening ever so slightly. He could see the looks from the lower level masters. They had pledged their full allegiance just as he had, but they were just as hungry for power and position as he. They would turn on him at the slightest hint of weakness. He knew how it was done. He fought hard to get where he was now and he was not about to give his position up without a fight. Especially not because of a woman! He would have to exert his supremacy.

He bowed down in his inner sanctum and began to chant. His incantations summoned reinforcements. He felt his powers being restored.

Urdang had noted her safe arrival with displeasure. He sent out messengers to the vital human puppets. How they despised those inferior beings who only thought they had power. The Great Enemy created them in His image so they were worthy of all the maltreatment that could be meted out.

They got a Redeemer, but Lucifer and his minions did not so they vowed to take as many as they could to eternal fires with them. They vowed to rub the Great Enemy's face in the depraved actions of His image-bearers who were now loyal to His enemy. Lucifer had a plan. He would ascend to heaven and raise his throne above the stars and make himself like the Most High Enemy. And when Lucifer won, they would all be rewarded.

It was do or die.

7

Saturday, September 30

Saturday morning was overcast and it was drizzling by the time Gary arrived in his pickup with the tow dolly. Abigail was prepared to go with him but he convinced her that it would not be necessary. The shop was only fifteen minutes away so he insisted on just towing her truck both ways. He was the kind of guy that went out of his way to help others.

"Okay, thanks," Abigail acquiesced, "I have plenty to do around here. You have fun with that."

Gary secured her truck onto the tow dolly with Dude's enthusiastic assistance and made his way down the driveway with his canine escort. Abigail returned to the house and decided to finish cleaning and straightening the basement. *That's what rainy days are for.* She brought her radio down with her to listen to praise and worship music.

There was a small window at either end of the unfinished basement which was one big room with the stairs nearly bisecting the space. The water heater was in one corner and the furnace was in the other. The circuit breaker was in another corner next to the cellar door. Some day she hoped to paint the dismal foundation walls to brighten it up. One wall was lined with shelves. Some were dedicated to canning supplies and equipment. Some were filled with her tools, painting paraphernalia, vehicle maintenance items, plumbing stuff, electrical parts, and sundry bits and pieces from old projects. There was a stained old workbench in the middle of the solid shelving.

She busied herself in cleaning and reorganizing the shelves to make room for the latest canning jars. Sometimes she did not take the time to put them up immediately so she still had several boxes of tomatoes and beans to label. She was pleased with the garden's yield this year. She still had some applesauce to make since the Arkansas Black apple trees had put out a good crop.

The battered car with the tinted windows cruised down the roads. He had a mission, but not a plan. He knew his effort to cause her accident or, more preferably, her death, had failed. His father was not pleased and when that man was unhappy, unpleasant things happened. This was his opportunity to show them. This was his opportunity to be advanced - maybe even over the old man.

He came from the south because he could now see through the stand of trees and determine whether or not her truck was there. If it was, he'd wait. If not … well, he would give her more than a little hint that someone had been there.

He drove past slowly and determined that her truck was not there. He looked to see if the nosy old neighbors were home but a glance up their back lane assured him that they were not home either. There was an abandoned trailer with a weathered barn about half a mile or so down the road. After checking the rear-view mirror and seeing no one, he turned onto the rutted lane and parked out of sight. It was an easy walk through the fields, across a gully, and back to the road directly across from her house.

It would have been much easier to just walk up the driveway, but he could have been seen too easily by anyone driving by. Instead he crossed to a point near the other corner that bordered the York's property and entered the woods. As soon as he stepped onto her property he felt his strength leave him and the skin on the back of his neck tingled momentarily. Ignoring it, he angled his way up to the house and patted the dog treat that was in his pocket. He didn't think that mutt would be a problem. He could kill him if necessary.

Coming out of the woods at a point that was even with the front of the house, crossing the leaf-strewn gravel driveway, he climbed the steps leaving wet footprints on the cement. He cautiously opened the screen door and tried the storm door. Unlocked! He slipped inside and began to rearrange things in her bedroom. Spitting on her mirror and walking back through the living room, he crossed the kitchen on his way to the back bedroom and the office.

Abigail heard the creak of the floorboards over her head. Her heart lurched as she froze. *It's too soon for Gary. Oh, Lord, what do I do? Oh, I'm such an idiot! I must have left the front door unlocked.*

She heard a man's sneering chuckle just before she heard a crash. *Why didn't I take Walther with me? Lord, what shall I do?* She prayed desperately as she slowly and carefully set down the jars that were in her hand

and looked around for a potential weapon. That was when she had the distinct impression that she should hide or flee rather than fight.

Okay, Lord, where do I go? I'm kind of trapped down here. She looked around the basement and her eyes fell on the cellar door. She had only opened it one time shortly after she first moved here. It was dark and creepy and full of spiders and cobwebs. But it seemed to be her only option at this point. The heavy crash overhead made her freeze once again.

Dude had been sleeping under the back deck. He was instantly roused by the unfamiliar clatter. Racing around the house, searching for the source of trouble, he barked menacingly. He sensed the intruder.

Footsteps creaked back across the kitchen floor. Suddenly the basement door opened. *He must have heard the music.* There was no time to get out through the cellar door now so Abigail ducked under the steps with her heart pounding so loudly that she thought the sound of it would give her away.

The stairway was made of thick, old wooden boards with treads but no risers. She would be able to see his feet as he was coming down but he would not be able to see her unless he was intentionally looking back through the gaps between the steps.

The landing creaked with the weight of the intruder. He slowly stepped onto the first step. Next his boots appeared as he cautiously descended to the next step. Abigail waited until he was about to step onto the next tread which was at her shoulder level. Quickly reaching through the gap, grabbing his ankle, she pulled back as hard as she could before all of his weight came onto that foot.

It surprised him and threw him off balance. He spun as he tried to grab the handrail and crashed down the remaining stairs in a backward somersault. The knife that was in his hand clattered across the cement floor as he sagged onto his side.

"Oh, Jesus! Oh, Jesus!" Abigail screamed loudly. She quickly came around the stairs and saw the blood seeping out from under his head. He was stunned or unconscious. Quickly looking around, she spotted the duct tape sitting by the paint supplies. Hurrying over to the shelf and then hastily back to the man, she peeled back the end of the tape and dropped down beside him.

Grabbing his left arm, wrapping duct tape around the wrist several times much like a rodeo cowboy tying up a calf, she hastily secured it. His other arm was wedged under his body and he moaned as she grabbed his wrist, yanked it out far enough, and taped it to the other one. She had wound it around his wrists and forearms at least five times when he began to stir.

"Wha … what are you doing?" the man slurred as he regained consciousness and quickly became alert. He began to struggle against his bonds and worked to get up. "I'll kill you!" he screamed and began to curse at her from his knees.

His eyes were ablaze with evil.

Abigail quickly stood and backed up. She saw him eye his knife and attempt to stand up. *He's going to kill me.* Even with his hands bound he could still wield a knife. She made her decision as he stood upright and stepped toward him. Pivoting on her left foot, she leaned back, pulled her right knee toward her torso, and then unleashed a crisp side kick to his knee. Her husband would have been proud, but the sound of the crunch sickened her.

He collapsed onto the floor and tried to cradle his damaged right knee. He let loose another string of curses as he screamed in pain, drawing Dude to the window, barking and snarling.

Abigail quickly darted toward the knife and kicked it to the far corner. She slipped past him taking the stairs two at a time, slammed the basement door and fastened the bolt. When she turned around she ran straight into a man's chest and screamed.

"Abigail! What's going on? I heard all this yelling and scream …" Gary did not get to finish.

"There's a man down there, he tried to kill me!"

"Whoa, slow down!" Gary grabbed her shoulders. She was shaking.

The man began to curse again and scream in pain. Gary unbolted the door, drew his .40 caliber hand gun and looked before he went down the stairs to where the man lay moaning and holding his damaged knee. He took in the pool of blood, the duct tape, and the man immobilized by the knee injury.

"Well," Gary looked up the stairs at Abigail, "it looks like you have it all wrapped up."

"Not funny, Gary," Abigail retorted from the top of the stairs.

He turned to the man, "Who are you? What are you doing here?"

The man unleashed another string of curses as he alternated his glares between Gary and Abigail.

"Ab, you call 911 and I'll keep an eye on him until they get here."

Abigail hurried to the phone in the living room and dialed 911. Gary went behind the man and removed his wallet from his pocket. Pulling his cell phone out of his pocket, he took a picture of the man's license. Then he returned the driver's license to the wallet and put the wallet back into the protesting William J. Wagner's pocket.

"911, what is your emergency?" the dispatcher intoned in a calm monotone.

"A man broke into my house, I need the police," Abigail said in a rush.

"Are you hurt, ma'am?" the dispatcher went through her prescribed interview.

"No, he is. He's still in the basement. Please hurry."

"Are you safe?"

"Yes, my friend is here and he's watching him." Abigail did not stop to fill in any more details.

"We have your address. I'll dispatch a deputy immediately. Please stay on the line until he gets there," the dispatcher instructed with a monotone.

Abigail did not want to stay on the line. "Okay," she said as she punched the loudspeaker button and set the phone down on the kitchen table. She poked her head through the basement doorway to check on the situation down there.

"They're sending someone," she informed Gary.

The man could only curse. "Shut up or I'll put some of that tape on your mouth," Gary threatened. He was twice the size of the young man and outraged at what he had done to his friend.

Abigail decided to go to the back of the house where she heard the crashes. "Oh, no," she put her hand to her mouth when she saw that the intruder had dumped the dresser over, scattering and breaking some of the antique mementos from her mother and grandmother. All of the photos of her husband and sons were knocked off the walls. Some of the glass was broken.

She went to the bathroom and saw that the toilet seat was up. *That might be the guy that was here before.* She was alarmed. She was angry. Going back to the basement door, she exclaimed, "Guess what, Gary! The toilet seat is up again. I think this is the jerk that was in here last week."

Gary was about to say something when they heard the sound of the siren coming nearer.

"I'd better go out there and calm Dude down." Abigail turned and hurried through the living room and out the front door.

"Dude!" she called. "Dude, come here!" Dude ran obediently to her side. She slipped her hand down to his collar and held him between her knees while she sat on the top step of the front porch. The siren was silenced just as the county vehicle crunched into the driveway. The blue lights continued to pulse. Dude wanted to exert his duties as the official greeter but

Abigail restrained him. She was not sure how he would react to the officer.

Oh no … Abigail's heart lurched as she watched Sheriff Roger Bynum exit his car. *Why is the sheriff here and not some deputy?* She stood on the sidewalk holding Dude but remained at the foot of the steps. Dude growled and flattened his ears. *Good instincts.*

Bynum slapped his hat on and strode over to her. "Is the intruder still here?" he asked with an official intensity that was alarming.

"He's in the basement. Gary McCord is down there watching him." She moved aside and pointed into the house. "The door is on the left as you enter the kitchen," she added.

Sheriff Bynum gave her a quizzical look but hurried past her and into the house. She let Dude go and followed him inside. His broad shoulders nearly filled the doorway to the basement. He peered down the stairs, quickly assessed the situation, and went down with his hand poised over his weapon.

He greeted Gary with a stony nod.

"Sheriff," Gary replied and nodded.

"What have we here?" Bynum asked.

"That man trashed my house," Abigail declared from the landing. "He probably thought I was not home because Gary was fixing my truck." She told him how she hid under the stairs and tripped the man when he came down looking for her. "I kicked his knife over to the wall," she said and pointed toward the south wall.

She watched as Sheriff Bynum looked up and located it. He walked over to the wall and picked it up with a cloth.

"Gary, I'd like for you go back upstairs while I secure this situation," Sheriff Bynum said evenly. "Don't touch anything up there until I take a look."

"No problem," Gary complied and joined Abigail in the kitchen.

Abigail noticed the phone on the kitchen table and picked it up. The dispatcher had apparently hung up so she returned it to its place in the living room. It rang immediately. "Hello?"

"Abigail, what's going on over there? Are you all right?" Jan and Earl had noticed all the commotion.

"Yes, I'm fine. Gary's here. I have an intruder. Come over when the sheriff leaves and I'll tell you everything," Abigail said quickly.

The man looked terrified as Bynum towered over him. Sheriff Bynum squatted down in front of the man as he removed a set of handcuffs from his belt. In a low voice he snarled, "How could you mess this up so bad? How could you let that woman get the upper hand like that?"

"I don't know," he was practically whimpering his whispered reply, "I ain't felt right since I set foot on this property, it's like all my power left me."

Sheriff Bynum did not want to admit it, but he felt the same thing. He at least had his gun, badge, and human authority intact. "Just shut up and I'll handle this." He cut away the duct tape and put the cuffs on the man securing his arms behind his back. The man tried not to groan. Much louder the sheriff sternly commanded, "Get up!"

"I can't! She busted my knee," he exploded with another string of expletives.

The sheriff took a closer look at his prisoner. His right knee was bent at an unusual angle and the blood seeping down his collar was leaving a dark stain on his sweatshirt.

He pressed the control on his collar unit and spoke into it. "I'll need an ambulance at my location and send a couple of the men to escort the suspect to the hospital." He received his confirmation, took out a second pair of cuffs and proceeded to cuff Billy to the post at the foot of the stairs. "You move one inch and you'll regret it," he instructed his prisoner. There was no place to go even if the man had wanted to.

Sheriff Bynum went up the stairs to survey the damage the alleged intruder did. Abigail pointed to the back bedroom. "I haven't checked the other rooms yet," she said. She did not like having that man looking through her home but she managed to disguise her repugnance while he casually went from room to room.

"It looks like all the damage was limited to that back bedroom," he said.

She decided that she was not going to mention the displaced toilet seat or anything about the previous intrusion and her suspicion about Billy having been here before.

"I'll take your statement while we're waiting for the ambulance," he said in his official tone. He took another glance down the stairs at his prisoner before he went to his vehicle to get his report sheet. He filled out the standard information and then asked for specifics about what she heard, saw, and did. "We'll get him checked out at the hospital and then he'll be processed into the jail. You will be notified about any court dates."

"Uh, thank you," Abigail was beginning to feel a bit disoriented by the events of the last hour. She was not immune to the effects of trauma just because she was a counselor.

The ambulance arrived with the additional officers close behind. They determined that the best way to get him out of the basement was to go through the cellar door. Abigail went outside while Gary secured the door from the inside once they were out.

"Dude! Come here, boy." Abigail wanted him to stay out of the way and she appreciated his presence as they sat together on the front steps once again.

Gary came onto the front porch. "You okay?" he asked with concern.

"Yeah, a little shaky, but I'm fine. This stuff is supposed to happen to my clients; not me!" she said ruefully. "Thanks for being here. That was such a God thing."

"Is your camera handy?"

"It should be on the kitchen window sill," she replied. She marveled at how calm he was. She was grateful to have someone watching her back and thinking logically when she was not.

He ducked back inside and took pictures of the damaged property and the blood-stained floor in the basement. "You never know if they might come in handy." He took out his cell phone and scrolled back to the picture of the driver's license. "Do you know a William J. Wagner?"

Abigail caught her breath at the name. "Wagner? Where does he live? I wonder if that's my counselee's brother, Billy." *Oh, that would make sense. He would be a part of the cult, too; probably much more willingly than Carrie Sue ever was.* When Gary told her the address in the nearby town, she knew that it had to be her brother. The age was right.

"How would he know where you live? Why …" his voice trailed off.

"Carrie Sue would have cult-loyal personalities, or, if not loyal, at least coerced into telling them anything they'd want to know. Besides, my name is in the phone book; it wouldn't take a genius to find me. And besides all that, I am followed quite often by their goons."

Gary was visibly startled by her casual comment.

"I get a lot of hang up calls, too. I suppose they want to know if I'm home or not. Or maybe, it's the alter of one of my SRA survivors who either has to harass me or chickens out when I answer or someone else switches in and hangs up so that personality can't talk to me."

Gary gave her a quizzical look that was mixed with concern. He knew of her work and prayed in general ways for her ministry, but he was now seeing just how close that real danger could come.

"Gary, it comes with the territory. I've been doing this a long time. God has called me to this ministry and I believe that no weapon formed against me will prosper. I mean, look at today – I should have been hurt or killed, but God gave me the way of escape. I know that there may come a time when the Lord permits something to happen, but if He does, I know He will redeem it and it will be for my good and His glory. I won't be stupid or presumptuous, but if I can't trust the Lord, I had better just quit right now."

"I don't know, Ab. Cindy and I pray for you. I guess I know more how to pray for you now. I just wish you wouldn't have to be at risk."

"Gary, I love these survivors. They're my heroes. They have been to hell and back and there is still a part of them that keeps trying. I can't give up on them. There are so few Christians who know how to help them. I can't quit … at least not until the Lord tells me to quit."

"I understand," he replied as he headed toward his truck. He stopped briefly, turned, and added, "By the way, I had my best mechanic look at your brake lines – they were definitely cut. They're probably quite disappointed that you didn't go flying off the road on one of those curves. God really does have His angels surrounding you." He paused when he saw Earl and Jan coming up the driveway. "You've got company coming, so I'll head out."

"Thanks for everything. Thanks for the prayers. I'll rest better knowing that he's in jail." Abigail did not want to think about the cult continuing to harass her. She did not like the creepy feelings she felt about Sheriff Bynum either.

Gary waited for Earl and Jan to park their car, waving to them as he made his way back down the driveway. Dude was torn between escorting Gary down the driveway and giving the newcomers a proper welcome. It had been a busy day for Abigail's clueless wonder. He was exhausted and flopped down on the front porch for a nap.

Abigail invited the Milners into the living room and began to narrate the events of the last couple of days. They assured her that they would be more vigilant when they left an hour later. This time Earl hugged her, too.

The prisoner was wheeled into the emergency room. His examination was expedited by the curious and slightly nervous staff. The laceration on the back of his head was cleaned and stitched. The X-rays came back negative for a fracture, so the physician had his knee wrapped and splinted. He was advised to see an orthopedic surgeon for further tests. He had likely torn the cartilage and one or more ligaments.

He was not permitted to have a pair of crutches so he hobbled between two deputies to the squad car. They took him to booking and processed him into the county jail. He was grateful to be able to lie down on the flimsy cot but he could not rest thinking about his fate. His legal fate was the least of his worries.

8

Sunday, October 1

The church parking lot was full again this week. It was the largest church in the county with an average attendance of nearly five hundred. Most of the community leaders and businessmen attended with their families. It may have been perceived by outsiders as the most prestigious church, but the spiritual leaders made sure that it was warm and inviting. Pastor Spalding made it a point to know everyone's name and tried to greet all of the visitors.

He was in the foyer when Abigail entered and greeted her with a warm smile, "I heard you had some adventures this week."

"Oh? What did you hear?" Abigail was not sure if he was referring to the brakes or the break-in or both.

"Gary mentioned that your brakes went out Friday. I'm glad you made it home safely."

"Thanks, me too," Abigail did not know how much he knew about what had happened. She didn't know if he really knew what kind of work she did. She wondered if he knew that he probably had Satanists attending his church.

He turned his attention to the next family and Abigail stopped to pick up the new church directory. It provided a good way to connect names and faces. Abigail hurried in so she could find Cindy and have a chance to talk a little before the service began.

As the last chords of the praise and worship song faded, Pastor Spalding bounced up the steps to the platform with his usual vigor. He always seemed to have a smile on his face and a twinkle in his eyes.

"Good morning!" his enthusiastic voice boomed over the auditorium. "Fasten your seatbelts because I have a lot to cover this morning. I'll talk fast and you listen fast and we can still beat the Methodists to the buffet line." The congregation laughed with him.

"I was talking to someone recently who had gone to church all of his life, walked the aisle when he was a young teenager, got baptized, and lived a pretty decent life. But he wrestles with whether or not he really is saved. He wonders if maybe he got saved and then lost his salvation. I wonder if anyone else wonders about that." He looked at his congregation.

"Well, I have to tell you that I was raised in a very strict, legalistic church that believed that some people were predestined for salvation and some people were predestined for damnation. They didn't even need an evangelism committee because there was no sense in evangelizing anyone since everyone was predestined one way or the other. It made me wonder if I was being good for nothing." Chuckles rippled across the room along with a few nods.

"Here's the problem, folks. We were each born with a sin nature. All we could do was sin because sinners can only sin. Some things might have looked good, but it was still sin. You can scrub a pig and dress him up, but you can't take the pig nature out of a pig, so he'll always go back to the mud. You can clean up a sinner and he can look good, but he still has a sin nature."

He went on to describe that at salvation, a person became a new creature in Christ. The old nature was eradicated and crucified in Christ. The Holy Spirit then comes in, but the person's behavior probably only changed a little bit because the regenerated spirit resides in a body that has old habits. "The soul - your mind, will, and emotions - still has stinking thinking and crumby feelings and makes bad choices. That's when the enemy begins to accuse you and so you look at your attitude and behavior and agree with his condemnation."

He paused to see if they were tracking with him. "This is our battle between identity and behavior. When you were a sinner by nature, you sinned. Once you became a saint - and yes, that's what the Bible calls born again believers - you still did acts of sin. But listen now, I want you to catch this! When you sin now, you are a saint who sometimes sins and not a sinner who sins." He could tell that this was a new concept for some of them.

"Look at the epistle that Paul wrote to the *saints* at Ephesus. He described their noble identity as saints in Christ and then a couple of chapters later he talks about their behavior. Don't steal, get a job. Don't lie, tell the truth. Don't be angry and sin. Don't let rotten words come out of your mouths but edify instead. Don't grieve the Holy Spirit. Does it sound like they were saints?"

He had them turn to Romans seven and concluded with the tension that Paul described between his inner man and outer man, his spirit and his flesh, his identity and his behavior. "Paul was distressed. The good he wanted to do, he didn't. The evil he didn't want to do, he did. He cries out in frustration as some of us do, *'Wretched man that I am, who shall deliver me from this body of death?'* I thank God that he didn't stop there. *'But thanks be to God through Jesus Christ, there is therefore now no condemnation for those who are in Christ Jesus.'* That's good news, folks! We have hope!"

They were following him. "If you are a born-again believer, you are a saint who sometimes sins. Do *not* let the enemy put doubt into your heart regarding your salvation. Never walk again with the king of condemnation." Pastor Spalding gave an invitation for anyone who needed prayer. The musicians played softly while most of the congregation moved to the aisles and began to disperse while others went forward to pray.

Daggett would never set foot in a church building unless it was for the purposes of desecrating it with a ritual. The regular congregants would be appalled if they knew what happened in their sacred buildings in the darkest hours. Every ceremony and every rite and every single sacrament that Christians celebrated was counterfeited by Satan's followers. Every revered Scripture was adulterated. Daggett wholly despised the followers of his Great Enemy in general and he was beginning to despise one of them in particular.

Daggett unlocked the door and descended the stairs to his lair. He removed his street clothes and donned his other black robe. After he picked up the black candle and lit it, he placed it precisely in the center of the Baphomet. Daggett softly intoned his incantations and felt his power being restored.

He felt more like himself again and was relieved. This was a busy season with the Equinox, the Feast Day, and Rosh Hashanah just past; and Yom Kippur, the full moon, and the Prep Days coming for All Hallows Eve. It would climax with their grand Halloween celebration and Demon Revels. Each year he hoped that his celebration would be honored by a visit from his king. This year was different. He had trouble and weaknesses that would bring him punishment rather than promotion. He would have to do something about that very soon.

Neither Carrie Sue nor Amy attended church services that Sunday. Carrie Sue was beginning to attend sometimes on Wednesday nights, but Amy was not interested at all. They had each been exposed to the counterfeit rites, ceremonies, and sacraments. Just seeing a communion table was enough to trigger flashbacks. Crosses, communion goblets, stained glass windows, choir robes, and so many benign symbols and accouterments which the various denominations utilized were used by Satanists to trigger unsuspecting survivors and drive them away from good churches.

They had too many unhealed parts who had been exposed to duplicity training. Over and over again, they would be told by a kindly person that Jesus loved them and would protect them. They were given opportunities to see demonstrations of "Jesus" doing just that for another child. They would begin to let their guard down and their hopes up. But any good they had experienced was always coupled with bad. They even believed that they were tainted by Satan from conception and God would never want them. Still they hoped that they were not a lost cause and so they would venture to believe and to trust a little bit.

Just a little.

After it was deemed that they believed enough, the double-binds with double meanings would reinforce their hopeless situation. The kind "Jesus" would turn his back on them, order their torture, or rape them himself. Then an emissary of Satan would rescue them and reinforce the notion that Jesus is bad and Satan is good. You will receive pain from Jesus. His followers are just as duplicitous.

You cannot trust anyone.

Helpless and hopeless, they miraculously continue their quest to be free and healed. However, they also would continue to test every so-called Christian that ever crossed their paths. It is as if they instinctively know that a true Christian holds a key to their release, but very few Christians had the expertise that it took to unravel the labyrinths that constituted their very complex systems, to dismantle the ubiquitous programming, and to bring full healing, deliverance, and integration.

Carrie Sue had been working with Abigail for over a year and she had experienced a great measure of healing. It was so very frustrating that just when she thought that she was close to being fully integrated, another group or level of personalities would emerge. Or she would discover to her horror that some part of her had taken them to another ritual and thus more splits with more programming were created. It was like trying to heal a never-ending abscess.

Amy only recently began to work with Abigail. While she had similar experiences - it was as if all Satanists used the same book and followed the same calendar - she came from a different area and was subjected to the peculiarities of that group. One of the masters in her area was also a wizard and was able to change into terrifying forms that were not human at all.

She was far more cynical when it came to her own healing and thought it would be safer to stay in the good graces of her masters. That was why she was willing to see Abigail. She would help the cult destroy her. She felt like a double agent – loyal to herself and loyal to her cult. What would she have to do to find peace? She finally decided to reschedule her session with Abigail.

Judge Roberts came out of his chambers precisely at nine o'clock as he did every working day. He had already been apprised of the day's load. He presided over cases ranging from domestic violence situations to non-violent crimes. Today was no different. He listened to motions. He dismissed several cases, he postponed a few, and he settled a few.

Toward the end of the day a wiry young man hobbled in with his attorney. The attorney made a subtle but deliberate motion with his left hand. There was a quick conference at the bench. The judge signed a document and handed it back to the attorney. He thanked the judge and returned to his client. The deputy acknowledged the document and released William Wagner.

In the hallway of the old courthouse the attorney said, "Let's go. He waived your bail. You just need to show up for your court date on October 16 at ten o'clock. Make sure you are here or your butt will be in jail."

"Yes sir, thank you," Billy said. He went with the deputy to collect his things and to arrange for a ride. His mother picked him up and they drove to their home at the edge of the county in silence.

9

Yom Kippur, October 3

Carrie Sue woke up with an ominous sense of foreboding. She looked at her calendar and noticed the small red print at the bottom of Tuesday, October third - Yom Kippur. *What was that Abigail had said? There's a ritual for nearly every religious holiday and every full moon, equinox, or eclipse. In other words, they used just about anything as an excuse to have a ritual.* Carrie Sue got her Bible, turned to the Psalms, and began to pray as Abigail had taught her. "Lord, You are my light and my salvation, whom shall I fear?" She continued until she felt the oppression lift.

She did not like to bother Abigail, but today she felt like she needed a little extra prayer support. Abigail had set some rules in place much earlier in their relationship when she had alters who would call her practically any time of day or night. She knew that the first question Abigail would ask was whether or not she had prayed. It aggravated her at first, but after a while she learned that she could do things that had tangible effects. She could be more than a victim; more than a survivor. All she had known were the powers of darkness. Now she was beginning to comprehend the surpassing power of the Holy Spirit. And that gave her hope.

She tapped in Abigail's number and waited as the phone rang. She knew that it would be a long shot to actually get her on a sunny day. Abigail would rather be outside than inside when the weather was nice. The answering machine clicked and the robotic voice gave instructions for leaving a message. "Abigail, sorry to bother you, this is Carrie Sue. I just wanted some extra prayer support today. I think there might be another ritual tonight and I don't want to get caught again. Thanks, lady."

Abigail was thinking about mowing the lawn today. *Maybe this is really the last time this season.* It didn't matter except the winds were getting colder. She spent the afternoon drifting from one task to another around the property. The compost pile was getting bigger as more and more plants were drying up after a good season. There were a few more concord grapes left on the vines, but she had already made several batches of jammy. What she made wasn't quite jam and wasn't quite jelly; but it sure was tasty!

She munched on a couple of grapes as she took a break and surveyed the area. Dude was sprawled on the deck and Buster was grazing contentedly. *I'll have to get some bales of hay for the winter.* She was blessed with a good pasture but sometimes she let Buster graze the yard when it got sparse in the heat of the summer. She'd hold up his blue halter rope and he'd trot over to the gate. She would slip it over his head and then open the gate. He stayed in the yard unless he happened to notice her and Dude going down to pick up the mail at the end of the driveway. At times he acted more like a dog than a horse. It amused Abigail and caused more than one driver to slow down to see her walk down the long front yard with her horse on one side and her dog on the other.

Deciding that it was time to get the log holder out of the shed, she dragged it to the front porch and placed it near the door so there would be dry wood handy when the cold and snow came. She walked over to the shed and opened the wide door. It was a semi-organized conglomeration of gardening tools and supplies, the tiller, mower, hoses, tarps, fence posts, axes and mauls. She grabbed the tools she would need to split the logs that had been tossed by the stack a couple of weeks ago.

Abigail removed her sweatshirt after ten minutes of work. After splitting and stacking nearly a rick of wood in the next row, she looked with satisfaction on the five plus cords of wood already in place under the large silver tarp. She estimated that the unsplit logs would give her the six cords she would need to supplement the propane fueled furnace. But that would remain for another day.

The cool breezes were beginning to chill her through the sweat-soaked shirt so she put the hooded sweatshirt back on. After putting the tools away, she closed up the shed and grabbed an armload of wood that she deposited in the log rack. "See you later, Dude," she bid her companion good-bye and went into the house.

Noticing the light blinking on the answering machine, she picked up the pen in case she would need to write something down. A gravelly voice threatened,

"If we can't kill you, we *will* ruin your reputation." Abigail dropped the pen. *Oh, Lord …* The machine clicked again and a second message came through. It was Carrie Sue's message asking for prayer support.

Abigail checked her calendar and realized that she had not thought about the probability of this being another ritual night. It was late afternoon and Carrie Sue had called earlier in the morning. *Lord, I'm glad that there's a Savior and it's not me.* Abigail decided to spend some time on her knees before she called Cindy for her prayer support. *I'd better practice what I preach!*

Moving to her bedroom and sinking to her knees by the bed, she prayed out loud, "Lord, I'm coming to Your throne of grace again to obtain mercy and grace in time of need. I am so tired of those jerks injecting themselves into my life and coming on this property. Your Word says that every place that I put the soles of my feet belong to me. They're trespassers. I ask for a fresh anointing of Your cleansing blood on this property and that You would send even more of Your warring angels to guard everything that You have entrusted to me if necessary. You are my light and my salvation. I will not fear them. No weapon formed against me will prosper. I pray in Jesus' name, amen."

She got up and promptly called Cindy. They prayed together briefly after Abigail relayed the newest threat. Cindy was worried about her friend's safety. Abigail had been followed and threatened before, but the intruders and the cut brake lines were an escalation that concerned both of them.

"Cindy, if I can't trust the Lord to keep me safe or to redeem my life from destruction, then I had better hang it all up right now - my salvation, the ministry, everything. And that is not acceptable. Not one of His choice servants went through life unscathed. We are going to encounter tribulations in this life, but Jesus said we're not to fear because He's overcome the world." Abigail asserted these things because she needed to declare them once again.

"Yeah, I agree, but you don't *have* to do this," Cindy objected.

"I think I do, Cindy. I feel like Jeremiah - it's kind of burning in my bones. Or like Paul - woe unto me if I do not. It's my calling and even though there are times when I would rather be a pew warmer and go slam hamburgers in a no-brainer job, I really can't *not* do this."

"I know," Cindy capitulated, "I just don't want to see you get hurt."

"Me neither, but you know what it says about these momentary and light afflictions."

"Yes, I know," Cindy agreed and tried to bring in some lightheartedness, "I just think Paul got hit on the head too hard when he said that."

"Well, I'm going to make a few changes to make it a little harder. I've been too predictable. I'll get some motion sensors that Dude and I and other critters will probably trip, but that's not all bad. So, I will be wise as a serpent and innocent as a dove. I'm praying for warring angels and I know you and Gary and Earl and Jan are praying, too."

"Okay," Cindy said, "just be careful! And if Gary and I can think of some other security thing, we'll let you know, like maybe a body guard or something."

"Thanks, I don't know what I'd do without my friends." Abigail and Cindy continued with some chatter about the kids before they hung up.

Abigail punched in Carrie Sue's number. She picked up on the first ring. Carrie Sue told her that she had been praying all day, but that sense of foreboding and oppression was just not going away.

"I have an idea," Abigail said, "why don't you come over here. We can throw something on the grill and hang out."

"Really?" Carrie Sue was excited. It had been a while since they had just hung out together. "What do you want me to bring?"

"Nothing, unless you have a taste for something. I can scrounge up enough to keep us from starving." They hung up and Abigail began to pull things out of the refrigerator and freezer.

Abigail believed that when a formal counseling relationship was concluded she should have a new friend. It was tricky to have a dual relationship and make that transition, but she firmly believed that the psychological model was not consistent with the biblical model of mentoring, teaching, and helping one another.

Carrie Sue did not take advantage of Abigail by making her "work" when they were together in a non-counseling setting. Abigail remembered with amusement some of the early times when Carrie Sue would come over and help her with the garden.

Invariably child alters would come out and Abigail would be asked over and over again, "Is this a weed or a plant?"

With all the healing and integrations, Carrie Sue stayed in adult mode more consistently and Abigail enjoyed her company. She was like so many of the other survivors who had vast areas of knowledge and creativity. The problem for many of them was that they could not keep those personalities in executive control reliably enough to hold down a job. But one day soon Carrie Sue would. Abigail believed it with all of her heart and was willing to work as hard as Carrie Sue did.

There was no rush to get their supper going and Abigail used these informal times to help Carrie Sue with the life skills that her mother never taught her. Carrie Sue was good at microwaving foods and opening cans. She could survive, but Abigail also wanted to encourage healthier choices and good domestic skills.

Carrie Sue did not believe that she would ever be married but Abigail did not rule out the possibility. No, she believed that everything that the enemy had stolen from Carrie Sue and others like her would be restored. Everything included a good marriage and children that were not birthed for ritual sacrifices.

It was not long before she heard the crunch of gravel, Dude's exuberant greetings, and the sound of a car door. Carrie Sue gave Dude the proper attention and ambled over to Abigail. They hugged briefly and went inside leaving Dude standing there with his tongue hanging out.

"I'm going to pre-cook the chicken and make some double-bakes. You want to start the salad?"

"Sure," Carrie Sue looked at the counter top full of romaine, spinach, raisins, sunflower seeds, bell peppers, tomatoes, and sprouts. She knew where Abigail kept her big purple glass salad bowl, cutting board, and knives. They began to chit-chat as they focused on their tasks. With the soft music in the background, this was the most relaxed they had felt in a while.

"Let's eat in the dining room, we can catch the sunset." Soon they settled down to their meal.

"Hey, my brother has to have knee surgery," Carrie Sue mentioned.

"Oh? What happened?" Abigail tried to sound surprised. She did not know what Carrie Sue knew and she knew that if Carrie Sue thought that she was in the slightest way responsible for the attacks on Abigail, she'd leave for good. She was amazed at the selfless loyalty of these survivors.

"He said he fell down some stairs."

"I know it doesn't sound very Christian, but after the way he's treated you, I'm not really sorry that he's finally on the receiving end of pain," Abigail said hoping to disguise the myriad of thoughts that were racing through her mind. "I just hope that puts him out of commission for a while so he can't hurt you."

"Yeah, me too," Carrie Sue agreed.

The sun had gone down and Carrie Sue was getting more restless. She recognized the all too familiar pulling of an alter or a group of alters who were programmed to take them to a ritual.

Abigail also discerned the uneasiness. "I think it might be a good idea to see if we can negotiate with whoever it is that is supposed to bring you to the ritual tonight." Abigail could not bear the thought of having to undo all the damage that would occur if she ended up at another ritual. How convenient for them that they are just down the road! T*here will be a lot of spiritual warfare going on tonight.* "Let me call Cindy and Jan and have them cover us in prayer, too."

"Are you sure?" Carrie Sue didn't want to intrude, but she was feeling more desperate with each tick of the clock.

"Yep! A stitch in time saves nine or something like that." Abigail made the calls and returned to the dining room. "How about we meet in the living room? It's more comfy. I'll go get my office out of the truck."

When she returned she looked at Carrie Sue and knew that someone else had switched in. He or she was looking around for clues as to where she was. This was probably an alter that had been shut down for a while. Abigail had the sense that she was in her late teens and was angry.

Hostile.

"Hello. I'm Abigail. This is my home and we just finished having supper together."

The personality had a quizzical look on her face as she shifted her gaze to the door and back again to

Abigail. It was as if she were measuring how strong Abigail was and whether or not she could get away.

"Carrie Sue has been seeing me for a while. You're safe here, I promise. And you can leave any time you want," Abigail stepped further into the room so that her path to the door would be clear, "but I'd sure like it if you wouldn't mind staying and talking a little."

"Carrie Sue!" she spat. "She's the one that got us into all this trouble! We hate her miserable guts and we're going to kill her."

"If you don't mind me asking … I'm not trying to be a smart aleck … but how will you kill her and not be dead yourself? You're a part of her.

"I am not! We'll kill her and she just goes away. We'll take over the body."

Abigail moved over to the easy chair. "Look, I know that you've shown up tonight because of the Yom Kippur ritual. You're supposed to go over there where they'll do their thing and reprogram you so that you continue to do their dirty work for them." Abigail knew that she risked an angry outburst, but she wanted to let her know that she knew. She also baited her with the comment about the programming and dirty work.

"I am not programmed! You don't know what you're talking about! Who do you think you are?"

"I'm just someone who is trying to get Carrie Sue and all of her parts free from the demons and the programming that dear old dad and his buddies have put on you so they could get their jollies." Abigail could see that despite the protests, this part was paying attention to what she had to say. Abigail also understood that the alters had to be hostile and convincing enough to their controlling demons or internal persecutors that they would not receive additional torment and pressure. She knew how the game was played.

"It's still early and you only have a mile or so to go, so why don't you hang here for a while and talk – after all, you have nothing to lose but a little bit of time," Abigail invited. She could see the visceral response to that statement.

"You're up to something. I don't know what it is but you're trying to trick us."

"I promise that I will do nothing without your permission. After all, if I pushed my agenda on you, I wouldn't be any better than your father and those Satanists. The door is right there and you can leave any time. Just remember, if you go there, all those little ones inside will be tortured again and I have a hunch that you really don't like to hear them crying." Abigail relied upon a combination of ample experience and discernment from God. She had been praying silently the whole time.

"All right then, I will. But if you try anything, so help me …" her threat trailed off unfinished. She sat in the recliner opposite of Abigail and stared at her with her arms folded.

"You got a name?" Abigail asked. She knew that often knowing someone's name meant having power over that part.

"You can call me Alexandra."

"Thanks; Alexandra it is. How about if I tell you some things that you may or may not be aware of and then you can think about it and then we'll figure out where we go from there?"

Alexandra nodded.

"Okay, first of all, I think you know that you are a part of Carrie Sue in some way. Don't get riled just yet. Let me tell you what I know and you can decide what's a fairy tale and what's true." She got another nod and Alexandra settled down again.

"Carrie Sue was born to Satanist parents. They were told whether or not they were allowed to let her live - probably by Prinz." Alexandra visibly startled upon hearing that name but Abigail went on. "They set her up for dissociating - splitting her into multiple personalities – by tormenting her while she was still in the womb. Yes, the mother has multiple personalities, too. Anyway, every time there was a ritual and torture, there were more personalities added. The original Carrie Sue kept splitting off new parts and each one had bits and pieces of her life. They have her strength and character. She emptied herself into the system. You are one of those parts."

Alexandra did not protest as much this time. She was curious.

"Your first memory and your last one were some doozies, right?" Abigail asked.

Alexandra looked thoughtful for a moment and then sighed, "Yeah."

"That's because the one that you split off of shut down and then you shut down after your last one. But you are here today because they programmed you to show up on the 2006 Yom Kippur ritual day."

Alexandra began to wince a little and adjust her position in the chair.

"They're tormenting you right now, aren't they?" Abigail asked gently.

"I can take it."

"That's not the issue. You shouldn't *have* to take it. You've had enough pain already. Do you want to get rid of them?"

"I can't. They're a part of me." She winced again.

"That's not true. Would you like for me to prove it?" Abigail offered.

"How?"

"I'll command them to step aside. I have authority through the true Lord Jesus Christ."

That got another reaction and Alexandra was listening to the demonic threats.

"I hate to say it, but they are not going to play nice anymore. They know that they're about to be ousted and they're not happy. What do you say? I'll just ask God to set them aside so you can think for yourself and you won't have to hear their trash talk."

"I can think for myself." Alexandra declared with less certainty and then began to writhe because of their torment. "Okay! Just make them stop!"

"You sure?"

"Yes! Do what you have to do."

"In the name of Jesus, I plead the blood of Jesus the Christ over Alexandra. Lord we ask You to separate all oppressing spirits that have been assigned to Alexandra and set them aside so they cannot speak or harm her in any way, shape, or form."

The result was immediate. Alexandra stopped her writhing and something very close to a smile came to her face. "Thanks. I'm sorry I gave you such a rough time, they were pretty tough."

"I know, and it ticks me off to see them hurt anyone. You want to get healed the rest of the way?"

"Yes!"

"How about the others in the Yom Kippur group?" Abigail asked.

"How did you know about them?" Alexandra did not hide her surprise.

Abigail pointed upwards, "He told me."

"Uh, yeah, they want to be healed too."

Abigail did not need to know names or numbers. She prayed big and let the Holy Spirit sort out the details. She asked the Lord to demolish all the strongholds associated with the verbal assaults, covenants, and programming. She prayed about all the direct and indirect unholy unions, soul ties, and flesh links from the sexual encounters. She prayed about all other traumas they had experienced or witnessed. She prayed for God's healing balm to cover all body memories and emotional pain. She renounced all the demons and asked the Lord to send them to a place where they would never afflict another person again. Finally, she blessed the parts with the fruit of the Spirit, with restoration of purity and innocence, and with recompense for everything that had been stolen from them.

When she finished praying she saw a wilted Alexandra. "Whew, I'm tired," she sighed.

"You've just been through a battle. There is one more thing. Most of the time the Lord indicates that the healed ones should be placed back inside where they came from. Sometimes He has one stay apart for some reason. What are you sensing for yourself and the rest of the group?"

"We're tired and just want to go in."

"Excellent! And that way, they can't access any of you anymore."

Alexandra flashed the first genuine smile of her life. "Let's do it."

Abigail prayed for the integration and was facing Carrie Sue before she finished.

"How are you feeling?" Abigail asked.

"Relieved. Lighter. I don't have that restless feeling like I have to go somewhere."

They got something to drink and chatted for a while longer. Then Carrie Sue announced that she felt as if it was safe for her to go back to her own apartment. It was located about half way between her parents' home and Springfield. Even though she was sometimes triggered and someone switched in to take them to a ritual or her parents' house, she was getting more healed and more secure. Able to move out of her parents' home about six months ago and enjoying the liberty, she was optimistic about truly getting free from the cult's clutches once and for all.

Pickup trucks, SUVs, and a county-owned sedan drove toward the farm. Night riders began to make their way down the trails along the river bottoms. They were all drawn to the site by an invisible force. Some of them came eagerly with blood lust; some came with dread.

The wiry young man with the limp was usually one of the former, tonight he was one of the latter. He had a sense of foreboding ever since that day he set foot on that woman's property. Everything was going wrong and there was no way to predict the volatile mood of this horde. Tonight, he was with his father and mother who knew that he had failed in his mission. There would be a price to pay for the fiasco with more than just a headache and a damaged knee. He was not sure if his father was being considerate - he did have a considerate side that surfaced on rare occasions - or if his father was making sure that he would be there. Besides, he still had not retrieved his car and had no transportation.

There was always a price to pay. They made it sound as if there was honor for enduring their so-called training. There was no promotion without training.

Prove that you are worthy.

Do not show pain because this is the ultimate survival of the fittest.

Blood did not matter. Fathers killed sons and sons killed fathers. Mothers betrayed daughters and daughters shed blood with the worst of them. Their sovereign came to kill, steal, and destroy. They would emulate him to the best of their ability.

They arrived well before the festivities were to begin. There were others who had been there for some time with more arriving at discrete intervals. They were all dressed in the proper attire.

Billy's foreboding punched him in the stomach when he noticed that a small cluster of people was gathered around a wizened figure giving him due honor. It was Prinz himself! Why was he at this little local gathering?

Prinz was the regional master. His jurisdiction encompassed the region extending hundreds of miles in all directions from the state capitol. Although he was known to show up at the local cult gatherings, he would normally convene at one of the larger, more prestigious regional or area gatherings.

His heart nearly stopped when he saw the judge. Daggett was talking to Prinz. His back was to Billy so he tried to nonchalantly fade back to the edge of the gathering. He needed to think. He needed to get away. He needed to get to his car that was still hidden by that weathered barn. It had to be less than two miles away. It did not matter how much his knee hurt, it would be less painful to walk two miles than to endure whatever was in store for him here.

He went back to his father's truck, gathered his belongings, and hid them under his robe. He skirted the edges of the group, being careful not to make eye contact with anyone. There was just enough dim moonlight to illuminate the trail down the back side of the hill that led to a series of fields. He kept to the edge and moved carefully so that he did not make any noise. He had to be able to drop out of sight quickly since there would be horseback riders and four-wheelers coming up this way.

After freezing in his tracks several times and awkwardly ducking down to avoid detection, he finally made it down to the field. He put his clothes back on and put his black hooded robe over them so he would be able to melt into the shadows more easily. He moved as quickly and quietly as his injured leg would allow.

On top of the hill the group began to congregate around the five-sided rock. A fire blazed nearby. Prinz signaled and they quieted immediately. He was not a large man, but he had a commanding persona. His eyes seemed to bore through each congregant.

No one knew his age. Some of them came from generations of Satanists and they had heard stories about his prowess from three or four generations back. He would have to be over one hundred years old by now. For the first time some of them noticed subtle signs of aging. His vitality seemed to be somewhat diminished.

He looked at Mastiff who instinctively stepped forward and gave the proper homage to his master. He had lost more weight in the last couple of weeks and had a gnawing pain in his belly that did not go away. "Where's your son? Where is that daughter of yours?" Prinz growled his demand.

"My son is here; the daughter is on her way," he tried to sound confident.

"Bring the whelp here." The group looked around and shifted uncomfortably as Mastiff searched for the miscreant. When Billy did not appear on his own, Zorroz and another man were dispatched to find him.

They summoned their powers and began to track Billy down the hill and onto a secondary trail that ran parallel to the field. They were able to move at a steady run. They did not have to hide the sound of their footsteps.

Billy had already crossed York Creek and was through the field beyond it. He picked up the trail that he had used the day he went to that woman's house. Ignoring his throbbing knee and screaming lungs, he scrambled up the rough trail. He was almost to the abandoned farm. His car was just over the ridge and through the sparse stand of trees. Two minutes; that was all he needed; just two minutes. Freedom was so close - a matter of seconds.

The unrelenting pursuers were like bloodhounds. They possessed a mysterious sense that kept them on the trail of their quarry. They easily navigated the creek, loped across the next field and up the ridge. Breaking out of the stand of trees, they spotted their prey and increased their speed.

Billy had to prop his injured leg on the passenger side of the seat and drive left-footed. Getting settled in the car took one extra precious minute.

They slammed into the car just as he was about to start the engine. Billy screamed in terror at the sudden shock. It caused momentary paralysis. Zorroz yanked the door open in a practiced move. There was no regard for the scapegoat. They hauled him out of the car with no consideration for injuries and hustled the captive back to the gathering.

Prinz was furious. He was enraged that Billy had run. He was angry that the father did not control his charges. He was livid because of another bungled mission. He was incensed because he also looked incompetent. Fear drove his anger. For the first time in his life he did not feel invincible. He would find and commission another female to seek the services of that damnable woman. This one would kill her.

A roughly hewn cross was produced. Billy was stripped, lashed to it, and hung upside-down. This was, after all, a day of atonement. His misfortune bought a reprieve for the intended sacrifice. They proceeded with their ritual and called on their powers. Covenants were ratified and demons were summoned. Blood was shed and curses were dispatched. It was a very dark night.

It was an exceedingly dark night, indeed.

Two demons escorted another damned soul to the place of torment. He could join that rich man and beg old father Abraham for a drop of water, too. They celebrated their success but now had to find a new host. Once a spirit was invited into a family it could move easily from person to person or generation to generation. It better served their purposes to slip over to his father since the female sibling was more of a challenge lately and his mother was a low priority.

10

Wednesday, October 4

The cloudless sky dawned brightly and promised unseasonably warm weather. Abigail was grateful. She would rather finish up the outdoor chores today. She still avoided going back into the basement even though the only sign of the attack was the blood stain that remained on the floor. She would have to use bleach or peroxide or something to get the rest of it out of sight - out of sight and out of mind. She may be a trained counselor but her brain also worked by association. Going down those stairs reminded her of that day.

Her humor was undiminished, however. She chuckled as she prayed, "Lord, if I were my own counselor, what would I say?" She knew the answer and decided to take care of it right away. She headed to her bedroom with her Bible.

"Lord, Your word says that You cover me with Your pinions; I'm safe under Your wings. You are my shield and bulwark. A thousand might fall at my side, but it will not approach me, I'll only watch and see the wicked recompensed. Jesus, You were there that day. Would You let me see You there with my spiritual eyes, hear You with my spiritual ears, or sense Your presence? I plead Your blood over that event and ask that You would bring me truth that will set me free from the anxiety and fear that I feel when I go down there."

Abigail then quieted herself and focused on the memory and allowed the emotion to bubble up. After several minutes she sensed words that were very similar to those found in Exodus 14. "Do not fear! You only need to stand by and watch Me fight for you."

Abigail immediately felt peaceful and praised the Lord with a song that she had made up years ago:

"I sing peace, peace be still.
Be still and know I am God.
I am God who heals you.
I heal you of all your pain."

She was glad that no one but God could hear her make a joyful noise. After she closed her Bible, she decided to test her healing by going to the basement. She went to the door and unbolted it. *No anxiety.* She opened it and stepped onto the landing and looked down at the stain. *It's just a stain.* She went to the laundry room for cleaning supplies and headed down the stairs to complete the stain removal.

"Thank You, Lord, for releasing me from fear and anxiety in this situation. Thank You for letting me take back this part of my life that was stolen by the enemy. Thank You that no weapon formed against me will prosper."

The phone rang just as she was gathering the cleaning supplies and heading back upstairs. It was Amy. Amy apologized for not calling sooner. She explained that she had been sick and in bed most of the weekend. "It must have been that flu bug that's been going around."

Abigail was gracious and made her appointment for their usual Friday afternoon time slot. She was always amazed at the excuses she heard - car trouble, illnesses, over-sleeping, forgetfulness, some kind of emergency for a friend or family member - they went on and on. Abigail took them at face value and only challenged them if she felt the Lord's prompting.

She had just hung up when the phone rang again.

"Hello?" she did not recognize the number on the display panel.

"Uh, hi, um, is this Abigail Steele? I, uh, I got your number from a friend. She said that you might be able to help me," a very nervous voice spoke.

"What kind of help do you need?"

"Uh, well, I heard that you help people who come from abusive families."

"Yes, I do. I see people on Fridays. How about if we set an appointment and we can talk more easily face-to-face? Do you work during the day?" Abigail would accommodate those who worked, but she really preferred to be home as early as possible.

"No, I'm on disability. I can come on Friday. What time?" she sounded a little less apprehensive.

"I have an opening at noon. Will that work for you?" After getting an affirmation, Abigail got her name and wrote the appointment down in her book. She gave the woman directions to the church and hung up. Friday would be busy with Carrie Sue at ten, the new lady at noon and Amy at two.

Abigail believed that each appointment was a divine appointment from the Lord. There were a couple of very rare instances in which the Lord told her not to work with someone or to discontinue one with whom she had already started. Abigail had a twinge of uneasiness after hanging up, but still sensed that the Lord would have her meet with the lady.

Abigail changed her mind about doing chores just then. *I think the boys and I need to go for a ride.* She got excited thinking about it and sometimes wondered why she didn't saddle Buster up every day. She grabbed her water bottle and a couple of snacks, then donned her boots and light jacket. Walther and her pocket knife were on her belt. Today she locked the back door on the way out and slipped her keys into her pocket. Any house could be broken into, but she did not want to make it easy.

"Buster!" she called. He was at the far end of the pasture grazing contentedly. His ears perked up at the sound of her voice and he began to trot up to the tack room. They went through their customary ritual and soon Dude joined them as they went down the gentle slope of the pasture to the back gate. She dismounted and opened it. Picking up the reins, she swung back onto the saddle and clucked as she gave a gentle nudge to Buster's flank with her heels to let him know that it was time to move and how quickly to move. He was a very well-trained horse.

They followed the edge of the corn field where wilted brown corn husks covered the drying grain. Their musky scent added to the aromas that were being borne by the soft breezes. It reminded her of an exotic tea. Dude was following his nose hoping to scare up a rabbit or a bird. Cutting through the break in the fence line, they soon entered the wooded river bottoms and followed one of their favorite trails.

Abigail gave Buster his head and he picked his way through the tree-lined trails. *This was a very good idea.* Abigail started to relax with the rhythm of Buster's gait and began a dialogue with the Lord.

They moved at a leisurely pace for miles before Abigail turned in her saddle and grabbed a granola bar. Riding in the crisp fall weather was invigorating and it always made her hungry. Dude continued to explore his own trails but returned from time to time with burs stuck to his fur and mud on his belly from splashing through puddles. Birds startled and flew away from them. She saw several box turtles on the trail. Skinks and other little lizards dropped off of rocks or logs and quickly disappeared into the grasses. Hawks soared on the breezes overhead.

It was finally time to head back home but Abigail did not give Buster his head then. She knew that he would gallop all the way home if he had his way. She let him pick up the pace and she truly enjoyed the thrill of the faster gait. They made the turn back into the cornfield and retraced their steps leading up to the back gate. Dude could not keep up with a quarter horse but when Abigail slowed Buster to a walk to cool him down, Dude would eventually catch up.

As they approached the gate Buster's ears flattened and his nostrils flared. He made a snorting sound and began to walk with that stilted gait. Abigail began to look around to see what might have Buster on edge. She saw a black shape in the center of the gate opening. It did not appear to be moving. *What is that?* She urged Buster closer.

By that time Dude had caught up with them. His curiosity never slowed him down. He boldly approached the black shape barking loudly. His hackles were up as he warily circled what appeared to be a sleeping dog.

It was dead.

Its throat was slit.

Abigail dismounted and led Buster through the gate. "Easy, boy, you're okay," she said comforting him. She tied the reins together and looped them over the saddle before giving Buster a gentle swat on the rump. She watched him race up to the tack room. He would be waiting for her there.

She turned back to the slain animal. "Dude!" she commanded, "Get back!" She was glad she had her riding gloves on. The dog looked similar to Dude. Of course, there were numerous Lab mixes in this area. But was it a message? This dog was not yet stiff. The blood was still oozing from the wound. She decided to drag it the hundred or so feet to the low marshy area that the farmer never planted. The coyotes and vultures would clean the poor thing up.

Walking back to the gate, she kicked dirt over the blood. Then she closed the gate and walked warily up to the tack room with Dude romping at her side.

Buster was waiting impatiently by his bowl so she went into the tack room and gave him another small measure of sweet feed to munch on while she put the saddle and tack away.

She spent some extra time grooming him. "When's the last time I cleaned your hoofs?" She started with his left front leg. She faced his rear and slid her hand down the length of his leg. He knew the drill and willingly let her put the hoof between her knees as she picked out the compacted mud, checked for tender spots, and made sure that Buster's shoes were still in good shape.

After she released his front leg she kept contact with his side and slid her hand down his rear leg. This time she had to make him extend his leg behind him. She repeated the procedure for the right side. He did not seem to mind the grooming. Indeed, he liked all the attention she gave him but he was finished with his sweet feed and ready to head to the water trough after he first dropped to his knees and lowered himself to the ground.

She looked over her shoulder in time to watch him roll in the dust, lurch awkwardly to his feet, and shake like a dog. As she neared the house she decided to loosen her jacket just in case she needed to introduce someone to Walther.

The house seemed to be undisturbed but she checked all the rooms upstairs as well as the basement. "Well, Lord, I guess it is possible to pray without ceasing," she mused.

Noticing that the message light was flashing, she stopped to see who it was. It was another hang up call.

She then called Cindy and filled her and Gary in on the latest developments of the day.

"It's a warning. Somebody is watching you, Ab. They would have to be. How else could they know you were out riding? Sounds like they timed it pretty well," Cindy's voice reflected her alarm.

"I suppose that there could be someone watching the property. The leaves are falling and it's easier to see through the woods from the road. Or maybe that was the reason for the hang up call. And it could be demonic watchers, too."

"What do you mean by watchers?" Cindy asked.

"The Bible talks about angels that have different assignments. Some are watchers. Some guard; others are warriors. There are messengers, too. Just because their character changed it doesn't necessarily mean that their assignments changed. They just work for the other guy." Abigail paused thoughtfully before she continued. "Well, actually, that's not entirely true. Like Hebrews chapter one says, '*are they not all ministering spirits?*' I think that *they* think that they're following Satan's bidding, but God hasn't fallen off of His throne. They probably do the dirty work like that celestial being in Second Chronicles eighteen."

"What's that one again?" Cindy asked.

"The prophet got a glimpse into God's council room. The hosts of heaven - angels - were on His right and left. That usually indicates fallen and unfallen. Lost or saved. Anyway, God asked that council how to entice King Ahab to go to battle. Ahab was evil and his time was up. God was going to use a war to kill him. One spirit came to God and offered to be a deceiving spirit in the mouth of Ahab's false prophets. God told him to go and be successful. He did it and Ahab died."

"Yeah, I remember that one now. I always thought it was a strange passage."

"Me, too. But with Psalm eighty-two and some other verses, I get the idea that God had appointed His council before Lucifer fell. When the angels rebelled, some of those on the council did too. Their original assignment did not change apparently because they were still on the council." Abigail concluded, "Maybe it's just me, but I don't think God would have holy angels deceive."

"Me neither," Cindy agreed. "So, if they relay a message or empower an evil person, they are not getting away with anything."

"Right. I have to believe that God has His own purposes. Like I always say, 'I don't always get it and I don't always like it, but God is God' and He doesn't have to consult with me."

"So, meanwhile, you have a dead dog with its throat cut by your back gate. That looks like Dude."

"Yes, but I think it's significant that it was not *on* the property. I think the Lord has stationed His warring angels around this property."

"What are you going to do?" Cindy asked.

"Well, I'm going to screen all incoming calls and leave a message to that effect. If that hang up call was someone trying to see if I was here, that would at least give him something to think about. I think I'll head to the hardware store and pick up those motion sensor units. I did a little research on line and they have solar powered ones. That way I can install them without having to worry about hard-wiring them. I'm going to get some timers and put them on some lights and the radio. And I'm going to keep praying.

"See you at church tonight?" Cindy asked.

"Yes, even though that would be one part of my predictable schedule. That's another thing I need to do - change up my routine." They talked about mundane things for a little while before hanging up. It was good to have a prayer partner.

Abigail went to the file cabinet and found the manual for the answering machine. After reviewing the instructions, she spoke into the speaker. "Hello, you have reached the Steele residence. Calls are being screened on this machine, but sometimes the lights are on and no one's home. So please leave a message and we'll get back to you. Thanks!"

Abigail decided that she needed to blow off some steam by splitting more logs. She put her old sweatshirt on and went to the shed to get her maul and wedge. After making a dent in the pile and stacking the wood up neatly, she put the tools away. She also decided to start that unpredictable schedule today. After a shower and dressing for church, she grabbed some extra cash from the gun safe. She would do her shopping first and then treat herself to supper at the Mediterranean Delights Cafe. Their stuffed crepes were outstanding and very nutritious. Her mouth watered just thinking about the spinach and feta cheese with all the wonderful spices.

She walked into the hardware store on the well-worn planks and inhaled deeply. There was just something nostalgic about the aromas in an old-fashioned hardware store. One of the associates led her to the back of the store and showed her the assortment of solar-powered motion sensor lights. She put five of them in her cart. Then she went to the next aisle and selected three timers. Passing the aisle of hunting supplies, she saw an advertisement for motion sensor game cameras. *That sounds like a good idea.* She got five of them as well. They were on sale. No-glow infrared game cameras with date and time stamped on the pictures. She could ask Gary about how to download the pictures later.

She made her purchases and went back to her truck. She loved the distinct look of the steel gray body with the black trim around the wheels attached with large shiny bolts. The black bumpers and the grill guard looked pretty good, too.

Her boys would have loved it. They would be driving by now. The thoughts saddened her, but she did not stop to mull over them. Her crepe dinner was delicious and soon it was time to head over to church. Tonight, she would try to park closer to the building.

When she entered the parking lot she noticed Carrie Sue standing by her car. She didn't come often, and when she did, it was usually because she was upset.

Carrie Sue angled to meet Abigail as Abigail headed to the front door.

"Hey, good to see you," Abigail greeted her.

"Thanks. And thanks for yesterday, too. I feel so much better. I don't know what's going on, but I feel freer. I want to start coming to church more - maybe on Wednesdays when it's less crowded."

"That's great!" Abigail rejoiced. *This is what makes it all worth it.* "Come on and sit with me, that is, if you don't mind being up front." Abigail liked to be up front because it was less distracting for her. Besides, she often said that if she was going to a concert, she would want the best seat up front and center. It seemed like it was the opposite for the church crowds which usually filled in from the back.

"Uh, that's okay, I think I'll find a spot in the back - I still may bolt and run, ya know," she said with a little half grin.

"Okay, I'll catch you later then." Abigail went down to the front and got ready for a time of worship. She was glad when it was time to break up into small groups for prayer. She did not want to go into detail but asked for prayers for safety. She told her little group about her brakes going out but did not tell them that it was intentional. She joined in praying for the others' prayer requests.

When the service concluded she noticed that Carrie Sue had already left. It was difficult for these survivors to trust. It was difficult for them to make eye contact with others. It was difficult for them to be touched in any way. Too many well-meaning church people would casually give a firm hug or a vigorous pat on the shoulder or a finger-crunching handshake. They did not understand that many of these survivors had fibromyalgia or chronic fatigue syndrome. They had been beaten and tortured beyond belief. Old injuries made it painful to be touched physically.

Abigail stopped to chat with some of her friends as she made her way out the door and back out to the truck. She remembered her purchases and started thinking about strategic places in which to install them. The solar panels would need to get enough sunlight to make the lights work. The cameras also came with batteries. They would need to be placed so that branches or shrubbery would not trigger them as they moved in the breezes. This could be a bit of a challenge. She was actually very handy with tools but she usually joked that she would cut it close, slam it in, caulk the gaps, and paint it.

11

Thursday, October 5

Mastiff woke up with an acute pain in his gut. Usually he was invigorated after a gathering, but he had been feeling worse and worse since Tuesday night. This had never happened before. He called the factory and let them know that he was too sick to come in today. Then he ordered his wife to make an appointment with his doctor. There would be no trouble getting in with Dr. Bacchus who was originally from Haiti. The doctor was part of a vast network of people in all walks of life who were dedicated to honoring the code of loyalty.

The doctor palpated his abdomen in a systematic pattern. One area was distended and firmer than it should have been. He wrote out orders for an X-ray and a CT scan and sent his patient to the imaging department in the hospital next to the physicians' annex. The patient was instructed to return to his office when the procedures were completed.

After the procedures were finished, Ron and Susan Wagner returned to the doctor's waiting room. Neither of them spoke. He did not want to eat and she would not dare go to the cafeteria without his permission. Soon he was called back into the examination room. Dr. Bacchus entered shortly afterward and came right to the point, "I'd like to admit you to the hospital. We need to do some more tests. The preliminary findings of the CT scan show a mass that we need to take a closer look at."

Carrie Sue heard a knock on her apartment door and was stunned to see her mother standing there alone. She looked over her mother's shoulder and saw her father's vehicle. She was rarely out alone. Something was afoot. "Uh, come in," Carrie Sue said warily. She peered over her mother's shoulder again to make sure that her father was not there to ambush her.

Her mother instantly broke down crying. This was her motherly mother. She began a rather disjointed, rambling narrative, "Your father's in the hospital. He's had that pain in his belly that's been getting worse and worse. I don't know where your brother is, he hasn't come home the last couple of nights. They say he might have a tumor and said something about his pancreas. Oh, I don't know what I'll do without him." Genuine tears rolled down the woman's lined cheeks.

At times like this Carrie Sue could almost forget that her mother had some mean personalities and some down-right diabolical ones as well. Today, she was closer to being the mother that she wished she could have had. Today, she felt sorry for this woman who seemed so terribly vulnerable.

"I'm sorry, Mom," Carrie Sue said sympathetically. "What are they going to do with him? When will you find out more?"

"I don't know. I just don't know about anything," her mother wailed. "Carrie Sue, you've got to come back home and help me. Billy's not there."

Carrie Sue was horrified at the notion. She had just recently gained a measure of freedom by moving into her own place and was determined to never be subjected to her father's or brother's demands again. "Mom, I'm sorry, I just can't. Billy has disappeared before and he always comes back. Besides, you know how mean Billy and Dad are to me."

Her mother stopped her sobbing momentarily and looked at Carrie Sue. Actually, a malevolent part of her surfaced and peered at her through her mother's malignant eyes momentarily. Carrie Sue saw it and redoubled her resolve to never live in that treacherous household again.

"Mom," Carrie Sue took a tentative step closer to her mother, "let me pray for you."

Suddenly her mother switched into the vicious personality. Carrie Sue was not prepared for the cat-like quickness that brought her mother close enough to slap her face hard. She rolled with the impact covering up her face and head as her mother continued to pummel her back uttering shrieks and cursing her for being such an ungrateful daughter.

The attack caused Carrie Sue's protector, David, to switch in. He deftly began blocking the punches and eventually grabbed both of their mother's wrists. "Stop it! Stop it right now!" he commanded.

She switched back into the compliant mom and looked at Carrie Sue with puzzled concern. "What happened to your face?" She could see the bright red cheek that had been subjected to the first blow.

David let go of her wrists and stepped back warily as Carrie Sue reemerged gently touching her face. "It's nothing, Mom. I think you'd better go now. Let me know what's going on with the dad, okay?"

"Okay, honey, I will as soon as I know something." Her diminutive mother left her apartment and drove off in the full-sized pickup truck. She looked as if she was doing a chin-up on the steering wheel so that she could see over the hood.

Carrie Sue wanted to call Abigail so badly. She felt so many mixed emotions. Mostly she felt triumphant because they had actually made their mother back down. A protector had switched in instead of a child. She felt pity for her mother. She felt vaguely guilty for being glad that the bio-dad was in a lot of pain and safely away in the hospital. She felt total apathy about her missing brother. "Good riddance!" *At least I didn't add, "May he rot in hell" like I used to.*

"Oh, Lord," she prayed, "I am such a slow learner. I can just hear Abigail quoting You about praying for those who despitefully use you and blessing those who curse you. God, I'm not there yet, please forgive me."

There was a light frost on the ground when she got up. Abigail waited for the sun to warm things up and used the time to read the instructions and hook up the timers. She plugged them into the extra radio, her grandmother's old lamp in the living room, and the tiffany style lamp that replaced the one that had been broken in the back bedroom. *I sure hope I set them right; I could scare myself and save them the trouble!*

Next, she looked at the instructions for the solar cameras and lights. The lights would pick up motion about twenty-five feet away for an arc of almost 180 degrees. The no-glow infrared motion sensor game cameras were good for about fifty feet, but the arc that they caught was only about ninety degrees. She had to decide how to set the intervals and whether she wanted a triggered shot or a set time lapse. *Maybe I'm not such a techno-tard after all.* She decided to put a light on one end of the front porch and a camera on the other. The porch extended across the entire front of the house. The door was in the middle so that would work out well.

She could forego putting on the porch light when she went out in the evenings. Then people would not know if she had forgotten to turn it on before she left or if she was actually home. *Good, another obstacle for the goons.* She dug the hardware out of the boxes, got the two-step ladder from the basement and went to work attaching the new equipment. Dude wandered around the side of the house and nosed around in the boxes before flopping down near his doghouse.

"Dude, I have a feeling that you're going to get your picture taken a lot." She took a break for lunch before installing a light and a camera to cover the back of the house.

She took her ladder, tools, and camera box down to the end of the pasture. Buster walked behind her with his nose touching her shoulder from time to time. He hadn't stepped on the back of her boot yet, but she was mindful that it was a possibility if she did not pay attention. Dude frolicked alongside of them until some tantalizing scent caught his attention and he was off like a shot into the woods. Buster got bored and eventually wandered off to graze.

Selecting a sturdy tree that was close enough to the back gate to capture the image of any intruder, she secured it and was satisfied that it would not be too easily detected by intruders. She knew that there were plenty of wild critters that passed this way and expected to see deer, dogs, raccoons, opossums, or coyotes. Buster would be getting his picture taken as he passed from the main section of pasture to the clearing in the southern corner. Wild berries were beginning to take over the area at the edge of the woods, but there was still plenty of good grazing.

Dude emerged from the woods and began sniffing at the ground where the dead dog had been slain. Giving an involuntary shudder, she commanded, "Dude, get out of there!" He trotted obediently up to her and then they wandered back up the pasture together when she was finished.

She decided to put a camera at the final turn of the driveway about fifty feet from the house and attached it to the utility pole there along with a light. She did not really think someone would be bold enough to drive up to the house now, but then, she had not expected any of the recent events either. She installed another light and camera duo on the tree that sat on the west side of the parking area. If someone tried to sabotage the truck, they would be filmed. It was getting dark earlier now and if nothing else, it would be handy to have the light. She had to think about the placement of the last light.

The sun had warmed the day nicely. *I'd better get those apples before a hard frost does.* Abigail went to the shed and got a five-gallon bucket and the fruit picker that was fashioned with a can, a pole, a string, and a wire hanger. She spent the rest of the day cooking and canning applesauce. She felt such contentment at times like this. "Oh, Lord, I have so many of the desires of my heart. Thank You for simple blessings." She sang along with the radio and relaxed.

12

Friday, October 6

Carrie Sue was waiting in the parking lot as usual but Marty, her driver, was not out. *She is healing.* Abigail gave a wave as she pulled into the space next to her. They entered the building together and Carrie Sue set up the CD player while Abigail took out her Bible and notebook. They usually warmed up with small talk, but today Carrie Sue was ready to jump right in. "I have a lot to tell you today," she said.

"All right, let's open with prayer." Abigail prayed and then added, "You know how I like to push you?" Carrie Sue rolled her eyes and groaned with mock dread. "I think that next time you should open with prayer," she hastily added, "just a little one" when she saw Carrie Sue shrink back a little. "I'm proud of you. You are growing so much lately. And it was good to see you in church the other night."

"Thanks. Thanks for being there for me," said Carrie Sue. "Something has changed. I can't quite put my finger on it, but something is different."

"I'm sensing it, too," Abigail affirmed. "So, tell me what's been going on."

Carrie Sue recounted the details of her mother's visit and reveled in Abigail's grin when she described how David came out and stopped their mom. She then related that her father was in the hospital and even though nothing was said, she suspected that he might have cancer. She also admitted that she was actually quite pleased that he was in a lot of pain and hoped that he had a long and painful death. She hung her head, "Yeah, I know, that *'vengeance is Mine says the LORD'* thing."

Abigail sighed, "Well, my flesh wants to cry out, *'God of vengeance, shine forth!'* sometimes, but we both know that it's not our job. And who's to say that this isn't part of God's judgment? Maybe he'll get saved when faced with death. And it's certainly an answer to our prayers to keep him away from you. Do you remember our discussions about reversing everything when you get healed? I have a sneaking hunch that your dad is losing a bunch of his power. I know of several survivors who lost their main tormentors not long after they got a significant amount of healing."

"I remember," Carrie Sue said. "He should rot in hell for everything he's done - and not just to me!"

"I can't say that I disagree. But you know that the Book says that *all* have sinned and fall short of the glory of God. We *all* deserve hell."

"It's not fair! He's killed and kidnapped. He's raped and beaten me so many times I can't count. He taught Billy to do the same thing. My life was hell on earth and he shouldn't get to go to heaven and get away with everything."

"No one gets away with anything. *'Righteousness and justice are the foundations of His throne.'*"

"But," she protested, "if he gets right with God at the last minute he gets to go to heaven. I don't want him in heaven with me."

"Let's look at First Corinthians a minute," Abigail turned to the third chapter in her Bible. "Paul gives an analogy that compares us to a building. He says in verse eleven that no one can lay a foundation other than the one which is laid, which is Jesus Christ. Then he describes how someone might build on that foundation with gold, silver, precious stones, wood, hay, or straw. Each man's work will be tested by fire in the believers' judgment. The wood, hay, and straw will be burned up. The rest will be refined and stand through eternity."

Carrie Sue was following Abigail, but the sour expression on her face reflected her displeasure.

"So, *if* your father would *happen* to get saved, he would have that foundation of Jesus Christ. All the rest would be burned up and gone."

"See! He gets away with it!" Carrie Sue protested.

"No, not really. Let's keep going. Verse fourteen says that if your work remains, you receive a reward. If the work is burned up, he suffers loss. He gets no reward; but he himself will be saved. That means that *if* he got saved, that's all he's got. No rewards.

"But he still made it to heaven and doesn't get punished for anything."

"Don't we still make it to heaven without having to pay for our sins? I don't know about you, but I'm really glad that all my wood, hay, and straw is going to be burned up. I have some gold and silver in my building, but I have a bunch of straw, too," Abigail continued to make her case.

Carrie Sue sighed, "Well, I don't have to like it, do I? I don't want to run into him in heaven."

"Carrie Sue, when all of his straw is burned up and all of your straw is burned up, you'll finally be able to have the father-daughter relationship that you've always wanted. Neither of you will have to change the subject or avoid each other. We'll all have new names, we'll all be wearing new robes, and we'll all be singing a new song. We will be able to love each other perfectly for the first time in our lives. Isn't that what you really wanted all along? A good daddy? It's hard to imagine that from this side of eternity, but God promised to wipe away every tear from our eyes. Somehow He will take the sting out of memories or bring divine forgetfulness."

Carrie Sue pursed her lips and processed that new angle in silence before nodding her head and sighing deeply. It was a few minutes before she said, "Oh, and another thing. Mom said that Billy hasn't been home since Tuesday night. He does take off like that sometimes, but, you know," she hesitated, "I just have a feeling that he's not coming back."

Abigail caught herself just before she was about to mention that he would have to be back for his court date. She did not intend to let Carrie Sue know about the reason for the court date. She would inevitably feel responsible for the attack simply because of guilt by association. "That's interesting timing. He might be losing his demonic power, too. The Lord's sending the reproaches back on them. It's beginning to make me wonder what's happening to some of the other masters in that group."

They fell into another thoughtful silence before moving on to other things. They finally ended the session and set up their next appointment.

Abigail had about fifteen minutes before the new lady would arrive. *Sherry something*. She tried to keep a time gap between counselees to help maintain privacy, but sometimes there was overlap. Soon she heard the outside door open and stood up to greet Sherry. Despite the signs in the hallway pointing to her office, some people missed them and wandered the wrong way.

Sherry strode into the waiting room. She was nearly six feet tall and her thick black hair, which hung loosely over her shoulders, was a stark contrast to her pale complexion. She carried a bulging tote that was the size of a beach bag. "Hi, I'm looking for Abigail Steele," she said with a boldness that surprised Abigail. This was not the same person that had made the appointment with her.

Oh, dear. I might just have another one with multiple personalities. Abigail smiled, "you've found her; I'm Abigail. Please come in and we can get started."

They went into Abigail's office where she had Sherry fill out a brief history and sign a consent disclaimer. Abigail noticed that Sherry hesitated several times and the expression on her face changed dramatically. When she reviewed the questionnaire, she noted that there were several distinctly different handwriting styles. *Another clue to dissociation.*

"You say that you are a Christian. Sherry, when did you get saved?" Abigail started with this basic question for all the new people. She would pray differently for someone who was not saved. She could do deliverance work with believers because the place vacated by strongholds and demons could be filled with the Holy Spirit. If one was not a believer, it would just be swept clean as the parable said, and demons could return and leave the person in a much worse condition.

"Well, I've been to church most of my life," a very sweet part of Sherry began. She described a couple of religious experiences but Abigail was not sensing that there had been a genuine conversion.

Abigail pressed, "I really want to be clear about this because it'll determine how we approach your issues." Sherry nodded but did not seem to grasp the full meaning. Abigail sensed that she was switching personalities rapidly and wasn't sure that she was still talking to the host personality or someone else at that moment but she went ahead and explained how we were all born with a sin nature because of Adam and Eve's sin and that we all need to be born again and receive a new nature. That only comes through the free gift God offered us through the death and resurrection of Jesus Christ.

She quoted verses from Ephesians two and ended with the passage in Colossians two. "You see, that the certificate of debt that consisted of decrees against us and which are hostile to us have been taken out of the way, having been nailed to the cross."

"Shut up!" a hostile personality shouted abruptly, "Shut up! I don't want to hear nothing about Him or none of that Bible stuff!"

"No problem. Who are you?" Abigail asked trying not to show any reaction.

"What's it to you, lady?" the newly switched in personality venomously demanded.

"Well, you are here in my office," Abigail replied evenly. She did not want to further inflame this one.

He considered her and then replied, "You can call me Damon."

"Damon. Thank you. Why are you out today?" It seemed like every Satanic Ritual Abuse survivor had a part named Damon.

"It's my job to keep her from hearing those lies," he spat.

"Well, then you've done a good job. You're being a good protector."

Damon looked closely at Abigail to see if she was being sarcastic. He was not accustomed to anything positive or complimentary.

"Yes I am," he asserted, "and you can't get to her."

"I'm not trying to get to her. I'm not going to be like whoever is controlling you guys and force my agenda on you." Sherry was looking like another SRA survivor.

"I'm not being controlled," he asserted angrily.

"Then who told you that it was your job to keep her away from the real Jesus and the real Bible?" Abigail knew that he had probably never considered why he did what he did. This was his life and his assignment and it was all he knew.

"Nobody."

"Do you mind me asking why you want to keep her away from Jesus?" Abigail continued to probe.

"It's just my job."

"I know, but *why* is it your job? Who gave it to you? What happens if you don't do your job?" She continued to press as matter-of-factly as she could. She could sense his tension and did not want him to be completely alienated.

"You sure ask a lot of questions, lady," he said with rising annoyance.

"Yes I do. I'm really not trying to irritate you. Feel free to step back any time you want." She knew that if she pressed him or reacted by trying to "win" the argument, she would lose him and quite possibly, all of them. At first, he appeared to be an adult, but with closer scrutiny, Abigail sensed that he was a teenager. She also sensed a word of knowledge from the Holy Spirit to the effect that Sherry was sent in to harm or distract her.

"I ain't going anywhere," he asserted. "Just what do you want, anyways?"

Abigail leaned forward slightly and looked him in the eye, "Damon, I'm going to be up front with you. I don't want anything from you. It was Sherry who called me and made the appointment to be here. But I also know something else. She was sent here by her master, probably Prinz, to mess with me and maybe even kill me." He looked shocked as she continued. "So, you have two choices as I see it. You can try to do what you were sent here to do or you can work with me and get free from your masters. It's your choice. I can help you if you want help but you might want to check with your inside leaders before you give me an answer."

"How do you know about them?" he demanded. He was thoroughly out of his comfort zone. He was accustomed to intimidating others. He had never encountered someone like this before.

"I have a bit of experience with folks like Sherry," Abigail continued. "You are part of a person who has multiple personalities because Sherry was subjected to trauma or abuse. There is a hierarchy inside and since you're a teenager, you are probably not the leader of your sector. Your leader put you out to mess with me and if that didn't work, someone else with more so-called power would take over for you."

Once Abigail had gotten that earlier confirmation from the Holy Spirit, she pressed harder. There was still a chance that Sherry would want to be set free.

Suddenly Damon bent over and reached into the tote bag. Abigail was praying furiously for direction from the Lord. When he sat back up again, it was evident that a bolder male personality had switched in. He was brandishing a large knife with a gleaming blade in his left hand. "I don't have so-called power, I *have* power and I'm going to kill you," the personality continued with a string of insults to her lineage and threats of what he would do to shut her "blankety-blank" cocky mouth.

Lord! I need some help here; he's between me and the door. Abigail continued to look him in the eye and said quietly, "Look, I'm really not trying to be cocky, but you can't do anything that the true Lord Jesus Christ doesn't permit."

He went into another tirade.

Lord, what do I say? What do I do? Abigail was amazed that the knife-wielding guy was still sitting in his chair as if he was glued to the seat. Immediately she found herself thinking about Gehazi, Elisha's servant. A passage in Second Kings described how the town was surrounded by an enemy army that was intent upon killing Elisha. Gehazi was frantic, but Elisha simply said, "Lord, open his eyes." Instantly the servant was able to see spiritual reality - the enemy army was surrounded by an angelic army in flaming chariots. "Oh," Abigail said aloud.

"What?" the personality demanded suspiciously.

"Lord, open his eyes," Abigail prayed out loud.

His eyes instantly widened as he looked intently at Abigail. Hastily flinging the knife down at her feet, watching it clatter ineffectually to a stop, he furiously back-pedaled, moving his chair backward several inches. He cried out, "Okay, I give; just get me out of here!" He sounded desperate.

Abigail was not sure exactly what he had seen. She hoped it was a flaming chariot and fiery angels, but whatever it was, it was good. He switched out and the pious one was back. She looked at Abigail and then to the knife and back again. She was trying to figure out what had just happened. She did not know that she had lost time when the other characters had switched in. She thought she was continuing where they had left off earlier. *But where did the knife come from?* It was just another in a series of mysteries that always seemed to surround her existence.

"Hi," Abigail recognized the switch. "I was just talking to another one. I didn't catch his name, but I think it was Damon's leader." She casually reached down for the knife, folded it and put it into her bag. She had a rule. If you pull a knife on me and I get it, it's mine and you're not getting it back.

The pious one's jaw dropped, "You talked to Damon *and* his leader? No one talks to them without getting hurt." She then realized the reason for the presence of the knife. How did this woman escape injury? How did she get the best of Damon and the other one?

"Yes, and I'd like to have another word with the leader guy, I think his name is Abaddon." Abigail most often got a word of knowledge when she was in a tight spot. That shook up the pious one even more. She switched out and Abaddon was back.

He was very wary as he watched Abigail. "I'm not trying to get you in trouble or anything; I just want to talk a little, okay?"

"Sure," he said nervously looking around. It was as if he was expecting someone to burst through the door and punish him.

"I'm curious, what did you see when I asked the Lord to open your eyes?"

He was very subdued as he spoke, "Um, you were, uh, are covered with the brightest, shiniest stuff. It covers your skin and looks like metal, but it's thin enough that when you move, it moves with you. I mean, I was going to slit your throat, but that puny knife won't cut through that stuff."

Abigail smiled, "It's called the armor of God. You can defect and have some of your own. Please let me help you."

"No thanks, I'm in enough trouble as it is. I, um, I really need to go now." With that he disappeared again and the poised one that originally walked in the door reappeared. She reached for the handle of the tote and stood up, towering over Abigail. "I'll be in touch," she said and quickly left the room.

Abigail sat there a little stunned for a few moments as she processed the last half hour. She picked up the sharp knife and looked at it again. *Another one for my collection.* She also had a considerable number of razor blades. Fortunately, the little observers of some of her former clients were able to slip in and alert her to a razor blade hidden in their shoe, wallet or other hiding place. Suicidal thoughts or gestures and acts of self-inflicted pain were constant companions that tormented these precious souls.

"Thank You, Lord, for protecting me. Thank You for warning me. Oh, Lord, it grieves me that she is a captive of the enemy. Lord please set that captive free." She continued to pray for Sherry for several minutes and then got ready for Amy.

Amy showed up right on time, exactly six minutes late. It amused Abigail. They started with their usual banter about anything and everything that really did not matter. But it was a simple way for Abigail to be somewhat transparent so that Amy would trust her.

It was also a way for Amy to avoid getting into issues. Today Amy was especially evasive. Abigail began to suspect that she had gone to a ritual on Yom Kippur. Amy was just beginning her healing journey so even though it was expected, Abigail was grieved that the damage continued. She was informed that Head Warden had nothing to say. Abigail tried several other tacks but was rebuffed or redirected down some meaningless rabbit trail.

Finally, Abigail closed the session, "Well, it seems like no one wants to work on stuff today, so we might as well call it a day. Do you want to make another appointment for next week? I hope that you're aware that next week is not only Friday the thirteenth; it's Prep for the Halloween rituals. It would save you a lot of pain if we could pray about it ahead of time."

"I'll be all right. I'll see you next week if that's okay." Amy stood up and reached into the front pocket of her faded jeans. Pulling out a wad of tip money, she placed five wrinkled singles on Abigail's desk as she left. "Sorry for today, sometimes I'm just not in the mood."

"No problem," Abigail smiled a little sadly, "some days are just like that!" Abigail watched Amy turn and disappear down the hall and heard the outer door click shut. As much as she loved to minister to people, she had a rule: I will not work harder than they do.

Sometimes she struggled with it. She knew that she could not want their healing more than they wanted it. The old saying, "you can lead a horse to water, but you can't make it drink" seemed apropos. *Lord, can we salt their oats?*

Abigail dutifully finished her paperwork and tidied up the office before heading for home. The weather was still nice so she could keep herself busy with fall clean up, splitting more wood, and finally going to pick up those bales of hay for Buster. Her list would keep her occupied until next Friday.

In keeping with her strategy to be less predictable, she took the long way home down Route 1950 and stopped at the tiny grocery store in Oakvale instead of the larger one in Kingston.

Stopping at the end of her driveway, she jumped out leaving the door ajar and crossed the road to get the mail. Dude saw her and raced down to greet her. He obediently sat with his front paws on the very edge of the road with his tail thumping wildly until she returned to the truck. "You want to go for a ride today, Dude?"

With no hesitation whatsoever, he scrambled past her and expectantly assumed his rightful place on the passenger seat practically before she had the words out of her mouth. *Oh, well, I need to clean the truck anyway.* There was no way Dude would not leave his nose prints and slobber on the window.

Meanwhile, the man in the full-sized sedan waited in vain in the parking lot of the Kingston grocery store. When it became apparent that she was not coming to this store, he uttered curses that dispatched messengers. But, once again, curses without cause did not alight.

Sherry lived with her aged grandmother who was becoming more forgetful and less able to get around. At least it was quiet here since Granny slept in front of the television most of the day and night. She never asked questions about Sherry's activities. She was in her own world and that world did not include Sherry.

Just after sundown the phone rang. A quick word was spoken and it had the desired effect. Sherry's eyes took on a slight glaze, as if she had gone into a trance. She moved almost mechanically to the door and left the house without explanation. Granny did not seem to notice anyway.

At the end of the sidewalk, she stopped. A full-sized sedan pulled up and she got in. They drove in silence to a sparsely populated area of the county and turned onto a lane. Daggett was already there. Prinz was relying on him to control the situation that was under his jurisdiction.

Daggett began to interrogate Sherry. He wanted to know what she had found out about the mysterious powers the woman seemed to possess. He wanted to know what happened in her meeting that day.

The assertive host began her report, "The pious one showed up right away when that woman started asking religious questions. I just remember that when she started praying and quoting that Book, Damon switched in. I don't know what happened until the end. She was actually talking to Abaddon just before I got back in control and got us out of there."

"Abaddon? How could she ...?" his voice trailed off. Abaddon was one of the deeper level alternate personalities. He was programmed. He was cult-loyal and ruthless. He would kill his own mother.

He used a pumper command and immediately Abaddon switched into executive control. Instantly giving honor to Daggett, he was trying to gain a measure of composure while bent over far enough that Daggett could not quite see his face.

Daggett inquired about Abaddon's encounter with the woman. While trying not to show any indication of weakness, he could not provide a good explanation for why he did not kill Abigail Steele. "She used her powers to take the knife out of my hand," he lied. "I was trying to slit her throat." Despite his resolve to appear calm, his pores were oozing sweat and his skin was beginning to glisten in the cold night air.

"What are you talking about?" Daggett demanded with a snarl. "You're much bigger and much stronger than twenty of her!"

"She was wearing some shiny metallic stuff all over her. The knife wouldn't have been able to cut through it." It even sounded incredibly lame to himself as he was saying it.

"Is that the best you can come up with?" he was angry. Fear drives anger. If Sherry failed, he failed; if he failed, Prinz would retaliate.

"She had body guards. They were bigger than anyone we have." He did not bother to tell Abigail about the three shiny sword-carrying men. They stood with their backs to her and warded off every attack from his allies. He wondered if she was even aware of their presence.

Daggett was alarmed. There were tales of such people. There were not many of them, but their number would increase as their King neared his destiny. He had hoped that he would not have to encounter one. Demon-slayers. Their words were as powerful as double-edged swords just like their King. "I will make my report to Prinz. You are dismissed."

Abaddon was stunned. Something unusual was going on. He had expected painful retribution, but it seemed that he would see the light of another day. He stepped back and Sherry reemerged. The man drove her back to her house in his large sedan where she resumed her evening routine as if nothing had happened. Granny was still dozing in front of the television and did not awaken when Sherry returned.

13

Saturday, October 7

Cindy answered her phone with a chipper greeting. "Hi, Abigail. What's up?"

"Fortunately, it's nothing bad this time. I hate it that every time I've called you lately it's been because of another little crisis."

"Little? I wouldn't exactly call them little crises! But don't you worry about it. What are friends for?" Cindy responded graciously.

"Well, I just miss being able to talk and pray about normal stuff so I have an idea. If you're not doing anything after church tomorrow, can you guys come over for lunch? The weather is supposed to be nice. I'll throw some dogs and burgers on the grill and we can hang out a bit. Gary can watch the game on my little television and the kids can play with Dude. We can even saddle up Buster and let them ride a little."

"Hmm, that sounds great," Cindy responded brightly. "There's just one little hitch. Gary's cousin is coming for the weekend. He's on his way from Montana and is in this area to visit relatives. Gary hasn't seen Lee in ages."

"Well, bring him along. He can watch the game with Gary and we can have a gab-fest," Abigail said.

"I think it will work but let me get back to you on that just in case Gary had something else in mind that I don't know about. You know how guys are."

"Okay, let me know. Don't worry if it's at the last minute because I'm prepared either way. Oh, yeah, I do kind of have an ulterior motive. I need for Gary to make sure I set up the cameras right and help me do the CD … DS … card thing. Maybe there are pictures of something besides Dude and Buster. Oh, and I got a notice about the court date for that guy."

"It's an SD memory card," Cindy giggled at her friend's struggle with electronic technology. It amazed her that someone could be so handy with tools and be mechanically minded and yet struggle with the newest gadgets that her children could operate. But then, if her sons were still here, she would have learned along with them.

"Yeah, that," Abigail giggled, too. "I'll catch you later, bye."

"Bye."

Abigail checked the clock. It was mid-morning on another glorious autumn day. *This is the day that the Lord has made!* "Lord, what are we going to do today?" Abigail did not think it was odd to consult the Lord about the big and little priorities of her day. Being the organized person that she was, Abigail decided to take the time to write out a list of things to do and purchase before winter:

Haul hay
Straw for the Dude house
Sweet feed
Dog food
Till the garden

Clean/check oil/add stabilizer to gas tanks
Last mowing
Clean mower/change oil
Clear fence lines
Split the rest of the wood
Stack wood on the porch
Gather kindling

She put down all the details so she wouldn't forget them. She would rather get things done ahead of time in the fall and not have to spend time doing prep work in the spring. She would rather gather kindling in the woods in the nice, dry weather than have to find something buried under wet leaves or snow.

Abigail decided to get the hay and sweet feed from the County Co-op Feed and Seed. It was located between Kingston and Oakvale on King Oak Road. They had just about anything a big or small farm would need. Their prices were competitive as well. *Better get some cash.* Abigail preferred to use cash rather than debit or credit cards. It made her feel more anonymous.

The settlement check was deposited in the bank on the first of the month and she usually kept enough in her checking account to cover the monthly bills. She did not do automatic payments. She did not like the idea of someone having access to any of her accounts. It felt invasive. So, she was going to go kicking and screaming into this new millennium with all the "time-saving" electronic technology. As far as she was concerned it was just a slippery slope for when the antichrist would demand a mark or a chip on the hand or the forehead in order to buy or sell.

Slipping her wallet into her front pocket, she grabbed the keys from the hook by the front door. Her heavy hooded sweatshirt would keep her warm enough. Dude raced to the front of the house when he heard the door open, racing hopefully back and forth between the truck and Abigail. "You're not coming with me today. Sorry Dude." She did not take him in the truck often, but she wanted to make sure that a trip to the veterinarian was not the only reason for a ride. He did not like the vaccine shots, but the treats sort of made up for it.

She turned right out of the driveway and took the back roads to town. As she travelled the first mile she slowed the truck slightly, looking for that blue roof and black barn combination again. Maybe with the leaves thinning it would be evident. After another mile, she assumed that the buildings were far enough away from the road that she could not see them. It would make sense that someone who had a secret night life would need that kind of privacy. *Oh well, I have better things to do.* She drove to town and got into the shortest line of the bank's drive-up.

She habitually looked in her mirrors to see if there were any familiar vehicles following her, but there were none that she noticed on the way to the Co-op. She made her purchases at the counter and then backed the truck up to the dock to get the three one hundred-pound bags of sweet feed. Then she went to the hay barn. She had learned over the years that she was comfortable with hauling twenty bales of hay at a time with the tail gate down. There was plenty of room in the mini-barn, even with its low ceiling. It was built with an outside back stair case that led to an upper room that she mostly used for storage.

Two trips were necessary each fall. The rest of Buster's hay would come from the round bales that she had delivered to the farm. She had gotten the name of a local farmer from the bulletin board at the Co-op several years ago and he was kind enough to make sure that she had what she needed. The three round bales from his last cutting were already by the pasture gate and covered by two large tarps.

She got home well after her stomach reminded her that she was late for lunch. Pulling into her usual parking spot, she then put the truck into reverse and cut the wheels so that she was heading back toward the gate to the pasture. She turned off the truck and went inside to eat. Dude was not there to greet her. *He's probably off chasing a rabbit*. Buster was at the far end of the pasture but was intent on his lunch and only looked up briefly before going back to grazing.

When she finished lunch, she went back out to the truck and opened the pasture gate. She was pretty good at driving in reverse using mirrors, but this was a little tricky going downhill. She couldn't see the ground without rubbernecking. She went slowly and carefully and finally came to a stop in front of the barn door. By that time Buster had ambled up to investigate the activity.

Abigail slid the solid barn door to the side. The rail was starting to get rusty and she would have to remember to ask someone if it should be oiled or lubed or if there was some special product for barn doors. She grabbed her work gloves from behind the seat of her truck and began to unload and stack the bales of hay. They were heavy and bulky, but she used muscle and leverage effectively. Her father always said that there was nothing wrong with working hard; just work smart.

By the time she got the hay unloaded and stacked, she was sweating. Taking a break on the tailgate, she wondered again about her absent dog. "Dude!" She gave a whistle. He usually came running when he heard that. She did not think he ever wandered very far away, but then, she was never quite sure. Buster was nipping at the three bags of sweet feed. The sound of his mischief brought her back to the task at hand. "Don't you tear a hole in that bag!"

She started the truck again and then realigned it in front of the tack room door. Boards that were left over from other projects were stacked along the back of the tack room. She selected a two by eight by eight foot board. It felt very heavy after the previous exertion, but she wrangled it so that one end was in the tack room and the other end was on the tailgate and she then got a second one. After dragging the first bag to the back of the bed, she flipped it so that it was centered on the boards. Then she jumped down and pulled it down the incline into the tack room. When all three bags were propped up against the nearest wall, she returned the boards, shut the tack room door, and moved the truck back to its usual parking place by the house.

Since there was still mowing and tilling to do, it made sense to wait to service those machines until later. She was too tired to split wood, so she went into the shed for a couple of five-gallon buckets and headed out to the woods to gather kindling since the wood stove would be needed very soon. Wandering down along the fence lines to see how much the vines and weeds had grown since the last time she cleared them, she filled her buckets before she got to the far corner. Once they were full she climbed the gentle slope back up to the house and deposited the buckets next to the log holder on the front porch.

The rest of the afternoon and evening was spent cleaning the house with a little bit more attention to detail just in case the McCords could come for lunch tomorrow. Burgers and dogs were transferred from the freezer to the fridge. Potato salad and "angeled" eggs were made. She did not do "deviled" eggs. She prepared a salad and cut up fresh vegetables and made sure that there was a fresh quart of applesauce in the refrigerator. The meat would be grilled tomorrow regardless of whether or not she had help. She could graze on it the rest of the week and not be at all unhappy about it. Yum!

About the time she finished in the kitchen she got a call from Cindy. She looked at the number before picking it up to be sure it was a friend. "Hi, Cindy, what's the word?"

"Gary said that he thought it would be a good idea. He'll miss his big screen, I think, but he and Lee won't mind watching the game on yours. You know how guys are - they relate by doing stuff together. They probably won't talk about anything personal and then walk away saying that they had a great visit." She laughed.

"Yeah," Abigail concurred and chuckled, too. "God sure did make men and women different!"

"What do you want me to bring?" Cindy asked.

"I've got the burgers and dogs covered, salad, applesauce, veges, and 'angeled' eggs. If you think of something the kids would want or something to drink besides cola or water, you can bring that."

"Sounds good. Maybe I'll come up with some desert - something ultra-chocolate," Cindy teased. She knew Abigail's weakness for dark chocolate.

"Perfect!" They talked a little bit longer before Cindy had to attend to Traci and Bryan. Traci was six and Bryan was three. They were like most siblings who either got along very sweetly or just the opposite. Today Bryan was not being very sweet.

Abigail set the dining room table and got everything as ready as she could for tomorrow's feast. Then she put on her jacket and went back outside to feed the boys. She filled Dude's bowl and then meandered down to take care of Buster. There was still no sign of Dude. *Lord, watch over that critter, please don't let him be hurt.* She went into the house and started her Saturday night routine.

14

Full Moon, October 8

Abigail sat in her usual spot near the front of the church. She did not see Gary and Cindy's family yet. They ran late sometimes and had to get the kids settled in the children's church so she did not think anything of it. Besides, they had a guest with them today. She had not thought about Gary's cousin until now and didn't know if he was married or single, old or young. She did not even think to ask Cindy. Perhaps since Gary was a little younger than she, maybe his cousin was too. Suddenly, she was a little anxious about lunch. *What if he's* ... She did not even want to finish the sentence.

Pastor Spalding was teaching about Jesus raising Lazarus from the dead today. After a very brief introduction and description of the account in John eleven, he got to the part where Jesus was standing near the grave. "The text says that Jesus *'was deeply moved in spirit and was troubled.'* The Greek words mean that He was agitated and indignantly angered. Now why would He be so upset? Four days before He had declared to the disciples that the sickness wasn't unto death and that it would glorify God. He already knew that in a couple of minutes Lazarus would be alive and well. Why the agitation and indignation? Why did He weep?"

He paused to let the congregation ponder this apparent inconsistency. He asked more questions.

"Was he upset because the disciples were clueless? Was He agitated because Martha and Mary questioned His timing? Was He indignant because the crowd was murmuring about this guy who opened the blind man's eyes but couldn't heal His own friend?" He let them think for another minute.

"I would propose that since Jesus was fully man, He was looking ahead to His own tomb very soon. But He was also fully God and maybe, just maybe, He was looking all the way back to the Garden of Eden. He was shaking with agitation and indignation while crying out in His spirit, 'It was not supposed to be like this! There was not supposed to be sickness and death, sorrow and grief!'" He paused to let them process these thoughts.

"Jesus then called for the stone to be rolled away. Martha protested because Lazarus was stinking dead by now. He reminded her of His promise and the stone was rolled away. Then Jesus called Lazarus out. Now you know that Lazarus had to hear Him with his spiritual ears because his natural ears were stinking dead." Pastor Spalding tugged at his right ear briefly.

"After Lazarus rolled out - he was bound hand and foot - Jesus told the friends and family to unbind him. Jesus could have rolled the stone away and gotten the grave clothes off Lazarus, but He allowed the friends and family to participate with Him. But those people could not raise Lazarus. That was Jesus' job." Pastor Spalding paused and looked around the room trying to catch as many eyes as possible.

"People, if I try to do Jesus' job, ministry would fail. And if I don't do what He's called me to do, ministry would also fail. We have the high and holy privilege of participating with God."

He concluded with one more question. "Is there something in your life that you think is so big and bad, so old and stinking dead that you think that even Jesus cannot possibly raise it up and redeem it? If so, come down to the front and our prayer team will help roll those stones away or help you get those grave clothes off." The music started and people began to move forward to receive prayer.

Abigail and Cindy were both on the prayer team this week and they each ministered to some of the ladies who came forward. There were muffled sobs as people were getting freedom from deep, old wounds. It was a good day in the house of the Lord.

Carrie Sue reluctantly went to the hospital with her mother that Sunday morning. At least he couldn't physically harm her. She had an internal meeting stressing the need for all protectors to keep their charges from being called out by the bio-dad. She led the prayer for their safety and for the strong host or a protector to stay in executive control at all times.

As the elevator rose, so did Carrie Sue's anxiety. She was deeply conflicted. She did not want to be here, but she felt an obligation to help her mother. She was grateful that her mother was in her pitiful needy mode. It was annoying but better than the mean one. The bell chimed its soft tone as the elevator whispered to a stop on the sixth floor. *Go figure! He's in room six.* Her mother led the way into room 606. Carrie Sue could hear her father's moans as he writhed on the bed. A nurse was adjusting his morphine pump.

They waited until the nurse had finished her task and then asked him if there was anything else she could do. He shook his head without opening his eyes. She turned and gave Carrie Sue and her mother a smile that conveyed her condolences as she exited the room. He did not look well. He was miserable and Carrie Sue had never seen her vigorous, strong father look so frail and vulnerable.

Susan awkwardly approached his bed. "Ronnie, Carrie Sue is here to see you today."

His eyes snapped opened and he scanned the room until they settled on Carrie Sue. "You! This is all your fault! You and that woman!" he hissed through clenched teeth. "I'd kill you right now if I could!" He tried to rise up in the bed but the pain was too great. He cursed as he thrashed weakly. Fortunately, the morphine began to have its effect and he settled down and closed his eyes in the drug-induced sleep.

David stayed in executive control for Carrie Sue. He was ready to do whatever it took to keep them safe. When the crisis abated, Carrie Sue emerged once again. "Mom, I'm sorry, but I need to leave." She turned and walked down the hall to the elevator. Her mother quietly followed her out of the room.

Gary and Cindy had to retrieve Traci and Bryan from children's church so Abigail had a fifteen-minute head start on them. She used the time to start the grill. She liked the old-fashioned kind that used charcoal and had a device that looked like a stove pipe with a handle on it which used paper instead of lighter fluid to ignite the coals. By that time she heard the minivan pull in next to her truck so she poked her head around the corner of the house and called out, "I'm back here getting the grill going."

Gary helped the kids out of the back seat on his side of the van. A gentleman emerged from the far side. He was not quite as burly as Gary but was slightly taller. "Hey, where's Dude?" Gary asked looking around.

Abigail's shoulders drooped a little, "I don't know. I haven't seen him since yesterday morning." She looked at his food bowl under the deck and noticed that it was still untouched. "I'm getting a little worried. His food is still in his bowl. That means he hasn't been home. I hope he's not hurt."

Or worse. Gary changed the subject. "Oh, I'm so sorry." Gary apologized for his poor manners. "Lee, this is our good friend Abigail. Abigail, this is my long-lost cousin, Lee Norris, from Montana."

"Welcome. It's nice to meet you. Make yourself at home." Abigail tried not to notice how handsome he was. It had been a very long time since she had felt these kinds of feelings. She was ambushed by them and that kicked her into action. "Come on, Cindy, we can get this food ready if you guys want to catch the pre-game show."

"Sounds like a plan," Gary grinned. "But let us know when the fire is ready and we can do the manly thing and take care of the grill." Bryan announced that he was going to watch football with the men. Traci wanted to help in the kitchen.

Traci was a big help carrying condiments to the dining room table. Beverages were poured and everything looked picturesque by the time the burgers and dogs were done. Abigail asked Gary to ask a blessing on the food and fellowship. After a frenzy of passing catsup and mustard, dressing and olive oil, salad and veggies, applesauce and eggs, the group fell into a contented hush as they savored the bounteous meal.

"Lee, what brought you to the area and how long will you be staying?" Abigail asked her guest. She hoped she was not obvious when she had glanced at his left hand that did not bear a wedding ring. She had worn hers for several years after Darryl was killed, but now she kept it in her jewelry box.

"I'll answer the second question first. I'm heading out tomorrow morning. As for the reason I'm here," he paused, "that's a little tougher. I guess I'm trying to figure out what I'm going to do with myself."

"Oh?"

"I just sold my ranch. I was running a couple hundred head of cattle, but it's getting too crazy with having to purchase grazing rights to federal land. And even though I love to ride horses, I'm beginning to think that my bones are not going to appreciate the long days in the saddle much longer."

"I can relate," Abigail said. "I'm good for a couple hours on Buster."

"You have just the one horse?" he leaned forward with interest.

Gary and Cindy gave each other a quick smile. This was not a premeditated match-making plot by either of them, but they sat back thinking that it might not be a bad thing for these two people that they both knew and loved. The conversations continued comfortably until the children were finished and wanted to go play.

"Is anyone up for desert?" Cindy asked as she got up to retrieve it from the kitchen.

A chorus of yeses immediately sounded, especially from Traci and Bryan.

Abigail got the desert plates and Cindy dished out double chocolate chunk brownies covered with dark chocolate icing. Decadent! They finished their meal and the women shooed the men out to finish watching the game. When they had tidied up the kitchen and dining room, they joined the men for the last of the game.

"Gary," Abigail said during the commercial - she knew not to interrupt a game, "do you think you could show me how to get the pictures from the cameras to the computer? There should be a bunch of pictures of me and Dude and Buster by now."

"No problem. Let's do it now. This game is in the bag already anyway."

Everyone wanted to take the walk down to the end of the pasture. Buster greeted the group with a snort and then pranced majestically in a wide circle around them. Traci and Bryan wanted to run up to him but each child was firmly held by a parent. "Let's just wait a while, kids, he's a little nervous with new people here," Gary said.

"When we're finished getting the pictures, we can put the saddle on Buster and let you ride a little bit," Abigail said with a smile. Oh, how her sons would have relished having a horse. She tucked that sad thought back inside.

They squealed with excitement and walked impatiently down the path that bordered the woods. Abigail felt like she was leading a parade. When she got to the opening near the gate between the two pasture areas she turned and pointed out the camera. It was well camouflaged against the bark of the tree.

"Oh, I forgot the step ladder," she said with dismay. Abigail had become very self-sufficient and independent. Sometimes she forgot that she was not alone and that other people were as pleased to be able to help her as much as she enjoyed helping others.

Lee stepped up and said, "No problem, Shorty, I can reach it for you." He was six feet four inches and easily reached up and unfastened the camera from the clips. He turned it over and deftly ejected the SD card and handed it to her. "What setting do you have it on?"

"I just left it on the factory setting. I thought that maybe Gary could help me figure out what would be best," Abigail replied.

"What's your goal here? What are you hoping to get pictures of?" he probed. He didn't want to be invasive, but he did need a little information to help her evaluate the best way to get the result she wanted.

That led to a discussion about finding a d-e-a-d c-a-n-i-n-e and the i-n-t-r-u-d-e-r. They spelled the words because Traci and Bryan were listening even while exploring nearby.

Gary and Lee decided that the motion activated setting would be the best and efficiently made the changes on the camera.

Abigail grinned at Cindy and mouthed the words, "Plan B."

Cindy was amused by her best friend.

"Let's walk back up through the woods," Abigail suggested. It'll be more interesting for the kids than the pasture. Heading through the gap and into the smaller pasture, she pointed out all the berry canes that grew in the far corner. As she pointed, she noticed the dark shape stretched out near the fence.

"Oh, God! Please no. Please don't let that be Dude ..." her whisper trailed off and she began to tremble inside and her knees started to buckle.

Gary grabbed her arm as she swayed slightly. "Cindy, why don't you take the kids back up to the house?" He tried to sound very calm so the children would not be upset. They could not see the animal from their lower vantage points.

"Okay; sure. Come on kids," she said with forced cheerfulness. "We're going to go up to the house while Daddy and Cousin Lee help Abigail with something.

They'll be up real soon and then you can ride Buster." She hoped.

They looked a little confused but obeyed without a question. Abigail could hear her divert their attention as they retreated back up the pasture. "Let's pick a bouquet of flowers for Mrs. Steele.

Gary was still holding Abigail's arm. He pulled her toward Lee and said, "Let me go make sure." She was numb with fear. Lee protectively put his hand on her shoulder. They watched Gary walk to the animal, stoop down, and put a hand on its side disturbing the flies that had survived the recent frosts. He stood up and turned around slowly. "I'm sorry, Ab, it *is* Dude. He's gone."

Abigail tried to make her legs move forward, but they felt disconnected from her body. Finally, she summoned the strength to go to Dude's inert body. She sank down near his head and buried her face in his neck. "Oh, Dude, Dude, Dude …" she wept for several minutes. Her world shrank down to just herself and Dude.

Finally, Gary moved close to her and put his arm around her shoulders. "I'm so sorry. I'm so sorry," he couldn't blink fast enough so he had to dab at the moisture that was collecting at the corner of his eyes.

Lee had followed Abigail slowly. He wanted to do something; he wanted to hold this grieving woman like he would have held a sister or a daughter. But, his thoughts raced, he had just met her and he was a man and she was a woman and he did not want to be presumptuous. So, he waited.

The ever-practical Gary finally broke the silence. "Abigail, we need to bury him." Fresh tears coursed down her cheeks. "Abigail, come on," he helped her to her feet and gave her a big brother hug. "Do you have someplace in mind or do you want me and Lee to pick one?" he gently pressed.

Abigail strained to refocus her thoughts. "I, uh, I have a little pet cemetery behind the shed in the big tiger lily patch … there's just a couple of stray cats and baby birds."

"Come on with me. Lee and I can take care of it," he looked to Lee for confirmation.

"I'll meet you up there with Dude," Lee said. He moved over to Dude and closed the dull blood-shot eyes. He noticed that the grass was flattened for several feet as if Dude had dragged himself using only his front legs. The grass around him was also crushed as if he had been thrashing around. He slipped through the fence and looked for tracks or footprints. He noted the tracks of a larger than average horse near the fence line. Lee came back through the fence and easily picked up the sixty pound animal and followed Gary and Abigail back up the trail.

Traci saw her daddy and Abigail coming up the path and sensed something. "Mommy, what's wrong with Mrs. Steele?"

Cindy and Gary never sidestepped difficult topics or situations with the children and tried to treat these things with age appropriate explanations. "Sweetie, she's really, really sad today. Her Dude died."

"Will Dude go to heaven?" she asked. "I hope so because I want to play with him when I get there."

"I don't know honey; I guess we'll find out when we get there." Cindy was not ready to go into a theological discussion about the eternal destiny of animals just then. It seemed that every parent had this discussion at some time.

Cindy walked down to the gate and embraced Abigail. They wept on each other's shoulders for a few minutes. Abigail wiped her face on her sleeve and took a deep breath. "Let me get the shovels for the guys and pick out a spot." She had to find something to do with her pent-up emotions. Her mind was racing. *Was he sick? Was he poisoned?*

Gary had already located the shovels in the shed and started digging in the place that Abigail had indicated. Meanwhile Lee had come up and after gently laying Dude on the grass, he took off his jacket and started digging, too.

She turned to Gary and Lee, "Thanks, guys. Let me know when the hole is done. I want to say good-bye before he's buried." Then she called out to the kids, "Hey, kids, I promised you a horse ride." She forced her voice to sound cheerful as she headed down to the tack room. This would keep her busy and the kids preoccupied.

At last Buster was saddled and the kids were settled on his back. They were beaming and the sight brought a smile to Abigail's lips. She handed the reins to Cindy who proceeded to walk Buster around the pasture. Fortunately, he ignored their cries of "giddy-up."

Abigail joined the men about the time that they were finished with the hole. She knelt down next to Dude and stroked his fur. "You were such a good Dude, so fierce and so friendly. I'm going to miss you." She bent down and put her cheek on the top of his head. She couldn't speak, and tears were seeping down her cheeks again as she straightened up and looked at Gary and Lee.

"Let me get his old blanket out of the doghouse, I'll be right back." Abigail hurried to the front porch and retrieved the dusty, shredded old blanket that Dude had wrestled with since he was a pup. She lined the hole with it and waited while the men brought Dude over and gently arranged his limbs to fit the hole. It looked as if he was sleeping. It was so surreal. She folded the excess material over Dude and nodded. They carefully filled in the hole. Abigail watched until the final shovelful was patted into place.

After coercing the children off of Buster and tending to him, Abigail joined her friends on the deck. There was an awkward silence for several minutes before Abigail remembered the SD memory card in her pocket and held it out to Gary. "Hey, maybe this thing can tell us something!" she almost shouted. They crowded back into the house and followed Abigail to the computer in her office.

Gary sat down at the desk and took charge of the project. Soon images came up on the screen. There were several pictures of Buster wandering between the pastures. A raccoon got his picture taken, too. Abigail wasn't sure exactly what area was being photographed when she first set it up and she was relieved that it did include the back gate as she had hoped. As they neared the end of the series of images, they saw someone ride close to the fence line. The next shot clearly showed him tossing something over the fence. The following shot showed the back of the horse as he moved away.

"Do you recognize him? What about the horse?" Gary asked.

"It's so hard to tell," Abigail said disappointedly. "Go back and let me see again."

Looking at the pictures several times, they noted his black cowboy hat. Zooming in only blurred the man's features. A dark braid of hair went down to the middle of his back. He had an average build. About the only thing distinctive about the horse was that he seemed big. A strap went around the front of his chest and attached to the saddle. A thin strap clipped onto the bridle and attached to that chest strap. It was used for horses that had a tendency to rear up to try to throw their rider.

Lee had tried not to intrude but he spoke up now, "I hate to say this, but I think that whatever he tossed over the fence was probably the poison that your dog ate." They looked expectantly at him and he went on to explain, "The grass was flattened like he'd dragged himself for several feet. I think he probably thrashed around some since the grass was crushed around him. Rat poison would paralyze his hind legs and cause seizures. It also causes hemorrhaging and internal bleeding. I'm sorry; it's not a very pretty way to die. Whoever did this is pretty depraved."

Gary deleted the irrelevant pictures and created a new file for the ones that he needed to save. "Let me and Lee go back down and reload that camera and check the others just to be sure." They spent the next hour with their project while Cindy rocked Bryan. He had dozed off in her arms. Traci cuddled up next to Abigail and napped giving Cindy and Abigail time to process things.

The men found a shredded baggie with remnants of meat that was laced with turquoise colored pellets. Dude was definitely poisoned. Gary was angry. Lee was mystified. Who was this poor woman? Why would someone do these things to her? Gary said that he would fill him in later. Lee showed Gary the hoof prints. Gary took out his cell phone and took pictures.

Just before it was time to leave Cindy suggested that they huddle for a time of prayer. "I could use it," Abigail sighed. "It looks like I have a stinking dead tomb that I need to invite the Lord to heal and I could sure use some stone-roller-away-ers and some grave-clothes-getter-off-ers."

She started, "Lord, I feel like Mary and Martha right now. I asked for protection for all that You've entrusted to me and I can relate to how they felt like You did not hear them or did not care enough ..." she continued to pour out her broken-heartedness. They each prayed for her and then left their friend with strict instructions to call any time of day or night.

Later that evening Abigail wandered out to the back deck and looked at the full moon. The sound of four-wheelers was in the distance and coming closer. It was another ritual night.

15

Monday, October 9

After a fitful night's sleep, Abigail woke to a cloudy day. The dreary weather reflected her own internal gloominess. Within seconds of opening her eyes the memories of yesterday cascaded down upon her. She rolled onto her back and looked up. "Lord," she said trying not to clench her teeth, "this is the day that You have made and I WILL rejoice and be glad in it. Lord I don't get it, I don't like it, but You are God. You are sovereign, and I trust that You will redeem my life from all destruction."

With that declaration she got dressed and tended to her morning chores - minus one. She wandered past the freshly dug grave on her way to tend to Buster. *Lord, thank You that he's okay. Oh, God, please ... I don't think I can handle it if something happens to him, too.*

After forcing some breakfast into her knotted stomach, she went into her office. She called it her ma'am cave because Darryl had had his man cave. She took out her Bible and began to appeal for justice from the heavenly court. She was not going to lie down and take it. During her intercession time she had an impression from the Holy Spirit. She needed to be on the offensive rather than the defensive. She needed to be proactive rather than reactive. She needed to be much more intentional with preventive strategies rather than mopping up afterwards. She felt strongly that this was about Carrie Sue.

Carrie Sue was surprised to hear from Abigail on a Monday morning. "Hello," she answered cautiously.

"Hey, it's me. I was wondering how you are doing - seriously," Abigail got straight to the point.

"Actually, I'm a bit uneasy. I don't know if it's the thing with the dad or my mom calling all the time or Billy still being gone or what. I'm just jittery," she said. "They told Mom that they want to put him in hospice." Carrie Sue did not want to admit that she was disappointed in herself because she thought she should be doing better by now with all the healing that was already done.

It was amazing to Abigail that despite a lifetime of horrendous treatment by their tormentors, most of the survivors have mixed feelings when they realize that their tyrant was about to die. Sometimes pent up fury arises from the knowledge that there will never be an apology or resolution or revenge. Often child parts emerge and yearn for their daddy.

"I have an idea," Abigail said, "actually, the Holy Spirit gave me the idea. If you aren't doing anything today, would you like to meet and get some more work done? I think it's important because this Friday is not only the thirteenth, it's another prep day for Halloween and we need to make sure that no one gets accessed. The Holy Spirit said that we need to do preventive work rather than wait until you get hurt and have to deal with it then."

"That would be great," Carrie Sue said with obvious relief. "Name the time and I'll be there."

"Ten o'clock?"

"Works. See you soon."

Abigail got to the church a few minutes before Carrie Sue and had the office set up. They did not engage in their usual small talk but opened with prayer right away. Carrie Sue actually prayed a short prayer and Abigail prayed in agreement.

"Lord, we are concerned about any parts that we may still not be aware of that could be triggered by the Friday the thirteenth date as well as the prep day ritual. We ask for favor with any protectors or other parts involved. Please start us where we need to start today, amen."

Carrie Sue looked up and said that she did not sense anything yet.

Abigail looked her directly in the eyes and asked, "Is there anyone who knows about the ritual coming up on Friday the thirteenth?"

Carrie Sue shifted a little in her chair and looked down. When she looked back at Abigail, there was another personality in executive control.

"Hi," Abigail greeted the newcomer. She sensed that it was a child. "Are you okay?"

The child nodded uncertainly but looked terrified and disoriented.

"Is there someone in there who is bigger than you that can talk to me about the Friday stuff?"

She nodded again and looked as if she were about to cry.

"You didn't do anything wrong, sweetie. I just need to talk to someone that can help me understand about Friday."

She gave another nod.

"I know you sent the little one out here to test the waters, but I really need to speak to someone who has some authority. Please just give me a couple minutes of your time," Abigail continued with the sensitive negotiations with someone who was listening but had not yet appeared.

Then she saw the shift and a deep voice said, "I'm here. What do you want?"

"I'll get right to the point. There's been a lot of pressure building inside because of the cult's plans for Friday. It's one of those 'double-curse' days because the prep day landed on the thirteenth. There are little ones who'll be called out and reprogrammed and tormented. I'd like to make sure that they can't do that."

The personality eyed Abigail suspiciously, "What's in it for you? Nobody does something for nothing."

"Let's just say that I have a personal reason for wanting them to be powerless and maybe even a little bit miserable," Abigail said a little bit evasively. She did not know who else might be listening in at this point and she did not want to upset them. They would take the blame for what happened to Dude and leave rather than expose Abigail to more danger.

"How are you going to do anything to them?" he eyed her with some disdain. On the outside, she just looked like an ordinary middle-aged woman.

"Actually," she plunged in bluntly, "it's not me doing the damage, it's what happens when we ask the true Lord Jesus the Christ to reverse the damage that was done to all of you verbally, sexually, and through other traumas."

"What if I like what they are doing?" he threw out a challenge.

"Oh, so you're like your father and brother and want to be just like them or worse?" Abigail counter-challenged him by taking his own argument to the extreme. Sometimes they needed to be shocked into seeing the implications of their position.

He let out a string of expletives regarding the bio-father and the brother.

"Okay, if you don't want to be like them, then why would you do their bidding and act just like them?" Abigail wanted him to think outside of the box to which he had been assigned.

"Look, lady! I don't know where you get off judging me. I just do what I want. This is what I want." He was getting exasperated.

"So, you're telling me that you like to hear the little kids crying. You like to help your father and the others torture little kids," Abigail pressed.

"Yes," he asserted and then reversed himself, "no. You're getting me all confused."

"That's not my intention, I'm sorry. I just want to be clear about what you want because I know what Carrie Sue Wagner does and does not want these days. Are you saying that if you had the opportunity right here and now that you would enjoy torturing some little kid?"

"No, I mean ..." he had run out of arguments. He had never been challenged to justify his life. He never had been given a choice and, indeed, still believed that he was without choices.

"Can I tell you what I think?" Abigail asked gently. She proceeded when he gave a slight nod. "I think that you have never been given the opportunity to do anything except what the cult wanted or you'd be punished severely. Even if you wanted to stop, no one ever told you that there was another option."

He was tracking with her so she continued. "I think that you're actually a decent guy who has been assigned to do a rotten job. If I could lay out a way to get free, would you be interested?"

He gave a nearly imperceptible nod. Abigail was accustomed to personalities who felt so endangered by even entertaining the thought of betraying their masters and their demons that they kept up the bravado and said whatever was acceptable and all the while they were hoping that Abigail would see their desperation and help them through it.

"I think I understand where you are coming from so I am going to do what I think you want," Abigail said. She then proceeded to plead the blood of Jesus over this one and all the others in his group that were like-minded and separate the demons from them.

"Whew! Thanks, lady. We were hoping that you picked up on it." He nodded to his right and said, "They sure are mad."

"I'll bet!" Abigail concurred. "Would you and the others like to finish up the healing?"

"Yes! All of us are ready – the Friday thirteenth group and the Preppers." Although many of the alters were unaware of what was going on in the outside world, their protectors and leaders had been emerging. They had observed previous sessions from their secret places inside.

Abigail prayed what she called her comprehensive standard prayer putting off the things of the enemy's kingdom and putting on things of God's kingdom. When she was finished she checked for stragglers or hold outs. There appeared to be none so she went on to discuss integration. They were all in favor and especially relished the idea that the masters would be frustrated by their inability to call out the parts that had been programmed for their diabolical pleasure.

Carrie Sue surfaced with a look of amazement and relief. "Whew! I'm whipped. Thanks, that was good. I had no idea that there were so many left. I was hoping that I was further along than that."

"They want you to be intimidated and hopeless when you look at the number of splits. Look at all they had to do and how long they had their way for decades. And in less than an hour God reversed it all. I'm glad that the Holy Spirit nudged me to make a preemptive strike. I think that we should pay closer attention to the ritual calendar and do the same thing before each ritual," Abigail wanted to encourage Carrie Sue. "You have a bunch of healing under your belt and each year gets better. We *will* come to the day when the Lord declares, 'It is finished' and then you'll just have to deal with the normal stuff that the rest of us have to have counseling for," she said with a smile.

They ended with a brief hug and left the building together. It was noon.

The nurse made her way systematically down the sixth-floor hall passing meds and checking her patients. She had finished her lunch break at 11:30 a.m. and unless there was a crisis, she should have all the mid-day meds passed out and documented on the laptop that now came with the multi-drawer med cart. But what shift ever passed without some sort of irregularity? She was dealing with people, after all.

She checked her watch. It was not quite noon when a woman burst out of room 606 calling for a nurse. She turned as she heard the commotion, quickly secured her cart, and moved down the hall to investigate.

"Hurry! I think he stopped breathing," Susan Wagner was desperately motioning for the nurse. "He just sat up all of a sudden and looked up at the ceiling like he was seeing a ghost and then he fell back."

The nurse entered the room and moved over to the patient's side. Placing her stethoscope on his chest, listening for a heartbeat, she heard nothing and called for a Code Blue. She lowered his bed and moved things out of the way for the team that would descend on this room shortly. She instructed Mrs. Wagner to go to the waiting room and she would come get her when her husband was stabilized. She felt bad for lying to the poor woman; this miserable man did not have long even if they could resuscitate him.

Lee had left Gary and Cindy's home well before dawn. He was a morning person and he wanted to get a good start on his long drive back to Montana. He missed the "big sky" but found that the rolling hills that he had been visiting were stunning in their own way. Actually, it was amazing to see the lush green fields. In Montana, each head of cattle needed many of the sparser acres to sustain it. Here, they required a fraction of the acreage.

He rolled through the memories of his short visit with his cousin and other relatives. It was good to be with family again, to reminisce, and to be pleasantly surprised at how like-minded they were. He had not seen their grandparents for years. Cards and phone calls were few and awkward. He was the family's last hold-out in Montana. Everyone else had made their way back east. Was it time for him to join them? He had several large and small decisions to make.

And then there was that intriguing woman.... He had convinced himself that if a woman as godly as his former wife was could fall away from the faith, then he could not trust that any other woman would not also fall away. He had tried dating briefly, but those supposedly Christian women weren't any more moral than those who did not profess to be Christians. He quit dating.

But that woman got his attention!

It is not good for man to be alone. "Lord; where did that thought come from?" He turned on the radio and tried to find a talk radio station.

Carrie Sue got the call from her mother thirty minutes after she got home from her session with Abigail. The woman was crying and hysterical one moment, and cold and logical the next. She alternately cursed her husband for dying on her and leaving her alone and then talked like it was no big deal.

She snapped at Carrie Sue, "If you were a good daughter, you'd have been there with me." She continued her venomous tirade about Carrie Sue's selfishness. Carrie Sue was speechless. Finally, David switched in and hung up the phone.

There were so many thoughts racing through her mind. There were so many mixed feelings. Relief was chief among them. It was hard not to resent being blamed for everything that went wrong.

She called Abigail and got the answering machine. "Hey, Abigail, I thought you would want to know that the bio-dad finally died. I'm not sure of the exact time, but according to what Mom said it was probably about an hour ago. Do you think …?" she did not voice the rest of her question about the timing.

Amy's daily routine was life as usual. Sleep - work - eat - watch television - play video games. It was about as uncomplicated as anyone's life could be. At least it appeared to be that way on the surface. Inside it was a totally different story.

Nicholai was very concerned about the mess that Head Warden had gotten them into. There was no immediate retribution from the masters, but he knew that they would never forget. He would have to be especially accommodating and wary at the next gathering. It was only a few days away and he was troubled. Some of the programmed child parts that were to be honored had disappeared on the day that Head Warden got suckered by that woman's smooth talking. If he could do something on Friday at their meeting, perhaps he could redeem their situation. Or was there still some way to play both sides and not get burned?

Abigail kept herself busy for the next several days. It was hard not to break down a little when she passed Dude's grave or when thoughts of the last couple of days surfaced. She hauled out the extension ladder and propped it up at the juncture of the front porch and main roof. Then she got the brush and assembled the twenty-five-foot handle so she could scrub the triple wall stove pipes. When it was cleaned out she sat on the peak of the roof and just enjoyed seeing far across the pasture and fields.

Later on, she hauled more wood up to the front porch and gathered more kindling. Her husband always said that one could never have enough five-gallon buckets. Indeed, she used them for everything from holding kindling to filling them with garden and orchard produce.

Wednesday night church was refreshing. She just needed to stand and hurt before the Lord in the midst of her brothers and sisters in Christ. Sometimes she could feel their worship lifting her to a place that she could not attain with the weight of her sorrow. *It is a process. I won't beat myself up.*

Pastor Spalding did a follow up teaching on John eleven. "I was glad to hear that a number of you got some significant healing from some of your big or little stinking old dead stuff. I love what Martha said to Mary in verse twenty-eight, '*The Teacher is here, and is calling for you.*' Mary immediately got up and went to Him. Folks, as we close, I'd like to invite you to close your eyes for a minute. Listen with your spiritual ears because the Teacher *is* here and He *is* calling for you, too. If you still have some unfinished business, come to Him. Don't wait. Be like Mary and run to Him for comfort. Be like Martha and witness the resurrection power of Jesus. Be like Lazarus and don't spend another day walking around in those grave clothes. The prayer team is here if you want to pray with someone."

The music began to play softly in the background and several more people came forward to pray. Gary and Cindy both found their way to their grieving friend and gave her hugs. Their compassion started a fresh round of tears.

"Well," Abigail sputtered as she simultaneously laughed and cried, "I always tell my clients that tears and snot are fruit of the Spirit."

Carrie Sue overcame her reservations and made her way to Abigail. She was somewhat distressed to see her counselor weeping. Abigail noticed her as she wiped away the tears, "Hey, you made it! I didn't see you when I came in."

Gary and Cindy only knew that the newcomer was Abigail's friend.

"I was a little late. Are you okay?"

"Yes, well, no," Abigail sighed, "Dude got sick and died Sunday. I'll be fine, I just wish that tomorrow, you know – the fourth day – Jesus would show up and resurrect him."

Carrie Sue and the others did not know whether they should laugh or not.

Prep Day Eve was a busy one for Prinz, Daggett, and Darod. They met in the same bleak building that they had met in nearly three weeks ago for a planning and strategy meeting. The windowless building was lit by dim lights and candles. There were many symbols and artifacts placed on walls, floors, and ceilings that added to the gloom and mystique.

Hordes of dark ones gathered wherever they went. Like vultures, they soared high overhead waiting for carcasses to fall. Some of them resembled prehistoric creatures. Many others had features that resembled enlarged insect faces. Claws and beaks, wings and distorted limbs, horns and fangs, scales and spines covered each of them in grotesque configurations. They did not resemble the glorious creatures that they once were. Magnificent voices formerly dedicated to praise now rasped and hissed.

Prinz continually alternated his fierce glare from Daggett to Darod. These figures were not friends in any sense of the word. They became associates on the same diabolical quest chiefly because of the chance geographical locations of their respective families.

Nationally and worldwide, men like them rose in their communities and held positions of esteem. Their social conduct was impeccable as they found mates, raised families, and contributed to society through their chosen vocations. They were law enforcement officers, judges, clergymen, entertainers, physicians, professors, military men, businessmen, congressmen, attorneys, and presidents. No one would ever suspect their dual loyalties and duplicitous lives.

Within the worldwide network of members, there was a hierarchy that corresponded to the one their Great Enemy would set up within His millennial kingdom. The Great Enemy reigned supreme followed by His Prince, the resurrected King David. The next level consisted of apostles and lesser princes. There were counselors and judges, the nation of Israel, and finally the gentiles who followed Him.

The glorious leader of these diabolical men was equal to the Great Enemy - or so they thought. They never acknowledged the fact that their leader was created by the Great Enemy before the fall. Their leader's antichrist would better his counterpart. He *must* surpass his counterpart. The Merovingian princesses and upper level masters were followed by those aspiring to be masters, and finally, there were all those who had not given allegiance to the Great Enemy. When the time came, their glorious leader would raise his throne above the One who had rejected him.

Meanwhile, this trio of men did all they could in their power to position themselves to rise in rank. They would steal, kill, and destroy. They had each endured torment that should have killed them. It was worth any momentary and light affliction to gain temporal and eternal glory.

Prinz cleared his raspy throat and began to beckon his dark allies. Daggett and Darod joined him in their preliminary negotiations with the ones who promised them everything that their Great Enemy had denied. Power was paramount. With power one could obtain any tangible or intangible desire.

Prinz did not have to outline what was at stake here. Tomorrow was Preparation for all Hallows Eve. Tomorrow's ritual must appease and please so that their glorious leader would choose to honor their gathering on Halloween with his presence. There were brides to present. Only the fairest, only the purest would suffice. How many golden-haired children with blue eyes ended up with their pictures on the milk cartons or plastered on the back pages of tax instruction booklets? Children of religious leaders were prime targets. They taunted their Great Enemy. He could not stop them.

16

Friday, October 13

Many people are triskaidekaphobic. They develop a morbid fear of the number thirteen. Do bad things happen on Friday the thirteenth? Yes. At least as often as bad things happened on other days.

Abigail was not phobic. She awoke and declared that this, too, was the day that the Lord had made and she resolved to rejoice and be glad in it. She continued her prayer that included petitions for safety for clients and for significant breakthroughs for each of them.

She was acutely aware that she walked alone to tend to Buster's morning routine. She was acutely aware that she did not have her escort when she drove down the driveway. She was acutely aware that there would be only half of a welcoming committee when she came home later that day.

Carrie Sue was waiting as usual. She seemed to be more and more composed as her system experienced healing, deliverance, and integrations of innumerable personalities. She was accessed much less, especially since her father was now gone. She wasn't out of the woods yet because the cult did not give up on anyone easily. As far as they were concerned, they created her, they programmed her, and they owned her.

Abigail asked, "What are you going to do about your father's funeral tomorrow?"

Carrie Sue knew that she would not be able to avoid being there. Her mother was depending on her since Billy still had not shown up. Her mother was very unstable and thus, very unpredictable. "I'm not sure, but I know I have to be there."

"Let's open with prayer and see where the Lord takes us today." Abigail prayed and when she finished, Lizzie, the five-year-old who previously did not want to go back to her critical memory, switched in. Abigail did not show her excitement but she had been hoping for Lizzie to be healed. Somehow, she sensed that Lizzie held a key memory.

Dissociation is necessary as long as the tension remains between personalities who knew the pain and those who denied the pain. As long as equal and opposite positions are held, dissociative barriers must remain. That is what allows a child to embrace the belief that her daddy is good and loves her very much while being equally convicted that her daddy is evil and hurt her.

"Hi," she said in her usual open way. "I think that now that the daddy is dead, I'm ready to let Jesus come with me to that memory. I'm not afraid that he'll find out. He said I would be punished if I ever told."

"You are being very brave. Are you ready to start praying?" Abigail asked.

"Well, I'm still a little scared," Lizzie admitted.

"Let's ask Jesus what you should do with that scary feeling, okay?" Abigail suggested. Although Lizzie believed that Jesus was not at that ritual, she still believed in Him. She was not altogether unlike many believers who receive salvation but hesitate to trust Him with everything.

Lizzie nodded, "Okay." She folded her hands and brought them under her chin like any five-year-old would and closed her eyes tightly.

"Jesus," Abigail prayed, "would You show Lizzie what to do with the scary feelings right now?" Abigail waited and watched Lizzie nod her head. She then unfolded her hands and cupped them as if she were carrying something. Slowly she lifted her hands a few inches and looked up as if she were offering the contents to someone who was standing in front of her.

Lizzie's eyes popped open and she said, "Okay, I'm ready now."

"Can you tell me what you just did?" Abigail was curious.

Lizzie gave her a confused frown. She assumed that Abigail could see the spiritual transaction that had just occurred. "Jesus told me to speak it into my hands and give it to Him, so I did."

"I saw that. What did Jesus do with it?"

"Well," Lizzie explained while making twisting motions with her hands, "He made it into a crown of thorns." She went on to make a gesture that imitated putting something on her own head, "and stuck it on His head."

Wow! Abigail took a deep breath. "Ready?"

"Yes." Lizzie went on to describe the terror and dread she felt after her father said the trigger word and she was suddenly in his clutches again. It was one of the few times she was ever out during the daylight hours. All she had known was night when darkness shrouded her world. She did not know that there was daylight and was amazed at how bright the sun was and everything she could see so far away. As amazing as it was, she felt a deep sense of foreboding that fateful day. "I was really scared."

"Do you want to give those yukky feelings to Jesus, too?" Abigail asked.

Lizzie nodded and made the cupped hand motion again before going on to describe her surroundings. "There was a little boy that daddy told me to take care of in the big barn. He was four. I'm five. Daddy gave us hot dogs and pop and chips. He never gave me stuff like that before. Maybe he was being nice because of the boy."

Abigail prompted her to continue with her story. She could envision the end of the story. How many times had she heard of the cult setting up a child to bond with a baby or another child only to have them witness the sacrifice of that child? And to make it even more twisted, the cult would blame the child - if you did this… if you didn't do that… if only - leaving the child feeling devastated and guilty.

At each turn in the grisly story, Abigail encouraged Lizzie to give the painful emotions to Jesus. Lizzie would make the cupped hand gesture as she offered her pain to Jesus. She finally came to the point in the story in which she and the little fair-haired, blue-eyed boy were approached by her mother and given some cookies. "Then the little boy fell asleep. My head was all swirly but I was scared to fall asleep."

Next, she described the muted sounds of drumming and chanting. The side door to the barn opened and sinister, hooded figures came in and took the boy. He woke and screamed for his mommy. Someone also grabbed Lizzie and pushed her along behind the hooded ones to the fire next to the big rock.

"Give it to Jesus," Abigail reminded Lizzie.

She nodded and then continued with her story. "The little boy was on the rock and the people were touching him. They took all his clothes off him. He was really scared. And that's when that big, bad man made me come over there." Lizzie was getting very apprehensive.

"You're being very brave, Lizzie," Abigail yearned to hold her and hug her because she saw the five-year-old rather than the grown woman.

"He had a great big knife and he made me hold it. It felt like I was a bad person, too, but I'm not. I didn't want to hurt the little boy!" Lizzie began to sob.

"Lizzie, it's really important that you give this pain to Jesus." Abigail was afraid that she would bail out with the stress.

"But He wouldn't want this. It's just too bad" she protested through her tears.

"Just try it and see if He takes it."

She tentatively held out her cupped hands. "Oh, He did. He did take it," she said with amazement, "and He smiled at me, but it was a sad smile."

"Good, keep going."

"The people were getting louder and excited. They were saying funny words that I don't know." Lizzie stopped and looked very puzzled.

"What's the matter?" Abigail asked.

"I always thought that I did it. But now I see the big man put his hand over mine. I tried to let go of the knife, but he squished my hand really, really hard and I couldn't." She pondered this new information. "Is that real?"

"Lizzie, remember how I told you that the bad guys keep you from seeing or knowing the truth?" Lizzie nodded so Abigail continued, "They didn't want you to know that the bad man made you hold the knife. Let's keep going and see if there is anything else different from the way you remembered."

Lizzie was more encouraged but became very upset as she described the next part, "The bad man almost pulled my arm off when he made me raise the knife up real high and then ..." Lizzie choked back a sob. "I don't like to remember the noise it made. I don't want to see all the blood ..." she trailed off and stared at something in the past with horror.

"Lizzie, give it to Jesus." Body memories were sometimes worse than the emotional pain and the rest of the memories. The sights and sounds, tastes and textures were constant until they were healed. It was much like Lady Macbeth, who could never wash the taintedness from her hands.

Lizzie stopped staring and gave the horrendous memory to Jesus and some of the tension left her. She stopped after describing the final acts of desecration that the evil man did to the little boy.

"Lizzie," Abigail asked gently, "do you see Jesus in that memory now?"

"Yes," she said softly, "He waved for two great big angels to come and get the little boy. They scooped him up just before the knife came down and took him to heaven. He's okay!"

"What else was Jesus doing?"

"Well, He was kneeling down next to me and He was crying and the blood was coming down into His eyes. I think He was sad for the boy and sad for me."

"I think so, too," Abigail agreed. "Tell me, Lizzie, why did Jesus have blood on Him?"

"Oh," Lizzie said, "He turned all the yukky things I gave Him into great big, sharp thorns and stuck them into the crown and they cut His head."

Abigail was astonished. What an amazing picture! She doubted that she would ever view the crown of thorns the same again.

"How are you feeling now?" Abigail asked.

"I'm mad that they tricked me, but I'm really glad that I didn't do it."

"Do you want to give those mad feelings to Jesus, too?"

"Yep. I don't want any yukky feelings." She gave that to Jesus, too.

"Lizzie, I have an important question for you. Do you think you are done now and can go back inside? You carried a really big load for Carrie Sue so she didn't have to."

She thought a moment and nodded. "I'm really tired and Jesus wants me to."

Abigail prayed and Lizzie was tucked back inside where she came from.

David emerged with a big grin, "Wow, we've been waiting for that for a long time!"

Abigail concurred, "I think a lot of it has to do with the timing. Now that the bio-dad is dead, I wouldn't be surprised to see a lot more of his 'creations' come forward and get healed now that he's not a threat."

"Oh, by the way," David said, "Queen is here." He was referring to the primary denial part. Queen was short for The Queen of Denial. She didn't like that name, but it was descriptive. And it was her job.

"Does she want to talk?" Abigail asked.

"No, she's just thinking," David replied just before he let Carrie Sue take over.

She and Carrie Sue prayed for their safety at the funeral. They prayed for a protector or adult to remain in executive control. They prayed that no kids would be triggered. Abigail promised to contact her prayer warriors for added cover. Carrie Sue promised Abigail that she would call her if things got dicey.

Sherry showed up for her appointment because she was not entirely sure that she was not supposed to continue her assignment from Prinz. Abaddon was hovering near the surface to make sure that things did not get out of hand like last time. He had mixed feelings about this meeting. On the one hand, he was intrigued by this composed woman who carried such authority and power. He had never encountered someone who could upset his masters like this one. On the other hand, he had his loyalties and he intended to pursue the plans his king had for him for a future and a hope.

Abaddon was amazed that Abigail could greet them warmly even though he had pulled the knife on her. Was she crazy? When Abigail opened with prayer, the Pious One showed up again and Abaddon could not have that. He reappeared and said, "We're not going to have any of that God stuff like last time."

"Okay," Abigail said evenly, "Abaddon?"

He was astonished that she recognized him. He was taken aback by her uncanny knowledge. He was very uncomfortable and all he could think to do was to try to preserve some of his dignity. "No offense, lady, but we're outta here." With that he got up and quickly left the room.

Abigail was very disappointed and hoped that she would see Sherry again. She hated losing anyone, but she also knew that the odds of a ritual abuse survivor seeing their healing through to the end was slim. It grieved her. She could not explain the love that she had for the most deeply wounded; the most severely traumatized people in the world. She counted it a privilege to participate with God.

Since Abigail now had ample time before Amy's appointment at 2:06, she decided to do her shopping. She could store perishables in the church refrigerator in the kitchen down the hall.

After locking up, she got into her truck, headed for her usual store and hoped that the irregularity in the time would throw off anyone who might be assigned to follow her.

She pulled into the parking lot and noticed that Carrie Sue's car was there. In fact, she was coming out of the store and heading her way. "Hey, small world!" she greeted Carrie Sue.

"I thought you had other people to see today."

"Well, I guess I need to go to charm school. I scared another one away." Abigail tried to make light of the situation. "Hey, do you have an extra minute? I've been meaning to ask you something."

"Sure." Carrie Sue was eager to help out her friend.

"I picked up the new church directory a while ago and I'm wondering if you wouldn't mind looking at the pictures to see if anyone looks familiar."

Carrie Sue looked a little puzzled, but then, she had come to know that Abigail probably had something in mind. Abigail found the directory where it had fallen partially under the passenger seat and handed it to Carrie Sue who began turning the pages. There were only a few names that started with the letter A and soon she was in the Bs. As she flipped the next page she was stunned and did a double take.

Abigail noticed the reaction. "Are you okay?"

Pointing at a picture at the bottom of the page she stammered, "Zorroz! That's Zorroz!"

"Sheriff Bynum. No wonder he creeps me out. I'm sorry, Carrie Sue, I shouldn't have asked you to do that today. You're already so stressed out."

"I'm okay, really, I just got a jolt for a second there. How could a Satanist go to church? Oh, never mind, of course they would go just to keep up appearances."

She took another look at the family portrait. "I think I've seen these little girls before." She and Abigail knew the significance of that and it grieved them both to realize that these precious little children were being abused and groomed for cult purposes.

"Let's not look any further today." Abigail tossed the directory back into her truck before adding, "Hey, call me tomorrow and let me know how it went." They talked a little more before Abigail headed into the store and Carrie Sue headed to her apartment. They were both distracted as they pondered the implications of Sheriff Bynum not only going to their church, but also being a Satanist. *And that man was in my house!*

Abigail made her purchases and headed back to the church. She just finished putting her perishables in the refrigerator when Pastor Spalding spoke from behind her, "Abigail, how are you doing these days?" He did not wait for her to reply, "For some reason the Lord has put you on my mind a lot lately. Is there something specific that I need to pray about?"

Abigail trusted this godly man, but she wasn't quite sure how much he would understand. Sometimes when she thought about her life, she believed that she could never write a biography; she would have to do a novel. No one would believe the crazy things that she had experienced. "Well, I could use some extra prayer cover these days. You know that I see those ritual abuse clients," she started cautiously. He nodded so she continued, "It's getting close to Halloween, one of the cult's favorite times of year to do rituals. There's just been a lot of spiritual warfare lately."

Pastor Spalding was rather discerning. He turned his head a little, raised his eyebrows, and looked at her out of the corners of his eyes and asked, "Is there something else?"

Abigail let out a sigh and spilled her guts, "My dog was poisoned. He died Sunday. I think it's connected to cult activities. I've been getting more threatening phone calls. Someone came into my house a couple of weeks ago and trashed it. Both brake lines on my truck were cut. And besides that, it's coming up on the tenth anniversary of the accident. But other than that, I can't think of anything," she tried to sound a little light-hearted.

"I don't know what to say," this was a lot to process even for a pastor. "I guess that's why the Lord has put you on my mind. I'll be very intentional about praying for you. Do you mind if I share with my wife so she can pray with me?"

"I can use all the prayer cover I can get; thank you," Abigail glanced at her watch and said, "I need to get back for my next lady, she'll be here in a couple of minutes.

"I can talk to Sheriff Bynum for you, if you want," he offered.

Abigail turned pale and stammered, "Um, no, no, please don't." *Think fast!* "Uh, actually, he was there when I reported the break-in." *Oh, boy; would that ever complicate things!* "Really, pastor, this is a spiritual battle and I think it'll all be resolved with our prayers."

He was a bit baffled by her response but agreed to limit his intervention to prayer. "You let me know if anything else happens." His protective big brotherly ways combined with his shepherd's heart kept him on his knees a lot with his growing congregation.

It was 2:06 when Amy walked in the door. She was more edgy than usual, no doubt because of the ritual date. They engaged in small talk and made an attempt at mundane banter.

"Let's open with prayer," Abigail suggested at last. Amy nodded and stared back at Abigail throughout the prayer. After she finished, Abigail asked, "Where are we starting today?"

"I don't know," the host Amy said, "I just feel a lot of nervousness, but I don't know why." The host's job was to reflect the outside world to the inside one and vice-versa. The host often felt emotions bubbling up from other personalities, especially if they were strong ones like anger or fear.

"Let's ask the Lord to show you where that kind of nervousness is coming from." She proceeded to do so when Amy gave her an affirmative nod.

Head Warden displaced the host. "It's me," he said with much more humility than he had during their last encounter. "I'm hesitant to talk; I don't want others to hear what we discuss."

"We can take care of that," Abigail replied.

"How?"

"I'll ask the Lord to put a protective shield around the two of us."

He gave her a look that conveyed his skepticism. "Do what you have to do." He sounded impatient but was actually feeling a bit desperate. He was feeling the pinch of trying to maintain his role while beginning to grasp just how much he had been duped over the years. He also knew what happened to traitors.

"Lord, I pray that You would …"

Suddenly Head Warden's voice snarled, "You can't have him, he's ours!" A demon fully manifested and took over Amy's body.

"In the name of Jesus the Christ of Nazareth, what so-called right do you think you have to him?" Abigail was accustomed to having demons manifest through her clients from time to time. It was not her favorite encounter, but it did not rattle her, either. She knew that when a demon manifested it was a desperate last-ditch effort to keep its assignment.

"Her father gave her to us," it glowered at her and made Amy's eyes look flat like shark eyes.

"I'm not going to argue with you. Your covenant is bogus." Ignoring its questions, she went on to pray, "Lord Jesus, Your Word says that every place that we put the soles of our feet belong to us. This place is under my rightful jurisdiction. I ask that You would evict this trespasser right now."

The demon did not budge. It looked triumphant as it continued to bombard Abigail with questions. She never answered a demon's question. By answering, it put the demon in charge because it was then making her answer to it.

"Lord, this demon is not in its assigned place, would You fill that place with Your Holy Spirit and evict it?"

The demon taunted her even more.

Abigail continued to pray as she turned in her Bible to several of the passages with which she had warred effectively in the past.

The demon taunted her, "You don't have the right verses. You'll never find them. I'll win."

"Fine," Abigail turned over to Genesis, "I'll just start right here. *'In the beginning God…'*" She continued reading the text even while being assaulted by the demon's tirade. *Okay, Lord, what am I missing here?* She listened with her spiritual ears while her natural ears were being accosted by the demon's diatribe.

"These momentary and light afflictions shall not be compared to the eternal weight of glory reserved in heaven for you." Abigail understood the Holy Spirit's message and smiled slightly.

"What?" the demon asked suspiciously.

"I just want to thank you for giving us such a rough time." She quoted the verse and said, "Since parts of Amy belong to the true Lord Jesus Christ, all of her will be going to heaven. Since you are tormenting her, she will get a better reward."

"You mean I'm helping her?" it demanded.

"Yeah, thanks." Abigail said brightly.

"Then I'm leaving!" The demon cast itself out.

Head Warden reappeared in full control once again. "Whew! That was amazing. I don't care what happens to me; I'm defecting."

Abigail spent the rest of the session ministering to the guards and other personalities that were under his jurisdiction on the above ground levels of the prison structures. There were many, including Caleb, who were not willing to go along with him, but hundreds did. Many more who were in the cells were set free as well. There were innumerable personalities trapped in the subterranean levels, including the original F. Amy Bolton. No one knew for sure just how many levels there were at this time. But for today, this was a huge turning point for Amy.

"Amy, I know that this is a big ritual day. How are you going to stay safe?"

"I don't know. I'll figure something out. I'll be all right. Besides, I have to go to work tonight. Friday night is a big pizza night."

They parted ways after praying. Abigail retrieved her food from the kitchen after locking the office and then took the scenic route home. The full-sized sedan was driving toward a different destination and its driver was not thinking about Abigail today.

October thirteenth marked the official preparation for All Hallows Eve and Halloween. It was the number thirty-one in reverse. It was time for the abduction, holding, and ceremonial preparation of individuals to be readied for human sacrifice.

It had been easy for Zorroz to supply the cult with suitable ceremonial sacrifices. He often came across homeless people, hitch-hikers, or petty criminals who had no ties to family or community. He could wear his uniform and drive the county vehicle outside of his jurisdiction and not be questioned. On that Friday the thirteenth he came upon a teenaged couple hiking through an isolated part of the county with backpacks and tents. They were unkempt and appeared to have come a long way. He stopped and questioned them. He ascertained that they were disgruntled kids who were basically running away from home. They began to get nervous under his intense scrutiny. The girl was particularly anxious and asked him if they could be on their way.

"No, I think I need to see your IDs and make sure you are not the ones who robbed the Gas N Go," he said sternly. Sheriff Bynum was a practiced liar.

"What robbery?" the young man was alarmed. "We didn't rob anyone. Check our backpacks. You won't find a thing."

"I will, but I need to detain you in the car until I do. Put your hands on the hood of my car," he ordered.

The startled couple complied. They were young and inexperienced, but something did not seem right about this encounter. She began to weep and the boy tried to hush her as Sheriff Bynum did a cursory pat down and cuffed both of them. He opened the back door of the squad and they awkwardly sat with their arms behind them. He buckled the young man in first and then went around and did the same to the girl. He did not search their packs; he just opened the trunk of the squad and deposited all evidence of their presence into it. He pulled out a small package that he kept hidden in the spare wheel well. Filling one syringe with a small amount of liquid, he grabbed the young man's arm and plunged the needle into it and emptied about half of the dose.

"Hey! What do you think you're doing?" the young man demanded and tried to jerk away. Sheriff Bynum was a very strong man and soon the teen was sitting there glassy eyed from the effects of the sedative. The girl began to scream and thrash as he went around to her side and did the same thing to her. He calmly closed doors and returned his syringe to the trunk and closed it. Then he drove them to their destiny.

Once again, the familiar pull tugged on the various cult members. A ritual as significant as this one would be held at the regional site closer to the capital of the state. The state park was conveniently closed to visitors after six o'clock. Sunset was at five-thirty tonight and there were not that many visitors at this time of the year anyway. The pavilion was nestled in the middle of a thick pine forest and afforded the group the privacy they required as well as ample parking. It could be easily cleaned when they were finished.

The sun went down and cast long, ominous shadows. Various "sacred" artifacts were brought out and readied. A dark full-sized van backed up to the pavilion and several men unloaded the aged but sturdy, blood-tarnished table. It would be stained again tonight because their blood-thirsty king had a voracious appetite that could not be satiated; it could only be appeased. Kill. Steal. Destroy. That would be done tonight with abandon.

Daggett and Darod, the area leaders; Zorroz and Herrak, the local leaders met with Prinz. They firmed up plans for the series of rituals and activities that would take them into the first week of November. The abductions had taken place and the ceremonial preparations would begin.

Women arrived alone or with their mates. Some of them were responsible for the proper preparation of the children of all ages who came with their parents. Some had been born at a ritual and were never registered or given a proper birth certificate. They did not exist as far as the rest of the world knew. They never went to school. They thought this was normal and that all parents dealt with their children like this. Tonight, they were in various trance states because of the potions that were administered by their guardians.

Little girls were being clothed in pretty dresses and told that they were being honored tonight in special ceremonies. They were excited and yet there was an ominous sense of foreboding. One prepubescent teen would be celebrating a rite of passage because of her first monthly cycle. She would become a fresh supply of innocent sacrifices as her innocence was sacrificed.

Tonight, there would be many sacrifices and one of the most anticipated ones would be a pre-born child of Prinz. The infant was conceived on March fifteenth. Beware, the Ides of March! Labor would be induced at the optimal time. This child would never see the light of day, but the angels of the Lord would escort this tiny life to the throne of the Creator of the universe whose brightness would outshine the sun. Here he would join other martyred souls under the alter who were crying out, *"How long, O Lord, holy and true, will You refrain from judging and avenging our blood?"*

There was much blood to avenge, and not just from this region of the world. Satan's loyal followers were scattered all over the globe. He was building the new world order in which he would be king and ruler. God's timing was and is and will be impeccable. The bowls of wrath were being filled and soon they would spill over in righteous judgment.

The night of revelry continued as planned and stirred up the heavenly hosts. By three o'clock in the morning curses were being released. Three o'clock – the darkest of hours and the counter-part of three o'clock in the afternoon when Jesus cried out, *"It is finished!"* They mocked and cried out, "It is not!" The head of the ancient serpent may have been cut off, but the rest of its body continued to writhe unaware that it was in its death throes.

17

Saturday, October 14

Amy was sore that Saturday morning. She could not remember doing anything that would make her feel like she had been run over by a truck. But then, this was yet another of the myriad of mysteries in her life. Amy thought she had put in her Friday night shift at The Pizza Palace and come directly back home. She was programmed in such a way that she did not notice time losses and thus, she could not know that others had switched in because of that programming. They had taken her to last night's ritual and she had fully participated in the revelries.

Head Warden was aware of the whole evening but stayed in the background. Several times during the night vulnerable female and child parts were called out and tormented. The torment had the desired effect of causing more dissociation. With every desecration, hundreds of new personalities were split out. Those wounded little parts were thrown into the internal cells that had been recently vacated by the ones who had been integrated the previous week.

Rather than the indifference that he formerly felt, Head Warden was sickened by the whole process. He and the other guards who were recently healed and yet remained dissociated had already met secretly. They believed that they could convince Nicholai and the other cult-loyal parts that they were still on board while finding ways to alleviate the agony of the little ones that would inevitably be placed under their authority. They had to tread carefully because of the cult-loyal guards. They would sell anyone out in a heartbeat.

Head Warden and the other defectors secretly comforted the little ones. Where they were formerly persecutors without conscience, they were now kind. They promised that they would get them help as soon as possible. That help would not come until Friday when they met with Abigail so they prayed that they could hold on that long.

Meanwhile Carrie Sue was dutifully preparing for a trying day at the funeral home which would also be followed by a graveside ceremony at the cemetery. She had refused to go out Friday night and knew that her mother would be hurt and irate because she did not go to the wake. She was praising God that the right parts remained in control so she was not accessed. Several of the vigilant protectors took turns staying alert while others rested.

Her mother had already called several times that morning. The first time she was the nervous, helpless mother. The second time she was the competent, assertive mother. Another time she was the mean, ill-tempered mother who berated her and disowned her.

Again.

When Carrie Sue could delay no longer, she finally made her way to her car and drove the short distance to the funeral home. She had been there before, but it certainly was not for a funeral or a wake. *Lord, I need Your strength.* She informed the attendant that she would not be riding in the limousine so she was directed to a position not far behind it. If her worthless brother ever showed up, he could ride with Mom.

Her emotions percolated wildly as a hodge-podge of thoughts and attitudes from the various remaining personalities surfaced and receded. There were some younger ones who did not have terrible memories. They wanted their daddy and were sad. Others were thrilled that their tormentor was dead and gone. *May he rot in hell!* Then there were parts that felt intense guilt about what they should have done. If only she had been a better daughter. Somehow it was all her fault. Some were angry that he died before they had the chance to tell him off.

Or worse.

But mostly, there was a great sense of relief.

Carrie Sue arrived just before the private viewing for the immediate family. She really did not want to see him again. She did not want to see her brother or her mother or anyone else for that matter. She had the ominous feeling that she would turn around and bump into some diabolical figure.

"Carrie Sue," her mother wailed when she saw her come through the double doors. "Your brother isn't here. He's never disappeared for this long. Whatever am I going to do?"

"He'll show up eventually, Mom, he always does," Carrie Sue said with little conviction.

Susan switched again. This personality changed the subject. "I don't know why *we're* here."

"What do you mean?" a puzzled Carrie Sue asked.

"Well!" some part that Carrie Sue had not met before huffed, "*we* didn't marry that SOB. Judith did."

"Huh?"

"Judith is the one who got swept off her feet by that smooth-talking jerk and married him. We told her not to, but she insisted that he loved us and we got dragged down the aisle anyway."

"Oh." It finally registered that one of her mother's personalities, Judith, had fallen for and married her father. Of course, that would make perfect sense in her mother's senseless world.

"*She's* the one that's been caterwauling all stinkin' morning!" she hissed. The intense disgust of this irate part was undisguised.

Carrie Sue just shook her head and tried not to laugh as she pictured the internal conflict that her mother - or some part of her - had just described.

Very few people showed up for the funeral. The Wagner side of the family was represented by several uncles and aunts. Carrie Sue nodded to some cousins whom she had not seen for years. Her mother's side added a few more to the scant crowd. They did not really have a church home. They were not at all close to neighbors. Two men who worked with Ron Wagner showed up. The funeral home had arranged for a local chaplain to come and say a few words. All in all, it was a dismal affair.

Billy did not show up and so Susan Wagner's two sisters joined her in the limousine. The graveside service was blissfully short and trite, but Carrie Sue did not care. She just wanted to get back into her car and get back to her apartment. Alone. She was grateful that her mother's sisters were able to stay for a while and keep the woman occupied.

And that was it. Her father did not even make it to sixty. What did his life mean? What kind of legacy did he leave? What happened to him that made him so anti-God, so mean? She never even got to meet his parents and he never talked about them. She knew her mother's parents were harsh, legalistic, and abusive. Her mother didn't talk about her childhood much, but one time she did mention an uncle who had molested her when she was very young.

Carrie Sue used her thumbs to get to the screen that had her pre-programmed phone numbers and tapped on Abigail's number. *Huh, even phones are programmed.* She grinned at her private joke that was not really funny when she thought about it.

Abigail made it a point to be inside so that she would not miss Carrie Sue's phone call. She wanted to be with her at the funeral, but then, she wanted Carrie Sue to be able to go through this difficult time and stand on her own feet. Abigail saw her role as one who initially did the majority of the work, encouragement, prayers, and so on during the early ministry times. As healing occurred, she began to shift the responsibility over to the counselee. She wanted to work herself out of a job.

"Hello," Abigail said. She picked up because she recognized the number, "how did it go?"

"Well, I made it. I think our strategy was good and I was able to say no to Mom even though it really made her mad … or sad … or mean." She chuckled as she alluded to her mother's multiple personalities. "Her sisters are with her for the rest of the day so maybe she'll leave me alone for a while."

"Good! I've been praying for you all morning. I'm proud of you, er, all of you." They chuckled together and then said goodbye.

Abigail was up early that Sunday morning and took care of Buster. It was hard to believe that Dude had been gone for a week already. She missed his loyal companionship. It seemed as if Buster missed him as well. His coat was starting to get thicker with the brisk night air. She was amazed at how quickly his winter coat could appear. It didn't seem all that long ago that she was currying and brushing away clumps of last winter's coat.

"We'll ride again soon," she said as she patted him on the rump on her way back up to the house. The month of October was already difficult with the anniversary of the accident. Now she had Dude's death to add to the pain.

She had worked through the intense pain and grief with her prayer partner, but she still honored their memory every year. They were her family and she would never forget them. The Lord had taken the sting out of the memory, but some years were more difficult than others. She determined to stay on her knees and press in even harder to the Lord.

The worship time was refreshing that morning as the congregation entered into the presence of the Lord. The song selection was meaningful and Abigail wondered how the Lord seemed to tailor the service just for her. Of course, she knew that others were touched by the songs, the testimonies, the teachings, and the other parts of the service as well.

"Today," Pastor Spalding opened, "I'm going to be teaching out of Second Peter. I want to focus on the life of Lot, Abraham's nephew." He paused as people turned the pages in their Bibles to follow along as he read verses from the second chapter.

"How many of you are kind of doing a double-take when you read the words 'righteous Lot' in verse seven? I know I did. And not only that, verse eight referred to Lot as 'that righteous man' and noted his 'righteous soul' being vexed or tormented by all the sin, sensuality, and lawless deeds. In verse nine, it says that the Lord knows how to rescue the godly from temptation. He is implying that Lot was godly and righteous." He let those words sink in for a few moments as he noted puzzled looks on some faces.

"Let's go back to Genesis and start in chapter thirteen and see just how righteous and godly this Lot was," Pastor Spalding continued. He brought them to the verses that showed how Lot selfishly took the well-watered valley and left Uncle Abraham with the poorer quality grazing lands before moving closer to the cities of Sodom and Gomorrah where he married one of the women. Then his children intermarried with them. He skipped up to chapter nineteen where Lot was visited by some angels. The men of the city wanted to have sex with them but Lot offered his two virgin daughters to them instead. And after Lot escaped with those daughters, he let them get him drunk and they each conceived a son by him.

"This is the righteous, godly Lot that Second Peter is talking about. Now, I don't know about you, but I did not see one righteous thing mentioned in Genesis about Lot. I don't mind telling you that I was a bit upset with the Lord for calling *that* man who did nothing but demonstrate selfishness, compromise, and perverseness a righteous man." He paused again to let that sink in. "So, I had to get down on my knees and ask the Lord to show me how He could call that apparently unrighteous man righteous.

"And do you know what He said to me?" he asked with raised eyebrows. He could see that he had their attention as many of them leaned forward slightly. "He said, 'Lot is righteous because I declared him righteous – just like I declared you righteous.' Oh!

"Folks, if we were honest, our history would not look much better than Lot's. We were selfish. Maybe we wouldn't have offered our daughters to strangers, but who has not compromised their values in order to protect their own reputation and hurt their family in the process? Maybe you haven't gotten drunk, but perhaps you did something that tainted your legacy." There were a few nods from the quiet crowd.

"Let's not turn there now, but I want to remind you of the people mentioned in Hebrews eleven. We call this the Hall of Faith. If you research their lives, you would find that many of them were right up there with old Lot. There were liars and deceivers, mockers and murderers, prostitutes and adulterers, but not one sin was mentioned in that chapter." He went into more detail about some of their lives that were documented in the Old Testament scriptures.

He concluded his sermon, "After the death, burial, and resurrection of Jesus Christ, their sins - and ours as well - have been taken out of the way and buried in the sea of forgetfulness, as far as the east is from the west. Folks, the good news is that when the Lord looks at us today, He sees a people that has been declared righteous. *That,* folks, is our identity, even though our behavior does not always match it."

When the service was concluded, Abigail and Cindy found each other and got caught up on the latest news. "Oh, by the way," Cindy said as they headed toward their respective vehicles, "Gary's cousin, Lee, is going to be moving out this way so he can be closer to family." She said it with a slightly conspiratorial smile. Abigail could see the match-making wheels turning in her friend's head already.

Abigail took the back roads home and tried to think about what she was going to do the rest of the day. Buster was especially frisky in this weather so it might just be a good idea to take a ride. It would be much different without Dude. She didn't realize how much she depended upon him for protection. *Lord, You are my shield and my defender, whom shall I fear?* The closer she got to home, the more excited she became as she thought about getting out into the woods again. She always felt the tranquility and the peace of the Lord whenever she meandered through His creation.

After a light lunch, she decided it would be a good idea to check the SD memory cards from each of the cameras. She got the two-step ladder and retrieved the ones from the front porch and the back deck and then got the one at the bend of the driveway. She did not expect to find anything unusual, but she did not want to take a chance.

She was right. There was nothing but pictures of herself coming and going. *That's a relief.* She replaced them and decided to return the one from the bottom of the pasture on the way back home. She could reach it easily from Buster's back and not have to drag the little ladder down there.

Buster greeted her when she finally made her way out to the tack room. The air smelled sweet from the fresh hay in the barn. She made a mental note to make another run this week to pick up another load. Saddling Buster, checking for dangers as far as she could see, she kept him at a walk all the way down to the back gate. He snorted impatiently as he waited for her to open the gate and remount. They soon settled into an easy lope and enjoyed the autumn sights, sounds, and smells. When they got to the opening at the far end of the field, she decided to go right instead of left. The trails were well marked and ran roughly parallel to the road.

Full only after a hard rain, smaller dried up creek beds crossed their trail at irregular intervals. She only slowed Buster's pace when the trail became tortuous just before the moderately sized glade. Buster startled briefly when they scared up a rabbit but he quickly settled down as she patted his muscular neck. There was a stand of pine trees at the far end of the clearing and she could hear the breezes soughing through the needles. The gentle pine scent added to the tranquil setting and soothed her soul.

After going down the trail for a while, they made another right turn onto a dirt road that headed back toward the highway. She did not want to ride on York Creek Road. She could easily cross over to the other side and go up the driveway of the abandoned farm, passing through a couple fields before eventually coming up her own driveway. After about a mile, the dirt road intersected with the highway. There was no traffic so they crossed the road and stayed on the shoulder until they came to the abandoned driveway.

As usual, Abigail watched for animal tracks. She was not expecting to see tire tracks. They did not look as if they had been made very recently, but it was hard to tell because of last week's rain. She did not think much of it; after all, it could have been anyone. Teenagers were known to find secret places to hang out and party.

Just as they passed the old trailer she saw the abandoned car with the tinted windows. Her heart lurched. *That's the car!* It always seemed to be in the same places that she was. She never saw the driver because of the deep tint. Covered in a thick layer of dirt with leaves accumulating over the windshield wipers, it was obvious that the car had been sitting there for some time.

In a bold move, she turned Buster toward the car and dismounted. She looked in the windows and didn't see much besides fast-food wrappers on the seats and floorboards. She did not want to disturb anything or leave evidence of her presence, but she really wanted to know who owned this car. Since she was wearing her riding gloves, she decided to try the passenger door. It was unlocked and opened with an ominous creak. Opening the glove box and carefully sifting through its contents, she found a worn and wrinkled registration card jammed in the corner. She straightened it out and read the owner's name out loud, "William J. Wagner."

So, this is where Billy left his car that day. Abigail began to piece together some things about that fateful Saturday. She really had not considered how he got to her house before. *I can't wait to tell Cindy and Gary*! She replaced the registration card and closed the old door. As she rode off, she prayed for a rain that would be hard enough to wash away Buster's trail.

Making their way through the fields and up the driveway, she leaned over in the saddle and deftly unlatched the gate. Buster balked a little at having to ride past his sweet feed and go all the way back down to the bottom of the pasture but he was patient as she dismounted, refastened the gate and remounted. She further confused him by coaxing him to stand close enough to the tree so she could get the SD card out of the camera. She slipped it into her pocket and finally let him head back to the tack room for sweet feed and a light grooming.

She checked the SD card and scrolled through the pictures like Gary had showed her. There were many pictures of Buster and various four-footed creatures. She was relieved that there was nothing suspicious to be seen. Putting the card back into her shirt pocket, stepping back outside, she checked herself as she almost called for Dude. *Lord, I really miss that Dude!* Abigail walked to the end of the pasture with the two-step ladder, inserted the card back into the camera and then trekked back up to the house.

Gary answered the phone, "Hey, Ab, what's up?"

"I had an interesting ride this afternoon."

"More interesting than my football game, I hope. Or, seeing as it is you, maybe I hope it's much less interesting than the game," he joked with her.

"I went riding and we took the trail toward the right and came up that old dirt road about a mile north of me. Guess what I found hiding by that abandoned trailer across the road from me?"

"It's hard telling," he replied.

"An old car with dark tinted windows – the one that I keep seeing practically every time I go out – it was abandoned back there. It was unlocked so I checked the glovebox. It was registered to William J. Wagner, Carrie Sue's brother."

"Your visitor!" Gary remembered the name.

"Yes." Abigail continued, "and the funny thing is that he has been missing for almost two weeks now. Carrie Sue says her mother is going nuts because he's never stayed away this long. Their father died last week and he didn't even show up for the funeral."

"Well, if he was gone," Gary said trying to think of some logical explanation, "maybe he wouldn't have known that his father died."

"But how would he get anywhere without his own car?" Abigail countered.

"That's a good question."

"I think that either he tried to leave without a trace - remember Sheriff Bynum is a …" she stopped her thought. "Oh, no, you don't know this. Carrie Sue looked at our church directory and she called him Zorroz. He's a cult member! That's why he creeps me out so much."

"No kidding!" Gary was confounded by that news for a moment. "That makes too much sense. So, Billy might figure that the sheriff could trace his car through other agencies." They fell silent as they pondered the myriad of implications.

"It'll be interesting to see if he shows up in court tomorrow," she said. "Maybe he's just keeping a low profile. Sheriff Zorroz sure didn't seem very happy with him that day."

"Or maybe there's been some kind of foul play," Gary conjectured. "Wait! Did you say Zorroz?"

"His cult name. And you're starting to sound like me," Abigail teased him back.

"Now that's scary. Hey, do you want to talk to Cindy?" He handed the phone over to his wife and went back to his game.

Cindy had caught his side of the conversation and was eager to have the blanks filled in. They talked about the new discovery for a while and then moved on to other subjects. Cindy said she would definitely be praying for Abigail at the hearing tomorrow.

18

Monday, October 16

Judge Roberts was in his chambers preparing for his long day on the bench. He considered the ten o'clock case and frowned. He needed to bury that particular case without raising any suspicions. He had done it before; it could be done again.

Abigail drove toward the courthouse and found a parking spot on one of the side streets a couple of blocks away. She noted the cross streets and made her way to the courthouse well before the assigned time. She was unfamiliar with the inside of the old building and was not sure how long it would take to pass through security. At least she had remembered to stow Walther in the truck.

Finding her way to the second floor where Judge Roberts held court, she slipped unobtrusively into a back row and watched the proceedings of a couple of cases that were quickly decided. She had expected something more like what one would see on TV, but this was not Hollywood and she soon found out that a defendant was allowed to request either a jury trial or a bench trial. Apparently, Billy had requested a bench trial. Maybe he knew the judge.

As each case ended, the attorneys, defendants, and witnesses exited the courtroom down the center aisle. She had no idea of what Billy's attorney looked like, but she would not soon forget her intruder. Another attorney in the string of lawyers appeared and sat at one table and busied himself in arranging papers. *He looks familiar. Does he go to my church?* She noticed him looking at his watch and glancing over his shoulder. She also noticed that the judge did not seem very happy about something.

Finally, Judge Roberts glared at the attorney and asked, "Where is William J. Wagner?"

Respectfully requesting that he be allowed to approach the bench, he was given permission. The two men had an intense, but hushed conversation. Geoffrey Evans returned to his table, packed his papers, and left the courtroom. The judge scrawled his signature on a document and summoned an officer. Apparently, it was an arrest warrant of some kind. Abigail heard the officer confidently make a remark about bringing him in.

The next case was called in and the new parties sat at the appropriate tables. Abigail slipped out of the courtroom and took the stairs down to the ornate foyer. Large portraits of several current and former judges were displayed on the walls. The Honorable Judge Jeffrey Roberts was among them.

She exited the building and made her way back to her truck trying to make sense of all the random pieces of information that she had rolling around in her mind. Billy had been gone for a couple of weeks. He was out on personal recognizance and did not show up for court – something that was sure to increase fines and/or jail time. At the very least, it would alienate the judge. His car was abandoned behind the trailer near her home. Something was wrong. She began to wonder if Carrie Sue's healing had anything to do with it. She wondered if he was the mysterious man on horseback who had tossed the poison over the fence. But no! That could not be because Billy did not have long hair.

"Lord, even darkness is light to You. Would You bring things that are hidden by darkness to the light?" Abigail was not entirely sure of why she felt the need to have Billy's whereabouts made known. Perhaps because if she had some idea of where he was, she would feel safer. But then, they always had back up people for everything.

When she got home, she called Cindy and let her know how it went at court. She had agreed to pray with Abigail about all the other issues. Abigail also remembered to tell Cindy that she did not find anything suspicious on any of the cameras the day before to set Cindy's mind at ease.

Abigail felt acute loneliness now that Dude was not romping around anymore but she could not bear the thought of looking for another puppy yet. Why is it that we want someone or something to be unique but when they, or it, is gone, we want an exact duplicate? How could another dog be better than Dude? Dad had a series of dogs over the years and he said that he appreciated each one. "Ain't wrong, just different," he would assert.

She spent some time cleaning out Dude's well-used doghouse, and finally she grabbed a five-gallon bucket and tackled Dude's dump in the front yard. He was definitely a retriever! Buster softly nickered as he wandered toward the front of the pasture area and stuck his head over the fence. Abigail met him there and stroked his powerful neck. He nuzzled her pocket for treats and when none were to be found, he went back to his grazing.

"You are so shallow," Abigail laughed quietly.

Susan Wagner was startled by a loud knock on the door. She was already on edge and not accustomed to having visitors. Cautiously peeking through the curtains in the window, she saw a county sheriff's car in the driveway and her tensions rose even higher as she opened the door to the uniformed officer.

"Ma'am, I'm sorry to bother you, but I am looking for William J. Wagner," he stated matter-of-factly while his eyes were busy scanning the room behind her. "Is he here?"

"Uh, no, no sir," Susan stammered and then boldly declared, "I haven't seen his sorry hide in a couple of weeks." She then began to cry, "He didn't even have the common decency to show up at his own father's funeral Saturday."

"I'm sorry, ma'am," the officer did not perceive the personality switches. He handed her a card and said, "Have him call us when he comes in."

"Yes, sir, I sure will," she replied. She remained in the open doorway until he drove away and then she called Carrie Sue.

Carrie Sue answered her phone with misgivings. She knew it would be another in a never-ending series of emotionally and mentally strenuous conversations with a very unstable woman. *Was I that bad?* Carrie Sue sometimes contemplated her childhood and now thought that anyone watching the erratic interactions between mother and daughter would be totally mystified. They must have switched personalities to adjust to or counter the switches in one another's personalities as they were triggered. Which was the "real" mom and which was the "real" daughter? Would they ever be able to have a normal - whatever that was - relationship?

"Carrie Sue, I just got visited by a sheriff. He was looking for Billy but he didn't say why and I didn't think to ask," she said with a rush. "Why would anyone be looking for him?"

"I don't know, Mom," Carrie Sue was careful not to stir anything up. *Keep it neutral; keep it short.*

"Where could he be?" Susan Wagner agonized.

"I don't know. I haven't seen him for a couple of weeks either." Carrie Sue kept quiet and there was an awkward silence for a few moments.

"It's all your fault, you know," an old, familiar accusing voice cut in. "If you had been where you were supposed to be, Billy would still be here."

"What are you talking about?" Carrie Sue was accustomed to the changes in her mother's demeanor, but she was sensing something ominous was coming.

"If you had been where you were supposed to be, you would know," her mother snapped.

Carrie Sue was scrambling for some explanation. What was she talking about? "Mom," she started and was abruptly interrupted.

"Let's just say," her mother's voice cackled as she pointed an accusing finger, "Billy will never come home. You're the one who had to go get involved with that woman. You brought all of this on us. You'll be the death of me, too. You're killing your whole family. I knew I should never have let you see the light of day!" The cult-loyal part of her mother launched into a vicious string of curses.

Carrie Sue was stunned as she began to put the pieces together. *Oh, Jesus!* She knew how diabolical the cult was. She had seen and experienced their depravity. Abigail had explained about the duplicity programming and the intentional double-binds that were constantly being woven into their set ups. But now it was personal, very personal. She hated Billy for everything he had done to her – but dead?

"Just what do you have to say for yourself, you ungrateful traitor?" her mother's voice taunted.

Carrie Sue had no answer. Her mind was reeling with what her mother had just told her. She hastily said good-bye and quickly hung up.

On the other end of the line, a docile and confused mother stared at the phone and wondered if she had been disconnected or if it was merely the end of a conversation or if she just forgot who she intended to call. She was accustomed to these mysteries. This happened to everyone, right?

Carrie Sue grabbed her keys and walked out of the door trembling with emotions. She did not quite trust herself to drive, so she headed to the nearby park. She used to go there to let her child parts play. She often got odd stares from the mothers who brought their children to play, but if she could restrict her little ones to the swings, she did not stand out very much. Today, she just wanted to walk so she angled toward the paved walking path that circled the athletic fields.

Carrie Sue needed to process the things her mother had said not only about Billy, but about her. How was she responsible for the deaths of everyone in her whole family? Abigail had explained about the reproaches going back upon the perpetrators. Her father was definitely the person who was the most responsible for orchestrating her torment so she could understand why he would have weakened to the point of death as she healed.

Billy was being groomed for leadership in the cult, but even though he was mean and mostly followed orders, he just did not seem to have the same kind of forcefulness as her father and the other masters. Well, now that she thought about it, even her father was not as powerful as Zorroz or some of the higher-level masters. They seemed to treat him more like a lackey. Her father sensed that and took it out on members of his own family.

What did Mom mean by saying that if I was there, Billy would still be here? Where? She racked her brain and prayed, "Lord, help me understand." She immediately had the thought that two weeks ago would have been that ritual that she did not attend.

Abigail had invited her over for supper and then they did a ministry session that took care of the parts that were programmed to go to that ritual. She had the alarming thought that whatever had happened to Billy that night would have happened to her if she had been there.

Her head hurt. She was grateful that she had so much healing already or she would not have known about the things that the other parts knew. As there was integration, there was sharing of knowledge and memories. Thankfully, the Lord took the sting out of the horrific memories, but sometimes realizing just how damaged she was made her sad. Abigail was right about the two kinds of pain - one came from the presence of trauma and the other came from the lack of good things.

Billy. Dead? And what did Mom say about getting involved with that woman? It had to be Abigail. Why kill him for her so-called offense? Was Mom dying, too? Was she being melodramatic by saying she would be the death of her, or did she have a feeling about something going on in the spiritual realm as well? She longed to talk to Abigail, but she knew that the first question would be how she had already prayed.

So, she prayed, "Lord, I'm reeling. I don't know what to believe about what that part of Mom said today. God, I don't know what to think or what to do. I'm so confused and I feel so alone." She poured out her heart to the Lord as she circled the track one last time before heading back to her apartment. She was calmer, but felt no closer to knowing what, if anything, she should do.

She called Abigail, left a message, and waited. She was too keyed up to focus on anything so she found herself drifting from room to room straightening things that were already straight and cleaning things that were already clean. Finally, she sank down on the couch and decided to have what she called a leadership committee meeting with several of the protectors and sector leaders of the remaining personalities. She wanted to see if any of them had ideas about what the mother had said. Did any of them have any information that would help all of them understand?

Finally, the phone rang. "Hey. I am so glad you called. I have to tell you what my mom told me a couple of hours ago." She proceeded to tell Abigail about the sheriff looking for Billy as well as the possibility that Billy was killed at that last ritual based on the strange things her mother had said. Rushing through her mental gymnastics and all the insane possibilities she thought of and how she had prayed, she ended with, "so what do you think?"

"Well," Abigail took a breath and measured her words, "that's a lot to digest. That could explain why Billy has been missing since that night. I really don't want to speculate right now. I think we should just keep praying about it. And keep praying for your safety and stability." Abigail would eventually have to tell Carrie Sue about her connection with her brother but did not want to do that over the phone. That dear lady had endured so much for so long.

Prinz was not a happy man. He had pulled off the last ritual with a wary eye toward those who would do anything to take over his position. He did not want to admit it, but he was beginning to feel his age and that was not a good sign. He had bargained very hard for a long and vigorous life. What did the Great Enemy's Book say about His prophet? When he died, his eye was not dim, nor was his vigor abated. Prinz claimed every gift and blessing that the Great Enemy gave to His people, but Prinz gained his gifts and blessings through his covenants with his own leader.

The Great Enemy's Book was useful. Its meanings and intentions could be corrupted and distorted. It was a never-ending source of inspiration for imitating and counterfeiting so many things. For every rite and ceremony of the Enemy, they had their own. *The Enemy baptizes in mere water, our leader calls for blood.* He scoffed that the Enemy's people used grape juice or even wine while they used blood.

Lucifer had his bride, too, and by her he would produce the seed that would bring the ultimate enmity against the Great Enemy's seed. For every book the enemy has, their great leader has his own. He has a book of Life; Lucifer has a book of death. He has a book of remembrance for those who fear His name; Lucifer has a book of remembrance for those who fear him. Critical verses could be twisted by changing or twisting, omitting or adding a word or two. Yes, it was indeed a source of inspiration.

All Hallows Eve was coming. He needed to come up with a way to not only protect the powers he had, but to enhance them. He both craved and dreaded the potential arrival of their great leader. He was known to visit as many gatherings as possible around the world on that day. He had heard the glorious accounts of his great and terrible visitations but had never personally been there when he appeared with his powerful minions. If a leader was favored, one of those elite spirits would be assigned to him. If he could engender that kind of favor, he could ensure his position for a long time to come. And to that end, Prinz entered the subterranean level of his dwelling place and applied himself to his dark arts.

Pastor Spalding was in his study putting the finishing touches on his Wednesday night teaching. He often sensed the darkness that invaded his community and the county at large. He had been a pastor for over twenty-five years, starting as youth pastor and later as an assistant pastor in some fine churches. He had some very good pastors who blessed him, encouraged him, imparted gifts to him, and mentored him. He also had the character-building experiences of having worked with some men who definitely should not have been in the ministry.

It had always been the desire of his heart to settle into a church and be instrumental in its growth in maturity as well as numbers. It was not a popularity contest and he did not want to "steal sheep" from other churches. He wanted his church to be known as a sanctuary for the lost and the wounded, the broken and the oppressed.

He wanted to "do the stuff" of ministry - preach the gospel, heal the sick, raise the dead, and cast out demons. He had not raised the dead yet, but it could happen given the times in which he was living. He wanted all of his members to be able to do ministry in the particular way each was called and equipped. In order for that to happen, he would have to mentor, bless, and encourage a team of leaders who could also do that in small group settings. His job was to equip the people to do the work of ministry. He was a servant leader.

As with any large church, there would be some who came to church out of obligation, habit, or to keep up social appearances. There would be some who were saved but seemed to have little desire to grow. In every church, he always found a remnant of dedicated people who wanted to finish their races stronger than they started. They wanted to be so closely attuned to God that when they passed from time to eternity, it would not be a culture shock.

Pastor Spalding felt the weight of leadership and of knowing that teachers would incur a much stricter judgment. He desperately wanted to hear his King say, "Well done, good and faithful servant." To that end, he applied himself to the Word and to prayer.

19

Wednesday, October 18

It was a brisk fall day, but Abigail wanted to take a ride on Buster again. It was still painful not to have Dude bouncing along. Buster seemed to miss him as well. She noticed that sometimes he wandered over to the fence closest to the back deck and snorted or nickered as if he was calling for his buddy.

She smiled as she recalled the times when Dude would bark at Buster and then take off as fast as he could to the far corner of the pasture with Buster chasing him. When they got close to the fence, Buster would rear up and paw at the sky before he pivoted and ran back with Dude chasing him. Back and forth they would go, Buster chasing Dude and then Dude chasing Buster.

When Abigail heard the pounding of the hoofs and the yips from Dude, she would go onto the deck and applaud and cheer them on. She laughed thinking about how Dude would duck under the orchard fence and take a shortcut when he got tired. He could not go as far or as fast as Buster. Eventually, they met at the water trough and then went their separate ways. Buster would invariably roll on the ground and shake off a cloud of dust before trotting down to find some choice patch of grass and clover.

Dressed in layers, she packed water and snacks, holstered Walther, and secured the house. She had already looked at the SD cards from the cameras near the house, so she took one of the cleared ones to exchange with the one at the bottom of the pasture. *That will save me an extra trip.* Buster met her at the tack room and only moved when he stomped a foot to chase away some persistent fly. She finished saddling him, double checked the cinch, and then swung up onto his back in a smooth movement.

"Where shall we go today?" Abigail asked as if she expected an answer. "Are you up for a long run?" She guided him down toward the gate but made a stop at the camera and exchanged the SD cards. She had to dismount and remount to get the gate opened.

A gentle nudge was all Buster needed to settle into a ground covering pace. Soon they were at the edge of the field and entering the woods where they slowed to a walk. She decided that since they went north last time, they'd go west this time and hook up with the trails that would take them straight west of the house. They had not been this way for a while.

Sometimes she would encounter other riders, but that was usually on the trails toward the south. She had never seen anyone else deeper in the woods, but that would make sense since there were no roads or houses back there, only woods and creeks for miles. She had been told that if she got on the right trail, she could ride all the way into the little town that was seven miles away. Of course, she would have to ford the Blue River and some of the larger streams that ran parallel to it.

It was a calming ride for Abigail. She used the time to ponder and pray about all the things that were happening with the Wagner family and how she kept encountering them in various ways. She also knew from experience that the evil that had culminated on Halloween would begin to crescendo in the natural as well as the spiritual realms. She prayed for protection for herself as well as her ritual abuse clients. She was very worried about Amy. She was sad about Sherry. She was encouraged but concerned about Carrie Sue this year. If she could just get past this season, she would be well on her way to healing. She prayed out loud as she and Buster moved down the vaguely familiar trails. Keeping the sun over her left shoulder, she was confident that they would have no trouble getting home. Of course, Buster could always find his way home.

She saw the typical deer tracks and a few dog or coyote tracks. None were fresh. Only a few squirrels rustled the leaves as they hid their acorns. She was enjoying the ride and reached back for a granola bar. As they approached a fork in the trail, she noticed fresh hoof prints that came from a branch of the trail that came from the north. One of the horses left large prints. The other one was typical in size. She stopped Buster. She was relatively sure that most riders were wholesome outdoorsmen and women, but she did not want to take any chances. Not today.

Buster snorted and flared his nostrils. His ears looked like radar monitors as they independently twitched and turned in different directions. He was sensing something or someone. Abigail patted him on the neck and then turned him with a small flick of the reins on his neck. "Let's get out of here, Buster," she whispered. He started off at a brisk walk and would have gone faster if Abigail did not restrain him. She definitely did not want him to fly through the woods on the tortuous trails and leave her scraped off on some limb. She did not want to end up like Absalom!

Buster sensed her tension and was more eager than ever to head for the barn. They quickly backtracked following Buster's prints and had no trouble finding their way to the corn field. When they came out of the woods, she let him go at a steady lope for about half a mile and then slowed him down as they neared the gate. He knew the routine and obediently stood while she fastened the gate before remounting and letting him trot up to the tack room.

She thought about the tracks of the two riders that she had crossed deep in the woods. Were they just a couple of people out riding on a fall day? Was it a coincidence that they were there on the same day that she was? Was that the same horse that left the large prints by her back gate? She decided to go back again at the next opportunity.

She showered and changed into something that was suitable for church. She looked forward to the worship and the messages from Pastor Spalding and got there early enough to chat with some of her acquaintances on the way inside before making her way down to her favorite seat.

Carrie Sue slipped in at the last minute so she did not have to interact with the people. They were nice enough, but she just felt awkward and did not want to answer any personal questions - especially not this week. She could just imagine a conversation, "How was your week?" And her answer, "Oh, fine, I went to my father's funeral and just found out that my brother was probably sacrificed at a ritual. And how was your week?" She upbraided herself for being so sarcastic and cynical. In church.

After the music faded, Pastor Spalding moved up to the platform. He smiled at the congregation and said, "I've been hearing about several families going through some tough times. Let's talk tonight about our response to the storms of life. Some of you might feel as if you are shipwrecked and your entire life has disintegrated. And whatever has not sunk is bobbing around on the surface of the sea. Maybe it's not quite that bad for others - just some mild boat bashing or tough tubing. Some of you have recently come out on the other side and some of you know that you will face uncontrollable circumstances soon."

He paused and looked out at the families. "I see the Moss family and we've been praying about their ailing loved one who was recently diagnosed with cancer. There are several in the hospital. I'm sure a lot of you are keeping much of your big and little turbulences of life quiet. But whatever the case, how do we, as Christians, deal with these stormy seasons of life? How do we face a world that looks on and says, 'If that's what God does for Christians, we don't want any part of it?' How do we respond to other Christians who judge our relationship to God by our fortunes - or lack thereof?"

He looked at the thoughtful expressions on the faces in the congregation. "Luke eight tells of a fierce gale that almost swamped the boat of Jesus and His disciples. Jesus was awakened by desperate men - and some of them were seasoned sailors, mind you - who thought they were going to die. He rebuked the wind and surging waves and restored calm. Now let's turn over to Acts twenty-seven for a look at another storm."

He waited until most of the page rustling quieted. "This is the account of Paul's shipwreck." He quickly outlined the highlights and salient points about how the sailing was dangerous as they encountered violent winds. The ship became barely controllable so they jettisoned cargo and tackle. They were lost without sun or stars to guide them. Finally, two long weeks later, they tried to get the ship into a bay, but ran into a reef. The prow got stuck and the stern began to break up because of the waves. However, everyone either swam ashore or floated in on debris and they spent the winter season there.

"It sounds like it was a complete waste. There was nothing salvageable. Why do you think that the Holy Spirit included these passages? What can we learn?" Again, he paused to let them think about the questions.

"You know," he continued, "we often look on storms or shipwrecks as God's punishment. He does not do that. He may discipline us or allow the natural consequences of our actions to manifest. And we also have to consider that in this sin-tainted world, bad things happen and bad people do bad things." He let that sink in for a few moments.

"So, let's look at the blessings of the storms and shipwrecks," he said with a smile. "I know you're scratching your head and wondering how any life-threatening circumstances and the loss of everything can be a blessing. Ask yourself this: Do you see a better or more complete revelation of God's character - His mercy, grace, favor, or some other attribute - in the uneventful proceedings of life or in the impossible situations? Would you know that God delivers if you didn't need to be delivered? Would you know He helps, protects, provides, shepherds, etc., if you didn't need that help, protection, provision, care, and so on?

"Here's another common question: Why did Jesus stop the disciples' storm but Paul had to go through his? I don't think Jesus *liked* the disciples more than He liked Paul. I don't think Jesus saved them just because He was physically in the boat with them and not with Paul. Paul could have rebuked the storm in Jesus' name and it would have abated. But he wasn't told to do that. God worked in Paul through the storm and He worked in the disciples by stopping the storm. It's going to be different for each of us, too."

He saw nods as the people followed him. "Folks, I have to admit something to you. I haven't always been the fine, mature leader you see standing here before you tonight." He smiled broadly as he accompanied that with a mock swagger.

"The picture of Paul's shipwreck reminds me of a vessel I have constructed, equipped, and captained.

Like the occupants of Paul's boat, I have had to make decisions in the face of my storms to throw things overboard that I have clung to and treasured. I put trust in strength, wisdom, and assets that were neither strong nor wise nor profitable. And as desperately as they tried to bring the shell of a ship into safe harbor, I have clung to an old scow that was too cumbersome to enter safe haven. Sometimes the only way to enter rest is to stop trying desperately to hold everything together and float into the haven using the broken bits and pieces that *can* reach shore. And when we get there, we gather the fragments and use them to fuel the fire that warms. We gaze around and realize that what remains is God and only God - and all the rest is immaterial."

They nodded as they related to his point. "God's mercy strips us of self-sufficiency and encumbrances of possessions and the futilities of life. Let us, then, in the midst of hardship, view it as an opportunity for God to restore peace and rest. Let's seek to enter His safe haven rejoicing that He has relieved us of false securities and broken foundations. Let's understand Hebrews twelve verse twenty-seven where the author reminds us that God is in the process of removing things which can be shaken in order that things which cannot be shaken may remain. He's able to calm any storm or bring us into that safe haven. Come to the front if you are in the middle of a storm - no matter how big or small - and let one of us pray with you."

The musicians played softly while several came up for prayer. Abigail slipped to the back and found Carrie Sue waiting for her. "Sounds like the teaching was customized for me," Abigail said with a smile.

"No," Carrie Sue countered, "I definitely think he was preaching to me."

"How are you doing? You've been through a shipwreck of a week. By the way, I'm proud of you for standing firm."

"Thanks, it means a lot coming from you," Carrie Sue replied. "I'm doing all right except for the mom driving me crazy with all her phone calls. I feel guilty for not answering sometimes and then I feel sorry for her and then I want to wring her neck for all the evil she didn't stop. I guess it was easier when I was really dissociated, I only had to deal with one emotion and let some other part take care of the rest."

"Well, congratulations," Abigail said with a gentle laugh and a wink, "how does it feel to be normal?"

"Great," she laughed. "I think."

20

Thursday, October 19

It was overcast, but it was not raining yet. It was supposed to storm in the afternoon but the winds had died down so Abigail thought their ride that morning would not be very uncomfortable. She put her camo rain poncho in the saddlebag just in case there was an unexpected downpour. She didn't mind getting caught in the rain in the summer time, but today it would chill her to the bone.

Buster covered the ground quickly because Abigail not only wanted to get her little mission completed, she loved the thrill of being in perfect rhythm with Buster in a full gallop. It was remarkably like sitting in a rocking chair. They slowed just before entering the woods and followed the same trail that they had taken yesterday. She could clearly see Buster's hoof prints going both directions where leaves didn't cover the moist dirt. There was still dew clinging to the leaves and branches so it wasn't long before Abigail's jacket and pant legs were damp.

As they walked across a stretch of clear trail, she was startled to see the large hoof prints once again. Two riders had come this far and then doubled back. They must have seen her tracks and followed her for a short distance. A small package was lying in the middle of the trail. *That was not there yesterday.* She wondered if one of the riders might have accidentally dropped something. She was curious, so she stopped Buster and dismounted. It was a shallow black plastic square container. She kicked it over with her boot and was startled to see an unopened box of rat poison.

Rat poison!

Her mind began to race. Was it just inadvertently dropped here? Why would a rider carry rat poison? Did they leave it here anticipating that she might return? Were they watching for her right now? Her pulse began to rise with the fresh surge of adrenaline. She listened intently as she scanned up and down the trail. As her gaze went back to the rat poison, she noticed a crudely drawn mark on the trail. It was an upside down T with a lightning bolt in the angle. She knew what that meant.

Remounting Buster and swinging him around toward home before her right foot was all the way in the stirrup, he sensed her tension so it did not take much to urge him to move faster than a walk. She still had to be cautious because of the branches and sharp turns. They broke through the opening and into the field. They were less than a mile from home and she let him have his head for most of it and then gradually slowed him to a walk. When she dismounted from Buster at the gate, she saw another square package in the middle of the gate. The same sign was etched there alongside the hoof prints of a large horse.

Abigail quickly looked around but saw no one. She took Walther from its holster and chambered a round before returning it. After securing the gate, she looked around once again and went to the tree and got the SD card. Yesterday's photos showed nothing but she and

Buster coming and going. Perhaps there would be something today. She kicked herself for not bringing another one to exchange because now she would have to walk back down to replace it after she scanned it.

Buster happily trotted back up to the tack room and waited for his sweet feed. It was beginning to sprinkle so she did a quick curry and hurried up to the house with her poncho and water bottle. She kept a wary eye out for any sign of an intruder. She did not think they would have come onto the property because she was confident that the Lord's angels had her surrounded, but she would still be as wise as a serpent and move cautiously as she entered the house and looked for signs of intruders.

There was nothing apparent so she holstered Walther and went to her computer to check the SD card. *There he is*! She saw the man on the large horse with the black hat ride up to the gate and drop the rat poison by the open gate. There was also a shot of him using a stick to make the mark on the ground before riding away in the same direction as the last time. "Lord, what do I do about this? Who can I tell?"

Abigail decided that she would walk down the trail that meandered through the woods to get down to the camera. It was the trail they were supposed to have gone up on the Sunday that they discovered Dude's body. It was a little more circuitous, but she loved the woodsy scents. Besides, it gave her more cover and it would be less predictable if someone was watching.

Retrieving the camera from its spot on the kitchen window sill, she grabbed the two-step ladder.

As she walked past the shed and slipped through the fence, she felt a pang of grief as she passed Dude's grave. *Oh, Dude! I miss you.* She remembered that a couple days after she got him she was sick in bed with the flu. She had made a bed for him with his blanket on top of the old plastic lawn chair outside of her window on the front porch. She slept most of the day but every time she looked out of her window, he was still there curled up in a puppy ball. She would talk softly to him and only his eyebrows would move as he looked up at her making him look so pitiful with those big brown eyes. He was in a new place with a new person and she felt so guilty for not being able to comfort him. Thankfully, it was only a twenty-four-hour bug and she was able to spend a lot of time with him after that. *Oh, Lord, I miss him.*

The rain started to come down a little harder as she walked the meandering path down to where it opened into the corner clearing. She was glad that she had put the poncho on for two reasons: to keep dry and to keep concealed just in case someone was still prowling around down there. She stopped just short of the clearing to look and listen for a few tense minutes. Nothing. She proceeded to the sturdy tree, propped up the little ladder, and reinstalled the SD card. Then she took the camera out and took pictures of the poison container and the mark on the ground before it was washed away by the rain.

Abigail was not usually impulsive, but she decided to stow the ladder up the pasture trail a little ways and then follow the large hoof prints. The soft, moist soil held the tracks well so they were easy to follow.

Obviously, the man was not concerned about hiding his trail. Abigail followed them about two hundred feet to the south and then they unexpectedly veered into the field. They angled toward that low-lying area where she had dragged that other dog's carcass. It had become overgrown with vegetation and scrub trees and was almost like a swamp.

Moving quickly toward the edge of it, she entered under a low canopy of trees. It did not take an expert tracker to read the signs. The man on the big horse had come here enough times that the undergrowth was trampled by both the horse and the man. Many cigarette butts littered the ground. She turned and looked back toward her property and realized what a good observation post this made.

These tracks were fresh enough to have been made within the last hour. He probably was watching for her reaction to finding the poison and the symbol. She took pictures of the tracks and was satisfied that she got a good shot of the boot prints. They were like so many others, but maybe someday they would come in handy. She was beginning to think like Gary and *that* was a scary thought. She smiled in spite of the tension she was feeling.

There was another trampled trail that angled south and west out of the area. She followed it warily back to the field and continued to track the horse to the south. She wished she was on Buster to cross York

Creek, but she found a log and a big rock that she could use to get across without soaking her boots.

The tracks led through the sparsely wooded area that was south of her immediate neighbor's property and turned up toward the highway. She was still within a half mile of her house when she crossed the road and went down into those fields. She had a hunch that they would lead back up to the place that had the ritual rock. She navigated the trails along the sides of the series of fields and when the tracks turned south, she decided that she had gone far enough. She was very sure that the neighbor with the rock was the man with the big horse.

Quickly retracing her steps, she followed the road to the corner of her property and entered the woods at about the same place Billy had a couple of weeks ago. Instead of going to the house, she turned onto the path that would lead her back down to the back gate so she could retrieve the ladder. At last she got back up to the house where she left her muddy boots near the back door and hung the dripping poncho in the back bathroom to drip into the tub. *Time to stoke up that fire!*

After the fire was blazing again, she called Cindy. "Hey, Cindy, is this a good time?"

"Sure, what's up? Wait! Do I want to know?" Cindy asked lightheartedly.

"Well, I took a ride again this morning," Abigail started and then continued the narrative about finding the trail and the hoof prints and the rat poison and the sign and the picture from the SD card. She ended with an account of the hike that brought her to the conclusion that the horse had come from *that* neighbor's place.

"Abigail," Cindy said, "I'm seriously worried about your safety."

"Well, I am too, but what else can I do? Hire a security guard?" Abigail was really not trying to be a smart alack.

"I don't know. By the way, what does that symbol mean?" Cindy asked.

"Well, it's a cult symbol. I've heard of two different explanations. The first one is that the horizontal line is supposed to be a time line. The perpendicular line means a point in time and the lightning bolt means something like judgment or revenge on a traitor. Basically, it's a death threat."

"What's the other explanation?"

"That it's an inverted cross of satanic justice. The lightning symbolizes imminent punishment."

Cindy sucked in her breath, "Are you serious? Abigail, what are you going to do? You need to get out of there!" She was in her she-bear, motherly, sisterly, protective mode.

"Cindy," Abigail said more calmly than she felt, "no weapon formed against us will prosper. I'm not going to run and hide. I'm not going to quit. I'm not giving up, giving in, or giving over to intimidation. It is unusual, though, for them to make the sign for a non-cult member. Most people don't even know what they mean."

"Well, they must know that you know."

"Did you happen to notice that they still do not come onto the property? I believe two things: One is that God has stationed protective angels around the property – nobody's been turning around in the drive or coming part way up and then backing out again since I prayed specifically for that. I think that they're being stripped of their demonic powers. And two, they are cowards. I'm not saying this to challenge anyone. In the natural, they have power and all, but these are a group of men who do things to drugged and incapacitated women and children primarily. Hello! That's not exactly macho in my book."

"Well, yes," Cindy conceded, "but they still cut your brake lines and someone still came into the house, and poor old Dude is dead."

"But even the guy who came onto the property couldn't do much damage. I think he must have lost his demonic powers but came up here anyway. And good old Sheriff Bynum looked pretty nervous himself that day.

They finished their phone call by praying together for a few minutes. Cindy assured her that she would tell Gary and both of them would continue to pray. "See you at church, then."

"Yes, you will, and thanks for all your support."

21

Friday, October 20

Abigail got up once in the middle of the night to add some logs to the fire. It felt good to wake up to a cozy house. She banked the fire effectively and was able to use her firewood more efficiently each year as she learned about how hickory burned hotter and how oak burned longer. She also learned that maple really burned hot and using it unmixed with oak is what caused her chimney fire last year. She and Earl intentionally cut oak and hickory, but if a maple went down in a storm, they would not waste it.

She went into her Friday morning routine and soon was pulling up to the church. She actually got there before Carrie Sue.

Pastor Spalding was waiting for her in the hallway. "Good morning," he greeted her. "Isn't it a beautiful day today?"

"Yes, it is," she heartily agreed and added with a twinkle, "and the weather is nice, too."

He chuckled, "How are you doing these days? Are there any new developments?"

"Well, just another pack of rat poison was dropped by the back gate with a cult symbol next to it," she said reluctantly. She knew that he would pry it out of her eventually now that she had told him about some of the other things.

"We'll certainly keep praying for your safety," he reassured her. "Oh, before I forget," he reached into his shirt pocket and withdrew a memo, "a lady called the church this morning and asked about counseling for her daughter. I told her that I'd have you call her when you got in today."

"Thanks; I'll do that right now before my first lady comes in." They parted ways and Abigail opened her office, started the CD player and went to the phone, punching in the numbers while she pulled her little calendar out of her bag.

The woman answered right away, "Yes, this is Nancy Taylor. Thank you for calling back so soon."

"You're welcome," Abigail responded, "How can I help you?"

"It's my daughter. I went into her bedroom to clean this morning and I found a bunch of bloody tissues in her waste can. I hate to snoop, but I just felt like I had to. I found her journal and it was smeared with blood. She wrote about cutting herself on purpose!" She was fighting back hysteria. "Why would my baby do that to herself? I just don't know what to do."

It was hard to stop the woman from rambling, but Abigail finally was able to speak. "Mrs. Taylor, I know that this feels very overwhelming right now, but this is very fixable if your daughter is willing to come in and work on it."

"Oh, she *will* come in," Mrs. Taylor said almost angrily, "I'll see to that. When can you see her? I'll pull her out of school if I have to."

They settled on meeting later that day after Twyla got out of school. Mrs. Taylor would pick her up and drive her directly to the church. This could be tricky. Teenagers were either incredibly great to work with or really tough. If her mother dragged her here and shoved her in the door, there would definitely be some resistance. It had happened more than once before. *Oh, Lord, I need favor with this one.*

Carrie Sue arrived and apologized for being late. "Mom called and I had trouble getting off the phone."

"No problem. It worked out okay; I had to make a phone call anyway."

They started their session with prayer and sensed that they needed to talk to Queen which was short for The Queen of Denial. Carrie Sue also wanted to talk about her mother and her missing and presumably dead brother if they had time.

"Is Queen available and willing to talk a little?" Abigail ventured.

"I'm here," a slightly different voice stated. She crossed Carrie Sue's arms as she sat there.

"Hi, thanks for coming out." Abigail began her negations with a very important part of Carrie Sue.

These highly complex systems of personalities could generally be divided into two main branches. One branch had personalities who carried the pain of the traumatic memories. The other branch did denial. There was a smaller buffer zone of personalities who were caught between them and were generally quite confused. They vacillated between believing the two compelling but opposite truths. One truth said, "My family let bad things happen to me." The other truth said, "I had a good family that protected me."

"What do you want?" Queen was not going to make it easy for Abigail.

"David said that you were hanging around last time so I was just wondering if you wanted to talk about anything in particular."

"I was a bit curious about what you were going to do with Lizzie."

"If you don't mind me asking, why were you so interested in Lizzie?"

Abigail did not want to offend this key personality. She may well be the primary denial personality who held a significant key to their healing. If the denial side accepted the pain side's reality, then dissociative barriers could be taken down. The buffer zone parts would settle down, and there could be more focus on healing the pain side personalities that still remained.

"Lizzie," she began slowly, "Lizzie is special. I don't know how to handle what she said about what happened to her. I know she wouldn't lie and she couldn't possibly have made that stuff up."

Abigail nodded. She understood that denial was the glue that held dissociation together. Queen had come a long way already. The first time they ever met, Queen denied the dissociation itself. She was stumped and disappeared when Abigail asked her how she accounted for the other personalities.

"Are you ready to face more hard questions?" Abigail asked gently.

"Yeah," she sighed, "lay them on me."

Abigail smiled, "All right then. Will you try to hang in here while you think about the answers?"

"I'll try, but I won't make any promises."

"Fair enough," Abigail agreed. "I guess that the burning question is: What would happen or what would it mean if what Lizzie and the other pain side alters say is really true?"

There was silence for a while as Queen thought about the question and the different ways she could answer. She finally sighed deeply and said, "I guess we would have to admit that we were unwanted and unloved. We didn't mean anything to our family. No one really cares about us. We're just losers."

"No one wants to believe that, Queen. No one likes to be rejected, and especially by the very people who should have loved you the best and the most."

"Do you hate me?" she asked.

"No! Why would I hate you?"

"For giving you such a rough time … for getting in the way…."

"You were doing your job. You were surviving in the best way - the only way - that you knew how. I admire someone who can make changes when they are given the facts."

"Thanks."

"What would you like to do now?" Abigail continued to push gently. She realized that Carrie Sue would turn a huge corner if the denial side parts were to be healed.

"We're tired. We know everything they said is true, even though some of it sounds crazy. We are ready to do like the others did that got healed and went back inside."

Abigail smiled warmly at Queen. "It would be my privilege to help you with that. Are you talking about your whole sector?"

"Well, I can't guarantee that there won't be any hold outs, but I think so."

Abigail prayed for Queen and the denial side personalities. She prayed for healing, deliverance, and integration. By the time she was finished, Carrie Sue had switched back into control. She was tired, but very happy. She said that she knew that they went inside, but she did not personally feel the integration. This meant that they probably went into the original Carrie Sue. This Carrie Sue was the host personality. She knew that she was not the original person, and that bothered her. After all, she had navigated life while the other Carrie Sue had taken off. But that was a discussion for another day.

Carrie Sue was relieved. She knew that this was a significant step toward her ultimate healing. "How much more before we're completely healed? When are we going to be done?" she asked, knowing that each time she pressed Abigail for an answer, Abigail would not and could not give a precise response. There were just too many variables to consider.

"I'm sure you remember that I told you that even when we think you're fully integrated, we still need to go at least another calendar year. We have to make sure that there are no stragglers either hiding or having been hidden by the cult. And even after that, there may be some parts who have been programmed to show up when you're old and gray." Abigail said patiently with a warm smile.

Carrie Sue nodded grudgingly, but quickly perked up. "That was really good. I'm not trying to give you a hard time, but I really want to be done. But then, I'm a bit apprehensive about what it will be like. I mean, when everyone has merged and the 'real' Carrie Sue has emerged from hiding, will she be able to recognize you and will you mean as much to her as you do to me? Once the healing is complete, will this affect *our* friendship? Will the real Carrie Sue know the same things the others do and I do? Or will her personality be so totally different that it will be noticeable to others? Just how drastic of a change is it going to be?"

Abigail laughed gently, "Slow down, it really is going to be all right. Do you remember how you were when we first met? Do you remember the subtle changes when some parts integrated into you? You got their knowledge and your personalities blended so that you changed a smidge? The original Carrie Sue is growing as each integration refills her. Everything that she 'divvied out' to the other personalities is coming back inside which gives her all the knowledge and character that they developed apart from her. So, she will know me. We'll still be friends. She'll know everything all of you know. Probably only the people who know you the best will notice any difference."

"Yeah," Carrie Sue acknowledged, "I guess that's what the mom is talking about when she says that I've changed since I started counseling with you."

"Maybe with your bio-dad out of the picture, she'd be willing to come and get some help, too."

Carrie Sue nearly spit. "Oh, I doubt it!" Then she softened and added, "That would be a miracle."

"Well, we can just pray for that miracle then. All things are possible with God."

They continued to talk a while about how her mother was doing. The subject of Billy did not come up. After making an appointment for their usual time next week, Carrie Sue left.

Abigail used her change of routine excuse to go to her favorite Mediterranean deli for lunch. She had a couple of hours until Amy showed up, so she also did her grocery shopping and stored the perishables in the church refrigerator. She still had plenty of time to catch up on some reading.

Amy walked through the door at precisely 2:06 and chirped her cheery greeting.

"Hey, it's good to see you. I've been praying for you a lot this week," Abigail responded.

"I'd hate to see what my week would have been like if you hadn't been praying," she said with her typical edgy humor. She was actually quite grateful, but somehow felt that it was not cool to admit it.

They opened with prayer. Abigail was not at all surprised that Head Warden showed up immediately. "Hi," he said softly, "can we do like we did last time with the secret meeting?"

Abigail prayed that the Lord would provide a "privacy bubble" for their time together. She prayed for their protection. She prayed that there would be no interference from internal or external sources.

"We ended up at that ritual last week," he said ruefully, "I couldn't stop it. I can't believe that I used to go along with all that stuff and not feel anything. I'm miserable. It just hurts so much to see all the damage being done. It's all so senseless." He was frustrated and ashamed, afraid and angry. "I'm not used to this. I never had feelings like this before."

"Well, let's see if we can do some damage control. We need to minister to the hurt parts and then do some preemptive work for next weekend."

"Yeah," he agreed, "I don't want to go through another week like this." Head Warden filled Abigail in on what had happened at the ritual and how his cell blocks got refilled with most of the newly split out, highly programmed, severely wounded personalities. Most of them were little girls. He gave her the update on the defected guards and the ones who were still cult-loyal.

"Does Nicholai ever come up to your level? I mean, does he have any authority over your jurisdiction? Does he know what goes on in your sector?" Abigail was praying for a strategy.

"He seems to know what happens, but I think that he has informants from my group or maybe there are some infiltrators. He's not my superior, if that's what you mean."

"Okay, that's good. Let's think like legalists," she gave a conspiratorial smile. "You have jurisdiction over the cell blocks and all the prisoners and guards on the surface, right?"

"Right, er, supposedly," he responded. "Oh, sorry, I forgot to mention that Caleb, one of my assistant wardens seems to be their ring leader. He's still cult-loyal, if you know what I mean."

"Well, you have the legal right and responsibility to do some things. Number one: have a strategy meeting with your fellow-defectors. You know your structures and rooms. See if you can find a way to get all the cult-loyal ones in one place at one time and lock them in."

Head Warden leaned forward with interest. It was obvious that he was mentally searching for that place by his eye movements and finally nodded. "I think I know of just the place." He suddenly moved from a defensive posture to an offensive one which better suited him. Lately, he had been walking on eggshells because of internal cult-loyal personalities as well as the external masters and demons.

"Good." Abigail continued, "Once you've gotten them secured, you can feed some false information to Nicholai about the status of your area."

"Isn't that lying?" he asked. "I thought that was supposed to be a no-no."

"All I can say is that David acted insane in order to save his life from the Philistines. And then there was Samuel who thought he'd be killed by Saul for going to anoint David and God told him to use a cover story that he was going to a special feast."

"Okay; what else?"

"Number two: once that's done, we can minister to the new ones in the cells and get them all healed and maybe integrated."

"Okay."

"Three: then you can find some of your guys to infiltrate the subterranean levels and start a rescue operation for the ones who are down there."

"Whoa!" He said in alarm. "You want us to go down there? That place is a hundred times worse than the surface levels!"

"First things first," Abigail said calmly, "but time is of the essence because there's that lovely five-day weekend coming up and we don't want a repeat of last weekend."

Head Warden gave her a look that conveyed that he thought she was out of her mind. All he knew was ritual after ritual, year after year. All Hallows Eve and Halloween were the biggest of the year.

"How soon can you get your guys to set up the trap?" Abigail asked.

"Just as soon as we can meet," he replied.

"Can you do it right now?" Abigail knew that conversations and maneuvers could be done in mere seconds internally, but if she were to have to mediate and talk to each of the players, it would take a very long time.

"Now?" he asked incredulously. "You don't mess around, do you lady?"

She flashed him a quick grin. "I'll pray for your meeting and the trap to be off the radar."

He rolled his eyes and then nodded. After several minutes he looked up and said, "It's done. We have them all locked down in one of the torture chambers - it's sound proof."

"Excellent," she said, "now can we pray for the healing of the new ones?"

He nodded in agreement and they prayed for physical, emotional, and spiritual healing. When it was ascertained that they were all fine, they prayed for their integrations as well.

Head Warden was relieved. "What now?"

"Let's pray that anyone who's been programmed to be accessed for the upcoming rituals will be - let's just say - unavailable." They prayed in agreement and he was noticeably calmer.

"What do we do with our captives? They're pretty mad and trying to tear the door down."

"Maybe you can start some negotiations with them. Be kind. Show them something that they have never seen before. Remember, there are no bad alters, just alters with bad jobs."

He went back inside and Amy came forward once again. She was able to observe the session from her vantage point inside and was encouraged by the progress. After they made an appointment for the following Friday, Amy left the building just as Twyla and her mother entered the waiting area.

Abigail greeted them with a smile. Nancy Taylor forced a polite smile in return; Twyla continued to text someone on her phone. "I'd like to have you fill out a consent form. Both of you can come in to start. Then I'd like some time with just Twyla. Come in when you're ready." She handed the form and a pen to Mrs. Taylor and returned to her office. *Lord, it looks like we'll be pulling teeth. Please give me favor. This girl is more than just a cutter.*

Twyla was cute, but very thin. She wore the baggy clothes that seemed to be anorexics' uniform, but it did not hide her thinness. Abigail noted her dry skin and pallor. Her hair was stylish, but dull and dry. *This girl has been starving herself for quite a while. Malnutrition! Anger! Control issues!*

Nancy Taylor handed the form to Abigail and sat tensely in a chair. Twyla spun into the other chair and slumped down as she continued to text. Abigail would have to ask her to turn it off if her mother did not say something first. She suspected that the mother was intimidated by Twyla.

"I'd like to ask a couple of questions before we get into anything. Twyla, would you mind turning your phone off for a little bit while we do this?" Abigail did not want to alienate the teen, but her mother did not address the issue. She realized that most of the time, these teens were all show and they just wanted to test the adult.

"No problem," she muttered as she powered it down and slipped it into an oversized side pocket on her baggy pants.

"Thanks," Abigail replied. "Twyla, do you know why you are here today?"

Her mother started to answer for her, but Abigail was ready and put her hand out to indicate that she wanted Twyla to answer for herself.

"I'm here because she," she rolled her forearm and gestured toward her mother with her thumb and balled up fist, "made me come here. She got all excited about a little bit of blood. It's no big deal. Everyone does it."

"Okay," Abigail chose her words carefully. "Mrs. Taylor, would you tell Twyla how it made you feel when you came across the blood?"

"Well, I suppose I was shocked at first. I wasn't sure where all the blood had come from. I was afraid that she had been hurt. Why wouldn't she come to me? I'm her mother."

"So, you felt shocked, confused, scared, and a bit rejected?" Abigail summarized.

"Yes, I guess you could say so. I just don't understand," she lamented.

"Twyla, how does that make you feel when you hear your mom talk about her reaction to finding evidence of your cutting?"

"I don't know," she side-stepped. "Mostly I'm mad that she was snooping in my room. You had no right to read my journal!"

"You are living under my roof, young lady, and it is *my* room," Nancy Taylor said sharply.

"Whatever."

"Mrs. Taylor, would you mind waiting in the other room while Twyla and I talk for a bit?" Abigail now had confirmation about the nature of the relationship between mother and daughter.

She didn't say a word, just gathered her jacket and purse, and closed the door firmly behind her.

"Twyla, I am going to be up front with you. I have a feeling that you appreciate straight talk." Abigail paused. There was no response from Twyla, but that was an indication that she was going to grudgingly listen. "Your mom indicated on this form that your father was killed in an accident about a year ago."

"What's that got to do with anything?" Twyla said defensively.

"Is that when you started the anorexia?"

Twyla looked shocked and gulped, "How did you know about that?"

"This ain't my first load of punkins," Abigail said with a gentle laugh. "I hate to say it, but I've seen a lot of teens go through a lot of stuff that they had no control over. Death … divorce … sicknesses … abuse … you name it. So, they kind of say to themselves something like 'at least I can control what does and does not go into my body' or 'I cut and it makes me feel better.' Does any of that sound familiar?"

Twyla grudgingly nodded and finally made brief but meaningful eye contact with Abigail.

"I have a hunch that you originally felt as if you were in control of both of those things, but now they kind of run you. So, instead of the dog wagging the tail, it's like the tail is wagging the dog now."

Twyla sat quietly and considered her situation. Her defenses were down a little, but she could still put them back up in a heartbeat and bolt. Teenagers were unpredictable.

"So, what do you want to do about these things?"

"I don't know."

"That's fair. I'm not going to pressure you into making a decision today. But would you let me talk to you about the hamster wheels that you are running on? Then you can make a more informed choice. I also want you to know that everything that's going on with you is fixable. And that whatever you say in here will be confidential, okay? I won't say anything to your mom unless you give me the okay or unless I think that you're going to hurt yourself or someone else, and then I have a legal obligation to notify the appropriate authorities."

"Sure."

"Let's start with the cutting cycle. It starts because some event really traumatizes you and makes you mad. For you, it was probably your father's death. The problem is that you can't be mad at your dad for being dead. Your anger has to go somewhere. Maybe you heard about cutting from a friend at school, or accidentally cut yourself and noticed that it distracted you from the emotional pain, or maybe you were just upset and happened to have a tool and cut yourself."

Abigail noted Twyla's expression that did not refute what she had said so she continued, "That's the set up. Now every time your emotions get triggered – maybe by an anniversary, or a thought, or something that reminds you that your daddy is not here anymore – you start thinking about cutting. The tension builds until you cut. Adrenaline surges through your body. When you cut, it starts to dissipate and you feel release and relief physically. So, you buy the lie that says, 'cutting makes me feel better.' But then you feel shame or guilt and promise yourself that you won't do it again. But you get triggered and you go around again only this time, you not only have the addiction to the adrenaline rush but you also have a lousy legalistic demon or two pushing you along."

Twyla's eyes widened at the mention of the demon and at how well Abigail had described what she had been going through. She sat up a little straighter in her chair.

Abigail continued, "Some cutters use cutting as a distraction. They have to plan. They watch the blood flow. They have to hide the evidence. They pick at the scab. The physical pain distracts them from the emotional pain." She paused and looked at Twyla.

Twyla spoke in a soft voice, "I cut so something worse doesn't happen."

Abigail nodded indicating that she understood. "Let me talk about the anorexia thing and then get you out of here. Are you a pure anorexic or do you do some of the bulimia stuff, too?"

Twyla was not accustomed to non-judgmental bluntness from an adult. "Uh, I just do the anorexia thing. I exercise a lot, too."

"That's real common. Basically, your anorexia is another thing that's driven by anger. Trauma gets it started and other things like perfectionism and control issues keep it going. It's yet another thing that distracts from the real pain - you desperately miss your dad."

Twyla had tried so hard not to think of missing her daddy, but it was something she could not evade today. She looked down and could not keep the tears from spilling down her cheeks. She sniffled and wiped her nose on the back of her sleeve.

"Twyla," Abigail said gently, "I'm so sorry you lost your dad. It's not fair. Would you be willing to come back and work through all this stuff?"

She dared not open her mouth so she just stared at the floor as she nodded.

"Thank you for hanging in there with me. I know this is tough, but I promise, it can all be fixed and you won't need to cut or starve yourself anymore."

"Okay," she sniffled.

"Well, what are we going to do about your mom?" Abigail asked. "Do you have anything you can say to her that will give her a little hope and keep her from being so scared about losing you, too?"

Twyla looked startled, as if she got a little glimpse into how much her mother must be suffering. "Uh, I don't know."

"Can I pray for you a minute before we get your mom back in here?"

"Sure."

Abigail prayed a blessing over her and asked the Prince of Peace to visit Twyla in her times of pain and trouble. Then Abigail went to the door and motioned for Nancy Taylor to come join them. Nancy noticed a more subdued daughter sitting in the chair.

"Twyla is willing to come back again next week. Will the same time work for you?" They made the arrangements and the mother and daughter left with a little less distance between them.

22

Saturday, October 21

It was another Saturday and another day to play. Today was unusually warm. Abigail had become very content with her life, but today was ten days from the tenth anniversary of the accident that changed her life forever. She accepted the loss of her family without slipping into bitterness. She was blessed to have a pastor who encouraged her to ask the right questions. "Don't ask 'Why?'" he said. "Ask 'for what purpose?'"

She still asked the question from time to time. "Lord, I still don't get it and I still don't like it; but You are God and You are Sovereign. You know the end from the beginning and I *will* continue to choose to believe that all things will work out for my good because I am called." She left it there and turned to her latest to-do list.

She decided that hauling hay would be the best thing to do so she repeated the same routine of going to the bank to get some cash before heading to the Co-op. The young men were polite as they loaded the feed and the twenty bales of hay and made sure the bales were tied down well with the ropes that Abigail kept behind the seat.

She made the trip home easily and backed the truck down to the barn. Buster wandered up to investigate and nibble on the hay.

"You have all that fresh grass and you want to eat this dried stuff?" The barn's sliding door opened grudgingly. *One of these days, I will oil that thing.* She loved the sweet smells of the hay, the distinct tang of leather, and the subtle odors of the wooden structure. She loved the sound of her boots on the worn wooden floor that was stained with oils and other spills that inevitably happened in barns.

She untied the ropes and lifted the first bale off the truck. As she approached the stack that was already there, she heard a slight rustling sound in the loose hay that was always on the floor. *Snake or mouse?* Abigail lowered the bale she was holding and spotted a fat copperhead curled up at the base of the stack of hay. It was watching her while rapidly flicking its tongue in and out.

"You just wait right there, I'll be back." Abigail hastily turned and ran up to the house where she grabbed her .22 rifle. She called it Thumper Bumper because she used it to pick off rabbits and other small critters that tried to destroy her garden.

The snake had not moved so Abigail got as close as she could without risking a strike by those venomous fangs. A bite would probably not kill her, but it sure would ruin her day. It was a single shot rifle so she flicked off the safety, carefully lined up the notch and pulled the trigger. The snake reacted immediately and began to crawl away. Abigail was disappointed to see that the bullet had struck the snake about ten inches from its tail. She did not have time to eject the casing and reload before it disappeared between the bales and the wall.

"Rats!"

Reloading the rifle, engaging the safety, propping it against the wall near the door in case there was another opportunity, she finished stacking the bales while attentively watching and listening for the snake. "God, I hate to hurt your critters, but I needed to do that taking dominion thing."

Finishing the task, she grabbed Thumper Bumper, repositioned the truck, got the boards, and slid the sweet feed into the tack room. She took one last look around before closing doors, returning the boards, and driving back up to the house.

She immediately called Earl.

"Hello?"

"Hey, Earl, it's me, Abigail."

"Did you just shoot something? I thought I heard a .22." Earl knew his weapons. He was a sharp-shooter when he was in the army and had taught Abigail to shoot. One time he brought out his .357 magnum and stood behind her. She thought he was joking when he said that he would catch her.

He was not joking.

"Yes, I did. I need to ask you a question."

"Shoot."

"Funny! So, if you shoot a copperhead in the butt, will he crawl away and die, or will he go find all his friends and family and come back for revenge?"

Earl exploded with laughter, "You just shot a copperhead in the butt?"

"Not on purpose! I was aiming for its head," she protested with a giggle.

"I guess if you start smelling something rotten in a couple of days, you'll know. If not, you might never know. My guess is that it will die eventually and hopefully in some hole in the ground."

"Thanks. Are you guys doing all right? One of these cool afternoons Jan and I need to have a cup of tea. Tell her I miss chit chatting with her." They talked for a few more minutes before hanging up.

Abigail made her lunch and ate it on the back deck while she enjoyed the warmth of the sun and the mild breezes. Leaves were turning quickly now that there were light frosts more often. Soon all but the oaks would be bare. She never bothered to rake leaves. The winds would blow them off her hill top in due time and whatever was left would be mulched by the mower in the spring.

She heard the phone ring and wandered into the house to see who was calling. She recognized Cindy's number and picked up. "Hey, Cindy, how are you?"

"I'm great. I was thinking, how about coming over for lunch tomorrow after church? Nothing fancy, it's just been so long since we've hung out."

"Let me check my calendar. Oh yeah, that's right, I don't have a life," she joked. "Sure, I'd love to come over. Do you want me to bring anything?"

"Just your appetite," Cindy answered.

Abigail's eyes popped open. "This is the day that You have made!" Sunday was her favorite day of the week.

It was a good day to rest and spend time focused on the Lord. She was excited about having lunch with the McCord family, as well. It had been far too long since they had just hung out and had a good gab-fest.

Deciding to take a peek inside the barn after taking care of Buster just in case the snake had returned, she was momentarily startled by the sight of a three-foot-long copperhead stretched out in the middle of the floor. *What a relief!* It was dead. She would have to remember to tell Earl that her shot did indeed kill the snake. Taking the time to find the tape measure, she was amazed at its length. "Oh, wow! Thirty-seven inches!" She grabbed an old shovel off of the wall and deposited the snake at the edge of the woods. *I'll bury him when I get back home.* Hurrying back to the house, she quickly got ready for church.

Pastor Spalding took his place behind the podium and opened his Bible. He paused like only preachers can and then looked across the congregation. "What is your name?" he asked and then waited a few more moments for the question to sink in. "Today we are going to look at a man who was asked this question two times. We know him as Jacob."

Pastor Spaulding directed the people to turn to Genesis twenty-five to review some background on Jacob and his older twin brother, Esau. He pointed out that they were named for their traits. "Esau was a red-head. Jacob was a supplanter. He had his hand on his older brother's heel as he was born, as if he was trying to pull him back in so he could be first."

Pastor Spalding outlined Jacob's manipulation to get Esau's birthright. He continued through the next couple of chapters until he got to the part where their father, Isaac, was old and blind and wanted to bless his oldest son, Esau, before he died. "Once again, younger brother, Jacob, supplanted his older brother by stealing his blessing."

He continued, "Isaac must have sensed something because he asked Jacob, *'Who are you, my son?'* And Jacob answered, *'I am Esau your first-born.'"* Pastor Spalding resumed the narrative and outlined the strife that developed. "Esau swore to kill Jacob once their father died so Mommy sent Jacob to her people to keep him safe."

They kept turning the pages and following the story of treachery against Jacob by his uncle. "He was getting a taste of his own medicine. Jacob prospered anyway, and in Genesis thirty-one God tells Jacob to go back to Isaac after twenty-some years. Uncle Laban was not happy, but God warned him not to touch Jacob when he caught up to Jacob sneaking out of town with his daughters and grandchildren."

He continued, "So now Jacob was heading toward his angry, ripped off brother, Esau, and heading away from his angry, ripped off Uncle Laban who was right behind him. That's when Jacob wrestled all night with God and told Him that he would not let Him go until He blessed him. Isn't it interesting that God wanted to know *who* He was blessing, just like his father did so many years before?"

He paused again to let the congregation think a little bit about the parallels. "God said, 'What is your name?' This time Jacob did not say, 'Esau,' rather, he said 'Jacob.' Jacob said, in essence, I am a supplanter. I strive with men. I am a deceiver. I confess that I am everything that my name implies."

Pastor Spalding brought the sermon to a close with a challenge. "What is *your* name? What do you call yourself? I'm not talking about the name that's been written on your birth certificate; I'm talking about what you call yourself when it suits your purposes. Jacob might have said to his father, 'My name is greedy because I want what is not mine. My name is fear because I am afraid that I cannot make it without your wealth. My name is jealous because my dad favors my older brother."

He closed his Bible and looked at the people that he had come to love over the years. He knew that many of them struggled with an assortment of issues. "Folks, I know many of you have wrestled with God about a variety of situations. You will continue to do so in the years to come because we will all encounter adversity. If you've come to Him without giving Him your real name, isn't it time to come clean? You look at your marriage and come to the throne of grace with Doubt written on your nametag. You see your child's addictive behavior and come to Him and call yourself Fear. Maybe you have given yourself the name Guilt or Shame or Regret because of something you did. You really don't want to ask Him to bless those given names. If you need to, please come today and wrestle with the Lord some more. Confess your old name and ask Him to change your name from Doubt to Faith, from Fear to Courage, from Guilty to Cleansed. You are a child of God, a co-heir with Jesus Christ, justified, sanctified, beloved, favored, and so on."

He continued to speak tenderly to them as several people made their way to the front to pray alone or with members of the prayer team. Abigail and Cindy were on the prayer team schedule this week and prayed together with several people. At last they made their way out of the church and met up with Gary and the kids before going to their separate vehicles and then heading to the McCord's home.

They had a tasty dinner featuring meatloaf and double baked potatoes with vegetables. Bryan loved her story about the copperhead, but Traci shook her head and said emphatically, "I don't like snakes!"

After dessert Gary retreated to the family room and became engrossed with the football game. Traci and Bryan ran in and out of the kitchen as they played together. Cindy and Abigail chatted about their week while they cleaned up the kitchen.

"Do you remember Gary's cousin, Lee?" Cindy asked coyly.

"Yes, how is he doing?" Abigail asked politely.

"Gary said that Lee has definitely decided to join the rest of the family and move back to this area. He's probably going to stay with their grandparents until he can find a place of his own."

Lee Norris felt peace now that he had made his decision to move back east. He loved the mountains, but he had to be practical. There were not many jobs available out here for an ex-rancher. He had been to college twenty-five years ago and had undergraduate degrees that had opened doors for him in the bigger cities but he was a country man at heart and found joy in the simple pleasures of God's creation. He could not foresee going back to Helena or Butte.

After revisiting the area in which his grandparents and cousins lived, he was reminded of the pleasant childhood memories from visits there and he started seriously thinking that he could easily combine his love of the farm life with a full or part time position to bring in a steady income. He began to think about which equipment, trailers, and farm implements he should keep. He wanted to take a couple of his favorite horses with him as well.

The move would not significantly affect his relationship with his daughter since he could visit her wherever she lived. Right now, she was in college near her mother in Colorado, but she could end up anywhere. She was in her senior year and might decide to begin her accounting career or she might decide to go back for post-graduate work. Yes, this was the right thing to do and he was excited.

23

Monday, October 23

Abigail knew from reports by previous ritual abuse survivors that this week would be filled with a flurry of spiritual activities. The local Satanists would be ramping up their doings which would climax on Halloween with their high unholy day. Preparations began in earnest on October thirteenth and the various groups would have already abducted their ceremonial human sacrifices.

Abigail shuddered involuntarily to think of the grief that so many unsuspecting families would endure. More pictures would be featured in tax publications or posted on neighborhood grocery store bulletin boards, but not a trace of these victims would ever be found.

That morning, after she attended to Buster, she intended to bury the snake and walked over to the spot that she had dumped the reptile. It was not there! Searching carefully through the leaves with the toe of her boot, she finally found a few inches of what was left of its tail. *Uh, oh, what's scarier? A copperhead or whatever eats them?*

Monday, Tuesday, and Wednesday were beautiful autumn days that she used to finish tilling the garden and turning the compost pile. She split the last of the logs and stacked them with the others under another large tarp. A stroll through the woods got two more five-gallon buckets filled with kindling. She changed the oil in the tiller and added stabilizer to the gas before she stored it in the shed. Finally, she went to the barn for the four-wheeler to which she hitched the cart. Buster supplied plenty of manure which she spread on the garden. She found one of Dude's old squeaky toys in the orchard and unexpectedly burst into tears.

Abigail remembered the morning that she was awakened to the sound of that squeaky toy. She was mystified because it seemed to be coming from the tall cedar tree near the yard light. Dude was running around the back yard looking for his toy. It took her a few moments to realize that it was a mockingbird in the cedar tree making the squeaky toy sound! She smiled a bitter-sweet smile, wiped her tears, and finished her activities.

She worked according to temperature rather than time in the cool fall days. She would start and stop at about sixty degrees. Today that would be about five o'clock when the sun was beginning to set and she would head down to take care of Buster before hustling back into the house. Dinner was generally something simple like soup and salad. Sometimes she would make a large quiche or vegetarian lasagna or eggplant parmesan and eat it for breakfast, lunch, and dinner until it was gone. These were some of the simple pleasures that she could enjoy.

She had to quit by five on Wednesday so that she could get ready for church. Someone had tastefully adorned the doors and hallways of the church with autumn decorations. Colorful posters announced the Fall Festival for the youth. It stirred emotions that she would rather not revisit tonight so she breathed yet another prayer. *Lord, I'm hurting. I miss my guys.* She had learned to take thoughts captive to Him and bring every distressing feeling to the Lord as soon as they hit. She had come to believe that one could, and perhaps should, pray without ceasing.

After a meaningful time of praise and worship, Pastor Spalding took his place up front and adjusted his lapel microphone. The small gathering looked expectantly to him. He was a source of wisdom and he was able to temper difficult subjects with humor so that there was not a sense of condemnation.

"Folks," he began, "there are a lot of verses in the Bible about sowing and reaping. If I were to mention all of them tonight, we'd be here a long time and I don't think any of us would want that. So, er, no pun intended, so, I would encourage you to get your concordance and Bible out and do a deeper study on this very relevant subject: Sow what!"

He went on to quote verses in both the Old and New Testaments. "I have to admit that as I was studying this, I was a bit upset when I was reading Jesus' parable of the sower in both Matthew thirteen and Luke eight. Jesus describes a sower scattering his seed in a field, but some of it randomly landed in rocks, some in thorns, and some landed on the hard-packed path. Jesus explained that the seed was the Word of God and that the different kinds of soil represented different kinds of people. The Word that landed on the good soil/people was fruitful while the other seeds either got snatched away, choked, or had nothing to nourish the roots."

He saw some nods as people were following him. "Did you ever want to cry out, 'No fair!'? After all, the different soil/people didn't have a chance. What if you were a rocky person? What if you were a thorn or thistle person? What if you were a hard-packed path person? You wouldn't have a chance to respond to the Word and grow."

He noticed that some had never considered this. "Well, once again I had to wrestle with the Lord about this unfair situation. Do you know what He told me?" He paused for a moment and proceeded to answer his own question. "He said, 'Keep reading.' So then," he caught himself, "oops, so I did. The first thing I noticed was that after explaining the parable, Jesus ran into a guy who was living in the tombs amongst the rocks. Hello! Here's a rocky guy who was transformed by Jesus into a fruitful man. Then there were the men who wanted Jesus to leave because He just ruined their pig business. And then there were others who scoffed because He said that Jairus' daughter was not dead. Do you think they might be a bit hard-packed? Jesus encountered others who lived in thorny situations like the woman with the hemorrhage. And on and on, Jesus encountered the various types of people. Some responded; others did not. I must conclude then, that we are not inevitably cursed or blessed because of our original situation."

Pastor Spalding talked about several other parables pertaining to sowing and reaping. "Let me conclude with three things, then. First, you *are* going to reap what you sow - blessings, curses, judgments, time, finances - both tangible and intangible things. You want to be sure you are sowing good stuff because you can't pray for crop failure after sowing wild oats. Secondly, you will reap *later* than you sow - that is, in a different season of your life, or perhaps it'll be in a different generation, or even eternity. And finally, you will reap *more* than you sow - you will reap a full harvest if you persevere. I think you can figure out that for your sake as well as for future generations, you must prayerfully sow what will both benefit you and glorify God."

He finished and dismissed them but always made a point to invite anyone who felt the need to come up for prayer. Most of the people began to quietly drift out of the sanctuary while some lingered a while in meaningful conversations. Abigail caught Cindy and thanked her again for Sunday. Cindy promised to pray for Abigail and the people that she was seeing in her ministry - especially for the SRA survivors.

A number of abducted people were being held in the windowless building. Besides a teenaged couple that had been brought in by Sheriff Bynum; there were two men who were mysteriously ordered to be transferred out of the local jail by Judge Roberts. The official paperwork would be lost in a labyrinth of red tape. There was also one of Herrak's young women who had been impregnated six months, six days and six hours prior to the upcoming Halloween night. Finally, there were the thirteen-year-old girls from various cult families who would be married to Satan or his representative when he showed up.

They were attended to by several different cult members in different parts of the building. Prinz came by often to assess the quality of the sacrifices as well as to supervise the ceremonial preparations for each one. He wanted to be sure that there would be no blunders for these critical rituals. He was certain that Satan himself would honor them with his presence this year.

Women were assigned to fit the female sacrifices with appropriate garments. There were potions and ointments that needed to be applied after ceremonial washings. The women were programmed and executed their duties with no natural emotions.

Levi was one of Darod's protégés who handled the men. He had a popular name within the cult because it was an affront to the tribe of priests of the Great Enemy, and it was also a rearrangement of the word evil. Levi was short for Leviathan. He lived up to his name and was particularly ruthless. Levi had a future in this group.

24

Friday, October 27

Abigail was prepared for another long day in a long week and was grateful for her prayer partners - Cindy especially. Tomorrow would begin five ritual days in a row. Her ritual abuse survivors would be battling the programming that too often overrode their good intentions. Parts, of which they were unaware, would be triggered and surface, allowing the Satanists access and control.

She arrived at the church a few minutes early and went directly to Pastor Spalding's office. Ginny, the secretary, told her that she could go right in. He greeted her with a warm smile and stood as she stepped into the room. "Come in; come in. Have a seat," he invited.

"I'm sorry, I really don't have time. I just wanted to ask for extra prayer cover today."

"You've got it," he readily agreed. "What can I pray for in particular?"

"There is just a lot of spiritual warfare around Halloween time for me as well as for a couple of my clients. Pray for safety for all of us."

He was a very discerning man of God. He looked at Abigail and asked, "How are you doing personally this Halloween?" He knew a little bit of her history.

"I'm mostly okay," she started, "and it gets a little easier each year. I remember my guys and do try to do something special, but this year just seems a bit tougher. I don't know if it's because it's the ten-year anniversary or if it's because Dude was killed ..."

"Dude?" He had forgotten about that.

"Someone poisoned him a couple of weeks ago," Abigail suddenly felt like she was in a confessional.

Pastor Spalding was quiet for a few moments before he said, "One of these days I'd like to sit down with you and hear more. I want to be able to pray more effectively for you. Do you think we can do that in the next week or so?"

"Yes, I'd like that," Abigail said, "I think there are things you need to know." She thanked him and then went to her office.

Carrie Sue Wagner came through the door on time. She looked better every week despite all the chaos swirling within her family. They quickly settled into their usual chairs and opened with prayer, sensing that there was much work that needed to be done in a short amount of time.

"I'm thinking that we need to pray preemptive prayers. There are still some parts remaining that have been programmed to show up at the rituals that are scheduled during the next five days."

Carrie Sue agreed. They prayed and after two hours of negotiations with sector leaders, they had covered some of the rituals. One key group was called the Halloweeners with a leader whose name was Samhain. They were very hostile, very cult-loyal, and very demon-loyal when first approached.

Abigail challenged them to think about new ideas. "You don't know what you don't know."

"We know everything we need to know," Samhain replied defensively. Arrogantly.

"Yes, everything that they want you to know and nothing that they don't want you to know," Abigail goaded, hoping to compel him to think outside of his limited box.

"We got along just fine without you, lady!" he was becoming agitated.

"I know – threats, pain, programming, demons – sounds wonderful." Abigail walked that fine line between provoking them into shutting down and spurring them to think about other options or another course of action and therefore a better life. She knew that they had only been exposed to evil and could not know that there were other possibilities.

"We can take it. We like what we do," Samhain asserted again.

"Oh? You enjoy being like the dad?" Abigail had a way of extrapolating the implications of their claims and taking them to the far end of the consequences.

"No, we don't! We aren't anything like him."

"You said that you like what you do. You do what the dad and the others programmed you to do. You do their dirty work for them. You help participate in the rituals. What am I missing?"

He grunted in frustration, "Yes. No. We do what *we* want to do."

"So, you're telling me that if you were given the choice right here and right now that you would gladly kill or hurt a child."

"Well, no …" He clearly had not thought about the repercussions of embracing his values.

"So then, you are not like your father. And if you are not like your father, why would you want to advocate everything that he stands for?" Abigail continued to push him to think.

"O-oh!" he grunted in frustration. "You are making me nuts!"

"Look," she said gently, "I know that you have never met anyone who was not a Satanist. Why do you think your father and all the others worked so hard to keep you from encountering a true Christian or being exposed to the true Lord Jesus the Christ of Nazareth? I mean, they talk about how God and Jesus don't give a rip about you, but really, why would they put so much effort into slamming God if He was truly inferior to Satan? Don't you think that they're protesting a bit too much?"

"Satan has power. We have power," he protested.

"I'm not disputing that," Abigail replied, "but they don't want you to know about the superior power of the true God. Satan and God are not on a par. God is the Creator. Satan is a created being. Powerful, yes, but still created."

"Well, I chose him," Samhain contended.

"Really? Someone really gave you an authentic choice when you were not drugged or a minor or outnumbered or programmed or threatened or put in a double-bind or tormented?" Abigail continued to challenge him.

"I made a blood covenant. I can't go back on it or else …" he let the sentence dangle unfinished.

"So," Abigail summarized, "you *were* coerced to make a covenant as a programmed minor while you were drugged and being threatened. And you are still under threat if you want to renounce it."

Samhain sighed, "Yeah, I guess so."

"If I were to tell you that the covenant could be undone and you don't have to go to the rituals that start tomorrow, would you be interested?"

"Maybe," he conceded.

"Would you listen while I lay out a strategy that will accomplish that?" Abigail asked.

He crossed his arms, conceded, and nodded his begrudging assent.

Abigail went into an explanation of how he was a part of Carrie Sue and how he was split out and programmed. She gave him a summary of the argument that there was a covenant previously established by God that made all the subsequent covenants bogus. She outlined the prayer for release from strongholds and demons that came through verbal and sexual assaults, traumas and near-death experiences. She told him that the physical and emotional pain would be healed and that many times God would take the sting out of memories and He often granted divine forgetfulness for some of the more horrific memories. "That's the stuff we 'put off'" she concluded, "then we 'put on' the good stuff from God's kingdom."

"What do I have to do?" Samhain said without animosity or frustration.

"Give me permission to pray for you. And, as the spokesman for the group, find out if the rest of them are on board so they can be prayed for as well."

"I'm in," he said wearily, "I'll check with all the others; I think they're tired and want to be done, too." He checked with the others and reported that they were all ready to be healed. No one ever wanted to go to another Halloween ritual.

Abigail was always amazed at how quickly the internal dialogues took place. Over the years she had worked with hundreds of survivors and noticed that the internal exchanges took a fraction of the time the external negotiations took. That was why she would often defer to whoever was in executive control. She did not ask about the numbers, but she suspected that the Halloween rituals had produced thousands of personalities. If she had to talk to each one, she could make a career out of one survivor!

"Let's do it," he said.

Abigail rejoiced but kept her composure, "Let's pray." She launched into the comprehensive prayer that she used so often with these survivors. When she was finished she checked with Samhain. His relief was obvious and he reported that there were a lot of smiles inside.

"Now what?"

"I think that it would be best for all of you to get put back inside where you rightfully belong. That way the cult can't access you anymore because you don't exist in the form that they created. Let's ask the Lord if everyone should go in or if you or one of the other leaders might need to stay separate for a while." They prayed and both had peace to pray for everyone to be integrated.

Abigail prayed for God to reknit them back into their rightful places with joy and unity in a bond of peace. She prayed that the Lord would recompense them for everything that the enemy had stolen from them. She prayed that they would experience the fruit of the Spirit and that the gifts of the Holy Spirit would be activated in them in such a way that it would bless and strengthen the whole.

Carrie Sue came forward again with a huge smile. "Wow! That was big!"

Abigail agreed. "Listen," she said, "it's lunch time. How about if we go to the Sandwich Shack and grab a bite and then put in another hour or so? I don't have anyone until two o'clock."

"Really? I mean, yes, I'd like that," Carrie Sue responded enthusiastically. She knew that there were still far too many vulnerable personalities inside.

They locked up the office and drove over to the Sandwich Shack in Abigail's truck. "Just kick that stuff back under the seat," Abigail said. She still had not brought the church directory and a few other magazines into the house.

"Do you mind if I look through this again?" Carrie Sue asked.

"If you are sure you're okay. I'm curious if there is anyone else you might know."

Carrie Sue occupied herself with paging through the pictorial directory. She stopped and held it up to scrutinize a couple. "This guy," she said pointing to the man, "I'm pretty sure I know him and his wife looks familiar, too."

"What's the name?" Abigail asked.

"Evans. Geoffrey and Brenda Evans."

"He's a lawyer of some kind. I don't know what his wife does." Her mind flashed back to the day that she saw the man in the courtroom when Billy failed to show up for his case. *I was right. He does go to my church. That is where I saw him.*

They fell silent as Carrie Sue continued to page through the directory. "Here's another familiar face. Edmund Parker. His wife's name is Eileen."

"Hmm," Abigail thought for a minute, "Oh, yeah, he and his wife own that appliance store not too far from here. I bought my refrigerator there. Someone from the church recommended that place."

By the time Carrie Sue had finished paging through the directory, they arrived at the Sandwich Shack. They ordered their sandwiches and sat at a table by the window. Abigail knew that Carrie Sue would not bring up the subject so she asked her how her mother was doing.

"Well, she's stopped calling me all hours of night and day and seems to have settled down but she's still Mom - one minute she loves me and in the next breath she blames me for every bad thing that has ever happened to her - including the bio-dad's death. I know it's the dissociation, but it wears me out never knowing which mom will switch in."

"Sorry."

"Did I tell you what she said at the funeral?"

"What?"

"Some part of her switched in and told me that she has a part named Judith. Judith married the dad and the others didn't. They've all been mad at her for dragging them down the aisle with her."

"Oh my! That is an interesting conundrum." Abigail giggled at the thought and then became more serious and asked, "What is she going to do now? Does she have any income?"

"She's on some kind of disability for mental illness. She'll get a little pension from Dad's work. She might be okay if she has someone in there who's financially responsible. I don't know if the house is paid off or what. I guess I'll find out sooner or later. I'm the only one left beside her sisters."

They conversed between bites of sandwich and nibbles of potato chips. When they were finished Abigail left a tip while Carrie Sue carried their tray and sandwich baskets to the trash can and put the trays and plastic baskets on the shelf above it. They exited the restaurant and got back into the truck for the short drive back to the church. Looking into the rear-view mirror, noticing a large sedan following them, she impulsively made a sudden right turn at the next light to see what happened. Carrie Sue looked at her questioningly.

"I think we have company," Abigail said. "I see that BFOMC around a lot. This is a small town, but I'm beginning to wonder how much of a coincidence it is."

"Uh, what's a BFOMC?" Carrie Sue asked as she looked over her shoulder to try to get a glimpse of whatever Abigail was talking about.

"Sorry. It stands for Big Fat Old Man Car. It's about the size of the car, not the driver. My dad drives one and I just noticed that practically every time I see one of them, an old man is driving it. Dad hates it when I tease him about it, but he says that they have a good ride and at this stage of his life, comfort is everything."

She watched as the sedan followed about half a block behind so she made another right and then pulled off the side street in front of a full-sized pickup truck that was parallel parked there. The BFOMC turned the corner and began to accelerate when he did not see her truck. When he passed Abigail, she pulled out behind him.

"Write down his plate number for me," Abigail instructed as she handed Carrie Sue the small tablet and a pen that she kept in the side pocket of the door. "Did you get a look at him?"

"No." His windows were deeply tinted so she could not tell much more than what his silhouette revealed. Abigail returned to the through street and drove back to the church. They resumed their session and were able to access more parts who would have been summoned to the upcoming rituals.

"Carrie Sue," Abigail said decisively at the end of their time, "I am not willing to take a chance on you getting accessed after all the work we've done. I know this sounds crazy, but how about if you pack a bag and spend the next five days with me?"

Carrie Sue nearly burst into tears as relief washed over her. They had gotten quite a bit of work done, but she was not entirely sure that they would not find some back door to get to her. "Are you sure? I mean, that would be such a relief. Thanks, how can I ever repay you?"

"Oh, I can think of all kinds of chores that need to be done," she grinned mischievously. "But, seriously, ministry is always a two-way street. You get yourself whole and healed and help someone else. I should be home by about five. I'll meet you there."

The driver of the large sedan cursed as he reported to Sheriff Bynum on his cell phone. "That broad was watching for me. She made me and ended up behind me. I have a feeling that she has my license number and is going to check up on it."

Bynum was not pleased with yet another glitch and let the man know in no uncertain terms. "Looks like you need some new wheels with new plates." He hung up on the protesting man. *Let him figure it out.*

Amy cruised through the door at her usual time and flopped down on the overstuffed chair across from Abigail. They exchanged greetings and then got down to business. Abigail noticed that underneath the thin veneer of the free-wheeling, care-free, semi-apathetic pizza delivery girl, Amy was beginning to get more serious about her healing.

Abigail wanted to touch base with Head Warden who responded immediately. "How is it going with your prisoners?"

"Well, they're not as angry as they were at first. We've been trying to talk to them and we've been bringing them good food and made sure they each had a mattress to sleep on. They keep calling us cowards and traitors. Caleb is there, too. He's been gunning for my position for a long time."

"Well, he sounds just like Lucifer who has been gunning for God's position for a long time. They don't know any better. I know it's hard not to take it personally, but they also might be trying to keep up appearances so their demons don't torture them for thinking about defecting."

Head Warden thoughtfully considered those possibilities. "What can we do about it?"

"Let's pray and ask the Lord to give us a strategy," Abigail replied.

They prayed and Head Warden slowly shook his head, "I have no idea."

"Let me run something past you, then," Abigail said. "I'm sensing that the Lord wants me to talk to you about your jurisdiction." He nodded and she continued. "You have the rightful jurisdiction over the above ground cell blocks and everything that pertains to it, right?"

"Yes."

"Who gave that jurisdiction and that assignment to you?" Abigail asked.

"Darod."

"Excellent! So, let's think like a couple of legalists. If you have jurisdiction and authority over everything that pertains to that assignment, then you can make decisions for the personnel as their leader."

"I do it all the time."

"So then, if you decide that your personnel need to be rid of their demons while they are under your jurisdiction, you can authorize that, right?" Abigail continued her line of logic.

Head Warden broke into a rare smile. "I think I see where you are going. I can't make a personal decision for them, but I can authorize the expulsion of their demons from my turf. You know, you'd make a great lawyer. I am officially asking you to pray for those guards to be rid of their demons." Head Warden and Abigail both liked the idea of using the very authorization that was granted by Darod, to dismantle the master's authority in Amy.

"My pleasure," Abigail beamed. "Holy Father and Judge of all, we come to You to ask that You would cover that room with all those captives with the blood of Your Son, Jesus Christ. We ask that You would separate every demon that has been assigned to each of those parts of F. Amy Bolton from them. We further request that You would send them with their entire hierarchies to a place where they will never afflict anyone ever again. We ask that You would do it in such a way that no one, inside or outside of Amy, would know what just happened. We pray that You would send Your Comforter to fill that place and bring peace that passes understanding to surround those parts. We pray these things in the name of Jesus the Christ, amen."

Head Warden was quiet for a moment as he went to check on the status of the cult-loyal captives. After reemerging, he reported, "They are all walking around wondering what just happened. What should we do now?"

"Let's ask the Lord," Abigail replied.

They prayed and then Head Warden said, "I think that they are ready to talk."

"Are they able to hear me?"

"Yes."

"Okay, then, do you need to be the middle man or will Caleb be the spokesman for the group?"

"I think you can talk directly to Caleb; he's ready."

Abigail asked Caleb if he would be willing to listen to a brief overview of the situation and the effects of programming. Caleb was amazed that he was able to think more clearly now and was ready to listen. He and his group had never known life without demonic oppressors. *That* was normal. They just assumed that what always was would always be.

"You will be even clearer once the programming is cancelled," Abigail encouraged him, "and then you can make an informed decision about what you want to do next."

After some basic negotiations, the entire group was finally able to understand about their history, the programming, the purpose of the torture, demonic oppression, and the way they were being used to do the cult's dirty work. They were all angry for being duped by the cult and were on board with doing whatever they could do to undo the damage that had already been done to them and by them. They readily agreed to Abigail's prayers.

Once they were healed and delivered, Caleb addressed Abigail, "I want to apologize for giving you such a rough time the last time we met."

"You are forgiven. I know you were just doing your job," Abigail freely extended forgiveness. "I'm glad you are on board."

"Thanks," a much humbler Caleb said softly. "So, what's next?"

"Well, I think we need to ask the Lord if any of the group needs to be integrated or if the Lord wants some or all of you to remain separate. And if so, what He wants you to do. I think I have an idea, but I'd rather have it come from Him."

"Okay."

Abigail led them in a prayer to inquire of the Lord for the specifics about this group of guards and assistant wardens. "What are you sensing?" Abigail asked after she prayed.

"I forgot to mention something," Caleb said. "We have a guy here named Zuard. He is from Nicholai's level and kind of got caught in the round up. He defected with us and is definitely a changed man."

"Isn't that interesting," Abigail mused. "I wonder if they've missed him yet."

"Maybe you should talk to him," Caleb suggested.

"Is he okay with that?"

"Yes." Abigail noted the instant switch.

"I'm here," Zuard said.

"Hi. Thanks for talking with me. What are you sensing that the Lord would have you do now that you've defected?" Abigail asked.

"I'm not sure exactly," he said thoughtfully, "but I know that I won't be missed. Nicholai has sent me topside lots of times." He was embarrassed, "I'm one of the reasons he knew what was going on up here. He's used to me being gone for a long time."

"Perfect!" Abigail said and then rethought her response. "Well, maybe not. I was thinking that you could do for Head Warden what you did for Nicholai, but I do anticipate one little problem: you've been transformed. You're not the mean, demon-driven, programmed guy they knew and loved. They'll bust you for sure."

"I think I can work around that, but," Zuard hung his head in shame, "I, uh, I need to get something right first."

"What do you mean?" Abigail was puzzled.

"Well," he confessed, "I got this uniform off of one of the guards after I ambushed him. I dragged him through the trap door and now he's a prisoner down there. I want to bring him back up here." He looked very distressed after realizing what he had done. "I have to make this right. Please!"

"Let's pray about it."

"Sure."

Abigail prayed for Zuard, asking God to bring him peace. She also prayed for a strategy for rescuing the ambushed guard as well as anything else God wanted him to do. When she was finished, she had a sense that God would send him down there and provide him with the cover that he would need. As usual, she first asked the prayer recipient what he or she sensed. She was then able to confirm whether or not the new impression was her own bright idea or an inspiration from the Holy Spirit.

"I think I am supposed to go down there and bring him back. For some reason I am getting the word 'peter' and I don't know what that means." Zuard answered with a puzzled expression.

Abigail smiled, "I think I know what the Lord is trying to tell us. Peter was one of God's apostles and was in prison one time. God sent an angel into his prison cell at night. The angel poked him in the side to wake him up and led him out. Peter thought he was dreaming for a while there. I think that God is confirming that you are to go get him out of his prison cell."

"Well, I am no angel!" Zuard said. "But I'll go."

"Let me ask a couple more questions before you go, if you don't mind." He nodded and Abigail proceeded to ask him about how many others from the subterranean levels would know about the trap door. She also asked him to reveal its location to Caleb and Head Warden so that it could be secured.

He said that he believed that he was the only one currently assigned to be topside and readily agreed to reveal where it was hidden. Abigail left it to the various personalities to work out the details of securing the trap door. It was located in the isolated pump room. He described a large pipe that did not carry water. It was a decoy and had a hinged door on the back side.

As usual, the internal work was done with speed that defied the imagination. Guards were dispatched to secure the pump room. Zuard was equipped with various items that he would need. Best of all, they prayed for his success. Zuard then went to the pump room, opened the door to the secret passage and slipped into the subterranean murkiness.

After a matter of minutes, he emerged with the guard he had ambushed long ago. The beleaguered personality was in poor condition with gray skin, dull eyes, and appeared emaciated. He was disoriented by the lack of oppression in the internal atmosphere. He, like Peter, wondered if he was dreaming.

"Zuard's here with the guard," Head Warden reported. "He's in really bad shape; can you pray for him, too?"

Abigail gladly prayed for the personality. She called it her "sozo" prayer. It was a Greek New Testament word that meant "saved, healed, and delivered." Technically, the cult and demon-loyal parts were saved because Amy professed to be a born-again Christian. There was only one spirit, one soul, and one body. There certainly was dissociation, but only one person. In a sense, those with multiple personalities were not much different from any nondissociated Christian who had not yet completely surrendered certain areas of their lives to the Lord. People with multiple personalities just showed the contrast more clearly.

The guard was immediately healed and wanted to defect from the evil kingdom and everything it stood for. He experienced and sensed evil so deep and so perverse that it felt as if he had absorbed it through his skin. When he was healed and then presented with the option of being integrated, he jumped at the opportunity. Abigail prayed for him and he vanished from their sight as the Lord placed him back into his rightful place.

"Now what?" Head Warden asked.

"Well," Abigail said, "I can think of a bunch of things that could be done as far as infiltrating the subterranean level or just waiting for someone to be sent up here. But I think the highest priority has got to be figuring a strategy to keep Amy from being accessed and sent to the upcoming rituals."

"How can we do that?" he asked.

"We can ask the Lord to give us access to the key individual personalities and groups who have been programmed for the high holy days that come before and after All Hallows Eve and Halloween night."

"We don't know who they are," he protested.

"But the Lord does," Abigail replied confidently and paraphrased a verse from Proverbs. "The spirit of the man is the lamp of the Lord and by it He examines the innermost chambers. We pray and He leads."

Head Warden admired her sure confidence. She demonstrated power that was superior to anything

Darod or even Prinz showed. They continued to talk about the complexity of the series of rituals that were coming up and then began the tedious negotiations. It seemed that most of the time either a lower level part or a child alter was sent out whenever a new sector was addressed. It took time and some give-and-take before Abigail was able to address someone who had authority to make meaningful decisions.

Unfortunately, they only had enough time to come to an agreement about the high holy day rituals that would occur on October twenty-eight and twenty-nine. Abigail, Head Warden and several of the others prayed for God to scramble the programming and keep Amy et al safe. Amy still naively believed that she would be just fine over the weekend and that all she was going to do was make good tips delivering a lot of pizzas.

After she left, Abigail had a couple free minutes to run to the kitchen for a snack before her meeting with Twyla Taylor. By the time she returned to the office, Twyla and Nancy were seated in the waiting room. Nancy was nervously paging through a magazine. Twyla was nonchalantly thumbing a text message on her phone.

"Hello," Abigail greeted them with a smile, "I'm ready when you are."

"Do you want to see both of us, or just Twyla?" Nancy asked.

"Is there anything you think we need to talk about?"

"No, not really; it's been a little bit calmer this week," Nancy said wearily.

"Twyla, come on in," Abigail invited.

The teen punched a couple more buttons and then turned off her phone. She ambled into the office behind Abigail and flopped down in the chair as only teenagers can do.

"Let's begin with prayer," Abigail said. Twyla folded her hands and bowed her head so Abigail prayed a brief prayer to invite the Holy Spirit to direct their time together.

Twyla looked up expectantly after the amen. That was a good sign. Twyla had gotten caught up in cutting and anorexia and did not know how to get out. She seemed to have some hope today.

"Do you have any questions or comments about the stuff we talked about last time?"

"No, not really."

"Did it feel like I was reading your mail?" Abigail asked with a smile.

"Yeah, kinda. I mean, the stuff you said made sense and all, but I don't see how anything is going to change any time soon."

"Are you willing to go along with me and see how we do? It's not hopeless."

"Sure."

"We need to look at the root, not just the fruit. It's like the anorexia and cutting are the symptoms and not the disease. I don't want to put a bandage on the symptom. I want us to have the disease completely healed so the symptoms go away for good."

She got another doubtful mini-nod from Twyla.

"Last time you got emotional when I mentioned your father's accident. Do you think you can talk to me about it a little bit today? I'm not trying to upset you, but it seems that your troubles with anorexia and cutting started right after that. They are related."

Twyla took a deep breath and puffed her cheeks out as she exhaled slowly. "What do you want to know?" Her voice was flat.

"Tell me about that day."

"It was a Saturday. Sometimes Daddy would let me ride with him in his truck when he made a delivery. He had a big dump truck." She paused as she gathered her thoughts. "I was supposed to go with him that morning, but Mom wouldn't let me because my room was a mess and she grounded me until it was cleaned up. I didn't have time before he left."

Abigail was beginning to understand some of the source of the hostility that Twyla held toward her mother. She could not be angry at her father, so it was directed at her mother. She let Twyla continue her narrative.

"Daddy went without me," Twyla paused and tried unsuccessfully to choke back her sobs. "That was the last time I ever saw Daddy alive. I should have been with him."

"You might have been hurt or killed, too."

"No!" Twyla said vehemently, "No! Daddy never wore his seatbelt unless I was with him. He always made me wear mine so I made him wear his." Her guilt poured out, "If I was with him we would have both been wearing seatbelts and probably woulda just got hurt a little. But he got hurt so bad when he was thrown around in the cab," she wailed. "It's all my fault. If I had cleaned my room like I was supposed to, I would have been with him and he wouldn't be dead." Twyla had held this pent-up guilt and sorrow since that fateful day. She sobbed and sobbed.

Abigail's mothering instincts were hard to resist sometimes. She wished she could hug the distraught teenager, but she knew that it would barely bring momentary consolation. "Twyla, can we take this pain to Jesus?"

Twyla stopped her sobbing with shuddering deep breaths and looked at Abigail, "How?" It seemed like an impossible load.

"Jesus is the same yesterday, today, and tomorrow. He was there that day even if you were unaware of His presence. Would you be willing to go back to that moment when you first started feeling all that guilt and pain and ask Him to bring truth about those feelings and thoughts?"

"I, I guess so," Twyla wasn't completely sure of what Abigail was talking about, but she was eager for any relief.

"Then you close your eyes so you're not distracted, and I'll pray while you focus on that memory. Let all the pain come up. You can't give it to Jesus if you stuff it; okay?"

Twyla nodded her head and closed her eyes. Tears continued to seep down her cheeks and she sniffed as she wiped her nose on the tissue she had found in the box on the table by her chair.

"I'm going to pray a little and then be quiet while you go back to the memory," Abigail instructed.

Twyla nodded again.

Abigail prayed, "Jesus, You were there the day that Twyla's daddy was killed in the accident. Lord Jesus, Twyla believes that it was her fault that her daddy died, that she could have prevented his death if only she was there. Jesus, would You come to Twyla right now in whatever way You choose and let her see You there with her spiritual eyes, or hear You with her spiritual ears, or sense Your presence as she focuses on that day. Jesus what do You have to say about the things that Twyla believes? Is it Twyla's fault? Could she have prevented his death? Jesus, Twyla is also feeling guilt and regret, anger and frustration, grief and loss. Would You lift that pain from her as she gives it to You?"

Abigail fell quiet and waited for the long, silent minutes that followed. She knew from experience that she could tell someone that it was not their fault until she was blue in the face, but unless Jesus told them, the pain would remain. When they knew the Truth, they would be set free. Abigail was praying in the Spirit while Twyla sat quietly in front of her. She watched carefully as the tears of bitterness stopped and then were replaced by a burst of tears of relief.

"What are you sensing in that memory, Twyla?" Abigail broke in gently.

"I saw Jesus in the cab with my daddy. He was holding him all the time. My daddy didn't feel pain. I,

I don't know how I know that …" she let the words trail off.

"How does your pain feel? The guilt and stuff?"

"Well," Twyla was laughing and crying at the same time, "Jesus looked right at me and He said, 'It's not your fault!'"

"What else?" Abigail sensed that there was another message for Twyla.

The teen gave a short sigh, "He said, 'Trust Me.'" Then she began to weep again.

"What does that mean to you?" Abigail asked.

"I think," she was unsure of what she was sensing, "I think it's something like, uh, well, um, I get the idea that Daddy was going to have, like, an awful disease like cancer or something and that Daddy had begged God to not let him die like his dad did." She ended the sentence with the inflection one would use if she were asking a question.

"How do you feel now that you said that?"

"Relief," she sighed, "like it was God answering Daddy's prayer. Do you think he knew he had cancer and didn't tell us?" Twyla's mind was racing with the implications.

"We may never know that until we get to Heaven," Abigail replied. "But let's go back to that day and the painful feelings. Do you still believe that it was your fault and that you could have prevented it?"

Twyla's eyes swept back and forth a couple of times as if she were searching for the guilt and then she broke out into a sheepish grin, "It's not my fault."

"Are you sure?" Abigail teased with a smile, but seriously wanted to hear it again.

"I'm sure," Twyla said with a smile of her own.

"Okay," Abigail said and then asked, "are you up for a little bit more?"

"Yeah," she agreed, but was uncertain of what Abigail had in mind.

"What do you want to do about your anger toward your mother?"

Twyla sucked in a deep breath and let it out slowly which puffed her cheeks out again. "I'm not mad at her any more. Maybe the whole thing with cleaning my room was the way God made sure I wasn't there."

"Sounds like you are beginning to trust Jesus a bit," Abigail observed with a gentle smile.

"Yeah," she said brightly. "Can I go tell her now?" Twyla was like any teenager who made impulsive decisions - sometimes impetuous and sometimes thoughtful.

"Call her in."

Twyla jumped up from her seat and gestured for her mother to come in. Nancy was not quite sure what to expect. She had not seen this happy side of her daughter for over a year. She sat down and Twyla began to recount what had occurred in the session up to this point. "Mom," she hesitated as she ended her story, "I'm so sorry that I've been mad at you and blamed you for Daddy's death by not letting me be there."

"Oh, honey, it's okay. I love you, baby." Tears began to fall again as the two hugged with genuine warmth and love for the first time in a very long time.

Abigail dabbed at the tears that formed unbidden in the corners of her own eyes. "Praise God!" she said. "This is a good start. Why don't we set a time for next week?"

Twyla gave her a look that said, "Good start?"

"We do have a little unfinished business with the matters that you came in with originally," Abigail reminded her with a gentle laugh. "This is a good step in the right direction, but I want to make sure that we take care of all the loose ends."

"Oh, yeah. Right."

Nancy and Twyla left together while Abigail finished the administrivia and closed the office. The sun was going down behind the low hills and made long shadows fall across the landscape. This was a good day, but it was not over. Carrie Sue would probably beat her to the house.

Abigail stopped at the end of the driveway and picked up the mail. Carrie Sue was at the gate petting Buster's nose and trying not to get nipped. Parking the truck, she called out as she opened her door. "Hey! You made it! I hope you haven't been waiting too long." They walked toward each other and hugged briefly near the yard light.

"I was just telling Buster how handsome he is. I think he was just looking for a treat and someone to rub him under his chin," Carrie Sue said with a laugh. She was clearly relieved to be in a safe place.

At that time the yard light started humming just prior to coming on. "We might as well get Buster his sweet feed as long as we're this close. Do you mind?"

"No problem. I think I'll wait here so I don't have to squeeze through the fence. I'm not quite as agile as you are."

"Okay, I'll be right back," Abigail said as she squeezed through the fence. Buster walked down with his nose touching her shoulder from time to time. Retrieving his large metal pan from where he nuzzled it after he licked up the last morsel of sweet feed this morning, she opened the tack room door and put a scoop into the pan. After locking the door, she patted him on the back. "Your coat is getting thicker," she said out loud. He was busy with his treat and ignored Abigail as she walked back up toward the house.

"He sure is a gentle horse," Carrie Sue said. "Do you remember how scared I was when I first met him last year?"

"I remember," Abigail laughed. "But I also think some of your little people really wanted to ride him."

"They did, but I was not about to let them do that! No way!"

"What about now? Have they been able to change your mind yet?"

"Nope," Carrie Sue said with finality and a little laugh. "No way!"

"Let me help you get your stuff inside and then we can rustle up some food. I think that the fire went out while I was gone, but it won't take much to get it rolling again. It's been getting pretty chilly at night out here lately. Did you notice how thick Buster's coat is getting?"

They chatted about ordinary things while Urdang and his cronies circled high enough above the angelic warriors to avoid a direct clash. Discussing their strategies, a battle was brewing in the heavenly realms. The prince of the power of the air was busy staging his minions in various battlefields around the globe. The Prince of Peace was dispatching His hosts to critical areas. Bowls of incense were being filled with the prayers of the saints and the answers were beginning to overflow and cascade back to the earth.

If humans could see into the spiritual realm as plainly as Elisha's servant saw the fiery horses and chariots they would be astonished at the dazzling colors and the vigorous activity. There were two statuesque angelic beings guarding the foot of the driveway who tirelessly wielded flaming swords in front of them. Their gleaming radiance illuminated the entire area. The lawn and buildings were covered with iridescent crimson blood. The air above the property was shimmering with the presence of the sacred blood as well. It was beautiful, not gory.

A look into the second heavens revealed the gathering of fallen angels. They were more grotesque than the most hideous ancient dinosaur. They were more repulsive than the most horrid reptile. Horns, scales, claws, bat-like wings, and fangs accentuated disfigured bodies that once graced the throne room of the Most High God.

Carrie Sue unpacked and made herself at home in the back bedroom. Abigail emptied ashes and found a small pocket of live embers. These she coaxed into a little flame with her kindling. She added larger sticks and finally had enough of a base to sustain a couple of small logs. By then Carrie Sue joined her.

"Are you hungry?" Abigail asked. "I'm starving! That was a good lunch today, but it's long gone."

"Yes, I am," Carrie Sue replied. "Can I help you with anything in the kitchen?"

"Sure. It's Friday night, so we have the week in review tonight. I have some quiche left over from Tuesday. There's the Grecian chicken that I made last night. There's plenty of stuff to make a good salad to go with them."

"Yum! It all sounds good."

"Well, there's no rule that says that we can't have a little bit of everything. I'll get things heated up while you set the dining room table. We'll dine in *fine* style tonight." Abigail exaggerated the word fine.

They each went about their tasks and soon there was a delectable dinner on the table. They bowed their heads and asked for the Lord's blessing on the food and their fellowship. After their initial hunger was satisfied, they began to talk again. Carrie Sue brought Abigail up to date on her mother. That led to a comment about her brother, Billy.

Oh, Lord I need wisdom for this discussion. "Do you think your mother is right about Billy being dead?" Abigail asked.

"I'm beginning to think that he was sacrificed at … what ritual was that, again? Yom Kippur? It's been nearly a month and Mom said that the sheriff was looking for him for some reason. She thought he was in trouble with the law again, but the sheriff didn't tell her anything. Or if he did, she hasn't told me. What do you think?" Carrie Sue looked right into Abigail's eyes. She was like so many of the survivors who had very keen discernment. There would be no fooling her even if she wanted to.

"I'll tell you what," Abigail responded, "I'd like to finish up dinner, stack the dishes, and then sit in some comfortable chairs around the wood stove before we go much further with this topic."

"Sounds like a plan," Carrie Sue agreed.

They had lingered over dinner long enough and quickly finished the last few bites that remained on their plates. Abigail put the leftovers away while Carrie Sue rinsed and stacked the dishes onto the counter near the sink. She wet the dish cloth and wiped down the dining room table and counter tops while Abigail threw a larger log into the wood stove. The fire was crackling nicely and heat was beginning to radiate from the black metal. She topped off the antique iron kettle which added some moisture to the air. They finally sat down in the comfortable chairs.

"So," Carrie Sue repeated her earlier question, "what do you think about Billy?"

Abigail paused and looked at Carrie Sue for a few moments before she answered. "I think your mother might be telling you the truth about Billy being gone. But, she's definitely not right about anything that may have happened to him being your fault." She stopped and looked Carrie Sue in the eyes, "You do believe that, don't you?"

"Yes, I do. I know he's not my responsibility," she answered with only a slight hint of misgiving.

"I know they blamed you for everything. Are you really sure you know that you are not to blame?"

Carrie Sue rolled her eyes at her friend before she reaffirmed her previous response.

"Okay, then, let me tell you what I found a couple of weeks ago when I was out riding Buster." Abigail told Carrie Sue about her ride that took her on a circuit which brought her past the abandoned farm across the road and not quite a mile away.

"Are you sure that was Billy's car? What would it be doing over there?" Carrie Sue only asked two questions but several more were tumbling through her mind.

"I looked at the registration in the glove box. It was registered to William J. Wagner."

Carrie Sue looked confused and distraught. "Why would …" her question trailed off. "Do you think it's still there?"

"Probably," Abigail answered, "I didn't report it and I don't think anyone ever goes up there."

"Can we go see tomorrow?" Carrie Sue asked. "I don't know why, I just want to see it."

"I don't see why not. The activity director has taken the weekend off, so we will have to figure out how to entertain ourselves," Abigail said with a grin.

"Funny."

They drifted into other subjects. They talked about Pastor Spalding and some of the friendly people at church with whom Carrie Sue was beginning to become acquainted. They talked about their vehicles and Buster and missing Dude. It was getting late and they were beginning to feel the effects of a long and stressful week.

"I don't know about you," Abigail said, "but I think it's time for me to take a shower and put my head where I'll find it in the morning."

Carrie Sue laughed, "Where did you come up with that expression?"

"In my former life, I worked in a nursing home and one of the sweet little old ladies would always say that. I thought it was funny so I stole it from her. You feel free to use the back bathroom. It's all yours this weekend."

"Thanks. I think I'll take my shower in the morning. And thanks for supper and everything"

"You're welcome. Sleep until noon if you want to. I'll get up and take care of Buster, but other than that, we can do whatever, whenever. Please feel free to raid the fridge or pantry. There is yogurt and some granola bars and fruit if you need a snack."

"Thanks again," Carrie Sue yawned, "I'll see you in the morning."

"Oh, wait," Abigail said, "we need to pray first."

"Good idea."

Abigail and Carrie Sue prayed together. Their vibrant rainbow-colored words streamed toward heaven where Jesus was also interceding according to the will of the Father. Abigail prayed a lengthier prayer, but Carrie Sue was beginning to be less self-conscious about praying out loud. Abigail added some logs to the fire and banked it. She would likely get up in the middle of the night and add more, but in case she slept the whole night, this would give her some embers to rekindle the flames.

Lee Norris was in a different time zone, but he was also preparing for bed. As a rancher, he was an early-to-bed, early-to-rise man. Lately he had been sleeping a little longer since he no longer had his cattle so he found himself staying up a bit longer, too. He still had his horses and his faithful old German shepherd, Bullet, to keep him busy. He was getting excited as he anticipated his move back east.

Prior to his trip to visit with Gary and Cindy and his other relatives, he only knew what he did *not* want to do. Now he believed that God was giving him a plan for what he should do. He would find some property that had a decent barn and hopefully a house as well as some acreage. He would keep three or four of his favorite horses and purchase livestock locally. He would not have the stress of *needing* to have a good herd. A small herd would be quite manageable. He liked the lifestyle that kept him close to God's natural beauty. He could supplement his income with a full or part-time job if necessary but his frugal life-style and the sale of the ranch released him from the pressure of having to find a job immediately.

His thoughts turned to the logistics of the move. He did not have much in home furnishings. His house was orderly, but sparsely decorated with some family heirlooms and items that his ex-wife did not take. Actually, it was now a bachelor pad. He had added a large desk to his office. Running a successful ranch was actually like running a small business.

He would have no trouble moving the household items, but the equipment was another story. Many big and small decisions must be made. Would it be wiser to sell it here and purchase replacements there, or would it be better to transport it? *Lord, give me the wisdom.* He decided that another trip back east to look at property would give him a better idea.

He would call Gary tomorrow.

25

Saturday, October 28

The Saturday morning air was cool and crisp. Abigail inhaled deeply as she stepped onto the back deck. It smelled like fall. It looked like fall. It was invigorating. There were some clouds forming in the west that confirmed the weather report. Severe thunderstorms should be rolling in by evening. Walking through the back yard, she left footprints where she crushed the lightly frosted grass. Buster trotted up and stamped his front hoof impatiently.

"Buster, this is Saturday. Give me a break, buddy. You probably want to get out of here, don't you?" Abigail wondered if Carrie Sue would be willing to ride with her on Buster to see Billy's car. Buster could easily carry both of them.

Carrie Sue did not sleep well. She could not remember ever getting a good night's sleep. When she heard Abigail moving around, she kicked the covers back and got up, selected some clean clothes and went to the shower.

Abigail heard the water running so she started to get breakfast items lined up. She was not sure what, if anything, Carrie Sue would eat. Some people were breakfast people and others were not but she decided to make it special anyway. This would be a good day for apple pancakes with plenty of cinnamon and vanilla added to the mix.

She chuckled thinking about what church people might think of her for making her home made vanilla extract from 100 proof vodka and a couple of organic vanilla beans. It took a few months for the vanilla to leach into the vodka before it turned a beautiful amber color. It was worth the wait for a better quality and much less expensive product.

Abigail diced one apple into the batter and made compote out of thin slices from another. By the time she was done, Carrie Sue was cutting through the kitchen on her way back to the bedroom.

"Mmm," she said sniffing the aromas, "something sure smells good."

"I had a taste for apple pancakes and some eggs. How do you like your eggs?"

"That sounds great," Carrie Sue said. "I'll have my eggs any way you make them."

"Well, they usually start out over medium, but sometimes end up scrambled," she answered with a little smile and a roll of her eyes.

Carrie Sue finished putting things away in her room and then set the little kitchen table. The tea kettle was whistling so Abigail whisked it off the hot stove top. "I'm making jasmine tea today," she said decisively. She already knew that Carrie Sue loved the variety of teas that Abigail served up hot or iced.

This was a good day for hot tea. Abigail selected the blue flowered bone china tea pot from her china cabinet in the dining room. "I just love these English teapots. They are so graceful and quaint." She said as she warmed the teapot with hot water from the tap before pouring it out after a minute. Finally, putting the jasmine tea in a tea strainer and placing it in the teapot, she added the boiling water and let it steep.

They finished preparing the meal and sat down to a tasty breakfast. Abigail asked for a blessing over their food and their activities. "And Lord, bless Carrie Sue as she takes her first horseback ride today, amen." Looking into the shocked and wide-open eyes of Carrie Sue, she burst into laughter.

"And just what first horseback ride would you be blessing?" Carrie Sue asked suspiciously.

"I thought that it might be a good day to take Buster for a leisurely walk over to Billy's car across the road. We can ride double."

"And just how will I get on that beast? My legs are not exactly as long as yours."

"You can get up on the tailgate of my truck and just hop on."

"Just hop on. Yeah, right! You make it sound so easy." Carrie Sue said with a hint of sarcasm.

"Seriously, think about it. It's a short ride and very safe. It'll be fun," Abigail coaxed her friend.

"I'll think about it," Carrie Sue conceded.

"You're a hoot!" Abigail observed with a gentle laugh. "You have been to hell and back a gazillion times and survived it, but you worry about getting on the back of a horse."

"Yeah, but, I didn't volunteer for that other stuff."

"Oh. Good point." They laughed and finished their meal. Abigail mentioned the weather forecast so they decided to go to Billy's car right after breakfast.

"I think it's not quite two miles round trip. Have you decided whether you are going to have sore feet from walking or a sore butt from riding?"

"I hate to admit it, but I still have some kids inside and they're screaming at me because they want to ride the horsey. We can ride Buster."

Abigail grinned triumphantly. "I'll go get Buster ready and you can meet me at the back of the truck. Go ahead and pull the tailgate down and climb up."

They parted ways and soon Abigail had the front gate open and rode Buster over to the truck. She guided him so that he was parallel to the tailgate and instructed Carrie Sue to grab the back of the saddle and slide her right leg over Buster's rump.

It was obvious that Carrie Sue was excited and anxious all at once and Abigail detected the switch into the child personality. Sometimes that was risky because coordination and judgment was definitely age appropriate, but the child part was able to get them seated without a mishap.

"Just hold onto the lip of the saddle. Keep your legs far enough out that you don't interfere with his back legs," Abigail instructed. "And relax! You want to try to go with his movement. Don't fight it, okay?"

"I'll try."

"Oh, and when we go down, lean back a little. When we go up, just lean forward a little."

"*When* we go down?" Carrie Sue was beginning to have misgivings about their little adventure.

"Just do what I do. You'll do great!"

Abigail gently nudged Buster and he started a steady walking pace down the dew-drenched front yard toward the end of the driveway. "How are you doing back there?"

"I didn't realize how high up we would be! This is pretty cool."

Abigail smiled as they clip-clopped across the road and entered the tall weeds that grew on the narrow shoulder of the road. She saw her opening in the brush that bordered the field and guided Buster down the incline. Carrie Sue tensed up with the downward direction but held on with white knuckles and didn't say anything as she leaned back a bit.

Abigail retraced the route that she took on the day she discovered the car and soon they entered a thin stand of trees that divided the field from the site of the abandoned buildings. When they emerged, Abigail pointed out the car.

Carrie Sue leaned forward and peered around Abigail's shoulders. "That's his car all right," Carrie Sue confirmed.

Riding right up to the car, Abigail had Buster walk completely around it. It seemed undisturbed since her last visit.

"Do you want to get down and take a closer look?" Abigail asked.

"I'd really like to, but how will I get back up?"

They looked around the property and Abigail pointed out an abandoned chest freezer. "I'll bet you could get up on that without a problem."

"Uh," Carrie Sue hesitated, "there's the matter of getting down, too."

"Let's go over there. If you can get off, you can get back on." Abigail proceeded to guide Buster to the old freezer and held him still while Carrie Sue got her left leg onto the freezer. Despite being a little stiff from the short ride, she was able to swing her right leg over Buster's rump and stand solidly on the freezer. She quickly sat down and hopped onto the ground. Abigail moved Buster away and dismounted herself. She held onto the reins as they walked over to the abandoned car.

"Billy bragged about ripping Mom and Dad off. He had a secret hiding place in his car. I think it was under his back seat. I'd really like to check."

"I'll help you," Abigail offered. She remembered looking for lost items under a back seat in days gone by. Her boys would invariably lose one of their tiny action figures or matchbox cars. She remembered how she had to kneel on the front edge of the seat to unlatch it from its rear fasteners.

Opening the doors, they reacted to the mustiness inside of the car. The driver's side window had been left open a few inches and rain had gotten in. The front seat was showing signs of mold. Unhinging the back seat, letting it fall forward, they were braced for whatever might be stashed under it.

Trash and plastic grocery bags.

Carrie Sue looked at Abigail uncertainly. "What do you think?"

"I sure don't want to leave here without finding out what he has stashed there."

Carrie Sue reached for the closest one.

"Wait!" Abigail warned. "I just had a paranoid thought. If there's something illegal in there, you don't want to leave your finger prints. We can wipe your prints off the handle, but I'm not sure about this stuff." She took her riding gloves off and handed them across the tipped-up seat to Carrie Sue.

Carrie Sue put the bulky gloves on and then picked up the first bag. She clumsily fumbled with it because of the gloves but managed to open it and peer inside. Her eyes popped open wide.

"What's in there?" Abigail demanded.

"Hoo boy! He really ripped off Mom and Dad," Carrie Sue said as she pulled out a wad of bills. They were stunned by the find. "I need to bring this back to Mom."

"Check the other bags, too."

Carrie Sue set the money bag down and picked up the next one. Looking inside, quickly dropping it, she pulled back and exclaimed, "Ew!"

"What?"

She had discovered his stash of marijuana. "I just found his whacky tobacky."

"Good thing you're wearing the gloves. Can you double-check to see if there is anything else in there, like maybe more of your mother's money?"

Carrie Sue picked it up again and opened it wide. Poking at the contents, she was satisfied that this bag only had baggies of marijuana in it. Reaching for the third bag, she looked at Abigail before she unfolded it and prepared to look inside. Metal shifted and made scraping and ringing sounds as the bottom of the bag tore and the contents clattered to the floorboard.

"Oh, Lord!" Carrie Sue yelped. She dropped the bag as if it was on fire. Hastily backing out of the car, she bumped her head on the door frame. "Ow!"

"Oh, my!" Abigail was also startled by the array of occult symbols emblazoned on some of the pieces.

Carrie Sue approached the pile again and looked closer. "It's a bunch of his jewelry - pendants and rings. Look! Those are his necklaces and chains and bracelet. It's the kind of stuff they usually wear at rituals but I've seen Billy wear some of this at home."

Abigail spontaneously launched into a prayer, "Lord Jesus, we plead Your blood over us and ask that You cleanse us for being near this stuff. We ask that You would demolish strongholds and get rid of any familiar spirits and especially the spirit of pharmakia associated with the drugs, amen."

"Amen!" Carrie Sue echoed. "Let's get out of here."

Abigail agreed. They quickly put the rear seat back into position over the marijuana and jewelry and heard it click down. Carrie Sue handed the riding gloves back to Abigail and held onto the bag with all the money in it. Just before Abigail closed the door on her side of the car she glanced down and saw a box of dog treats. "Did Billy have a dog?"

"Not that I know of; Mom wouldn't let him have one at home for sure. She's a cat person," she paused and then asked, "Why?"

Abigail pointed to the box of dog treats.

"That's weird," Carrie Sue said. "Why would he have dog treats and not have a dog?"

"I don't know for sure," Abigail hedged. She put the gloves on and used them to wipe her prints off of the door handle and then did the same on the door that Carrie Sue had opened.

"Come on, let's get out of here."

She got back onto Buster and guided him back toward the chest freezer. Carrie Sue climbed up and got onto Buster with less trouble and less trepidation than she did the first time. Turning him toward the trail, they rode home in near silence as each was lost in her own thoughts.

Buster stood obediently at the back of her truck while Carrie Sue dismounted still clutching the bag in one hand. "I'll meet you back in the house after I take care of Buster."

Carrie Sue walked up the steps to the back deck but decided to wait for Abigail out there so she could enjoy the view. She was somewhat bewildered when she saw that Abigail rode Buster down to the end of the pasture. Soon Abigail came back up to the house after putting the tack away.

"Grab something to eat or drink. I need to check something on the computer real quick." Abigail went into her office and turned on the computer. She inserted the SD card with a more practiced move and quickly scanned the images. Nothing suspicious showed up. She put the card in her pocket and joined Carrie Sue in the kitchen.

Carrie Sue had taken the money out of the bag and found that her brother had accumulated nearly two thousand dollars. "Mom should be glad to get this money back."

"What will you tell her?"

"I don't know. If I tell her that I found it in Billy's car, she'll wonder how I knew where to find his car," she paused to think about her options. "Do you have any ideas?"

"Not right now, but we can pray for a creative solution." Abigail paused for a moment and then said, "Maybe you can hang onto it and just use it to help her out with groceries or bills."

Carrie Sue gave a short laugh, "I could just drop a twenty in her purse every now and then when she's not looking and she'd never know where it came from. She's so scattered most of the time."

They moved to other subjects and then Abigail told Carrie Sue that she needed to go back to the bottom of the pasture and then fill up the water trough for Buster. "Feel free to come out with me or kick back up here," she invited.

Carrie Sue chose to stay in the house. Abigail unreeled the hose and started to fill the water trough before she went to the end of the pasture. She had already purchased another two-step ladder so she could leave one down by the lower camera. The new fiberglass one would not rot like her old wooden one would have. By the time she came back up, the trough was full enough so she turned the water off and rewound the hose. That was still not her favorite chore even with the crank-handled unit which neatly stored the hose.

The rest of the day was spent doing little chores together. Sometimes Carrie Sue went to her room and tried to take a nap. She was disturbed about Billy and kept turning a multitude of troubling thoughts over in her mind.

Abigail refilled the wood rack on the front porch before the rains started coming. There was a buildup of towering thunderheads in the west. Abigail loved to watch the storms come across the fields but she was a little uneasy today, especially since the lights had already flickered from time to time. She was hoping that she would not lose electricity. *Oh, Lord, I pray for Your protection over us all.*

She went to the closet and pulled out candles. She went down to the basement where she gathered two lanterns and the bottle of lantern oil. *Pray for the best. Prepare for the worst.*

Abigail popped left over quiche into the oven in the late afternoon. There was enough salad left over from the previous night. It would be a simple meal, but nutritious. The winds were getting stronger. Gusts blasted small limbs and leaves out of the trees. She happened to glance at the clock on the stove at exactly six o'clock.

It went dark.

The electricity went off for about a minute and flickered back on before remaining off.

Carrie Sue hurriedly groped her way out of her room about that time. "I don't like storms."

"I don't like them this strong." They could hear the rain drops pecking at the back door and windows. It was quite dark especially without the yard light.

"It's the end of October, so I'm not expecting a tornado, but these winds can do a lot of damage." She was praying in the Spirit as she placed one of the lanterns on the kitchen table. She put the other one on the end table in the living room. After finding a small flashlight for Carrie Sue, she used her own little flashlight to find the matches in the junk drawer in the kitchen. She had several candles that came in jars with lids. They placed one in each bathroom and one in each bedroom just in case they needed them later.

"The quiche is as ready as it'll ever be, let's eat it while it's hot," Abigail suggested.

"We might as well." Carrie Sue was clearly worried but grateful that she was not alone.

"The front will pass and things will calm down." Abigail tried to sound confident. "Hopefully, the crews will be out soon and fix whatever got broken. Maybe a tree fell on a line."

They finished their meal and sat in the living room where they tried to relax. The wind did not die down. They thought they heard hail. Something clattered along the side of the house and they heard a crash in the woods.

"Do you think we should go into the basement?" Carrie Sue asked nervously.

"It might not be a bad idea to set it up in case we really need to. Why don't you grab this lantern and I'll get some candles?" They each took their load down and set them on the workbench.

"I'll be right back with a couple of folding chairs and a couple of blankets. If we need to be here, we might as well be comfy." As she dashed back up the stairs she breathed a prayer. "Lord, is there anything else we might need?" Nothing came to mind, so she returned to the basement door and handed things down to Carrie Sue. They returned to the living room and continued to talk. Neither one was ready to go to bed quite yet.

The battle in the first and second heavens was engaged. Those who were once allies and unified worshipers of the Lord of hosts were now pitted against one another. The Judge and God of all had heard the petitions of the saints. He sent His warriors to defend those in jeopardy. The warriors at the end of the driveway led the battle. Their swords were effective. The guardians positioned to the west of the house were unmovable.

It was ten o'clock p.m. in human time and the daily sacrifices were being prepared in that region. The malevolent chanting of evil men and women invoked curse after curse. They were unleashed like torrents of rain and hail as the messengers were dispatched.

Curses and hexes, spiels and chants were directed at Abigail Steele and Carrie Sue Wagner. They were vicious and incessant. Those women were the cause of all their recent woes. How infuriating that they were being made impotent by women.

Women!

How the demons hated women!

There was an all-out assault on femininity and motherhood. Defile their innocence! Promote their careers! Destroy their unborn! How they were despised! Demons had triumphed over the successful destruction of all the children of these two particular women. One had them torn from the womb. The other lost them in one fell swoop. These demons celebrated the death-days with exultation.

Satan had once petitioned the Great Enemy to destroy Job's family and possessions. He was then permitted to blow their house down. They would do it again; with or without permission. They were focusing their powers on the farmhouse on the hill. The sacred iridescent red surface was shimmering and fluttering like a disturbed pond as the forces of evil bore down on the property.

It was ten o'clock when they heard another crash in the distance but the storm seemed to be abating. The electricity had been off for about four hours, but they were cozy by the wood stove. The lantern cast odd shadows against the walls and ceiling when an occasional draft caused the flame to flicker. "I think it's safe to head for bed," Abigail said. "Let's pray together before we turn in."

"Good idea; I'm whipped," Carrie Sue agreed and they prayed briefly.

"I know I'll be warm enough with my bedroom this close to the wood stove. Feel free to crash on the couch if it starts to get too cold back there." She got up and pulled an extra quilt out of the linen closet for her guest.

"I'll be fine. I'd rather be too cool than too warm."

"Knock on my door if you need anything," Abigail said. She blew out the lantern and then lit the candle in her bathroom and in her bedroom to give her enough light to go through her bedtime routine.

They slept peacefully.

It was nearing midnight. The runaway teenage girl was presented to the high priest. She had been prepared with drugs that rendered her incapable of clear thinking. It did not take these experts long to brain-wash their victims during the preparation weeks. She was in a hypnotic trance. And although mercy was not the goal of any Satanist, her present mental and physical state was merciful. She would be tormented and defiled beyond imagination to the point of near death. She would be used for the insatiable pleasure of men and women. When they finally used her up, they would end her life and gain more demonic power for having done so.

Prinz was wearing his festal robes. His external appearance did not betray his internal cheerlessness. Conducting the ritual flawlessly, he was certain that his king would be pleased. By three a.m. curses were dispatched and the crowd dispersed. There were four more rituals to perform. Each one would be better than the last and by the time Halloween night was finished, Prinz would be vindicated.

This would be the year.

He was sure.

26

Sunday, October 29

Abigail woke up at six-thirty just after sunrise. It was overcast and there was still no electricity. She had gotten up a couple of times to keep the fire going so it was about sixty-five degrees in the living room and about sixty degrees in the kitchen. The back bedroom and bathroom would be even cooler. Grateful for the woodstove, Abigail stoked it up and then donned her jeans and sweatshirt to take care of Buster. She was very curious about the crashes they had heard during the previous night.

She pulled on her boots and grabbed her winter coat off its hook. Today she zipped it up all the way. It was chilly! The first thing that she noticed was the cedar tree near the shed. The once magnificent tree looked as if some giant hand had twisted it off of its trunk and thrown it onto the ground. Approximately eight feet of splintered trunk remained upright in the midst of a jumble of branches. She quickly called for Buster. He nickered from the lean-to.

Thank you, Lord!

Abigail made her way down to Buster and checked him over. He seemed a little bit skittish today so she talked to him and stroked his damp coat. Apparently, he had gone out at some point to graze despite the wind and rain. He settled down quickly after she gave him a measure of sweet feed. Everything was right in his world.

On an impulsive whim, Abigail took the trail a short way through the middle of the woods and saw that a couple of large trees were also twisted off of their trunks. *This is weird.* Abigail had never seen that kind of damage from a wind storm before. Maybe it was a tornado after all. Whatever it was, she and Earl would be busy cutting up firewood again next year.

She decided that she would wait until later to explore more. As she approached the house, she noticed that the gutter on the northwest corner was dangling. The trash cans were blown away from the south side of the house and one of the shutters was off. *That must have been all the clatter we heard.* Her truck and Carrie Sue's car were plastered with leaves. They didn't seem to be damaged, but they would have to do a closer inspection later.

Turning around in a full circle, she tried to assess the damage. Aside from several mutilated trees on all sides of the house and what she had noticed about the house, there appeared to be nothing else damaged. The shingles on the roof were lying flat and were unscathed as well.

"Lord, this *is* peculiar. What happened here last night?" She immediately sensed that the Lord had stationed angels in V shaped lines that went from each corner of the house to a point just beyond the orchard. They diverted the winds and kept the house from being torn apart. She also realized that the winds had come from the large city directly west of her home.

This was more than a storm in the natural realm! She went back into the house feeling very thankful.

Carrie Sue was up and dressed by the time she came back inside. "How bad is it?"

"It looks like Earl and I have some trees to cut up next spring. Other than that, I only saw some minor damage to a gutter and a shutter. The trash cans blew away somewhere, but I'm feeling very blessed and protected by the Lord."

"That's good to hear."

"I'm just sorry about your car, that's all," Abigail said with a straight face.

"What? My car?" Carrie Sue looked stricken until Abigail laughed.

"I'm sorry, I couldn't resist. Your car is fine other than being plastered with leaves. We need to take a closer look, but it seemed to be okay," Abigail was still smiling.

Carrie Sue huffed at Abigail, but underneath it all, she thoroughly enjoyed being able to joke around with someone. "You have to sleep sometime, you know," she fueled the lighthearted moment.

"Truce, truce." Abigail put her hands up.

"Truce," Carrie Sue agreed.

Abigail's stomach rumbled a little and reminded her that they had to figure out what to have for breakfast. "I guess we're having cold cereal or yogurt or fruit or granola bars for breakfast. Are you ready for breakfast?"

"Yes," Carrie Sue replied. "I could go for a little yogurt with some of your granola cereal on it if you still have that kind."

"Coming right up," Abigail said and turned to gather the items for breakfast. "Let's eat in the living room by the wood stove." They settled in their chairs and ate a quiet breakfast.

"Do you think the church has electricity?"

"That's a good question. I think I'd like to go to town and find out. If it's closed we can turn around and come back home. I'm a little curious about the storm damage."

"Me, too," Carrie Sue agreed. "What time do we need to leave?"

"If we're going down the driveway by about nine-thirty, we'll get there in time."

They finished their breakfast. Abigail added more wood to the fire, using some shag bark hickory to make it burn hotter. She would put oak on it before they left so it would burn longer. They went their separate ways to get ready and were soon seated in Abigail's truck and heading down the driveway. There were trees down along the road that Abigail had not seen from the top of her hill. Her neighbors seemed to have been hit pretty hard, too, but the further they got away from Abigail's farm, the less storm damage was evident. It was as if her farm was the target.

The church parking lot was not as full as it usually was. Either people overslept because their alarm clocks did not go off or they thought that the church was not open. Fortunately, this section of the county was fed from a different power line and the town still had electricity.

"I'll sit in the back with you," Abigail offered.

"You don't have to," Carrie Sue countered.

"I'd like to just in case some of the people you saw in the directory come in today. I know Bynum's family usually sits in the balcony, but I'm not sure about the others."

They found a place in the back corner. Abigail secretly wondered whose pew they had usurped. There were invisible name tags on all the pews. Sometimes she liked to move to a different area just to get a little rise out of her fellow-parishioners. She was a bit feisty like that. The service started and Abigail closed her eyes to keep from being distracted during the worship.

After the announcements, Pastor Spalding moved to the platform and turned on his microphone. "Good morning!" he greeted the congregation with enthusiasm. "I trust that the storm didn't do too much damage. I heard that there was a lot of damage east of here." He made a few more comments and then launched into his teaching.

"It's kind of interesting that I'm preaching from the book of Nehemiah. He rebuilt the walls around the city of Jerusalem in only fifty-two days. I suppose he didn't have to wait for permits." The congregation chuckled at his reference to the red tape that slowed down modern construction projects. "I want to very quickly go over some of the things Nehemiah did as a leader that made his construction project successful."

He had them turn to the book of Nehemiah and began to systematically point out what Nehemiah did well. Pages were turning as Pastor Spalding moved through the chapters rather quickly. Soon he had completed his overview.

"I realize that was a very quick overview of the entire book of Nehemiah, so I want to encourage you to go back over it sometime soon. Let me conclude with a list of all the things a good leader does and does not do. Are you ready?" he asked with a mischievous smile. Heads nodded.

"First of all, Nehemiah had a great deal of passion for the project. He mourned, fasted and prayed. He confessed the sins of his people and reminded God of His promises before he asked Him for success and favor with the pagan king. Nehemiah asked for help from the king and from God. Then the first thing he did when he got there was to assess the damage. He laid out the challenge to the leaders and gave specific goals. He shared his testimony about how God gave him favor with the king. He expected opposition and prayed vicious prayers." He paused to check for a reaction on that point before he continued.

"Nehemiah handled criticism that came from his own camp. He set up a guard day and night and had them work with a tool in one hand and a sword in the other while he continued to encourage them. He worked, modeled dedication, didn't abandon his post, and wasn't distracted by internal or external conflict. He knew the law and was discerning. He was prepared to handle false accusations, gossip, and slander. He kept praying and did not give in to scare tactics. He was secure in his own identity. And when the wall was completed, he encouraged the people to occupy the city, live in obedience, and maintain security. He also delegated responsibility to faithful men. Finally, he could throw a party to celebrate."

Pastor Spalding ended with exaggerated panting after his brisk summary. "Folks, I want to invite you to come up for prayer for your leadership decisions. It doesn't matter if you run a business or are the head of your home. Be like Nehemiah and ask for help if you need it for any reason."

The music started playing softly in the background and some people made their way to the front of the church. Abigail and Carrie Sue slipped out the back where they ran into Cindy and Gary.

"Hey, Abigail," Gary said, "I got a call from my cousin, Lee, a couple of days ago. You remember him, right?"

"Sure do; he saw a bunch of drama that Sunday," she replied. She was a little curious, a little excited, and a little confused with her unfamiliar emotional response.

"He asked me to ask you a question and told me to first ask you to pardon his presumptuousness."

"Okay," Abigail said slowly, curiously, "what's the mystery question?"

"He's travelling here with four horses that he doesn't want to part with. He wonders if he can put them in the pasture with Buster for a day or two until he can find a place to board them or rent a pasture." Gary delivered the message and then added, "He said he'd get extra hay and that they were up to date on all their tests and shots and stuff like that."

"Oh, well, uh," Abigail had not expected that and paused a moment. "I don't see where it would be a problem if they were mares - Buster might not want another guy in there with him."

"I'll check to see what they are and get back to you," Gary said.

"Good," Abigail said, "because I really would like to help him out if I can." She did not voice her next thought: *because I really would like to see him again.*

Continuing their conversation, exchanging news, laughing about a few light-hearted anecdotes about Bryan and Traci, they enjoyed the camaraderie.

Abigail told them what the Lord had shown her about the storm.

"Interesting," Cindy responded. "There are still three more ritual days besides today, right?"

"Yes, that's why I'm having Carrie Sue stay with me," Abigail affirmed and smiled at Carrie Sue. "We have put in way too much work to have them snatch it away. I think we can relate to good old Nehemiah with all the opposition and distractions and stuff."

Carrie Sue and Abigail made their way out to the parking lot without running into anyone that would have triggered Carrie Sue. They were both grateful.

"Maybe the power will be back on by the time we get home," Abigail said hopefully. "If not, I'm going to get that wood stove roaring once we get there."

They wound through the town with Abigail being extra vigilant for any vehicles that might be following them. She decided to go straight home and not worry about evading anyone. *Why should I waste my time and gas today?* Besides, she was hungry. Even if the electricity was not on, they could still light the gas stove with matches and cook something.

Carrie Sue pointed to the house when they were half way up the driveway, "It looks like you left your lights on."

"Hallelujah!" Abigail said, "That's a relief!"

The house was warm throughout because of the furnace. A couple of lights were still on so they turned them off and then began to make lunch. After their light lunch they sat in the living room near the wood stove sipping tea.

"I need to ask you something," Carrie Sue ventured.

"Sure," Abigail replied.

"Actually, I have a lot of questions about Billy's disappearance," she paused and looked intently at Abigail and then continued when she got the nod. "Why would Billy's car be up there? Why would they sacrifice him when they were supposed to be grooming him for leadership? Why would the sheriff be looking for him? You know? I mean, none of this makes much sense."

"I have a theory," Abigail offered. "But you have to promise me that no matter what I say, you will not blame yourself for one bit of it or make any rash decisions." She looked just as intently at Carrie Sue and waited for her response.

"I won't. I promise. I know that Billy makes, uh, made his choices."

"Okay then. On the Saturday before the Yom Kippur ritual, my friend, Gary, was working on my truck. He took it to his shop. I was down in the basement straightening stuff up. Someone came into the house and started knocking furniture over in the back bedroom. He probably thought I wasn't home because the truck was gone. But then he came downstairs probably because he heard my radio going. I hid under the steps and when he came down far enough, I grabbed his ankle and he fell hard enough to be knocked out. When he tried to stand up, I kicked his knee and took him out. By that time Gary had come back with my truck and he watched him until Sheriff Bynum got here. Gary pulled his wallet out of his pocket and got his name." Abigail paused to let Carrie Sue connect the dots.

"Billy?" she said in shock. "Billy came in here and did that?" Her voice trailed off. "Why ..."

"Yes, he was probably sent on a little mission by the cult. You remember how your father was going downhill, don't you?"

Carrie Sue nodded.

"I think either he or someone above him sent Billy on a mission to mess with me. I would guess that all the masters and others who had significant input in your torment and programming are also losing their powers. We're messing up their plans."

"I had no idea; I mean, I believe everything you told me and I saw dad go downhill just like you said, but I didn't think about what it might do to all the others." Carrie Sue frowned as she processed this information and the implications.

Abigail continued, "He was supposed to be in court on that day that the sheriff was looking for him. I was there and he didn't show. No one told me anything, but the judge gave an order to a sheriff so I assume it was an arrest order for contempt or no-show or whatever it was that ticked off the judge."

"But why would he leave his car up there?"

"I don't know. Don't forget his leg was pretty messed up. You said that he needed an operation. I would imagine that he wasn't about to say, 'hey Dad, can you give me a ride to get my car from where I left it when I screwed up that mission.'"

Carrie Sue gave a weak chuckle, "No, I guess not. He sure wouldn't ask me either."

"So, the best I can guess is that he went to the ritual with your folks and had hoped to get it then."

"What do you mean?" Carrie sue was confused.

Abigail was taken aback a little, "Don't you know where that ritual took place?"

"I never know where they are," Carrie Sue said, "they either have that stupid hood over my head or they have some other part of me switched in. It's dark and I always seem to get drugged somehow so nothing seems real anyway."

"Oh. Well, then, here's a shocker for you. I went for a ride across the road about a month ago and explored some of the trails along the fields to the south and went up a hill toward the road hoping to see who lived up there. I found a pentagram shaped rock up there." Abigail did not want to give specific details to avoid the risk of implanting ideas in Carrie Sue's mind. "Apparently, one of my neighbors about a mile down the road is a Satanist." She let the news settle in for Carrie Sue.

Carrie Sue had enough internal information from healed and integrated personalities who had been to the rituals. Even though she did not "personally" experience them or "own" the experiences, she still assimilated the knowledge and knew that it was true. "So then, I was at rituals just down the road from you?" She paused and let that disconcerting thought sink in.

"I see pictures in my head like that … the rock …" She made hand gestures that roughly matched the dimensions of the rock Abigail had seen. "And I remember a huge tree at the top of the hill. There were always lots of people coming up on horses or four-wheelers. And I remember a barn …." Carrie Sue shuddered involuntarily.

They remained silent for a few minutes as Carrie Sue remained deep in thought. "Are you okay?" Abigail asked.

"Are *you* safe? I mean, if a nearby neighbor is a Satanist aren't you in danger? If Billy was sent here to hurt you, won't they send someone else? Is that why you're always looking in your rear-view mirror? Oh, it's all my fault!"

Abigail tilted her head and raised her eyebrows as she rebuffed the unsettled woman sternly but with a smile, "You broke your promise."

Carrie Sue was distressed thinking that she was responsible for her friend's troubles. "If you didn't know me, they would just leave you alone."

"Not true! You are not my only SRA survivor. I'm working with a couple of people who also fall under the regional master in the big city. Besides, I've been doing this for a few years and it is my choice to be in ministry. These momentary, light afflictions shall not be compared to the glory waiting for me some day."

"I still don't like it," Carrie Sue grumbled.

"So, let's get back to Billy," Abigail suggested. "He apparently displeased the masters and was taken out. You know it's a dog-eat-dog world. Someone always has to pay."

Carrie Sue nodded. "So, what do you think we should do about his car?"

"Is it worth anything to you or your mom?"

"Not to me, but maybe Mom could sell it and get something for it." Carrie Sue suddenly giggled at an errant thought, "Mom might need the weed."

Abigail laughed, too. The image of Mrs. Wagner lighting up a joint was humorous just then. "We could put in a call on the anonymous tip line. I'd do it from a pay phone though."

"One more question," Carrie Sue said. "Did my brother kill Dude? Is that why Billy had the dog treats in his car?"

"I don't think it was Billy. He was poisoned though. Gary and his cousin found a container of rat poison. Apparently, they put the poison in some meat that he ate. We found him near the bottom gate."

Abigail did not mention the surveillance cameras, but she was sure that Carrie Sue would have noticed them by now. SRA survivors were some of the most observant people she had ever encountered. Far too many times personalities would switch into executive control and not have any idea about the situation that they just inherited.

They would use every sense they had of necessity to piece together as many clues as possible about their present predicament. Was it day or was it night? Who was with them? What season of the year might it be? Were they in a house or another kind of building? Were they safe or not?

These survivors tried not to make their switching obvious but Abigail was very astute when it came to sensing that a different personality had switched in. She would notice the nonchalant eye movements as they checked out Abigail and her office. She would quickly introduce herself to assure the alter that he or she was safe.

"Well, I'm glad to hear that it wasn't him. I'd want to ki ..., um, slap him myself for doing that to Dude and you. I know you miss your dog."

They continued to talk about more pleasant things. Abigail put an occasional log on the fire. She yawned and eventually went into her bedroom for a short nap. Carrie Sue did the same. Later they met back in the living room where Abigail picked up a book she was reading and Carrie Sue leafed quietly through a magazine. They sipped steaming cups of tea. It was a pleasant way to spend a Sunday afternoon.

Other people were just stirring after their blood-intoxicating orgies of the previous night. Some were attending to the next human sacrifices; others were securing the ritual site and beginning to reassemble the various implements and animals.

The young man who was to be featured at the ritual tonight fought the drugs that were regularly being injected into his system. Dr. Bacchus supplied them with the necessary drugs and medical supplies. The young man was angry. He was repentant. He wept. He bargained with God. He demanded to see his girlfriend. He suspected that he would never see her again. He suspected that he would eventually share her fate, whatever that was. He begged to be released so he could go home.

He would not tell.

No, he would never tell.

The robotic attendants were accustomed to these weaklings. Did they not know that it was an honor to be chosen? They continued to prepare their naked bodies so that they would be presentable. Their own masters must be pleased or they, too, would suffer. They did not apprehend the double standard.

Urdang and his entire hierarchy were madly circling and swooping in the second heavens. These days were the culmination of the autumn season and they anticipated escorting many accursed souls to their final destiny.

Occasionally one would dart toward the earth and afflict one of the Great Enemy's image-bearers. A filthy fiend would whisper lewd thoughts into another believer's ear. The image-bearers did not suspect that their own voices could be imitated. Others stood on their doctrines. "Demons can't put thoughts into our minds," they would insist.

Demons screeched their dark mirth as they did their utmost to kill and steal, deceive and destroy. "We got King David to number the people! We got Ananias and Sapphira to lie to the Holy Spirit!"

27

Monday, October 30

Monday dawned shrouded in heavy clouds. Abigail lazily stretched as she debated as to whether or not she wanted to get up or try to get a little more sleep. She was frustrated that she was too tired to get up and too awake to go back to sleep.

Her mind began to process the conversations of yesterday afternoon and she drifted to the unwelcome thoughts about her family. *Ten years tomorrow.* For some reason this was a more difficult year than usual; maybe because it was ten years. She tried to picture what Darryl would have looked like by now. The gray at his temples would probably have invaded the rest of his hair. The boys would be shaving. They might have girlfriends.... Abigail did not want to go down that road right now. Pulling herself back into the present, she pulled back the covers and headed to the bathroom and began her day.

Carrie Sue slept fitfully again. She had nightmares nearly every time she fell asleep. That was one reason she resisted sleep. Sometimes they were nightmares. Sometimes they seemed much more like flashbacks. Sometimes the other personalities would leak their memories, especially if they were triggered by a date or some programmed or unprogrammed prompt. Last night's nightmares centered on Halloween and All Hallows Eve and other demon revels.

Carrie Sue gathered her things and got ready to take a shower. Glancing at the photographs on the wall, she felt a pang of sadness because of her friend's tragic losses. She did not know how long ago they had died. The older two had a strong resemblance to their father, but the youngest one definitely favored Abigail. The Bible talked about life being a whisper, like a blade of grass or a flower. It did not seem like it to her when there were so many heart-rending events.

After Abigail took care of Buster, she began to set things out for breakfast. Carrie Sue was still in the shower but was soon finished and joined Abigail in the aromatic kitchen.

"Hot tea?" Abigail offered.

"Thanks; that sounds good. I could sure use some caffeine this morning."

"One of these days you will get healed and have no more nightmares," Abigail tried to encourage the sleep deprived woman. "Do you think that parts are being triggered because of tonight's rituals?"

"That must be what's going on because that's all I dreamed about last night," Carrie Sue said with hint of disappointment.

"We have all day so why don't we plan on setting some time aside to work?"

"I hate to make you work on your short six-day weekend," she said with a slight grin.

"I know it'll be hard to go to work Friday with only a two-day weekend, but I think I can handle it," Abigail said with mock seriousness.

After clearing the breakfast dishes, they settled down in the living room to address the personalities who were created for the All Hallows Eve rituals. Carrie Sue and Abigail were both relieved that the leader of the group as well as all the personalities who were a part of that group were weary of Satanism. They had been peeking in on some of the previous sessions and saw the impact that the healing had on those groups. They wanted the same thing. Within an hour most of them had been saved, healed, delivered, and integrated.

The ones that remained had peculiarities that were not covered in the prayer that Abigail and Carrie Sue prayed for the group. It was a consistent pattern that Abigail had recognized in all of her SRA survivors. Some of the parts had to deal with pregnancies that were terminated at various stages of gestation. Some of them had to deal with other traumas that brought them to the edge of death. There always seemed to be those that had been subjected to crucifixion, drowning, hanging, suffocation, or burial. One of the little ones was thrown into a freezer naked. Not one of them escaped sexual encounters with men, women, goats, and/or demons. There was no end to the depravity and perverseness to which they were exposed.

Abigail prayed with each one. She was humbled by the call on her life to participate with the Lord in the healing of these amazing survivors. Abigail was able to understand Jesus in more profound ways through the eyes of these broken-hearted ones. When they went back into the memory, Abigail asked Jesus to manifest in that memory.

A little one named Kizzie was put into a coffin and buried. She felt herself beginning to black out. She became conscious again in the memory and saw Jesus with her spiritual eyes. She reported, "He was there and He was glowing so it wasn't dark and scary anymore. He kept blowing into my face so I could breathe."

There were similar stories from each part who described how Jesus was with them and kept them alive. Soon they were all healed and integrated. Carrie Sue described a deep sense of peace. "I didn't realize how restless I was. I think a bunch of them would have tried to get to tonight's ritual somehow." Her brows furrowed, "Do you think that they'll be having it down the road?"

"I don't know, but I suppose that if we hear four-wheelers after dark, we can assume they are heading over there. I'd think that for a ritual this important they would have it at a regional site."

"Yeah, that makes sense. I'd just as soon not think about a ritual going on less than a mile away." Carrie Sue caught her breath and said, "Are you sure we're safe here?"

"Absolutely," Abigail said with conviction. "The Lord has stationed His angels around us. The blood of Jesus Christ and the word of our testimony overcome the enemy - both in the spiritual realm and the natural realm. Think about it: Billy wanted to hurt me and he got hurt. The guy who poisoned Dude didn't get on the property but did manage to lure Dude to the fence to get the poison. That storm should have wiped out the house, but God protected us. The guy who follows me got busted. And there are probably a bunch of other things they tried that I don't even know about that the Lord has stopped." Abigail did not want to mention the cut brake lines.

"Yeah, I guess you're right," Carrie Sue took a deep breath. "If you don't mind, I'm tired. I think I'd like to take a nap."

"Sweet dreams," Abigail said with a smile. "That was hard work. I'll just be doing my little projects."

Prinz was feeling more powerful as he orchestrated and participated in the recent rituals. He anticipated more of the same for tonight and the ones that followed. He had sired many children over the years. They currently ranged in age from infants to adults. As their father, he had the authority to make covenants which gave him increased demonic power. There was no natural paternal affection. He did not care that he caused his offspring to be excessively demonized, programmed, abused, and sometimes sacrificed. They were simply the means to an end. Just as the Great Enemy's image-bearers looked forward to rewards in the next world, so he was working toward his own rewards. Rewards meant power and privilege. That was his ultimate goal.

Tonight, Prinz was surrounded by his leaders. They were all wearing their robes. Sinister eyes peered out from under dark hoods. The various implements of torture had been arranged as meticulously as any church laid out its furniture, baptismal pools, and other items that enhanced worship. The young man had been properly prepared, but he still had some fight left in him. His untimely death was particularly grisly. Satanists believed that extreme diabolical and vicious torment attracted the more powerful demons. They craved that kind of power and Prinz was no exception.

Yet again the activities of the ritual crescendoed. Demons were duly granted to the feverish throng. Messengers once again tried to deliver the curses to the farmhouse on the hill. Again, they were rebuffed by the superior forces of the Great Enemy and the lack of cause. Toward dawn, the human assembly removed any evidence of their presence. Returning home spiritually energized and physically depleted, they eagerly anticipated Halloween night.

28

Tuesday, October 31

Abigail woke up at her usual early hour on Halloween morning. She despised Halloween for several reasons. It was the forever anniversary of the death of her husband and their three sons. It was a day in which the Satanists would inflict untold damage to so many people. And she was also upset that most believers did not know about or, perhaps, forgot the early Christian celebrations and focused on trick-or-treating instead.

She was glad that she lived in a rural area where she could turn off her lights and pretend that she was not at home so no one would come knocking at her door. She felt somewhat hypocritical since she had worn costumes and gone trick-or-treating as a child with her brothers. Back then, it was a merely a time to plunder the neighbors for candy while dressed in their benign costumes. Hobos and clowns, cowboys and Indians were popular back then.

When she became involved in counseling Satanic Ritual Abuse and Witchcraft Ritual Abuse survivors, she stayed away from it as much as possible. She avoided going into stores that were decorated with witches and goblins, ghosts and skulls.

At least the day dawned a little brighter than Monday and Abigail was grateful that there would be sunshine today. She would have had a more difficult time if it was as gloomy on the outside as she felt on the inside.

"Lord, I miss my guys. Abba, Father, I have prayed this so many times and I'm praying it again: I don't get it and I don't like it, but I choose to trust that You will redeem and recompense for all that the enemy has stolen from me. Show me Your glory."

She and Carrie Sue had fallen into somewhat of a morning routine which would likely continue until she went home on Thursday. Five ritual days in a row was brutal. When Abigail finished feeding Buster she stacked more wood in the holder on the front porch. Carrie Sue was out of the shower by that time so Abigail started breakfast. She knew that Carrie Sue was still a bit of a people-pleaser and would eat almost anything that was prepared. This was a good day for a steaming bowl of oatmeal. She liked to add raisins and cinnamon while it cooked and then top it off with a little brown sugar and too much butter. *Yum!*

She heard Carrie Sue's cell phone ring and could hear Carrie Sue's end of the conversation.

"I'm okay, Mom. I've been staying with a friend."

"I'm sorry; I didn't mean to worry you. I didn't think you would stop by."

Carrie Sue was getting a little more defensive, "No, you don't know her."

Carrie Sue listened to her mother for several minutes before saying, "Mom, you aren't going to lose all your children."

She wandered into the kitchen pointed to the phone and mouthed "Mom" before she went back into her bedroom and eventually ended the tense conversation.

"Is everything all right?" Abigail asked. She noticed a slight shift in Carrie Sue's demeanor and wondered if her mother might have used a word that triggered programming or caused another personality to begin to emerge.

"Apparently the mom has been driving by my place the last couple of days. She is worried that she'll lose all her kids and be totally left alone. Isn't that interesting? Now that my brothers are gone she finally pays attention to me."

"Brothers?" Abigail asked. "I thought Billy was your only brother."

"No, I had an older brother. He's been dead a few years. I don't think about him very much. We didn't exactly have a loving brother-sister relationship," she said ruefully.

"Did he … I mean … did the cult take him out, too?" Abigail asked.

"No, actually, he died in a wreck. Maybe they made it happen. Who knows? I remember someone saying something about his brakes failing. But he was always driving too fast."

That startled Abigail. She thought about her own cut brake lines.

Carrie Sue continued, "I think he was trying to get out of the cult. He was the oldest and was supposed to carry on the family tradition, but he was a drunk." Carrie Sue had never talked about her older brother to anyone before. Many of the personalities in her system did not know him. Those that did know him hated him. Even though he did not want to rise within the cult, he still preyed on Carrie Sue and caused her to fragment into additional personalities.

"I'm sorry. I had no idea," said Abigail just before frowning. "Actually, this is confusing; I don't know if I'm glad or sad about your brother. It's sad that his life was so dismal, but I'm glad that he's not around to torment you."

"Yeah," Carrie Sue said, "it's a lot easier in your case. I was looking at the pictures of your family and there is no doubt that it's sad and seems like such a waste. It's not fair. How long has it been?"

"It was ten years ago today."

"I'm really sorry," Carrie Sue said and then looked distressed. "Are you sure you want me to be here?"

"Absolutely. It's nice to have someone around. I'm glad you're here."

The oatmeal was ready so they sat down to eat. Both of them were lost in their own private thoughts. Abigail cleaned up the kitchen when they had finished their breakfast. Carrie Sue still seemed a little edgy and said that she would be in her room.

Abigail would have to find out what was bothering her whenever Carrie Sue was ready. It was probably a combination of things - her mother's phone call, the conversation about her brother and his death, and then there was Halloween programming. It was a lot for one person to sort through.

Abigail's thoughts were interrupted by her own phone ringing. Recognizing Cindy's number, she greeted her best friend, "Good morning, my friend." Cindy was the sister she never had.

"Good morning to you, too, my friend. I wanted to see how things are going with you." Cindy was never one to hedge, "I know it's the anniversary and I just want to keep tabs on you. Are you doing all right?"

"I am. This year is just a little tougher because it's been ten years. I woke up wondering if a large portion of our budget would be going for shaving cream and razors … if they would be making plans for college or marriage … if they'd be jealous of my fine ride …" Abigail tried to lighten up the conversation.

"I wish I could fix it," Cindy said.

"I got my morning cry and complaint session with the Lord finished already. I'm so glad that David said in that Psalm that he complained morning and noon and night. I can relate. I will get through this. I will trust the Lord even when I don't know the end from the beginning."

"I'm so proud to be your friend. You should write a book."

"Right. I'll call it 'Character-Building 101 - Don't Flunk It Because You'll Have to Repeat It.'" They laughed lightly together.

"How is it going with Carrie Sue?"

"Great. We took a ride on Buster. I showed her where I found her brother's car. I'll have to talk to you and Gary about that later. We've done a couple of sessions and gotten good healing. Pray for us today. Her mom called and I think something got triggered. I'm not sure if it's programming for tonight or if some part got triggered by the mom. Anyway, she's been a bit on edge since the call."

"You got it," Cindy agreed. "Oh, by the way, I thought you might be interested to know that Gary's cousin, Lee, called him over the weekend and he has decided that he is definitely moving out this way. He's going be coming sometime in the next week to start looking at property."

"That's what Gary said when he asked about the horses. I'm glad he made his decision. It seemed that it was weighing on him from what I remember of the conversation. That will be nice for Gary, you know, having his cousin around again. I got the impression that they got along well."

"Yeah, Gary is excited," Cindy paused and then changed the subject. "Sorry, I need to referee a couple of short people. Call me if you need to - seriously, any time of day or night."

"I will, but I'll be fine," Abigail could hear Traci and Bryan bickering in the back ground, "bye."

Sitting for a moment and considering what she would do next, she finally drifted into her office and dropped to her knees in front of the tan four-drawer metal filing cabinet that she inherited from her dear grandmother. She tugged on the bottom drawer and pulled it all the way open. For some reason she felt compelled to dig out the old accident report.

Important papers and documents that were seldom used ended up in this drawer. There was a file for the manuals that came with appliances and tools that she would never read. There were old documents for the purchase and sale of cars and houses. Looking past the genealogy file that contained her sons' heritage from both sides of the family, she found the manila envelope that contained the accident report.

"Abigail?" Carrie Sue called.

"I'm back here; I'll be right there," Abigail called back and set the envelope down on her desk and found Carrie Sue in the living room.

"Can we pray? I'm feeling so nervous. I feel like I just want to run."

"We sure can. Did that start after your phone call with your mom?" Abigail asked.

Carrie Sue thought for a minute. "Yeah, I think so. I don't know why that should have bothered me so much. I mean, she's aggravating, but we didn't talk about anything weird that I remember."

"Let's pray and ask the Lord to take us to the root of this nervousness." Abigail led the prayer and then waited quietly for Carrie Sue to let her know what thought or what memory came to her.

"I think it has something to do with my oldest brother. I don't know, I'm just feeling responsible or guilty and I have no idea why."

Abigail was accustomed to hearing similar things from her survivors. The host personality would quite often feel the feelings or think the thoughts of other personalities who had not yet made their presence known. She took a calculated chance and addressed the unknown part, "Is there anyone who knows about these feelings or anyone who has something to do with your brother?" She waited silently for several seconds.

Carrie Sue's head dropped and she shifted self-consciously in her chair before she drew her knees up to her chin. "I do," a soft child-like voice answered.

"Can you tell me about it?" Abigail said gently. "You're safe here and you are not in trouble."

"My daddy said that I would be in big trouble if I ever told," the little one said sadly. She was caught between the threat of the father and the need to be released from the pain that she was carrying.

"Do you know that your daddy died a couple of weeks ago?" Abigail asked.

"No, he's not dead. I see him all the time. He's telling me right now that I need to be quiet," the little one insisted.

"Okay," Abigail said, "I don't want to get you into trouble, but I think I can find a way to help you feel better if you would let me."

"How?"

"I can ask the real Jesus to let you know some things that will help you feel better. Do you know the real Jesus?"

Her eyes widened in alarm and she blurted, "He's bad! Daddy said that He's bad."

"I know you love your daddy, but he tricked you. There's a pretend Jesus and there's the real Jesus. Your daddy didn't want you to know the real Jesus."

Abigail had had variations on this conversation with innumerable alters in hundreds of survivors. The survivors' worlds had been restricted to exposure to Satanism only, but they were led to believe that they had comprehensive knowledge. The child alters also had an enormous need to believe that their daddy and mommy were good and would never lie to them. They also experienced or witnessed the consequences of disobedience. Double-binds and duplicity training abounded to keep them locked down.

The little one sat there indecisively. She was feeling the tension between her experience and her intuition. But did she dare trust this woman with the soft brown eyes? Tears were brimming in her eyes and her chin quivered as she looked at Abigail. "I didn't know there were two Jesuses."

"Would it be okay if I ask the real Jesus to let you see Him?"

"I would be scared."

"How about if I ask Him to let you see Him from far enough away that you still feel safe?"

Deciding to take a chance, she said, "I think that would be okay. What do I have to do?"

"I'll ask Him. You close your eyes and just look around inside and then you can tell me what you see." Abigail could tell that the little one was not quite sure about why Abigail couldn't see as clearly into the spiritual realm as she did.

"Okay," she said uncertainly.

"Jesus, the real Jesus Christ of Nazareth, would You come right now and reveal Yourself to this little one in such a way that she feels safe. Thank You, amen." Abigail waited quietly for a few moments.

The little girl's eyes soon opened wide and she exclaimed, "He's got kind eyes like yours. That's not the Jesus my daddy told me about." She let her legs down and sat up straighter.

"I'm sorry that your daddy tricked you about that. I have a feeling that he probably tricked you about other things, too."

"He tricked my brother."

"Is that what makes you feel so bad?" Abigail took a not-so-wild guess.

"Uh huh," she replied.

"Can you tell me about it?" Abigail noticed her shift uncomfortably and look toward the ceiling. "Is that daddy guy bothering you?"

"Uh huh," she nodded.

"Why don't we ask the real Jesus to keep you safe from getting into trouble? I have a sneaking hunch that the daddy that you are seeing is another trick."

The little one considered that briefly and then nodded her head.

"Jesus, would You take the mask off of the daddy guy and keep this little one safe from him?"

The little girl startled as she saw something that was not visible to Abigail. "Ooh!"

Abigail could visualize the disguise coming off of a demon that masqueraded as the dad and exposing the hideous being that he was. "Shall we ask Jesus to get rid of him?"

"Yes!" she vigorously nodded.

"Jesus, we plead Your blood over this demon that has been tormenting this little girl. We ask that You would send it to a place where it can never hurt anyone ever again. Would You please let Your Holy Spirit fill up the place where it was assigned?" She paused and then asked, "How's that?"

She took a deep breath and said, "Good."

"Do you feel safe enough to tell me about the stuff that's bothering you?"

She nodded and then began to tell Abigail about a past Halloween day. "Daddy said it was trick-or-treat day and he wanted to trick Danny because he drives his car too fast. He went down on the ground next to Danny's truck and used a tool to do something. It looked like a funny kind of scissor. He did it on both sides and when he was all done he gave me a big wink and said that it was our secret. And if I didn't tell Danny, I would get a treat. Daddy laughed and said that Danny gets a trick and I get a treat." Then she put her head down and looked like she was going to cry again.

"What happened?" Abigail asked.

"Danny got into his truck after supper and drove away fast like he always does. He got in a bad wreck and died. I think Daddy broke his truck," she broke into tears. "I should have told Danny but I wanted the treat. I didn't know he would get dead. It's all my fault," she wailed.

"Why is it your fault if your daddy did it?" Abigail asked gently.

"Daddy said that if I didn't want the treat so bad my brother would be alive still. But he told me not to tell …" she trailed off in the confusion of the double-bind that her father set up.

"Let's ask Jesus to help you with this, okay?"

"Uh huh."

"Jesus, You were there that day. This little one is feeling like it's her fault that her brother died. Would You please let her see You with her spiritual eyes or hear You with her spiritual ears or sense Your presence in that memory? Please bring her the truth that will set her free." Abigail remained silent while the little one closed her eyes and peered into her past.

Finally, she opened her eyes and wiped tiny tears from the corners of her eyes and gave Abigail a small smile. "I saw the real Jesus by my brother's truck. He looked sad when He looked at me but He looked mad when he looked at Daddy. He shook his finger at my daddy because he was being naughty."

"Do you still think it was your fault?"

"Nope," she shook her head decisively, "it was Daddy's fault. He tricked me too." She hesitated again and then said in a tiny voice, "his treat wasn't nice … he made me …." Her voice trailed off as she made a face like any child would after being forced to swallow something distasteful.

"Let's ask Jesus to take away those yukky feelings, too." Abigail prayed a simple prayer asking Jesus to release this little one from all the body memories associated with this trauma.

"I'm okay now," she announced. "I'm tired."

"You had a really tough job and I know that Carrie Sue is grateful that you carried that terrible memory for her so she and all the others didn't have to. Do you think you are ready to go back inside where you came from?"

"Uh huh."

Abigail prayed a thorough prayer that covered this part's memories and then asked Jesus to reknit her back inside where she rightfully belonged. When she said amen, Carrie Sue was back.

"So that's why I felt so messed up about Danny's death. Wow! Dad was so evil! How could a man do that to his own kids?" She shook her head as she continued to process this new information.

"Do you still feel like you want to run?"

"No. I'm calm. Thanks. You don't know how much I appreciate this."

"Well, you relax for a while. I think we still have some more work to do because of tonight's and tomorrow's rituals. I'm going to just check emails and write my bills and whatever.

"I don't know why you do what you do, but I'm really grateful."

Abigail's lips formed a soft smile, "I guess my worst fear is insignificance. A missionary named William Borden once said, 'No reserve, no retreat, no regrets.' I want to be able to say that, too. I want to leave a great big spiritual footprint on this earth so everyone will know that I was here with an eternal purpose. It's not about me; it's about God and His kingdom."

Abigail got up and returned to her office. Seeing the envelope, she picked it up again and played with the fastener. She was not sure that she wanted to go through it right then, so she set it back down and checked her emails. The afternoon passed quickly.

Lunch was grilled cheese sandwiches and tomato basil soup. Dinner was a pot roast with potatoes and carrots. It would be a very cool evening so Abigail began to stoke up the wood stove after she returned from taking care of Buster.

"Okay," Abigail said to Carrie Sue, "I think it's time to do some more praying for any parts that might be affected by the rituals tonight and tomorrow."

Carrie Sue agreed. They found their comfortable chairs in the living room once again. The Halloween personalities were called the Trick-or-Treaters. There were thousands of them that had been created over the decades. A representative personality described a ritual in which there were several other children who were also from cult-loyal families. They were each given a choice of receiving a trick or a treat. She observed that those who chose the treat were given some tasty food, but they would soon become very drowsy. Once they fell asleep, an adult would carry them off behind a curtain.

She decided that she would choose a trick instead so she was brought to the curtain that had three ropes hanging in front of it. She did not know what was behind the curtain. She was given the choice of pulling one of three ropes to receive her prize. She chose the middle rope. When she pulled it, the curtain opened revealing three small dazed children sitting in chairs. A large blade suddenly fell from behind the curtain and sliced through the child sitting in the middle chair. The gleeful adults taunted her, "You chose the wrong rope. You murderer! Go on! Pick up your treat."

There were many other memories that involved diabolical variations on the trick-or-treat theme. The personalities were riddled with intense emotions and it took several hours for Abigail to negotiate the healing that they so desperately needed. Finally, each one of them was healed, delivered, and ready to be integrated back inside.

They took a few minutes for a bathroom break and a snack before they delved into the November first Satanist high holy day ritual. There were more pain-ridden personalities. Within an hour the Lord had ministered to these groups of alters as well. It was good work; it was hard work, and Carrie Sue was exhausted. She thanked Abigail and went to her room for the night.

Abigail returned to her office and intended to finish writing out the bills. The envelope caught her eye. She kept being drawn to it for some reason today. Sighing as she sat down, deciding to take a quick look before she returned it to its place, she gently shook the papers onto her desk top and began to sort through them with no particular goal in mind.

There were newspaper clippings and condolence cards, funeral notices and life insurance policies, receipts and several legal papers. The accident report was near the bottom. She had never had a reason to look at it very closely before but tonight she wanted to know who the officer was that worked the scene. To her great relief it was not Sheriff Bynum. Zorroz. Her eyes then fell on the name of the driver who was charged with a DUI.

Daniel W. Wagner.

Abigail shook her head and blinked her eyes and stared at the name and checked the address. Daniel W. Wagner. It was the same address as Billy's. *O Lord! Carrie Sue's brother killed my family? No! Her father killed my family!*

She was in a bit of a shock as she pondered the convoluted implications of this discovery. How ironic, then, that Abigail's work with Carrie Sue was the catalyst for her bio-father's demise! *It's gone full circle. God, I don't know what to think!*

Abigail had to clear her head. Moving to her closet, finding her gloves, stocking hat, and scarf on the shelf, she grabbed her coat and went out onto the back deck. Drawing in the cool air, she released it in a little cloud that quickly dissipated.

It was quiet outside. Most of the crickets and frogs had retired for the season. A half-moon was partially hidden behind clouds. Buster nickered his greeting and went back to his grazing. Somewhere beyond the pasture and beyond the field in the deep darkness of the woods along the river Abigail picked up the faint sound of four-wheelers making their way along the trails. She ached knowing what that meant and wept before her Lord while the fury of Satan reverberated in the raucous shrieks of his minions somewhere beyond the first heavens.

Somewhere deep in her spirit she heard the words that sounded like they might have come from the book of Revelation, *"Behold, the tabernacle of God is among men, and He'll dwell among them, and they'll be His people, and God Himself shall be among them, and He'll wipe away every tear from their eyes; and there shall no longer be any death, or mourning, or crying, or pain; the first things have passed away. But for the cowardly and unbelieving and abominable and murderers and immoral persons and sorcerers and idolaters and all liars, their part will be in the lake that burns with fire and brimstone, which is the second death."*

"Lord, I'm overwhelmed." It was the only prayer that Abigail could breathe at that late hour. She went back inside and prepared for what she hoped would be a good night's sleep. Tomorrow would be the fifth ritual day in a row and there were sure to be loose ends that needed to be tied up with Carrie Sue. She turned out the lights, banked the fire, and crawled into bed in her cozy pajamas.

The star of the morning, the son of the dawn was disguised as an angel of light as he plunged from his domain in the second heavens through the earth's atmosphere and suddenly appeared at the first of his many stops for that night. He was not omnipresent, but he was swift and determined to grace as many gatherings as possible on this great celebration night.

It did not matter if it was called Hoo Doo or Voo Doo, Witchcraft or Satanism, Umbanda or Macumba, Kabala or Black Mass. They were his worshipers. It was his night. He dominated it and he would instill the respect and fear that was necessary to build his kingdom. He must fulfill his destiny to overthrow his Great Enemy.

It was midnight in Hawaii. What a choice place to start. That state was rededicated to him by political leaders in a so-called healing ceremony to repair the damage done to Hawaii by Christianity. From there he and his entourage stopped at several islands before entering the next time zone as the minute hand ticked from 11:59 to midnight. He surged through Cairns, Darwin, Pyonpyang, Tokyo, Shanghai, and Hong Kong before he swept into the next time zone. He skyrocketed and plunged as he met the assemblies in Astana, Islamabad, and New Delhi. He escalated his pace as he crisscrossed mountains and oceans, countries and states. He ricocheted through key cities where brides were presented for his pleasure. They were surely wrinkled, spotted, and blemished.

On and on the corrupted one soared as the midnight hour struck each new time zone - Kabul, Tehran, Moscow, Baghdad, Jerusalem, Damascus, Bucharest, Minsk, Rome, Tripoli, London, Monrovia, Dakar, Roykjavik, Sao Paulo, Brasilia, Washington D.C. and the Pentagon. His minions wheeled and circled in and around the rituals.

He swept into the next zone and visited some of the larger and more perverse cities. Detroit was building a temple to worship him. Oklahoma City was hosting an exorcism of the Holy Spirit from a follower of the Great Enemy. He met his ardent followers in Denver, Calgary, Phoenix, Tijuana, Spokane, Las Vegas, and Juneau.

Gathering his strength to finish his race around the planet, having reinforced his new world order, his itinerary ended with a surge through Fairbanks, Anchorage, and one of the Aleutian Islands.

Exhausted, and yet unable to quench his insatiable appetite to kill, steal, and destroy, he finally ascended to the second heavens where he sought rest in his lair.

Prinz was not a happy man. He had put forth his best effort. He had drawn from his vast knowledge and experience in order to attract the attention of his master. Midnight came and went. Three a.m. came and went. He kept up all appearances despite the absence of his anticipated guest of honor.

"That damnable woman!" He vowed vengeance on her and those wretched women that fell under her powers and failed in their assignments. Tomorrow was their All Saints Day. He would show those wretched saints a lesson or two after he gained more power, more status, and more stature. Tomorrow was his Satanist high holy day and this time he would triumph. He was certain.

Prinz contacted Zorroz and ordered him to fetch Susan Wagner since she was the most useful remaining link to Mastiff's daughter now that the miserable men in that family were gone. He gave his instructions and dire warnings for failure to carry out those desires. Zorroz was accustomed to being summoned by Prinz, but he was not accustomed to the slight hint of desperation that he detected in the powerful man.

Was he losing his powers, too?

Were they all?

29

All Saints Day, November 1

It was Wednesday, the day that the Lord had made, and Abigail was looking forward to refreshing herself at church that night. She realized that this could still be a very long day even though she and Carrie Sue had worked hard and gotten good relief for many of her key personalities. But there was still the likelihood that there was some latent programming with which they would have to deal.

Abigail was encouraged by the steady progress that Carrie Sue had made over the last couple of years and Abigail anticipated full recovery from all of the effects of having been abused so severely on a daily basis. Unable to bear the thought of anything but full recovery, she respected these survivors, and was amazed at their tenacity for life, humor, and persistent pursuit of healing. No wonder they were so loyal to those who could effectively minister to them.

Abigail heard the shower running in the bathroom and shook herself from her thoughts. "So, Lord, what are we going to do today?" She answered her own question by throwing back the covers and getting dressed before stoking up the fire, adding water to the kettle on top, and heading outside to tend to Buster. From the far end of the pasture Buster galloped up the incline, tail and mane streaming from his magnificent body, muscles rippling under his thickening coat, majestic head proudly tossing as he slowed, snorting his greeting and impatiently prancing around Abigail as she opened the door to the tack room and scooped out his morning ration from the big barrel. He began blissfully munching his breakfast as soon as it hit the pan and she knew he would have it finished about the time she got back into the house. He would come back from time to time during the day to see if he had overlooked a morsel.

Abigail unsuccessfully resisted the urge to continue dwelling on the myriad of troubling thoughts that had been tumbling through her mind since finding out that Carrie Sue's brother had killed her family ten years ago. Was it a diabolical assignment? Was it purely an alcohol related accident? Was it a chance combination of carelessness and speed? Or did they conveniently blame it on that while the actual cause of the accident was loss of control due to brake failure? And what were the odds that he would be on the same road as her family?

It did happen on the blind curve not far outside of town. Abigail was working with a couple of SRA survivors back then but had not yet started working with Carrie Sue. Of course, it would be reasonable to assume that some or all of those survivors fell under the jurisdiction of the regional and local masters that were likely still in the area. They would likely have felt effects from the healing that some of her counselees experienced back then and somehow orchestrated the accident.

Could they do that?

Unfortunately, she was not as knowledgeable or as skilled in the early days as she was now. Most of the survivors were like Sherry and quit working with Abigail well before getting any significant healing, but there were three women who were quite persistent in their healing before moving out of state.

Carrie Sue greeted Abigail amiably from the kitchen. "Good morning! It's another beautiful fall day." She faltered a little and her eyes misted before continuing, "and I can't tell you how grateful I am to be here today."

"I'm glad you're here, too. I've invested too much time and energy to let the jerk-face Satanists take any territory back from you. Besides, it's nice to hang out and have a gab fest with someone other than Buster." Abigail flashed a quick smile before bending over to take off her boots.

Carrie Sue was busy heating the water for their morning cup of tea.

"Hey, what do you have a taste for?" Abigail asked as she came into the kitchen. "I am thinking about making an omelet."

"Sounds good," Carrie Sue answered, "what can I do to help?"

They busied themselves gathering a variety of ingredients from the refrigerator and spice cabinet, chopping and dicing, mixing and whipping them into a palate-pleasing aromatic creation. They soon settled down to their breakfast and relished each morsel. At last they pushed back their plates and sipped their steaming cups of tea.

"What do you want to do today?" Carrie Sue asked, hoping that it would include another session.

"I have some bills and paperwork I need to tackle and then I'd like to make sure that we won't have any more surprises later today. Maybe we could plan on a prayer session after lunch. You'd probably have a better idea of the issues that we need to take care of by then." She paused for a moment and then asked, "What would you like to do today?"

Carrie Sue nodded thoughtfully, "That sounds like a good idea. I mean, I'm okay right now, but I sure don't want any surprises either. I'll let you know if I start feeling anything. I'd like to get outside for a while today and maybe take a walk. Of course, I need to start packing, too."

"How about taking another little ride on Buster?" Abigail asked with a mischievous grin.

"Uh, no thanks," Carrie Sue replied, "My butt's sore from the other day, but you feel free."

"You know, I might just do that. It's such a beautiful day, and I know Buster would love to fly through those fields. This brisk weather energizes him. I'll wait for it to warm up a little, though."

They cleaned up the kitchen and went their separate ways. Abigail went into her office and Carrie Sue walked toward the back bedroom to begin packing. Abigail, not hearing Carrie Sue's phone ring or Carrie Sue's end of the conversation, moved through her bills and prepared for her ride on Buster. She would have plenty of time to have a good ride, work up a decent appetite for lunch and time it about right for their prayer session.

Susan Wagner stared at the beeping phone that was still in her hand. She was not entirely sure if she had just made a call or had just answered one. In either case, the phone was making that annoying sound that indicated a call was dropped from the other end. She hung it up and immediately a very self-assured personality switched into executive control as she displaced her. Gathering up her purse, thrusting her arms into her coat, snatching the keys off the hook by the front door, Dorkas swept out of the house.

She swung into the truck as if she had driven it every day of her life. Any of her neighbors who may have witnessed this would have been mystified by the abrupt differences between this confident display and the tentative actions they usually saw.

Heading down the highway, she negotiated the turns that brought her to the road that led due west of the little town of Kingston. That road would connect her with another tortuous road and her destination at the secluded windowless building where she would receive instructions reinforced in ways that only master Satanists could dispense.

"Carrie Sue," Abigail called, "I'm heading out for my ride. Is there anything you need before I go?"

"I'm good. Have fun," Carrie Sue replied coming out of the back bedroom, "I'll finish packing and then I'll probably take a short walk."

"I'll be back by about noon," Abigail said. "We can do lunch and then pray a bit."

"Sounds like a plan. I'm sure that I'll be back way before noon." Carrie Sue returned to the bedroom.

Abigail finished gathering her water, granola bar, and Walther before putting on her boots and jacket. She remembered to grab the SD card from the back-deck camera and went back into the house to take a quick look at all the pictures of herself and Carrie Sue going in and out of the back door. *Well, it's good practice for me, anyway.* She tucked the SD card in her pocket and planned to switch it with the one by the back gate on her way out.

Buster nickered his greeting as she strode across the back yard, slid through the fence, and jogged down to the tack room. They went through their customary routine and were soon walking down to the end of the pasture. Abigail had Buster stop by the camera where she switched out the SD cards before walking over to the gate. *I need to devise a latch that won't involve me getting off of Buster every time.* Abigail dismounted, opened the gate, and remounted the impatient beast. He was as anxious to roam the woods and trails as Abigail was. She often thought that he must get bored with their limited woods and pasture.

She missed Dude.

They broke into a comfortable lope that Buster could maintain for a long time and instead of entering the woods at the far edge of the field, Abigail turned

Buster to the left with a subtle movement of the reins. They headed south along the well-worn trail that bordered the woods and followed field after field for a couple of miles. Encountering a larger creek, they had to slow down to negotiate it. Buster was not a big fan of walking through deep water, but this creek was low right now and it didn't quite come up to his knees. Abigail did not know the name of this creek, but she guessed it ran roughly parallel to York Creek near her house and assumed that it, too, eventually dumped into the Blue River.

Buster seemed eager to continue at their previous pace which suited Abigail. They scared up a deer as they crossed the rough area between fields. Buster seemed unsure of how to react until Abigail nudged him and said, "Let's go!" He kicked his pace into a full gallop and followed the deer. Stunned at the speed of the deer, Abigail watched it quickly pull away and then disappear into the brush and woods.

She slowed Buster down patting his strong neck as he pranced to a walk. The trail narrowed and led through an overgrown area where a dilapidated old house barely stood surrounded by a number of crumbling sheds and other weathered buildings that once made up a homestead. Finally, they came to a gravel road, turned right, and headed slightly west toward the rusty one-lane iron bridge that crossed over one of the main branches of the Blue River.

Abigail stopped Buster in the middle of the bridge and dismounted. Adjusting the cinch and giving her hips and knees a little break, she enjoyed watching the river flow. It calmed her soul. "Oh, Lord, this is the day that You have made and I am rejoicing and being glad in it! I am so blessed and so thankful for so much – friends, church, Pastor Spalding, fulfilling work, Buster, and so much more." Abigail paused and then apologetically added, "But Abba, having someone at the house is reminding me of how alone and lonely I feel sometimes. I'm just saying…."

After praying some more about the Wagner family connection and the mystery that surrounded her family's demise, she continued praying for Amy and some of the other SRA survivors who would most certainly be tortured tonight. Sighing, she remounted Buster, noting the time. "Come on, Buster, we can explore a couple more trails and then we have to head h-o-m-e." She spelled the last word because he really did know that word.

Carrie Sue had already packed her suitcase most of the way so that when she left in the morning it would take a minimal amount of time and effort. She found that she had become much more organized since becoming so much more healed and integrated. She often joked that it was tedious to operate by committee since the dominant personalities seemed to have their own opinion about what was the right way to go about anything and everything.

When she "lost time" because someone else had switched in, she would have had to search for an item that she knew she had put away. It didn't matter if it was clothes, keys, spices, food, or cleaning supplies. Things were constantly being rearranged or lost or else she would come across something that she knew she had not purchased. Did someone else in here buy it? Or did we steal it? Life was becoming less and less mysterious; more and more predictable. Carrie Sue was really looking forward to becoming whole.

Soon!

Grabbing an apple from the bin, she went out the front door and relocked it behind her, knowing that Abigail left the back door unlocked. She did not have a particular goal in mind and so she meandered down the broad front lawn toward the end of the driveway. It reminded her of the last time she went that way on Buster's back and so a germ of an idea sprouted in her mind. *I wonder if I can find my way back to Billy's car to see if it's still there.* Soon she stepped off the property and onto the road looking for the break in the growth where they had stepped through previously.

Urdang shrieked his great delight and summoned his cronies. This was a choice opportunity to get at that woman while she was off of that forbidden property. He looked warily at the sentries which remained stationed at the foot of the driveway. They appeared distressed but did not budge from their assignment.

Carrie Sue had walked through the first field and was half way through the second field when she started feeling uneasy; more uneasy than when she first stepped onto the road. She rationalized that she was just a little nervous about what she might find. Her discomfort subsided somewhat as she breathed a prayer and then continued through the wooded area while crunching the fallen leaves. *I'm almost there.*

Deciding that she was probably on edge because she was not accustomed to being in relatively untamed places, she rationalized that she was a city girl and used to streets and sidewalks and not woods and fields. Soon she broke through the woods and was able to see Billy's car in the distance. Glancing at her watch, she was proud of herself for getting this far in less than thirty minutes. I'll just take a quick look around and then head back. She covered the last hundred yards quickly and was just about to peer into the car when she stumbled badly and was unable to catch herself in time to keep her forehead from striking hard against the driver's side door.

Urdang was proud of his strike at Carrie Sue's feet. He evaded one of her protectors and pounced on her inert back, digging his claws into her ribs and causing her to moan. He sent one of his messengers to guide the mother to Carrie Sue's location.

"Ha, ha!" He screamed with glee, "We have you now." Urdang licked his dry fangs with his hot tongue as he anticipated his rewards for this triumph. They would get to that other woman now!

Susan was guided onto the back road that connected to York Creek Road. Driving rapidly around the bends and hills as if she were on an urgent mission, she passed the ritual site. A mile later she passed that woman's house, and finally, within another mile she neared the abandoned driveway. Slowing to make the turn, she drove up the rutted lane and followed the same tracks that her son had followed about a month ago. She skidded to an abrupt halt just short of Carrie Sue's still form.

Abigail judged that it was about time to head back home so she turned Buster as she softly said, "Let's go home." Buster immediately responded to the light pressure of the rein on his neck and turned around in the trail. They retraced their path and soon the rusty iron bridge, the abandoned homestead, and field after field were far behind them. They entered the pasture through the gate where Abigail dismounted, once again thinking that she needed to come up with a better system for opening and closing the gate. Buster patiently waited for her to close and fasten the gate and moved out just as her right foot was firmly in the stirrup. He had sweet feed, water, and a roll in the dust on his mind.

Unsaddling a sweaty Buster and giving him his expected treat, Abigail went up to the house after finishing a thorough grooming. Stepping into the house and hanging up her coat, she removed her boots, and called out for Carrie Sue. When she did not get an answer, she walked softly down the short hallway to the back bedroom expecting Carrie Sue to be napping.

She was not there.

Oh well, she's probably enjoying her walk and will be here pretty soon. Abigail proceeded to stoke up the fire and made preparations for lunch. Having worked up a good appetite, she hoped that Carrie Sue would return soon. Meanwhile, she used the time to look at the SD card and was relieved to find that there was nothing out of the ordinary on the pictures.

That cult-loyal, demon-driven personality of Susan Wagner, Dorkas, opened the full-sized pickup truck door and jumped down to the ground. She stalked over to Carrie Sue and roughly rolled her onto her back. Carrie Sue moaned and started to come around. She had a hematoma forming over her left eye which was nearly swollen shut.

"Carrie Sue!" Dorkas shouted as she kicked Carrie Sue in the ribs. "Get up!"

Carrie Sue stirred and attempted to sit up. She was dizzy and disoriented and in pain as she tried to focus on the woman who was standing in front of her.

"Mommy?" A child alter, triggered by the sight of the woman and the strange circumstances, switched in. She had no idea of the depth of the peril in which she found herself; she only knew that she wanted her mommy because she was hurt and scared.

Dorkas recognized the switch and used it to her advantage. She stooped and said as soothingly as she could, "Oh, honey, let me help you up. Here, look right here in my eyes and then let's get you in the truck and we can take care of that boo-boo on your head." The eye contact had the desired effect and the little one offered no resistance as Dorkas helped her into the passenger seat of the truck, buckled her in, and drove off spitting dirt and gravel behind them.

David, the protector, was inside screaming, but to no avail. Neither he nor any of the other protectors nor the host Carrie Sue were able to switch back in.

Abigail finished the lunch preparations and looked at the clock. Again. It was now after one o'clock. She wandered into the living room, pulled back the sheers, and looked down the driveway hoping to see Carrie Sue. She was beginning to worry.

Drifting back into the kitchen, she decided to eat her lunch without waiting for Carrie Sue. Carrying her soup and sandwich into the dining room, she positioned herself so that she could watch the end of the driveway. "Lord, please keep that woman safe from accident or critters … or worse."

It was after two o'clock and Abigail began to be very uneasy about the situation. Something was wrong. She called Cindy and they prayed for a few minutes. They both sensed that Carrie Sue was in serious trouble.

"I'll continue praying," Cindy said, "and I think it would be a good idea for you to look for her. Surely she wouldn't be very far."

"Yeah, I doubt that she would go too far or explore any new places. It's just not like her."

"Do you think she might have gone to see if her brother's car is still there?" Cindy suggested. She, too, was not always sure if her thoughts came from her own mind or if they were from the Holy Spirit.

"That's a good thought," Abigail confirmed. "I'll look at the SD cards from the other cameras and see if I can get a hint as to which way she went. Then I'll saddle Buster up again and head out. I'll call you when I find out anything."

She was energized and immediately went out the front door, noting that it had been locked, and got the SD card from the porch camera, the camera that covered the bend in the driveway, and the camera that covered the vehicles. The one from the back porch would be irrelevant.

She rushed back into her office and inserted the first one into her computer. She saw Carrie Sue exiting the front door and making sure that it was locked behind her. The camera lost her image as she moved out of its range, but Abigail now knew that Carrie Sue had started out by going down the front yard. The other two SD cards did not have any pictures of her so she was fairly certain that Carrie Sue was headed toward Billy's car.

Abigail hurriedly put her boots and jacket back on, chambered a bullet in Walther, grabbed her phone, and headed down to the tack room once again.

"Buster!" she called and then whistled.

She heard twigs snapping as he came up the trail through the woods. He was as excited as usual to see her, being doubly energized when he saw her open the door to the tack room.

"I know, we just got back, but we're on a mission." She talked to Buster while trying to calm herself down a little. He had rolled his sweaty body on the ground after their first ride, so she had to spend extra time on his grooming before placing the blanket and saddle on his back.

Past denial, Abigail was seriously concerned and began to pray quietly in the Spirit inserting passages of Scripture that she had tucked away in her mind. She customized the verses from Isaiah, "Lord, You have been a defense for the helpless, a defense for the needy in distress, a refuge from the storm, a shade from the heat; because the breath of the ruthless is like a storm against a wall. Lord, defend my helpless, needy friend in her distress. Lord speak peace to the ruthless storm; give her refuge." She prayed until she finished saddling Buster.

Buster sensed her mood and seemed more alert than usual. They maneuvered through the upper gate and crossed the back yard. Abigail took a quick glance at Dude's grave and felt a momentary pang of grief before forcing herself to focus on finding Carrie Sue. Fortunately, the trees had been shedding their leaves and it was fairly easy to see where Carrie Sue had shuffled under the oak tree and through some of the thicker accumulations.

Crossing the road, Abigail prayed, "Which way, Lord?" She looked up and down the shoulder of the road that had not been mowed by the highway crews lately and noticed a trampled area. Nudging Buster closer, looking from that vantage point, it was easy to see the freshly flattened path that Carrie Sue had recently made as she walked through the opening that they used just a few days before.

She was fairly certain that Carrie Sue had gone to Billy's car so she guided Buster in that same direction, going slowly enough that she could confirm freshly bent weeds and recent footprints. Crossing the first field, she quickened Buster's pace, being certain of her destination. Buster quickly covered the next field and entered the wooded area where the displaced leaves and trail debris confirmed that Carrie Sue had walked this way fairly recently.

Abigail was still hoping that her friend was safe. *Maybe she took the driveway out to the highway and turned the wrong way.* Abigail was hoping against hope. "Lord, let me find her safe."

They broke into the overgrown clearing and she could see that Billy's car was still there. Nothing appeared to have changed – at least not that she could tell from this distance. Galloping the final stretch, she stopped Buster about ten feet away from the car and dismounted. Letting the reins fall to the ground so that Buster would not roam, she carefully approached the car and noticed the disturbed ground near the door. She noted the place on the door that looked as if someone had taken a hand and wiped it clean just above the low-lying trim, but she did not want to step closer until she looked at the ground to see which way Carrie Sue might have gone.

Abigail saw the footprints. No! There were two sets of footprints. "Oh, Lord!" She followed them a short way and then noticed the tire tracks. One set of prints disappeared and the other went in a semi-circle and then they, too, disappeared.

She got into a vehicle with someone! Stunned by the realization, Abigail's mind whirred with questions. Did she intentionally meet someone here? Was it a coincidence? Did she call someone on her cell phone? Was someone watching her? How would they know she was here?

Abigail speed-dialed the McCord's number and got Gary. "Hey, whatcha up to?"

"Hey, Gary, did Cindy tell you that we're worried about Carrie Sue being gone too long?"

"No, I just got home."

"I'm here at the abandoned farm down the road where Billy's car is and I followed Carrie Sue's tracks here. It looks like she might have been on the ground the way everything is flattened, or maybe she got in a fight with someone. From the footprints, it looks like she got into another vehicle with someone. I think she's gone."

"Whoa, slow down," Gary interrupted. "Are you thinking that it's foul play or that she met someone there on purpose?"

"I don't know," Abigail was distressed.

"Okay," Gary tried to calm Abigail down, "look around and tell me what you see by the car again."

Abigail described Carrie Sue's foot prints that approached the car, she described the clean mark on the car door, and the flattened area by the door.

"Get close to the car and see if you can see anything else - maybe she dropped something and had to look under the car." He waited while she followed his instructions.

Abigail stooped down and reported, "Gary, I see something. There's some dark hair caught in the trim at the bottom of the clean streak."

"That doesn't sound good," Gary said. "I wonder if she tripped or was shoved into the car."

"I don't know," Abigail was even more distressed.

"Okay," Gary interrupted her, "Tell me about the vehicle tracks." He waited while Abigail stood upright and walked over to the tire tracks.

"Well, they leave a clear pattern, like they're fairly new and they're wide - wider than my tires."

"Are they further apart than your truck tires? I mean, you have a mid-sized truck. Are these about the same or do they look like they might be from a full-sized truck?"

"Yeah, they're definitely farther apart than mine. I'm looking at Billy's car and it seems like they're about two feet wider."

"Okay, how big are the footprints of the driver?" Gary continued to ask questions as if he was a seasoned detective. "How do they compare to Carrie Sue's size or yours?"

Abigail looked again at the footprints. "Gary, they're pretty close to the same as Carrie Sue's and both of them are smaller than mine. I'm a size nine and these must be eights or less."

"It sounds like the other person might be another woman or else a guy with tiny feet." Gary confirmed what Abigail was thinking.

"Oh, wow! I wonder if it was her mother!" Abigail was suddenly struck by the thought. "She's been driving her dad's big pickup truck and they're about the same size and ..."

"Abigail," Gary interrupted her train of thought, "I think you need to get out of there. Take one more look around and then get home. Call me when you get there."

"Okay, I'm on my way," Abigail pressed the red button and disconnected the call as she walked past the car and over to Buster, taking one last look behind her. Grabbing the reins, she swung onto his back and directed him down the abandoned lane and out to the road. When she got there, she noted that the truck had come from the south and returned the same way.

She drove right past my house!

Twice!

Guiding Buster back home along the rough edge of the road, covering the ground quickly, she took an extra second to stop by the mailbox on the way up. Once she had Buster settled, she called Gary to let him know that she was home and that Carrie Sue definitely was not.

Carrie Sue's battered head was throbbing. She had opened her eyes, but it was completely dark and she had no idea where she was or what time of day or night it might be. The last thing she remembered was tripping over something just before she got to Billy's car. Carefully reaching her arms above and to the side, she but felt nothing but the cold cement floor upon which she was unceremoniously dumped.

Lifting her head rewarded her with a stabbing pain above her left eye. Gingerly touching the area, she realized that her eye was swollen shut. Bending her stiff knees to try to ease her aching hips shot a sharp pain through her back.

"Oh Lord, what happened to me? Where am I? Jesus, I need You."

David was co-conscious with Carrie Sue and they began an internal conversation. "Carrie Sue, I'm so sorry; I couldn't switch in and stop the bio-mom from taking us."

"Mom? What happened?" Carrie Sue asked. They did not need to speak out loud because they were able to hear each other's thoughts and could converse as clearly as any two ordinary people; but they could convey their thoughts at a blistering rate.

"I'm not real clear, but one of my people said that we were being tailed by some big demons once we left Abigail's property. She said that the leader made us trip. That's how we stumbled and hit our head on Billy's car."

"Yeah, we have a nasty bump," Carrie Sue replied, "and I think our eye is swollen shut."

David added, "And she also said that the demon pounced on our back and dug his claws in."

"That explains the pain back there. Never mind that, we've been through worse. Where are we and how are we going to get out of here?"

David and Carrie Sue continued a long internal narrative that included the information David had gleaned from the little one who only wanted her mommy. They surmised that they were now in the windowless lodge and that they were probably going to be featured at tonight's ritual. They also found someone inside who was willing to carry the body pain so that Carrie Sue, David, and some of the other key leaders would not be distracted. That was one of the perks of dissociation.

They tried to encourage each other. "I know that Abigail will be praying for us and she will get her intercessors to pray, too." They were determined to pray and stand firm no matter how bleak it looked.

Abigail looked at the time and decided to go to church as planned. There was nothing she could do here except wait for someone who was not likely to come home, at least, humanly speaking. She was praying for the miracle that Carrie Sue desperately needed. After eating a small meal that she did not taste, Abigail went to church. She sat with Gary and Cindy tonight and received some puzzled looks from those who knew that "her" seat was up front.

Abigail worshiped. She pressed into the presence of God as intensely and intentionally as ever. As she drew near to Him, He drew near to her and she began to feel the tension seep out of her soul and body by the time the worship team was finished. Pastor Spalding thanked the group as he opened his Bible, placed it on the podium, and then moved on to his teaching for that night.

"I was reading in the book of Luke this week and came across a couple of verses in Luke twelve that are both alarming and comforting. You don't have to turn there because I'll be focusing on the book of Daniel tonight. Luke says, *'When they bring you before the synagogues and the rulers and the authorities, do not worry about how or what you are to speak in your defense, or what you are to say; for the Holy Spirit will teach you in that very hour what you ought to say.'* These really are comforting verses because we know that the Holy Spirit will be there for us; they're also alarming because he says *when*, not if."

He paused and then continued, "I started thinking these verses are very relevant to our day and time. They're not just about the disciples, or Stephen in the book of Acts; it's for us too. Most of you are aware of our brothers and sisters in Christ being martyred today in alarming numbers." Pastor Spalding went on to enumerate several recent events in North Korea, China, and the Middle East.

"I think that these verses represent two sides of one coin. God's empowering us is on one side and our choosing to cooperate with Him is on the other side. Let's turn to the book of Daniel and look at some examples of men who illustrate this. I like Daniel," he said with a twinkle, "and not just because we share the same name." He paused until the rustling of pages died down and then he gave a brief overview of the circumstances that Daniel and his three friends faced as very young men.

"Actually, these four young men were called youths in verse four of the first chapter. They may not have even been teenagers yet. They were from royal families with no defects, they were handsome, and showed intelligence. I would imagine that they went through very thorough inspections of body and mind. Can you imagine yourself marching from Jerusalem to Babylon - a distance of several hundred miles - separated from your family and then being interrogated and tested? Can you imagine facing a whole different future as the son of a nobleman than what you had come to expect?" Again, he paused to let his audience ponder the questions.

"Apparently, Daniel could handle being taught the literature and language of the Chaldeans. He could handle being a captive and being forced to serve a pagan king, but he could not, no, he would not violate his deeply held convictions when it came to the food and wine he was being forced to partake of. Look at verse eight. *'But Daniel made up his mind that he would not defile himself with the king's choice food or with the wine which he drank; so, he sought permission from the commander of the officials ...'* Daniel didn't throw a childish tantrum, but I believe through the wisdom of the Holy Spirit, he was given the words to say to the official. He was able to negotiate a deal because God granted him favor and compassion in the sight of the commander." He paused to give time for reflection.

"I want to ask you some questions: do you think God gave him favor because he was so special? Or do you think that God gave him favor because He knew about Daniel's unwavering resolve to be godly?" He let the questions go unanswered and then proceeded to his next point.

"Turn to Daniel chapter three. Here we find that King Nebuchadnezzar had made a ninety-foot golden image of himself and demanded that whenever the music played, everyone was required to fall down and worship or else be thrown into the fiery furnace. I'm not sure where Daniel was at this time, but his three friends didn't bow down so they were turned in and were brought to the king. Like it says in verse six, they were threatened with death if they didn't obey. The king seemed to want to give them one more chance even though he was enraged at them."

Picking up his Bible, he dramatically pointed to the next passage and excitedly read, "'*O Nebuchadnezzar, we do not need to give you an answer concerning this matter. If it be so, our God whom we serve is able to deliver us from the furnace of blazing fire; and He will deliver us out of your hand, O king. But even if He does not, let it be known to you, O king, that we are not going to serve your gods or worship the golden image that you have set up.*'"

Putting his Bible back on the podium, he walked to the edge of the low platform. "King, we have already thought about this. We will not be defiled! God will deliver us … or not!" He gave a broad smile as if he was proud of his own sons who had predetermined that they would not cross the line.

"Folks, when I looked at the passage in Luke twelve, I kind of had the idea that the Holy Spirit would give them something nice to say that would placate the king, you know, something diplomatic like Daniel did in the first chapter. But no-o-o" he exaggerated, "they signed their own death warrants with those words."

He paused as he heard a few chuckles. "Seriously, these guys didn't even have to think about it. There was no question, no doubt. They were absolutely not going to worship any god but the true God. Period. Do you think that they chatted about their response on their way to see the king that day? I doubt it. I think they were talking about it even before their first day of indoctrination when Daniel spoke for them about the food. I think they were discussing it while they were walking those long, dusty miles from Jerusalem to Babylon. I think they wrestled with their commitment to God when captivity was looming. I have to believe that their parents knew of their imminent deportation and prepared their sons. And that is what made it possible for them to respond to the promptings of the Holy Spirit in their day of trial."

After making several more observations and pointing out other plausible possibilities, he then directed them to Daniel six. "Daniel had his test as well and he passed with flying colors again. He simply prayed three times a day as he always did and got rewarded with a night in the lions' den." Pastor

Spalding made several more comments and then laid out his challenge and invitation to come up for prayer.

"Let us be praying tonight for our brothers and sisters who have to make these kinds of stances in the face of persecution. Let us pray that God would join them in the furnace or shut the mouths of the lions or grant them supernatural favor as they respond to the Holy Spirit. Let us also pre-determine what our own response will be if we face similar situations. Before God, you must know the point at which you are being defiled and stand firm no matter what the outcome." He spoke a little further and then dismissed them, walking down to the front to pray with people.

Abigail moved down to the front with Cindy and lingered until Pastor Spalding was free. He instantly sensed her distress and gave her his full attention. Abigail began to blurt out the prayer request, "Carrie Sue never came back from her walk today. She's been staying with me until this ritual week is over. I followed her trail and I think the cult grabbed her."

"Oh, dear," Pastor Spalding had an inkling of the implications. "Let's pray then," both he and Cindy lightly placed their hands on Abigail's shoulders as they stood by her, "Oh, Lord, we lift up Carrie Sue wherever she is and ask that You would shut the mouths of the lions, that You would quench the fiery furnace, that You would set her free, that You would not let her be defiled. Oh, Lord, send Your warring angels to protect her, to set the captive free …." He continued to pray for several more minutes after which Cindy and then Abigail prayed in agreement.

"Keep me posted," Pastor Spalding instructed as she and Cindy turned to find Gary.

"Keep me posted, too," Cindy added.

"You know I will," Abigail replied. "I just want to get home and keep the lights on. I'm going to pray all night if I have to."

Abigail hugged Cindy and then quickened her pace as she headed out of the church and across the parking lot. Keys in hand, she efficiently started her truck and moved through the parking lot and onto the road that led home. She was feeling more peaceful now but was still anxious for this to be over for Carrie Sue. She had grown to love this tenacious, spunky survivor.

The drive home was uneventful. It was quite dark by the time she wound her way up the driveway and parked the truck next to Carrie Sue's car. "Oh, Lord Jesus ..." Abigail could not form words to convey the angst her spirit was feeling for her friend. She went to the phone and called Earl and Jan. Jan answered with her usual cheery greeting.

"Jan," Abigail got right to the point, "I need for you and Earl to pray for Carrie Sue, the lady that has been staying here for the last couple of days."

"Sure, what's going on?" Jan asked.

"Well, she's one of my SRA survivors, and today she took a walk while I was out riding Buster and never came back. I tracked her to the abandoned farm just across the road from you and it's pretty clear that she got into a truck with someone. Maybe her mother because it doesn't look like she struggled. Anyway,

I'm sure they will get her to a ritual tonight and it won't be pretty." Abigail took a breath.

"Oh, my, we sure will be praying. Are you sure that you are safe, dear?" Jan asked.

Abigail had not thought about her own safety. "Well, of course, I mean, I know they've tried things and done things, but no weapon formed against me will prosper."

"Do you think they'll try to use her to get to you?" Jan asked an even more insightful question.

"That's a good question," Abigail answered thoughtfully, "I'm not sure how, but then, they're a pretty creative bunch. I had no trouble getting to church and back, at least, I didn't notice anything unusual, but then I was a bit distracted."

"Well, you just call us if you need anything, and I mean anytime," Jan's motherly instinct surfaced, "and don't you worry, dear, God's got this handled."

"I believe it; I just wish I knew the end from the beginning on this episode."

Carrie Sue, David, and several other key personalities used their time in the dank, dark room to pray and strategize. They realized that they would more than likely be subdued with drugs; they would definitely be outnumbered and overpowered by those demon-powered men who were bigger and stronger than them in the natural.

"We're not going to get out of this mess by our own strength. We need a miracle. But we're not going to give in no matter what they do!" Carrie Sue voiced this declaration with all the conviction she that could muster.

"That's right," David encouraged her and the others, "if God delivers us or not, we're *not* going back to Satanism!"

"We need to make sure that the little ones and some of the cult-loyal ones that might still be around won't get accessed," Titus added. Titus was a quiet one, but very strong and determined to follow the true Lord Jesus Christ. He had been transformed after his rescue from his cult-loyal assignment.

They called on all the known observers inside Carrie Sue's system of personalities. From the information that came forth, they surmised that there was a pocket of parts that was primed for tonight's ritual. They were beginning to get restless and did not know anything but November first rituals.

"Like Abigail says," Carrie Sue reminded them, "there are no bad parts, only parts that have a bad assignment. Let's ask God to show us a way to help them or else to keep them from having to go through a ritual again."

They went to prayer and Titus had an idea come to his mind. "I think I'm sensing that God wants me to go to their leader and, well, kind of ambush him and integrate with him so that he'll know and understand everything that I know and vice-versa. Then we can separate again and see what happens. I think it'll work out good."

No one else received anything specific, so they prayed for his success and Titus went deep into the recesses of Carrie Sue's mind and found Ichabod with the help of the observers who knew where he was hiding. Ichabod was not expecting Titus to show up in his domain and was unprepared for his sudden appearance and equally sudden ambush. Leaping onto Ichabod, arms and legs wrapping around him, Titus disappeared completely into Ichabod.

Stunned by the unexpected turn of events, Ichabod shook himself and turned around to see who had accosted him. No one was there. He felt strange. It was not quite like being programmed, in fact, it was not quite like anything he had ever experienced before. He suddenly knew things that he did not know before. He felt things he had never felt before and realized that it actually felt good. *What is going on?* He was aware of the kingdom of God, he knew that there was a true and a false Jesus; he knew about programming, he felt strangely peaceful.

Titus was having an equally strange experience, however, having been cult-loyal before, he knew experientially what Ichabod had imparted to him by their integration. He understood everything that made Ichabod tick. Stirring and pushing to the surface, Titus emerged from Ichabod and stood before him face-to-face like any two ordinary men would, only unlike ordinary men, they had just exchanged a full download of each other's life experiences.

"Who … who are you?" Ichabod was stunned. He already knew, but he did not really know. *Bizarre!*

"I'm Titus," he replied, "hey, man, I'm sorry about the unexpected visit, but it was the best way I knew how I could show you what you need to know."

"Well, I know a bunch of new stuff," Ichabod conceded slowly, "but just what am I supposed to do about it?" He was still in a bit of a shock and was not sure if what he thought and felt was real or some kind of trick. He had been exposed to so much wizardry and demonization and programming that he was not quite sure that this was genuine.

"Would you be willing to meet with some of the others?" Titus invited.

"Sure," Ichabod was not sure why he agreed, but he was feeling more and more confident that Titus held a key to more answers about their mysterious meeting. Somehow, he trusted Titus and he was not quite sure why. All he had ever known was the savagery of competition in his dog-eat-dog world.

Carrie Sue and the others were warily accepting of Ichabod. They answered all of his questions and he answered theirs. He came to realize that he had been duped and they reassured them that they had also experienced much of the same treatment.

Their internal discussions took mere seconds and soon they had prayerfully laid out plans for keeping Carrie Sue as safe as possible. The child alters were prayed for and integrated into their respective protectors, programming was cancelled, and prayers were winging their way to heaven, joining those of Abigail and the other intercessors.

Deciding that the greatest mockery would be to torture the last remaining Wagner spawn under the very nose of that enemy, that infuriating woman, Prinz arranged for the festivities to take place at their site just south of her property. His blood pressure rose just thinking of her, and how she had eluded his traps. Yes, there was some incidental damage, but he wanted to make her pay and pay dearly. Undoing all the work that she had done was just the ticket. Carrie Sue would be shattered into thousands of newly dissociated and programmed parts before the cock crowed in the morning. Gleefully reviewing his plans, he set out for the farm with the five-sided rock.

A few minutes before ten o'clock activity increased in the windowless building. The large van with the darkened windows pulled up near the rear door. Blindfolded and hooded, gagged and bound, Carrie Sue was hauled out to the van. She did not waste her energy resisting and her protectors were co-conscious with her. Unknown to these goons, Ichabod was among them. He would do his best to convince them that he was still cult-loyal if necessary so that they could seize upon any opportunity to escape.

The van was not designed for human cargo so the ride from the lodge to the farm was noisy and jarring, especially since Carrie Sue, acting as if she had been drugged, was brusquely thrown onto the cold metal floor next to some of the furniture that would be employed tonight. Carrie Sue was glad that she did not have to feel the pain from the swollen eye and she breathed a prayer for the part of her that volunteered to feel the pain for them. There would be much to sort out if she made it through the night.

If.

For some odd reason she was remembering the story of Daniel's three friends who were faced with bowing to an idol or being thrown into a furnace. They had predetermined that they would not defile themselves and she prayed that they would have the same resolve despite drugs or hypnosis and whatever else they did to her.

The van lurched to a stop after bumping over the pitted gravel driveway that led to the barn on the back side of the property. Doors were jerked open and hands roughly grabbed her by the ankles and pulled her until she could sit up on the bumper. Escorted by two silent bodyguards, guided by their hands on her elbows, shoved through a doorway, she fell free as they let her trip over the threshold with the door slamming behind her.

Carrie Sue assumed that she was in the barn by its smell and her recollection of having been at this ritual site numerous times every year of her life. She slowly righted herself and was eventually able to stagger to her feet awkwardly despite the blindfold and her bound arms.

Listening carefully, she ascertained that she was alone in the old barn. She groped her way slowly until she came into contact with a wall or partition of some kind. It was made of rough wood so she gently pressed the right side of her head against it hoping the material would snag and allow her to get out of the hood. After struggling and failing several times, she cried out to the Lord, "Oh, God, please get this thing off of us!" When she went back to the task, she found a nail sticking out of a board just far enough that it worked. She immediately put the nail to work in removing the blindfold as well.

It was pitch dark because it was night time, but there were cars coming up the driveway which momentarily flashed strobe-like beams of light between the gaps in the old, weathered boards. Carrie Sue was able to see farm equipment outlined against the wall not too far away. Delighted to find that it was rusty, she leaned hard against a rough section of metal on some old piece of machinery and sawed the ropes from her wrists.

Gratefully rubbing the circulation back into them, she commanded herself to think. *Don't panic.* She didn't know what was planned, but she was certain that she would not have much time before they came for her. Hiding would only delay things; she needed to get out of this barn without being detected.

Abigail stepped out into the chilly night air and was able to see fairly clearly when the nearly half moon was not blocked by a cloud. It was past her usual bed time, but she was not sleepy as she kept her prayerful vigil for her friend. Heart lurching, she heard the sound of four-wheelers in the distance. Their sound travelled freely across the barren fields and swept up her hill. *I'll bet they're just down the road. Carrie Sue is right there.* She knew it would be futile to saddle up Buster and go charging into a satanic ritual, but that is what she wanted to do more than anything.

Instead, Abigail increased the fervor of her prayers and petitioned the Most High God, the Judge of all, the Lord of hosts to intervene on behalf of Carrie Sue. "Oh, God, You transported Philip from one town to another, You sent an angel to break Peter out of jail, You sent an earthquake to spring Paul, You gave Joseph favor, You blinded Elisha's enemies, oh, Lord God, show Yourself strong on behalf of the weak." Abigail assailed the throne of grace with impassioned prayers that rose to the heavens as her breath rose in the cool night air.

Prinz arrived shortly before midnight and sensed something unusual in the atmosphere that was almost tangible. It was not good. His smug certainty that this would be a very satisfying ritual was ebbing away as he approached Daggett and Zorroz near the rock. "Where's the woman?" he snarled his demand.

"They've got her in the barn. We were waiting for you to let us know when you wanted us to bring her out," Daggett replied with forced bravado. He did not want to admit it, but his strength was waning and no matter how much he petitioned his lord, his strength was not like it once was. Something was wrong. Something was different.

"Get her!" Prinz growled. He turned sharply and glowered fiercely at Zorroz.

Zorroz immediately strode toward the barn with his hooded black robe fluttering around him and the hood flopping on his back. Two men guarding the door stepped aside in unison even though there was no audible communication between them. Turning on his flashlight, Zorroz stepped into the barn. The beam settled on Carrie Sue.

"Hello, Sheriff Bynum," Carrie Sue said evenly. He had pushed back the oversized, droopy hood because it blocked his vision. He did not expect her to be standing there without her hood, blindfold, or bonds. *Did no one drug her?*

Zorroz was taken aback; indeed, he stepped back before he regained his composure and then hastily approached Carrie Sue. Grabbing her right wrist with his large hand, cursing under his breath, he yanked her out of the barn and marched her hastily up the path toward her destiny.

Carrie Sue summoned the boldness to twist away and authoritatively demand, "In the name of Jesus Christ of Nazareth, let me go!"

Zorroz was again taken aback and turned to look at the woman in the dim night light. At that moment David switched in. He was left-handed even though Carrie Sue and most of the others were right-handed. He swung his tight left fist as hard and as fast as he could and connected with Zorroz' exposed windpipe. Pinching a small artery between the hyoid bone and the windpipe cartilage, blood slowly but steadily flooded the folds of the larynx.

Hearing the crunch, struggling for breath, stunned by the attack, Zorroz reflexively released his iron grip on Carrie Sue's tiny wrist and instinctively clutched at his own throat. Coughing and gagging, wheezing and rasping, he dropped to his knees, calling out for help with a high-pitched rattling voice. The men who followed them at a discrete distance did not see what had happened; they only heard the labored rasp of his breathing as they approached Zorroz.

David wasted no time in backing away and soon disappeared into the shadows. He was a faster and more coordinated runner than Carrie Sue, so she let him stay in executive control. The leaders were co-conscious with each other and the consensus was that they should follow the driveway back down to the highway and then head north to Abigail's house. They knew that the trackers would be coming after them very soon. The commotion was becoming more indistinct the farther they went, but they were literally not out of the woods yet.

"Oh, Lord, please keep any human or demon from being able to track us!"

It was nearly midnight. Abigail had come back into the house an hour before after listening to the night riders moving through the river bottoms. She stoked up the fire and decided to leave the front and back porch lights on. For some reason, the yard light was not enough tonight. She was not afraid, she just had a feeling. When she had a feeling, she learned that it was a good idea to go with it.

Once again, she was on her knees with her Bible open to her favorite warring scriptures, feeling more like a child than a warrior. She periodically turned from passages in the Psalms to some verses in the book of Isaiah and customized them for tonight's situation. Praying until she could pray no more about Carrie Sue, she petitioned for Amy and Sherry and so many others who were also under the spell of the kingdom of darkness.

Physically exhausted from the strain of the long day and the late hour, she crawled into her bed, pulled the covers up to her chin and settled into a comfortable position. Her mind, percolating and bubbling, took a little more time to calm down as she sifted and drifted through myriads of thoughts.

She half thought and half prayed, *I miss Dude, how can anyone be so cruel? How can anyone be a Satanist? Both Billy and Danny dead ... and their father... crazy connection between Carrie Sue's family and my family ...* Abigail nearly fell asleep shortly after three in the morning but was awakened by the sound of a noisy vehicle on the road followed by several more.

Random thoughts began to flow again. *Lee and his horses ... Buster will love the company ... I might, too, I am lonely ... got to remember to talk to Pastor Spalding ...*

Peaceful sleep finally came to the woman who found herself in the eye of the storm as winged messengers from opposing kingdoms clashed in the heavens far above her.

COUNSELING RELATED E-BOOKS BY THIS AUTHOR:

I am a Cutter, Please Help Me

Yo Soy un Cortador Ayudana Por Favor (Spanish version of I am a Cutter)

Emotional Abuse and Verbal Assaults through Lies, Vows, Curses, and Judgments

Battling Anorexia, Bulimia, Binge Eating, Health Food Obsession

Panic and Anxiety Attacks

Heaven or Hell – Have I Lost My Salvation?

Mad at God, Self, and Others

Dissociative Identity Disorder

What's in Your Family Tree? Battling Generational Curses and Familial Spirits

Spiritual Gifts – Discovering Your Spiritual Gifts

Seeing, Hearing, Sensing God through His Brokenhearted Children

FICTION SERIES OF E-BOOKS BY THIS AUTHOR:

Ritual Abuse – Autumn

Ritual Abuse – Winter

Ritual Abuse – Spring

Ritual Abuse - Summer

PAPERBACK EDITIONS BY THIS AUTHOR:

Dissociative Identity Disorder

www.ingramcontent.com/pod-product-compliance
Lightning Source LLC
Chambersburg PA
CBHW050915030726
47503CB00007BB/2300

* 9 7 8 0 9 9 8 1 5 3 8 1 0 *